I0524437

HELL FAE
COMMANDER

USA TODAY BESTSELLING AUTHORS
LEXI C. FOSS J.R. THORN

This is a work of fiction. Names, characters, places, and incidents are either the product of the author's imagination or are used fictitiously, and any resemblance to actual persons, living or dead, business establishments, events, or locales is entirely coincidental.

Hell Fae Commander

Copyright © 2023 Lexi C. Foss & J.R. Thorn

All rights reserved.

Editing by: Outthink Editing, LLC

Proofreading by: Katie Schmahl and Jean Bachen

Cover Design: Covers by Juan

Cover Photography: Wander Aguiar

Cover Models: Sophie, Alex, Philippe, Forrest, and Camden

Chapter Header Art: Nathan Hansen Illustration

Ornamental Chapter Art: Ricky Gunawan

Chapter Watermark for Ajax, Cami, Az, and Typhos: Claire Holt

Chapter Watermark for Melek: Covers by Aura

Published by: Ninja Newt Publishing

Print Edition

ISBN: 978-1-68530-306-8

To Baby Foss & Little Thornie, your mommies are always thinking of you, even while they work. <3

About Hell Fae Commander

"I'll never trust you."
The words resonate in my very soul.
They make me feel like death.

Of course, I can't actually die.
I would just burn to ash and wake up again with the same
damn problem swirling around in my heart and mind.
My inner beast thinks it has imprinted on a Halfling Hell Fae.
Without my permission.

Now all I want to do is hold her. Kiss her. F-ck her.
Claim her.
But I can't.
Not until we solve this mystery going on with the Hell Fae
Source and these rogue portals that keep popping up
everywhere.

The Hell Fae Realm is in chaos, and my potential mate might be to blame.
Warden Ajax and Prince Melek think she's innocent.
The Hell Fae King is sure she's not.
And I'm too busy dealing with my panting Phoenix to pick a side.

All my animal can think about is biting his intended.
Meanwhile, all I can think about is how to stop him.

Camillia should have a choice.
Only, she doesn't seem to want to choose...

A NOTE FROM LEXI & JEN

Thank you for picking up *Hell Fae Commander*! We hope you enjoy this dark world as much as we do.

For those new to the series, we strongly recommend reading these books in order, as it is a continued story.

Just a note of caution: This series contains strong sexual undertones, violent scenes, and themes of dubious consent. There are also several strong male-on-male relationships in this world, and these men absolutely love to fuck each other. But they'll be inviting Cami to join them... once she proves her worth. ;)

However, Cami isn't the type of heroine to bend over and take it. She'll fight until the bitter end.

Her mates have a lot of work ahead of them.

As well as some groveling to do along the way.

Their journey won't be easy. But it'll be deliciously sinful.

So continue your journey through the Hell Fae world. Be careful who you trust. And watch out for the infamous mirages.

Nothing is what it seems.

Just like our Hell Fae mates...

INTRODUCTION

The Black Phoenix's flame burns eternal.
Darkness descends and ash is spread.
Who will rise will determine fate's end.
—Az

HELL FAE REALM

A REVEALED PAGE FROM LUCIFER'S BOOK, VITA

Once upon a time, an angel Fell. His feathers were stripped, his light was extinguished, and he landed in the fires of a broken land.

But this was no ordinary angel.

He knew his world was about to end before the ultimate betrayal arose, and inside him, he hid the source of his light. His true power. His ultimate revenge.

From that fiery ember of energy, he created a new world—the Hell Fae Realm. And within it, he accepted all the creatures every other fae realm rejected.

Nightmare Fae. Abominations. *Monsters*.

As his new court grew, various kingdoms were established. Each one is ruled by a protective Mythos Fae, and beneath them, various Fae Kings.

This entry is considered to be an index of those kingdoms and known species within. It changes and grows daily, but I am Vita, Lucifer's prized book. I know all. I document all. And now, I'll share that knowledge with you, dear reader...

Barren Lands: Desertlike dry areas with rocky landscapes and little to no water sources. Centaurs, Manticores, Minotaurs, Air Dragons, Griffins, and Boggarts make these lands their home. It has also recently been used to house the Hell Fae Bridal Candidates within a unique paradigm.

Hell Fae Kingdom: A centralized kingdom that Typhos Lucifer calls home. All non–Nightmare Fae creatures reside here, as do Lucifer's infamous Hellhounds.

Marsh Lands: Murky waters and swampy plant life make this an ideal home for Nagas and Unseelie.

Morpheus Kingdom: This is the land of dreams, where Nightmare Fae feed on terror and fear. Ghouls and Stigori call this place home, but one of Lucifer's personal creations lives here, too—the Kuntilanak Fae.

Netherworld Kingdom: Darkness and wisps of dull moonlight haunt the graveyards of this kingdom, making it an optimal home for Corpse Fae and Death Fae.

Underwater Kingdom: Vast oceans and coral-like castles paint this kingdom in a sea of unique colors. Kelpies and Water Dragons call this kingdom home, but some of Lucifer's personal creations, like Sirens, reside here, too.

HELL FAE REALM

MARSH LANDS

HELL FAE KINGDOM

MORPHEUS KINGDOM

UNDERWATER KINGDOM

BARREN LANDS

NETHERWORLD KINGDOM

PROLOGUE: AZ

I FUCKED UP.

The three words echoed in my mind, the voice one I barely recognized. Mostly because it sounded contrite. And I didn't do contrite.

Yet, I felt... conflicted.

It wasn't like I'd enjoyed seeing Cami in that cage.

Well, no, that wasn't entirely true. A dark and twisted part of me had thoroughly appreciated the view.

That same part of me had also wanted to join her in that cage, remove the chains, and fuck her in front of the room. Claim her in a base way to inform all those hungry fae bastards that she was *mine*.

Except she wasn't mine at all.

Which made the craving that much more confusing.

Fucking Phoenix, I muttered. *She's not ours, you stupid fucking bird.*

A low growl escaped me as I ran through the Marsh Lands, pursuing a runaway bride. This was the absolute last thing I wanted to be doing, but I didn't have a choice. She was injured and needed to be returned to the bridal camp.

"Veronica!" I shouted, irritated as hell that she'd taken off through the marshy underbrush.

The entire kingdom was falling apart from some unknown magical spell, and this female had decided to try to escape.

Escape to where, I had no idea. If the Unseelie found her, she'd sorely regret the decision to flee.

I shouted her name once more, not that it seemed to be doing me any good.

My Phoenix hummed, my tracking ability fully engaged. The bridal candidate was only a few meters ahead, the smoggy air concealing her from view.

It was thick and damp, the swamp-like surroundings popular with the Unseelie and the Nagas of this realm.

I much preferred the fire and brimstone of the Hell Fae Kingdom.

"Veron—"

Typhos's fury washed over me in a hot wave, causing me to pause midstep. My Phoenix perked up, distracted from our hunt, as I turned slowly toward the Hell Fae King's presence.

I couldn't see him; he was too far away. But I could feel his power rippling through the air.

What is it? I thought at him.

No reply.

Yet his anger was growing with each passing second. Typhos didn't typically emit emotion, and especially not in such a palpable manner.

Frowning, I engaged my Phoenix and dissolved into ashes. Veronica would have to fend for herself for now.

I'd hunt her down later. Or I'd send someone else to do it.

The courtyard—or what used to be the courtyard, anyway —appeared around me as I took on a solid form again.

Chaos reigned in the sky, a massive portal sucking everything around it into its obsidian depths, all while Nagas and Unseelie worked together to try to close it.

Fuck. It'd grown since I'd arrived, the vortex resembling a dangerous black hole that was threatening to rip this kingdom apart.

Typhos was in the air, his fiery wings glowing furiously at his back while Melek shouted up at him from the ground. However, Typhos's focus wasn't on his princely mate but on a beacon of power in the distance.

Camillia, I realized in a breath. She was emanating energy, her brownish-blonde hair appearing lighter than usual as vitality swirled around her.

Typhos started toward her, the portal in the sky a glaring hole behind him.

Oh, shit... Camillia's accessing the Hell Fae Source. I could hear the confirmation of my thoughts in Typhos's mind, his anger a hot whiplash of smoldering ire.

She was too lost in his power to notice, her attention seeming to be on the sky.

Blinding light appeared in the next second as she unleashed a ball of warm energy, the power flowing directly up into the portal.

The ground shook in response, the sky seeming to splinter. Only... only the vortex closed in response.

And disappeared.

Fires, I breathed.

Had Camillia just used Lucifer's power to heal the breach? *How...?*

That... that shouldn't be...

I swallowed. *Fuck.*

Typhos looked ready to kill her. He'd warned her not to touch his source again.

His demand had nothing to do with possessiveness and everything to do with protectiveness. He'd been burned before in the worst way possible. By a woman. By one he'd trusted. One *I* had trusted, too.

Vivaxia.

Just thinking about her made my skin crawl—a sensation that worsened as Typhos landed on the ground in front of Camillia.

Shit. He was going to rip her apart in this state.

I started toward them, only to curse as he grabbed her and disappeared.

Melek immediately followed, his expression holding a touch of concern—an uncharacteristic trait for the usually carefree prince. I only caught it for a second before he disappeared, but it was definitely there.

And it rivaled my own concern.

Typhos very rarely lost his temper. He also preferred sensual punishments, like the one he'd inflicted upon Camillia earlier tonight.

But his current mood wasn't playful or charming. It was deadly.

And Camillia had just earned the full force of his wrath.

Fuck.

Fuck.

Fuck.

CHAPTER 1

CAMI

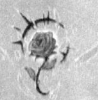

IF DEATH HAD A FACE, it would be Typhos's face right now.

The Hell Fae King paced before me, his magic resembling invisible binds around my wrists and ankles. I supposed it was better than the snake-vines Ajax had used during my last interrogation, but I still wasn't thrilled by it. Mostly because I was naked and entirely exposed.

And also because Typhos Lucifer looked like he was about to kill me. Truly. Like rip me apart with his bare hands and burn my remains to ashes.

Not a great way to die.

Especially considering all I'd done was *help* him.

I tried to say that, but my lips refused to move. *More magic*, I muttered to myself. *Awesome*.

He didn't utter a word as he walked around me in a slow, deliberate circle.

Like a predator evaluating his prey.

Red embers glittered in the backs of his unblinking eyes, making him all the more intimidating.

I helped you, I thought at him, unable to speak, thanks to whatever spell he'd cast over my mouth. I couldn't move much either. Just my neck and head.

Alas, it wasn't like my plea would stifle his rage anyway. I'd touched his source—something he'd explicitly told me not to do again or he'd kill me. Yet he hadn't done much other than grab me by the nape and teleport me back to his palace.

The moment our feet had touched the opulent carpets, he'd released me to begin his pacing.

Back and forth.

Silent steps.

Wicked eyes.

Deafening silence.

You're the one who wrapped me up in your power, I muttered, aware he couldn't actually hear me. *It's not technically my fault that your source decided to alter and manifest inside me. I was just trying to save the Hell Fae Brides.*

He paused, then slowly crouched before me.

Uh, maybe he did hear me.

No. He can't read my mind.

Unless... Can he?

Those eerie red embers flickered in his deep oceanic eyes, his gaze assessing.

His perfectly tailored suit stretched around his muscular torso, revealing a crisp white dress shirt underneath. Thanks to his power, or maybe the magic of the fabric he wore, he didn't look like he'd just come out of a war zone.

Whereas I, on the other hand, was naked and vulnerable before him.

A swallow stuck in my throat as those fiery-ember eyes met mine from mere inches away. He still didn't say anything, just tilted his head, reminding me a bit of Az's Phoenix.

Except this was the King of Hell, and he looked like he was about to rip my head from my shoulders with his bare hands.

I didn't do anything wrong, I attempted to say with a look.

Naturally, he remained silent.

So I essentially battled his murderous gaze with my own.

That portal was sucking in your *people, and* you *were making it worse. I was able to fix it, so I did.*

Not that I understood the intricate details of *how* I'd fixed it, but it wasn't like I'd been trying to hurt anyone.

"Don't try to sit there and look innocent, Camillia. You touched my *source*," he hissed, his hot breath kissing my skin. "Do you remember what I said I'd do if you ever did that again?"

You'd kill me, I thought darkly. *But obviously I wasn't doing anything nefarious. I was saving people.* Your *people.*

A warm gust of air sent my hair rippling over my bare shoulders. I didn't break Lucifer's gaze to see who had joined us. I knew better than to look away from the predator in front of me.

Any weakness could forfeit my life.

"Don't," Melek said, clearly talking to the Hell Fae King. His single word held an edge to it, one that sounded a lot like fear.

That can't be a good sign.

A rare flurry of desperation stirred in my gut, but I pushed it down before I did something stupid—like try to run.

Not that I could break free of Lucifer's powers. Nor did I really have anywhere to go.

"Don't what?" Lucifer asked him, his white teeth flashing with a cruel smile—one that appeared particularly wicked, thanks to the eerie light glittering off the lavalike palace walls.

"You need to calm down before you deliver a verdict," Melek continued, ignoring the ominous tone that lingered from Lucifer's reply. "Think about what this will do. Think about *us*."

"I *am* thinking about us," Lucifer replied, anger deepening his tone. "I'm thinking about all of Hell Fae kind.

9

The *source*. You know, the very power that she just tapped into and *used*." A hint of magic warmed the air as he uttered that last word.

I flinched as the invisible binds around my wrists and ankles squeezed in response.

But I refused to cry out or make a sound.

Another disturbance in the air told me someone else had entered the room. Lucifer didn't move, but his jaw flexed as Ajax and Az appeared in my peripheral vision.

Great. Everyone is here to watch my execution. My jaw tightened. *Oh, and by the way, you're all welcome for saving the Marsh Lands.*

Ungrateful asshole fae.

"Bride casualties?" Lucifer asked, his question unexpected, as was his bored tone.

One minute, he was seething. The next, he was all business.

Because, apparently, his rage could be temporarily set aside for his precious brides—a title that no longer applied to me, thanks to Lucifer's announcement in his club.

The mere memory of the incident renewed my rage, the burning emotion swiftly chasing away any residual fear I'd felt from Lucifer grabbing me and bringing me here.

Because how fucking dare he.

It wasn't like I'd meant to touch his source the first time or the last time. I was literally just trying to survive in this hellish realm.

He had made the deal with my father that then forced me to be here. I had no interest in the Hell Fae Source or Lucifer's powers. I simply wanted to go home.

But the damn book kept talking to me.

And that portal had been killing innocent brides.

What the fuck was I supposed to do? Sit down and watch while Lucifer made it worse?

No.

I'd realized what needed to happen, and I'd fixed it.

That was not a response worthy of death or any other punishment. This bastard should be thanking me. Especially as I'd done it after he'd spent the evening ridiculing and shaming me with that damn chain dress.

Energy danced over my skin, the power belonging to Lucifer. Which would probably just infuriate him more, but I couldn't control it.

All I could do was embrace it.

"Six," Az said, drawing my focus back to the conversation about the bridal casualties. "King Viper says we lost four in the portal, and two others in the landslides."

I glanced sideways to see Az reading a message off a translucent screen, suggesting he'd sent Lucifer's bridal count question off to someone—probably the King Viper he'd just mentioned—for an update.

"And one is still missing," he continued. "The rest have been retrieved and are being treated."

"Seven," Lucifer corrected, his voice low and deadly.

Az tilted his head in a birdlike gesture, one glittering with confusion.

"The casualty count," the Hell Fae King continued. "You said six dead brides, but it's actually seven." Lucifer kept his eyes on me, the promise of murder in his gaze.

I continued to stare at him, a thought taunting the back of my mind. One that I was glad I couldn't voice aloud, as it would probably earn his wrath.

I'm not a bride anymore, remember? was the thought. *You denounced my title in front of a club of horny Hell Fae.*

Yeah, that wasn't an argument I wanted to have right now.

Silence filled the room around me as blistering waves of energy simmered through the air like a precursor to the flames about to consume me.

A chilling presence followed, one that settled over my skin like a cooling blanket.

I swallowed, uncertain of whether it was real or fabricated in my mind, only for Lucifer to glance sharply over my shoulder.

"You promised not to hurt her," Melek said as if it was a reminder of an agreement between them.

A shiver ran up my spine at the thought of Melek vouching for me. I wasn't sure what I had done to earn his protection, but I was grateful for it right now.

I was not a damsel to be rescued, but sometimes a girl could use a little support.

Especially if that support came in the form of a delicious Hell Fae Prince.

"I promised not to hurt her unless she proved to be a viable threat," Lucifer responded. His eyes flared with heat. "I'd say she sufficiently proved herself to be a threat today."

Ajax and Az visibly stiffened in my peripheral vision. And the chilly sensation strengthened against my exposed skin.

"Sometimes the lines between a perceived threat and a true asset can blur, my king," Melek said softly.

"And sometimes a king has to make difficult decisions in order to protect those he cares about," Lucifer returned. "Particularly when those he loves are blinded by lust."

Az visibly bristled, the reaction one I didn't expect. Especially since he'd done nothing while I'd been locked in that cage on display. But now he appeared to be restraining himself.

Why? I wondered, my focus shifting to Ajax. *Is he holding you captive again?*

The Midnight Fae's nostrils flared, suggesting that perhaps Az was controlling him like he had at the club.

I swallowed, my heart giving an aggrieved thump in my chest. While I didn't know the whole story, I'd sensed the pain in Ajax's voice when he'd spoken to Az in the Marsh Lands. His fury had been most evident in his tone and words, but an agonized past had shadowed his statements.

A past involving an old Midnight Fae monarch who had killed Ajax's family and friends in front of him, while incapacitating Ajax with magic and forcing him to watch.

He'd told Az that what he'd done to him in Lucifer's club had been similar, noting that he would never forgive the Commander for his actions.

And now it seemed Az was doing it again.

Strong fingers wrapped around my throat, choking off my air supply. My eyes widened, my heart skipping several beats as he began to squeeze.

And not just with his hand, either.

The magical bindings around my wrists and ankles tightened, too, the burn seeming to travel along my limbs to my torso.

A whimper escaped me, the treacherous reaction one I couldn't fight. But the invisible enchantment covering my mouth muffled the sound. However, Lucifer caught it, as evidenced by the cruel grin in his gaze.

Asshole, I thought at him as I fought to breathe. *You. Are. An. Asshole.*

"Stop!" Ajax demanded, his sudden appearance at my side shocking the hell out of me.

Okay. Maybe he wasn't bound after all.

Or he'd somehow broken free of Az's hold.

Except the Commander didn't appear to be trying to stop him. If anything, he looked even more tense than before.

Fire blazed around me in the next blink, the heat nearly singeing my eyebrows and forcing me to focus on Lucifer.

And the ashy wings at his back.

Oh...

They beat once, cascading embers all around us, then disappeared.

I'd seen those fiery feathers when he'd attempted to close the portal in the Marsh Lands. They'd been magnificent in the sky. Witnessing them here in this closed space, however, was more terrifying than magnificent.

"Who are *you* to command *me*?" His voice boomed, shaking the very walls as I stiffened my spine.

Ajax didn't budge. He didn't even flinch. He simply stared the Hell Fae King down, his blue-black gaze as hard as granite.

Melek's cool energy swirled around me as his palm went to my shoulder, his thumb drawing a line up my neck to trace over the Hell Fae King's fingertips.

The talisman hanging between my breasts responded to his caress, sending another chilly wave across my skin that chased away Lucifer's hot touch.

But I still couldn't breathe.

"I realize you never agreed to specific terms, my king, but I'm imploring you to take a step back," Melek said, his calm tone underlined with a seriousness I rarely ever heard from him. "Particularly before you do something irrevocable that may result in lasting consequences."

Lucifer's jaw flexed, his sapphire eyes narrowing.

However, he didn't release me.

He simply stared down the man behind me.

"There is more than her life at stake," Melek added. "She closed a portal, one that likely would have destroyed the Unseelie capital had she not intervened. Now we need to handle the cleanup. We also need to focus our efforts on finding the culprit responsible so this doesn't happen again."

"She used *my* source to close that portal," Lucifer told him, his grasp unyielding.

I tried to swallow but couldn't. There was no room. No

air. *And wow, now I'm seeing spots,* I thought dizzily. *Not good. Not good at all.*

"Because you couldn't close it," Melek returned, a note of steel underlining his tone now. "She *helped* you. And this is how you're going to repay that assistance? By throttling her?"

Az cleared his throat. "He's right, Typhos. She didn't make things worse; she helped. Let go of her."

Lucifer startled, his gaze flying to his Commander. "You, too?" He shook his head, his long hair waving over his thick shoulders. "Fucking ridiculous. This female has captured you all by the balls." He released me so suddenly that I would have fallen had Melek not been behind me.

His arm instantly came around my waist, holding my back to his chest as I greedily gulped in air, the world spinning around me through each breath.

Lucifer measured up his prince, bewilderment battling with his fiery rage. "She can access the Hell Fae Source. Not only that, but she can *use* it."

"Yes, and she did so to close a portal that was growing wildly out of control because *you* couldn't close it," Melek replied.

I froze. Pointing out Lucifer's failure probably wasn't the best way to handle this situation. Yet I couldn't help thinking, *He's not wrong...*

"Cami resolved a potentially realm-destructive portal," Melek pressed on. "These are unprecedented times, my king. Acting rashly will only put your kingdom in more danger."

"You mean *our* kingdom, little prince."

Melek merely shrugged, causing an eerie quiet to settle in the air around us.

I continued to breathe, my lungs stinging with each inhale.

All the while, Lucifer focused intently on the male behind

me, the two men seeming to have fallen into some sort of staring contest.

Or perhaps they were speaking telepathically now. I wasn't sure. But Melek appeared to have Lucifer's undivided attention, the Hell Fae King's gaze sparking with unresolved fury while he glared at the other fae.

As they continued their silent debate, Ajax subtly moved closer to me.

I pretended not to notice, something that became decidedly difficult as his magic slithered over me, the sensation reminding me of the snake-vines from his interrogation. Only, a warm kiss of power immediately followed the slithering sensation, the impact causing my shoulders to relax.

Ohhh, I thought. *That... that feels... nice...*

Healing magic, I understood after a beat. *Ajax is healing me.*

I blinked at the Midnight Fae, but his focus was on Lucifer and Melek. Yet his magic continued to wash over me, each stroke making me feel lighter—*freer*—than before.

Because Lucifer still has a hold on me. I'd thought he'd released me from his power, but he hadn't. He'd merely physically let go of my throat and loosened my bindings enough to knock me off-balance.

Fucking bastard king.

He still had an invisible bind over my mouth, too. A bind that Ajax's magic had yet to touch. *Because he's purposely leaving me mute.*

I nearly glared at him, but I didn't want Lucifer to notice.

Ajax was providing me with some relief, perhaps even trying to free me from Lucifer's mental grasp. I didn't want to risk the king discovering Ajax's interference, as it would surely not end well.

Which left me wondering, *Why is Ajax doing this?* He'd

already pissed off Lucifer by telling him to stop. And this... this certainly took that defiance to a new level.

"Just because the portal is closed doesn't mean there isn't work to be done," Melek suddenly said aloud. "You should be channeling your energy into rebuilding what was lost in the Marsh Lands and guiding your people when they need you most."

"*Our* people," Lucifer corrected, seeming to grow weary of reminding Melek that they were supposed to be united. Still, the fires eased in his eyes as he spoke to the prince, leaving his piercing eyes smoldering like the low burn of a blue flame.

"Our people," Melek agreed with a nod, his arm loosening a little around my waist as he moved to my side. "Thank you for protecting *our* people, Camillia."

The Hell Fae King made a noise in the back of his throat.

"Yes, thank you for closing the portal," Az echoed.

Lucifer just shook his head and took another step backward, his power still caressing my skin.

My naked *skin*, I thought, swallowing—a motion that hurt, thanks to Lucifer's manhandling.

Everyone stood there watching me now, like they were waiting for me to speak.

Which I couldn't.

Because of Lucifer.

However, had I been able to speak, I probably would have said, *Now would be a great time for someone to offer me some clothes.*

Silence fell upon us again, all four men exchanging glances.

This seemed to be a pivotal moment. One that would determine my fate.

Either the Hell Fae King would pass judgment on me now, which every fiber of his being clearly wanted to do, or he would listen to the Hell Fae Prince and head back to the Marsh Lands.

Melek wasn't wrong. I'd seen some of the devastation caused by the portal, as well as the impact of closing it. The shock wave had rushed out for miles. As king, Lucifer was absolutely needed at this critical time.

The Nightmare Fae relied on him for protection and acceptance. Without him... Well, I wasn't sure. From what I could tell, the Nightmare Fae were seen as abominations by other fae, making them homeless.

Lucifer had given them a place to nest, to run free, to be *alive*.

But someone, or *someones*, had attacked that safe haven.

It was Lucifer's job to heal the kingdom and the Nightmare Fae who resided within it. I'd done my part. Whether grateful or not, the problem was temporarily solved. *Because of me.*

Which was why I didn't deserve to be treated like this.

I didn't deserve his *judgment*, especially when all I'd done was assist him.

Willing myself to meet his gaze, I lifted my chin as he gave me one last evaluation. His expression changed, and I wasn't sure how to read him.

There was a sadness there, definitely frustration as well, and a hint of concern.

But there was also something else, something I couldn't quite place.

To my surprise, he was the first to break eye contact. His focus went to Ajax, then to Az, and finally landed on Melek. He gave them all a slow once-over, almost as though he was trying to figure something out. Whatever it was, he didn't comment on it. Instead, his lips flattened as a weird vibration touched the air, one that caused the hairs along my arms to stand on end.

Is something coming? I wondered, my gaze flickering

around the room—the same one Ajax and I had been relegated to in Lucifer's quarters.

I waited for someone or something to appear, but nothing happened. That odd reverberation just continued, the echo of it infiltrating my thoughts and buzzing down my spine.

What is that? I glanced at Lucifer to see if he'd sensed it, and instead found his attention entirely on me, his gaze flaring with renewed embers.

All of the emotions in his features had fled, leaving only rage behind.

Oh, shit. He's decided to kill me, I realized.

Melek's arm tightened around my lower back, reminding me that he stood at my side, while Ajax's power flared to life across my skin.

Lucifer growled under his breath. "She's not yours to protect, Warden."

"That's not for you to decide, Hell Fae King," he returned, the title one he voiced with a hint of something that seemed to startle Lucifer for a beat.

The vibration intensified, causing my head to spin. Dizziness washed over me a moment later, and the edges of my vision grew dark.

Is Lucifer doing something to me?

Despite the tightness growing in my chest, the electric humming continued in my head in a steady repetition.

It's... it's repeating like a cell phone vibration.

Or a pager?

The latter was something I'd never seen in person, but I'd read about them in books.

"Watch her," Lucifer said as the world surrounding me went black.

Melek's arm flexed around me, my feet suddenly floating in the air.

Because he picked me up? I thought tiredly.

"I'll be back to finish this later," Lucifer added, leaving me alone in the darkness. *No, alone with Melek. Maybe.* Except... I felt... a new strength around me. *Ajax?* Had Melek caught me, only to hand me off to the other man?

No one spoke.

Or maybe I could no longer hear them.

I was... cast... into the night. Alone. Hearing only Lucifer's final words reverberating in my head. *"I'll be back to finish this later."*

To finish what? I wondered. *Finish off my life?*

He could try.

But I wouldn't make it easy for him. That was for damn sure.

Because whether Lucifer realized it or not, he needed me.

And I'm going to make sure he fucking knows it.

CHAPTER 2

TYPHOS

My Warden held the unconscious female while my Commander's nostrils flared.

Clearly, they didn't approve of how I'd handled this situation.

And neither did my prince.

The disapproving glint in his multicolored irises made me growl. He arched a brow in response, daring me to comment or do anything to counter his disapproval.

Goading me, I realized, *He's fucking goading me.*

He should know better, especially in my current mood.

"Be glad I didn't kill her," I snarled before engaging my teleportation ability and leaving them all in the room.

One of them could watch the girl. I didn't care which of them did. They were smart enough to keep her out of trouble until I returned.

To finish this.

Whatever the fuck that meant.

I reappeared in the hallway of my palace, my fury no doubt palpable to everyone in my path. Which explained why all the Hellhounds took several steps back, eager to give me distance.

Smart Nightmare Fae.

Unresolved rage pushed against my mental barriers, stirring Hellfire in my veins. Sizzling energy crept along my skin, the power unintentionally singeing the palace floor as I stormed down the corridor.

It had been instinct to bring Camillia here after feeling the invasion of her presence in my mind.

In my soul.

In my *source*.

If Melek hadn't appeared, I would have killed her. And then what? Would I expect my prince to forever stare at the place where I had murdered his young mate?

He's the one who chose to tie his soul to hers, I mentally muttered.

Of course, that didn't mean I wanted to see him suffer.

Fuck, all I ever desired in life was Melek's happiness. However, I also valued his life. And Camillia had threatened that today.

Threats were something I dealt with swiftly and mercilessly.

Except, this pretty little threat had a magic cunt that had spellbound all of my men.

Fuck.

A growl reverberated in the back of my throat. I should just turn around and kill her.

Or I could... I could try to understand her, I considered. *Determine why all of my men are so infatuated with her. See if there's a way to shatter this damn spell she's woven around them all.*

I snorted at the inane thoughts.

Camillia De la Croix was a mystery no man would unravel without forfeiting his soul.

I kept walking until I entered the trophy room. I bypassed the skulls and mementos from my many victories and went straight to a dimly lit corner that showcased my favorite piece of art.

This was where I went when I needed to think. When I needed to get my head on straight. When I needed to... *calm down*.

Grazing my fingers over the ridges of the painting, I drew in the memories of when Melek had created this piece. It depicted a wall of flames that wouldn't mean much to others but represented how Melek viewed my love.

All-consuming.

Passionate.

And never ending.

My love for Melek and my people was a fire that burned for eternity because I deemed it so.

However, Camillia's presence here endangered everything I'd built. Everything I adored. *Everything I am.*

I'd felt her elegant fingers delicately unwinding my soul like the frayed ends of a tapestry, threatening to make it all come undone.

My fingernail caught the edge of one of the flames, and the paint broke off, revealing the glittering gold base canvas underneath. Frowning at it, I decided I didn't like the metaphor that small action represented.

She's going to strip me down to my core if I continue to allow her to breathe.

And then what? What use would I be to Melek if a simple Hell Fae Halfling could manipulate a power that would otherwise be eternal?

There's something more going on here that I'm missing.

But I didn't have time to pick apart everything right now to find that missing piece. As Melek had pointed out, there were more important items to be concerned with at the moment.

Such as the kingdom that had just been nearly ripped apart by foreign magic. And the Naga King that had paged me for a conversation.

She sensed that page, I recalled, my gaze narrowing.

I'd seen it in Camillia's features—she'd felt the vibration of magic that had shimmied in the air when Viper had tried to reach out to me. No one else had reacted, just Camillia.

Was it because she was still connected to me?

Or was she continuing to access my source without permission?

Even if she wasn't doing it on purpose, it was a violation that couldn't be tolerated. I'd cast her into a deep sleep to prevent her from meddling further. It was a mercy she didn't deserve when I should have made her heart stop instead.

She needs to die.

Yet my men clearly disagreed with that verdict.

Fuck.

With a growl, I formed a portal back to the Marsh Lands and slipped through it.

I stepped through the wall of liquid fire and sank into the soft, damp soil of a world rocked by a portal I'd been unable to close.

No. The Hell Fae Halfling had done it for me.

Fucking Camillia. Her presence haunted my every step, causing my teeth to grind together in frustration. *How did she know what would close the portal?* She'd hit it with heat rather than water, which was counterintuitive to putting out a fire.

Yet she'd done it with ease and without hesitation.

Does she know who created it? I wondered as I moved across the murky earth. *Did she create it?*

A flurry of colorful wings had me glancing left as a group

of Unseelie took off in a scatter, likely trying to avoid my presence.

Wise.

Destruction spanned out everywhere I looked. I'd shadowed to the other side of the Unseelie castle in response to Viper's summons.

The lieutenant—whom the Nagas referred to as their king—appeared at the gate. As a Naga, and a Nightmare Fae, he could take either a human form or his monster one.

He'd chosen his human one to speak to me in, even though his long tail would be better suited to work through the marsh. But it was a measure of respect to come to me in a suit, which was what he wore now. Although, he wasn't wearing a shirt underneath the unbuttoned vest.

He wasn't wearing shoes, either.

He looked more like a warrior with his bare feet sunk into the muck and the lower half of his silky pants damp from walking through his territory. He didn't seem bothered by it. His pants hung low, revealing muscles that betrayed his strength.

As a Naga, he likely spent most days scaling the kingdom's rocky cliffs and slithering through the marshy terrain while hunting invading creatures. That took skill, athleticism, and a specialized talent for seeking out prey.

The Unseelie and the Nagas had a few natural enemies in the Marsh Lands that kept them busy. Given the Nagas' declining population, the alliance between the two Nightmare Fae species had served them well.

But clearly, Viper played his part. He rippled with well-used muscles that put some of my spoiled Hellhounds to shame.

I'd once considered Viper for the post of Warden. He'd been the perfect candidate, given he could track any creature and tame any beast with his hypnotism ability.

But he excelled as King of the Nagas and would not have accepted the coveted station, nor would I have expected him to hole up in the dungeons in the palace's dry underground.

"Thirty-five Unseelie deaths," he informed me quietly, as was his style.

Now I understood why he'd called me. Most of my lieutenants—who were all considered kings among their faedoms—normally waited for me to contact them.

However, the incidents of late were unprecedented.

And Viper was well within his rights to page me after today's destruction in his kingdom.

I should never have left after the portal was closed, I realized. *But I'd been too caught up in Camillia's show of power to think it through.*

That was what Melek had been trying to tell me—that I had other priorities to consider right now.

Priorities like Viper.

"And Naga?" I asked him, already fearing what he would say. There had been a reason he'd started with the Unseelie death count rather than that of his own people. It must be a high number; otherwise, he would have led with that first.

His jaw ticked before he answered. "Almost a hundred. Ninety-eight, to be precise. The portal opened near a Naga cavern."

I bowed my head, my eyes falling closed as I whispered an ancient prayer of condolences to him in the Naga tongue.

He answered in kind, then silence fell between us.

I waited several beats, aware of the quiet rituals his species favored.

Part of the bridal test today would have revolved around sound, or lack thereof, and a bride's capacity for hearing the truth in unconventional ways.

Alas, that part of the trial hadn't happened.

I swallowed and gave a nod of my head. "Their losses will be avenged. I swear it."

"Thank you, my liege," he replied, his soft tone deepening with an emotion I understood—the need for revenge.

Alas, that required knowing who was responsible for this.

Camillia certainly appeared to be guilty, especially since she'd known how to close the portal. However, we'd intimately connected when she'd tapped into my power, and I'd sensed her genuine desire to help. But that could have been a manipulation of some kind. It also still didn't explain how she'd known what to do.

Maybe she's working with someone, I considered.

If that was true, then I needed to find out who was helping her.

Or using her, I added, frowning. The thought had been instinctual, almost as though my source had whispered it into my mind.

This woman is fucking with me, everything I hold dear, every piece of me—magical or otherwise.

Clearing my throat, I refocused on Viper and asked, "Have you seen Erebus?"

The Naga King sneered when I mentioned his Unseelie counterpart, which was out of character for Viper.

He and Erebus were friends. Their camaraderie was why they successfully shared the Marsh Lands territories.

Even the Unseelie castle held caverns and an underground lair for the Nagas to use as they wished, caverns that linked up directly to the Nagas' central domain.

Other kingdoms lacked the homeostasis these two kings had established.

Of course, having a shared enemy—the soulless creatures that plagued this kingdom—had linked the Nagas and the Unseelie, giving them a common enemy to fight.

Sometimes I helped, but usually I stayed out of their way.

Alas, I'd failed today.

And already I could see the damage my failure had caused.

Not just the destruction of stone or the loss of lives—but the fracturing of a kinship that should have lasted for thousands of years.

"The last time I saw Erebus, he was chasing a bride," Viper hissed out as a slithering sound entered his words. He clearly disapproved.

That must be the runaway bride Az mentioned from the status update, I thought.

"Was she hurt?" I asked Viper. Because while King Erebus was many things, he would not abandon his people over a rogue female. He'd need a much better reason to pursue the errant bride, such as a need to heal her.

"*All* of the Marsh Lands are hurt," Viper replied, his long tongue snaking out before he reined it back in. "Wounded are being gathered in the medic quadrant. Survivors are still being found, and it was just discovered that there are Nagas trapped in collapsed tunnels."

"They can't dig themselves out?" I asked. The Nagas were the ones to build those tunnels in the first place; it seemed strange that they could be trapped underground.

"The blast rendered many of them unconscious," Viper explained. "They're helpless and losing air, so unless we do something, the casualty number will rise."

"I see." This must have been why Viper was frustrated with Erebus—the Unseelie King would be able to use his magic to move the stone. Yet he was off pursuing a female. "Are Erebus's people unable to reach him?"

Some of the Unseelie possessed telepathic capabilities with their king; they should be able to find him fairly easily.

"As I said, he's chasing a bride. When Erebus doesn't want to be found, no one can reach him."

I nodded. "I will speak to him after we save your Nagas."

Viper's shoulders relaxed as if he was afraid I would choose to join Erebus in the hunt for a female instead of helping his people.

No. I just abandoned you temporarily over a different woman instead, I thought guiltily. *Camillia De la Croix is a problem.*

One I really needed to stop thinking about.

"I've tried to dig through the debris, but it won't be fast enough." Viper bowed his head, the gesture one of respect. "If it pleases you, my liege, I request your aid."

Unleashing some of my Hellfire energy sounded like a brilliant idea.

"Of course, Viper," I said, returning his formal gesture with a slight nod. "Show me where they are."

CHAPTER 3

TYPHOS

IT WAS a simple matter to unearth the trapped Nagas. Simple did not mean easy, per se, not in my current mood. It took more effort than I cared to admit to limit my blast radius so that Viper and the other Nagas could begin digging.

The goal was to save the survivors, not obliterate them.

Which gave me some satisfaction for my task now to rebuild a wing of the Unseelie castle. With the rescues out of the way, it was time for rehabilitation. Something I would normally task the subjects of the affected territory with doing, but this was my fault.

I'd failed to protect them.

Now, I would fix the damage.

Starting with destroying this portion of the castle so I could work from a clean slate. Maybe it was overkill, but it suited my task.

My fist met cracked stone, blasting through it with ease as Hellfire turned a portion of it into molten rock. The rest evaporated completely under my unrestrained rage.

The shock wave rippled through my senses and hit my

chest just as the familiar scent of burned stone overtook my senses.

It wasn't like the molten rock of my palace, but something a bit muskier and heavy with moisture native to the Marsh Lands. It added steam to my building stone fire, blotting out the murky sky as I released another blast.

This one was accompanied by a roar of rage that held a shock wave of its own. The sound came straight from my soul, holding all of my frustration that everything I'd built was slowly crumbling down all around me and there wasn't anything I could do about it.

Unlike stone and structure, I couldn't rebuild Melek's heart if Camillia's death broke it.

I couldn't even protect my own damn people, hence my current predicament.

Out of instinct, I checked in with my source once again, finding it content. The sensation baffled me. I could *feel* Camillia's intrusion.

It was wrong. Unacceptable.

And something I would deal with after I finished in the Marsh Lands.

While I muddled through a perpetual sea of frustration, the source practically purred. It had *enjoyed* her ministrations, approving of her interference.

Which was incredible, really. My source never liked anyone except me. Because it was *mine*.

Is it because she was able to close the portal? I wondered at the source. *Is that why you're brimming with pride?*

Sighing, I leaned into the burning pile of stone I'd created, my forehead falling to the broken, heated rocks.

Who did this? I whispered to the kingdom. *How have my walls been breached?*

Both figuratively and literally.

The only ones powerful enough were the Virtuous Fae, but what could they possibly want with me? With my people?

To prove a point?

To make me look like an incompetent king unable to protect his own?

If so, they were succeeding.

But why would they breach my walls now? After all this time?

What if I've been betrayed? I pondered, a sour taste building in my throat at the possibility. *Is someone trying to take over my realm?*

Someone like Camillia?

But what would she have to gain?

I frowned, my mind returning to the concept of her working with someone—or her being *used* by someone.

Is she just a pretty distraction?

My men were obviously influenced by whatever bewitchment she'd cast over them. Perhaps she was unaware she was doing it, but the evidence was there.

My orders had already been defied. Without swift repercussions, disobedience could turn into something more sinister.

Melek would never betray me, I thought. *But Azazel, after everything we've been through. Would he be capable of it?*

Maybe not on a regular day. But he was with Ajax. And Ajax was young and unstable. His broken soul made him malleable, something I intended to use to an advantage. To make my Warden strong and unstoppable. The revoking of his title was only meant to be temporary. I'd expected him to earn back his place.

Just like the Unseelie castle, I could rebuild what was broken if given a clean slate.

But my punishment had only seemed to further break my

Warden, thus creating a potentially irreparable situation. He'd told me to *stop*. Like he was suddenly in charge, not me.

Fuck, Az had taken his side as well. Melek, too.

All three of them were against me.

For her.

Melek's bond to her made him unreliable in terms of a decision where Camillia was concerned. Ajax... I sighed. This was too difficult for Ajax to bear, what with his history and what Constantine had done to him.

And Azazel, my Commander, was linked to Ajax. His Phoenix had also imprinted on the girl, which was enough to confuse my Commander, at the very least.

They were my inner circle. The only three who could really hurt me.

But was this enough for one of them to betray me?

No.

They might stand up to me, but betrayal...

No, I repeated to myself. *No.*

Yet I couldn't help thinking about the last time I'd been betrayed. That memory existed behind a solid barrier I never took down.

But now, I chipped away at those walls like fragile paint over golden canvas, exposing the raw truth underneath.

Vivaxia's was the last Virtuous Fae presence I'd felt near my gates. She was the treacherous bitch who'd caused my fall. Her threads of power had been unique.

She'd siphoned my energy. Attempted to use it for her own purposes. Weakening me. My abilities. *My being.*

I hadn't seen it at first.

I'd been blinded by my faith in her. In our friendship.

But Az... he'd seen what was happening. He'd warned me. However, by then, it was nearly too late.

A vision of air—no land, just an abyss—formed in my

mind. The strain of my shoulders as I tried to ignite wings that no longer existed.

Just a bone skeleton.

Too diminished to form feathers. To fly. *To survive.*

My fist hit a structure column, sending the whole segment crashing around me. With a rush of flaming power, I protected myself from the weight of the stone, causing my fiery wings to appear and brush my shoulders for a brief second. They were merely a remnant of what they used to be.

What could never be again.

Because I'd been betrayed.

Ash rained down while the rumble of destruction spread out around me like a crack of thunder.

My chest heaved with the exertion. It felt *good*.

But it wasn't enough.

I was about to resume the havoc when Melek's crystal gaze cut through the demolition, his irises radiating his disappointment.

"Are you done throwing your tantrum?" he asked.

Tantrum, I repeated, grunting inside. Of course he would see it that way.

I started toward him, crunching my way through the broken stones. "Once I finish rebuilding here, I will find who is responsible and *finish this*."

He cocked a blondish-brown eyebrow. "Does that mean you still intend to kill Cami?" A bold question. But I expected no less from my prince. However, I really wasn't ready for this conversation yet, something he should know, as I was clearly in the middle of *throwing my tantrum*.

"She's a threat," I growled at him. "End of discussion."

"A threat that helped fix the breach," he returned, ignoring me. "Seems incredibly dangerous." The deadpan quality of his voice had the hairs along the back of my neck standing on end. It was almost mocking in nature. *Rude*, too.

"She accessed *my* power to do it."

"And it worked. What's the problem?"

"*What's the problem?*" I repeated, irritated by his continued nonchalance. My temper flared, power echoing with each step I took toward him.

Melek didn't seem fazed, yet anyone else in his position would have run in terror.

Granted, no one else would be brave enough to face me in this state.

My nose brushed his as I fisted the collar of his flawless dress shirt. "Did you not hear me?"

"I did," he said softly, his breath a provocation on my lips. "Did you not hear the part where I pointed out how she *fixed* the breach?"

My frustration easily turned on my prince as I slipped my hand up his hard, muscled chest and wrapped my fingers around his throat. I was still furious, mostly because of what had occurred tonight—and over the last month and a half.

But I was also angry at Melek for refusing me my outlet earlier.

Camillia was a problem that should have been swiftly dealt with.

Instead, she was alive, and my prince was here, leaning against a column like some sort of offering.

Hmm, I hummed, considering him again, the word *offering* repeating in my mind.

Because that was exactly what he was attempting to be— an alternative outlet.

Oh, I see. He wants to play.

A dangerous proposition, given my mood.

I blocked him in with one arm, making the stone behind him heat to dangerous temperatures. My hips grazed his, keeping him in place as my violence quickly turned into arousal.

Which was probably exactly what Melek had anticipated.

"Why are you goading me?" I asked him, finally seeing through the haze of my temper enough to realize what he was doing.

Melek grinned against my mouth. "Is it working?"

I bit his lip in response, hard enough to draw blood. He didn't flinch. Instead, he licked his tongue over the small hurt as if begging for more.

"You need an escape, Ty," he said, softer this time. "I denied you an escape earlier. If you need to take out your anger on me, I will gladly bear it."

I thought back to the flames Melek had painted, an accurate depiction of my love right now. Anyone close to me was prone to being burned.

"I don't want to hurt you," I whispered against his lips, already shoving my tongue into his mouth.

He took my violent thrusts, only speaking when I moved to his neck to mouth his pulse. "I was made for you, Ty. There's nothing you could do to me that you haven't done before."

I doubted that.

I couldn't remember a time I had been quite this angry.

This pent-up.

When Melek whispered a spell that rendered him naked before me, all muscle and man with an erection leaving little doubt of his willingness, my resolve faltered.

"You told me to fix the problem here," I reminded him, my senses slowly dissolving into ash. "Now you're distracting me."

"Because you've been here for hours, Ty. It's going to take weeks to rebuild the castle on your own. You need to take a break."

"I need to find out who did this."

"Yes," he agreed. "But you're not going to accomplish that

in this state. You need to calm down first. Think clearly." He grazed my lower lip with his teeth. "Fuck me, my king. Escape for a little while. Empty your head of everything except us."

I narrowed my gaze at his beautiful face. "I can't tell if you want me to use you or if you're distracting me from something."

"Both," he admitted. "I want you inside me. And I want to distract you from killing Cami tonight."

I rolled my eyes. "It's all about her these days."

"It's not," he whispered. "It's about *you*. But you don't see it yet, Ty. Someday, I hope you will. But to do that, you need to focus. And I know a good way to help you do that."

"Sex."

"Sex," he agreed, his fingers running up my arms as I tightened my grasp around his throat. "No limits tonight. Anything you want."

My blood heated with the prospect of playing with my prince in such a manner. He was a gift. A prize to be cherished. *The perfect mate.*

I am, he agreed, clearly having heard my thought. *Now indulge me, my king. Otherwise, I'm going to go find an Unseelie to play with.*

My eyes narrowed. *Taunting me isn't advised, little prince.*

Who says I'm taunting you, my king? Maybe I mean it.

You don't.

He lifted a shoulder. *I will if you don't—*

I squeezed his throat as I engaged my teleportation talents, our bedroom appearing around us in the next instant. "I have half a mind to tie you to this bed and keep you there for hours."

His full lips lifted at the edges. "Yes, please."

"Always so troublesome," I said as I pulled him onto the mattress by his throat.

"It's my middle name," he replied against my mouth. "Now stop talking and use me."

I was the strongest fae in this realm, and yet I was incapable of resisting Melek's demands. Sometimes I wondered who was really in charge here. Because it certainly seemed as though he dominated me in ways I could never dominate him.

Lowering my mouth to his, I whispered, "As you wish, little prince."

CHAPTER 4

AZ

A FEW MINUTES EARLIER

FOUR HOURS OF SILENCE.

No commentary.

No replies.

Nothing.

Just me talking to a fucking wall that happened to resemble Ajax.

"This is ridiculous," I told him. "You forgave my Phoenix for unduly attacking you, but you can't even consider forgiving me for doing my job?"

Ajax simply twirled his wand in reply, his gaze on a still-unconscious Cami. He wouldn't even look at me, let alone acknowledge my presence.

He just kept pacing, his eyes lingering on the female sleeping on the couch. The Midnight Fae had held her for a good two hours before finally laying her there to rest. He'd also conjured a blanket to cover her naked state, his movements protective as he'd tucked her in with it.

Then he'd started walking back and forth.

Back and forth.

Back and forth some more.

All the while acting as though I weren't sitting in the armchair catty-cornered to Cami.

Ajax endlessly twirled his wand as magic sparked around him like angry little fireworks. He didn't have to tell me again that he wouldn't forgive me for this. His body screamed it.

The effect left me feeling breathless, as if my lungs refused to give me all of the oxygen I required. Defenses of my actions —and inaction—tingled on the edge of my tongue, but all of them fell flat into silence.

He wasn't going to listen to me anymore. I'd crossed some invisible line for Ajax, and now I wasn't sure how to find my way back to him.

I'd never seen Ajax this furious. His anger nearly rivaled Typhos's current state, but the flame behind it couldn't have been more different.

Typhos feared what Camillia would do to the Hell Fae Realm and the risk she posed to everything he had built. I'd been with him from the very beginning. No one understood his concern better than I did—except for Melek, of course.

But Ajax was much younger according to supernatural standards. He didn't have the weight of millennia on his shoulders.

Cami was the first spark of life that he'd allowed to flicker within his emotional walls. He'd granted me a glimpse inside those walls, too, but Cami was different. She was... *more*. A breath of fresh air. A soul for him to save.

A soul like Emelyn's.

In many ways, Ajax's view of this was simplistic.

Camillia was his. Therefore, she must be protected.

My Phoenix bristled in the back of my mind, clawing at the barrier of my soul in firm agreement. He wanted to fix this.

Whereas Typhos, my king, wanted to *finish* it.

That was something I wasn't sure I could accept. Which was why I'd stood against him tonight. I'd felt his shock at my taking Melek's side, but on this, I agreed with the Hell Fae Prince. Killing Cami would be rash. I'd witnessed her burst of power, her enigmatic energy, and saw an ally, not an enemy.

She'd helped fix the barrier.

Yes, she'd used Typhos's powers to do it, but she could have used them for something far worse. Why punish her for doing the right thing?

I sighed, my gaze wandering to the little Halfling at the center of all this chaos.

She appeared so fucking innocent on the couch. He'd tucked the blanket over her bare breasts, but the material was thin enough to give me a full view of her luxurious form. Her beaded nipples disturbed the folds of the fabric, begging for attention.

My mind easily slipped back to when she'd been essentially naked in the cage at the club. All of her delicious skin had been on display and—

Grrrr.

My Phoenix growled in the back of my mind, interrupting the memory, but not just because he wanted me to fuck her. No, it was more proprietary than that. His perception was possessive. *Instinctual.*

And *pissed* that so many other fae had seen *his* female in such a vulnerable state.

I studied her features as I tried to understand this fascination that my Phoenix held for her.

Well, maybe not just my bird, but me, too.

She was stunning. Intelligent. Strong. A survivor.

Despite her disqualification from the trials, she was a Hell Fae Bride by every definition of the term—but she was something so much *more,* too. Her multicolored hair didn't seem to agree if it should be blonde or brown, the mixture of tones intertwining the silky strands together as they framed her angelic face.

She appeared so vulnerable while asleep, but her brows furrowed as if even her dreams weren't free of endless trials.

The urge to smooth the worry from her brow all but consumed me. Yet, my loyalty to Typhos, my mate and my king, kept me in place.

Mate, my Phoenix echoed, but his word was intended for the beauty on the couch, not for Typhos.

The divide in my loyalties shook me to my core, making me tremble with indecision.

My Phoenix pulled me toward the female, while my past demanded that I follow orders.

Mate, my Phoenix insisted again. My teeth ached with his desire to bite her.

But that would mark her as mine—*permanently.* It would be a betrayal that Lucifer would not forgive because it would put him in an even more delicate situation. He already had Melek to contend with; he didn't need me involved, too.

Besides, I was stronger than my primal instincts, wasn't I?

Maybe.

The desire seemed to be growing by the day, my Phoenix irritated by my refusal to listen to his irrational need. He'd been this way since he'd taken over the other day, his cravings blending with my own and confusing my senses.

If I bit her, I could truly protect her, but the claim would destroy everything I had built with Typhos in the process.

My chest tightened as I struggled to breathe again.

My bird saw it as a simple claim, but I knew better. Nothing about this was *simple*. Not to mention the fact that she wouldn't even accept my claim now anyway.

I'd fucked up.

But I was just doing my job.

I didn't even know how to begin to explain myself. Not to her, and certainly not to Ajax.

The latter of whom shifted into view as he placed himself

between me and the female on the couch, blocking my sight of her. When he didn't move, it became clear he was doing it on purpose.

"You act like I'm going to hurt her," I accused. I didn't hide the sting or the annoyance in my voice.

He cocked an eyebrow in return. *Aren't you?* his eyes seemed to say.

Did he not fucking understand what had happened?

"We had orders," I snarled, ignoring the sensation of my Phoenix clawing at my skin. "No fucking the candidates. That was broken, so the consequences were what happened at the club." Typhos was a fae of his word. He couldn't be blamed for punishing us for our sins. It was what the Hell Fae King did.

If he hadn't followed through, then he wouldn't have been the steadfast leader the Hell Fae Realms required.

The Nightmare Fae Kingdoms and the Hell Fae were a stone's throw away from dissolving into disorder without a powerful and predictable king. Typhos was the one who had brought organization and peace where there had only been suffering and despair.

I would know. I was one of his first projects.

I stood and took a step closer to Ajax, my chest brushing his. Breathing seemed almost impossible when his heat bled through my clothes, but I needed to make him understand.

He didn't back down as his dark eyes burned with deep blue flames of defiance. Instead of engaging with me like he normally would, he remained a solid fucking rock that was not going to bend.

"Typhos also said what would happen if Camillia touched his source again," I reminded him.

While I hadn't been there for that exact conversation, Typhos had echoed the words into my mind and Melek's.

I had carefully listened to every word because Typhos

Lucifer worked in deals, which made the terms of each one important.

Despite my resolve to explain the complexities of the situation to Ajax, I desperately wanted to find a loophole in this situation between Cami and Typhos.

It was the only way to achieve any sort of peace without betraying my loyalties.

The alternative was to go against everything I stood for and believed in. Typhos had freed me from a life of posture and servitude. I'd been nothing more than a glorified pet. But ever since I'd become his Commander, my life fucking meant something.

He deserved my eternal and unwavering loyalty.

But somehow, Camillia had changed everything with her mere existence.

Ajax showed his teeth against my attempts at rationalization. My Phoenix responded to the gesture in kind, snarling in my head. A gesture not meant for Ajax but for me.

Because he agreed with the ex-Warden.

This is driving me fucking mad.

"Do you always blindly follow orders?" Ajax finally asked. His words were barely a whisper but lined with deadly knives. He flicked his finger against my head. "Is there a brain somewhere up there? Or is it all made of feathers?"

My hackles flared in response. Ajax and I had never been at odds like this. We'd fought before, but usually it was because my beast had been a little too rough and had physically hurt him. An instance like that was easily soothed by sensual pleasure.

Now, my normal methods of apology clearly weren't going to cut it.

He stabbed a finger back at the female on the couch. "I told you what Camillia meant to me. I said it once, but apparently, I have to fucking repeat it for you. She's the first female to make me feel anything more than death in the last decade. I was charged with her protection, and yet she was put on fucking display for all the Hell Fae to see. Then, when she helped us close a destructive portal, the thanks she received was a threat on her life."

His hand dropped to his side as his fingers curled into a fist.

"I told you I'd never forgive you for this, and that was *before* you watched Lucifer almost execute her right in front of us. If I didn't mean it after the club, then I fucking do now." His nose brushed mine as he snarled in my face. "I won't forgive you, Az."

Shit.

Pain stabbed my heart at the thought of losing Ajax, as well as Camillia, and the sensation surprised me.

I'm royally fucked.

Because I couldn't betray Typhos, either.

Luckily, Melek seemed intent on keeping Camillia alive. I would use that to my advantage and trust him to reason with the Hell Fae King.

In the meantime, I would follow the order I'd been given.

To watch her.

Which required Ajax and me to mend this schism before it became irreparable.

Assuming it's not too late.

The words felt foreign as I forced them to roll off my tongue. "I'm sorry," I grated out, being the first to back away. It was a concession in both my words and my body language that felt wrong and unfamiliar. "Is that what you need me to say? *I'm sorry.*"

Two words I rarely uttered to anyone.

Yet it was the second time I'd apologized to Ajax in a matter of days. Only this time, I was saying the words aloud instead of in my mind.

I wasn't sure what kind of response I expected, but Ajax turning and putting his back to me was not it.

My teeth ground together because it had taken *a lot* for me to apologize.

"And I *did* say something to him earlier. I didn't just stand there and watch as he nearly executed her," I corrected him. "I... I probably could have said more, but I did defend her."

He snorted. "Verbally, perhaps. But physically, you would have rolled over and let him proceed."

"You don't know that," I told him, frustrated by the accusation and his inability to understand. "You're also not the only one who didn't have a choice at the club. Typhos is my mate. My oldest friend. I will always put him first."

It was a vow I had made over a thousand years ago, a vow I could never betray. Even if a part of me wanted to.

"I know," Ajax finally replied, his voice flat. "That much is very clear."

Reaching up with the desire to touch him, I caught myself just before I brushed his shoulder. I forced my hand to return to my side.

"That doesn't mean I don't care about you, Ajax." Fuck, I more than cared. I considered him to be *mine*. "I did what I had to do to protect you." How could he not see that? Why couldn't he understand?

"And what about Cami?" Ajax demanded as he began to pace again, his wand reappearing to resume twirling. "Were you protecting her, too? Letting her stand up there for everyone to gawk at? Watching her lose her fight all for some sort of fucked-up punishment?" He scoffed at that, his wand moving faster now. "Just fuck off, Az. We're done talking about this."

My frustration burned into flames of my own, making me prowl forward. A flare of arousal didn't help. When Ajax and I fought, it often ended in sex.

But I realized the thrumming sense of lust wasn't only coming from me. A surge of heat burst through my mate-bond with Typhos, making me snarl.

Typhos and Melek are playing. Great. Just what I fucking need.

It wasn't the normal playful sensation I felt when the pair fucked one another.

This time it was primal, violent, and *dangerous*.

The frustration and turmoil over the whole damn situation, mixed in with so much aggression and arousal thrumming through my body, mingled together into a determination to *make* Ajax understand.

Force him to talk.

To *forgive*.

Ajax's wand snapped, sending magic wrapping around me in response. He knew the look in my eyes when a fight was coming on.

But this time, his fist came next, connecting with my jaw and sending a burst of blood from my lip.

My Phoenix was at the end of his patience, flaring to life within me as dark shadows exploded all around my form. I roared in response, angry at both my beast and Ajax. I dove for the ex-Warden with a blow that held nothing back.

He was ready for it.

He dodged, easily slipping into a warrior stance where he let his emotions rule. His fury unleashed an array of attacks, some in the form of tiny daggers that were embedded into my skin only to dissolve a moment later and others in the form of physical brute force.

We crashed into a writing desk, demolishing it into a pile of splinters before Ajax's fist created a new hole in the wall.

A single sound forced us both into an immediate standstill.

I held Ajax's wrist while he dug his fingers into my hip, but we were now focused on Camillia.

She'd gone deathly pale, and the small sound had been a moan from her plump lips. The kissable feature should have been deliciously red, but it was now a sickly blue.

An unspoken truce settled between Ajax and me as we untangled from one another and rushed to her side. Ajax rested a hand on her shoulder, and he didn't stop me when I bent over the couch on the other side to investigate the cause of her distress.

My Phoenix's growl slipped through my lips when I felt a strange, magical energy slithering all over her skin. A single tear rolled down her cheek, startling me.

Cami wasn't the crying type.

"Is Lucifer doing this?" Ajax demanded.

"I don't know," I answered honestly.

I could still feel the effects of Typhos and Melek engaged in rough, primal activities. Perhaps Typhos's magic was retaliating in some way.

I met Ajax's gaze. The blue flames in his obsidian eyes had only grown hotter, and I didn't blame him. "I will find out what's going on," I promised him.

Thankfully, Ajax gave me a curt nod of approval.

At least we can agree on something.

Turning on my heel, I left Camillia in his care while I hurried down the hall to face Lucifer.

I'd never physically interrupted him when he was being this intimate with his prince. I'd never had a reason to.

Typhos Lucifer was my mate in a platonic sense. He protected me, honored me, and I served him in return.

Mate, my Phoenix echoed in my head, referring to Camillia and all the justification needed to interrupt the Hell Fae King.

"I know," I told him as we reached Typhos's door. I paused as I prepared myself for what I would face within.

This was a small act of defiance. One I worried was a precursor of things to come.

The ancient vow I had once uttered to Typhos rang out in my mind, feeling fragile now as my hand hovered over the doorknob.

I pledge my fealty to you, Typhos Lucifer, my mate, my king. Your enemies are my enemies. Your allies are my allies. Your desires are my desires. In this, we are bonded together as the equals you claim us to be—a title none of your kind have ever proclaimed for one of mine. My Phoenix will never again taste ash. My soul will never again burn because your source burns for us all. You have my eternal loyalty. My eternal love.

Nothing will break my vow.

This I promise in blood.

All hail the Hell Fae King.

CHAPTER 5

CAMI

A BOOM SOUNDED, the echo reverberating my chest and knocking the wind out of my lungs.

What...?

My eyes blinked open, the sensation of sleep tugging at my lashes and blurring my vision.

I rubbed at my face, only for my nose to scrunch at the briny texture left behind.

That's... weird.

I lowered my palms and blinked again, this time my surroundings coming into view.

Oh... what the...?

An ocean.

Vast. Deep. Spreading out before me like an infinite blue landscape.

And I was sitting on a stone dock of some kind.

Where did the boom come from? I wondered, glancing over the waves and the mist spraying all around me.

Except, the mist wasn't from the water. It was coming from the sky.

Or maybe... it's from me?

No...

Scrambling to my feet, I squinted against the murky sun to get a better look at the sky in front of me. The air was swirling as if a portal had just closed, leaving the water twisting underneath it in a vortex that was growing larger—not smaller.

A swallow stuck in my throat as I turned around to see if I could run. Being trapped in a vortex ocean of death did not sound like an appealing way to die.

But I was met with Lucifer's visage when I spun to find out where the stone dock led.

No land anywhere in sight. Only a massive statue glowering down at me with disapproval.

What. The. Fuck?

It was an island.

An island dedicated to Lucifer's disapproving face.

Is this another trial? I wondered, noting that the platform was large enough to hold a significant number of people.

Like what was left of 666 brides.

Except I was all alone.

And I'm no longer a bride.

This place also didn't feel natural.

The air twisted around me, yet I felt nothing. No warming kiss from the sun. No chill from the oceanic breeze. No moisture from the mist.

It was as though a numbness had taken over, leaving behind a strange sensation of being encased in an invisible bubble.

I should be freezing, my exposed body—because of course I was naked again—on display for the elements.

Yet I sensed nothing.

It was almost like there was a burning heat deep inside my soul that was keeping me warm.

Lucifer's power, I thought with a frown.

Cami, a distant voice echoed, sounding eerily like my mother's.

My eyes widened as I turned in the direction of the voice, only to find the vortex shimmering in the air again. Except it was bigger now, more intense and swirling with angry waves of power.

Um...

A lightning bolt jolted from the center in the next breath, hitting me straight in the chest. I screamed, the sound lost to the waves crashing against the stone.

Fuck!

Heat blistered through my being, pushing power to somewhere deep within my soul. I rubbed my chest, my heart beating far too fast. My veins burned. My breathing became labored.

Then it... *settled.*

Electricity hummed through my body as the ground beneath my feet fractured, the stones turning to pebbles.

What is this? I marveled. *What's happening?*

Follow it, my mother's voice whispered back. *Follow the power.*

I blinked. *What?*

Am I going insane? My mother can't be here.

She was human.

And she wasn't exactly the nurturing type, either.

Is this a dream? I started to wonder, my gaze searching the seascape for answers. *Or is the voice contrived by magic within the trial? What's the purpose of it?*

Maybe Lucifer was trying to manipulate me into making a mistake? Trying to convince me to touch his source again so he could burn me alive with it?

Because this couldn't be a trial.

I'm no longer a bride.

So why—

The pebbles beneath me dissolved into dust, creating a grainy texture that engulfed my feet, causing me to sink into the ground.

A vortex.

One that resembled quicksand.

Another scream lodged in my throat as I fell through the stone with the sky looming ominously overhead.

No. Not sky.

Water.

Shit!

I stole a deep breath and held it right before a wave crashed over my head, the texture lacking temperature and giving me pause once more.

This... doesn't make any sense.

I should be wet. Cold. *Shivering.*

Yet... I felt... nothing.

It didn't matter, because I was falling, looking up into a cloudy sky before water rushed over my head.

I could also see, almost as though that bubble around me acted as a magical shield.

My lips parted on a tentative breath, my mind fully prepared to cough. Except I didn't imbibe water; I inhaled air.

Blinking, I glanced around, startled by the sea-like environment. Not only was there a strange source of light—which shouldn't exist this far underwater—but I wasn't alone.

Sea creatures, I marveled, eyeing the humanlike beasts with fish tails. Some of them reminded me of the sirens I'd come across in Ajax's dungeon, but the others seemed different. They also appeared to be avoiding the vortex swirling around me, making them too far away for me to see their auras.

Still, I tried to spy any colors surrounding them.

Only for everything to go pitch black in a blink.

My eyes widened as a subtle glitter invaded my vision. No. Not glitter. *Scales.*

Is that a fucking water dragon?

I kicked my feet instinctually, wanting to get as far away from that thing as possible. Except there was nowhere for me to go, the whirlpool having too tight a grip on my form to allow me to escape.

Not that I even knew how.

I was trapped in this damn portal-like swirl, sinking lower and lower into the sea.

Am I going to hit the bottom? I wondered, looking down. *How are there still glimmers of light around me?* Now that the scaly creature had moved, some of the sunbeams trickled in from above. Yet I had to be at least fifty feet underwater by now with how fast I was sinking.

This... defies logic.

I should be drowning.

Yet this magic bubble was protecting me—apart from propelling me downward instead of upward, anyway. *Where are we going?* I asked it. *Why are you yanking me to the bottom of this ocean?*

Follow it, yes, that's it, my mother replied, her words not making any sense. They were an echo in my head, whirling around in slow repetition, almost as though she were underwater with me and speaking through the waves. *You're doing so well, Cami. Keep going.*

I frowned. *What?* Her praise suggested I was doing this somehow. But how? *Why?*

Darkness continued to ebb and flow, my surroundings murky and bright in sequence. Breathing felt labored, mostly because it was unnatural. Yet oxygen flowed without issue, my temperature remained regulated, and there were even some familiar scents around me.

The latter had my brow furrowing.

Hold on...

That... that shouldn't be possible either. Hell, *none* of this should be possible. But... that fragrance...

I closed my eyes and inhaled deeply, the aroma of minty aftershave mingling with pine needles infiltrating my senses.

Ajax, I recognized, my eyelashes fluttering once more as I looked around for the source. Only, I was still lost in this sea of perpetual darkness.

A dream, I thought. *I must be dreaming.*

Unless it was another trick of the mind.

But why water? Why here?

And even if I was dreaming, that didn't necessarily mean I wasn't in danger.

As if to confirm my thought, a massive creature swam past, but it kept its distance as electricity began to hum across my being. It seemed to be coming from below me.

Another glance down revealed nothing of consequence, but I could feel the volts trickling over my body, causing the hairs along my arms to rise on end.

It reminded me of Lucifer's source, the waves of power leaving familiar kisses along my bare skin.

Odd that I could feel that and nothing else.

Unless it's really happening outside of this dream, I thought, my lips curling down. *Is that possible? Or is this all some warped punishment?*

With Lucifer, it was hard to tell. But it seemed like the solution was to absorb more of that magnetic energy. Because each tug felt empowering. Refreshing. *Right.*

I was starting to better understand Lucifer's source. It was a wild, uncontrollable beast and a reflection of Lucifer's heart.

Which wasn't bad, I decided. Just cautious, passionate, and a bit unfettered.

Maybe that's why his power likes me, I mused. *Because I'm all of those things.*

I didn't take any shit, but I also believed in balance.

Meanwhile, Lucifer seemed to believe in control—as evidenced by the portal he'd tried to dominate into submission.

Sometimes one had to go with the flow of energy in order to properly tame it. That was the lesson I'd learned all those years ago with the fire my father had started—the magic had wanted a partner, not a dictator.

I sighed, reveling in the kiss of energy against my being, the vitality making me feel that much more alive. I could almost ignore my surroundings, almost forget that none of this was realistic or natural.

Just float, float, float, I whispered, content.

Wait.

I glanced down.

Not float... sink.

That... hmm.

No, I want to float.

Yet my feet were anchored by the bubble, an invisible strand yanking me in the wrong direction. Almost as though I were being controlled by some indefinable force.

I don't want to go that way, I told it. *Let me up.*

The vortex didn't listen, my mother's voice saying, *Don't fight it,* a constant mantra in my mind.

Knowing Lucifer, the whole point *was* to fight it. To break through the facade. To find the real meaning of this... this... whatever the fuck it was.

A punishment. A dream. A trial. *Death.*

Who the hell knew, but I didn't want to continue going with the flow. I wanted to break through the barrier, to fly, to be free of this bizarre hold.

I kicked my feet, my motions strengthened by the electricity flowing through my veins.

Everything around me rippled, the spiral faltering for just a moment.

More, I decided, tugging on the essence that gave me strength. *I need to take in more.*

I inhaled heavily, Ajax's scent whirling around me as Lucifer's source embraced my call.

Lightning rained down through the waves, confirming that this was no ordinary sea. The sea creatures scattered. The whirlpool slowed.

Now, I thought, giving another resounding kick that shot me out of the bubble and into the icy texture around me. My skin cooled, my insides protesting at the shock to my system.

But I wanted *out.*

I kicked again.

And again.

And again.

My lungs burned, the water threatening to enter my mouth.

Maybe leaving the comfort of my spiral was a bad idea, but if this was one of Lucifer's mind tricks—of which I had no doubt it was—I needed to break free. To unweave this dreamlike spell. *To wake up,* I realized.

My legs strained with the effort to reach the surface, my speed slowing as the energy seeped out of me.

Give me more, I told Lucifer's source. *Help me.*

My fingers brushed Melek's talisman between my breasts, the crystal the only item I seemed to be wearing. The necklace hummed in response, my lungs suddenly full of air once more, as though it was protecting me and reviving the life within my veins.

I clutched the object in my hand as I propelled myself upward, my eyes closing along the way. Lucifer's magic swam over me, seeping into my being, his wild essence revitalizing me to my core.

Yet it was Melek's talisman that seemed to ground me. To guard me. To *guide* me.

His charm helped me tame Lucifer's magic into usable strands as well. Which was a feat, considering Lucifer's source was literally a ball of burning Hellfire.

I wove the magic into a ladder of sorts, using it to help me climb back to the world above.

Only then did I notice the strange strings whirling around me—strings that appeared to be tied to the vortex below.

They jerked on my feet and legs, trying to force me down while I clung to the invisible rungs of power that led up.

It was a delicate dance, the magic warring within the waves to create an odd sense of pushing and pulling that left me dizzy. That, coupled with the lack of oxygen, and I started to see stars.

Just keep going, I thought tiredly. *Almost... there...*

You're going the wrong way, my mother informed me. *The core, Camillia. Go to the core.*

It's a trick, I told myself. *Don't listen to her.*

Camillia, she said, my name holding a hint of warning in it.

No.

Do as I say, she demanded.

No.

Camillia De la Croix, stop this nonsense and go back down.

No! I shouted as I reached the surface with a gasp, the strings around my ankles snapping free and floating off into the abyss.

I grabbed the rocky island, noting the crumbling statue above.

Lucifer's eyes weren't staring down at me in disapproval anymore. They were nonexistent. As was his face.

Whatever I'd done had dismantled his mirage, leaving behind a pile of stones instead.

My mother's voice no longer whispered in my head, her

presence seeming to have disappeared into the depths of the sea.

Using my mother as a way to guide me had been Lucifer's primary downfall. She would never care enough to help me survive. All she'd ever done was watch my father torture me. A few times she'd told him to give me a little assistance, but it was nothing ever truly helpful. Just a way to pretend to be a parent. To pretend to care.

I'd learned long ago that I only had myself to rely on.

Hell Fae Rule #4: Don't Trust Anyone.

It paired nicely with *Hell Fae Rule #6: Only Look Out for Yourself—No One Else.*

Pulling myself up onto the rocks, I shook out my hair and shuddered at the intense breeze touching my damp skin.

Whatever bubble had been protecting me from the elements was long gone.

Yet I'd won. I could feel it in my soul that I'd burst free from whatever hold Lucifer had cast over me. Now I just needed to wake up.

"I'm done with this shit," I informed Lucifer as I picked up one of the stones and crushed it between my fingers. "Now let me wake up."

No response.

I stood and crushed more of the rocks beneath my feet, the gravel feeling more like sand than rocks. Yet it was sturdy enough to allow me to climb up to where his head used to be.

When I reached it, I stared down at the indecipherable mass.

He'd put me in this mental prison as some sort of punishment or lesson. Now I intended to break free.

And I would start by destroying what was left of his face.

I slammed my palm into the stone, causing it to dissolve just like everything else.

"Let me out," I demanded.

The irony of the word choice wasn't lost on me. Just hours ago in the Marsh Lands, I'd been demanding he *let me in*. Now I wanted out. Away from him. Away from this place.

His power warmed my skin, responding to my call. But rather than free me, it surrounded me, filling me with heat and energy and vitality.

Embrace me, it seemed to be saying. *Embrace me and we'll set you free.*

I growled, irritated by all these mind games. Frustrated by Lucifer's incessant need to test me. Or punish me. Or whatever the fuck he called this.

"Yeah, I touched your source," I told him. "To *help* you when you needed it. You're fucking welcome."

Probably not the wisest thing to say to the Hell Fae King, but I was over this bullshit. Over him. Over his deals. Over his torture. Over his *everything*.

If he wanted to castigate me for doing something good, then he could face me himself. Not leave me stranded in this dangerous trial-like world and taunt me with crashing waves.

I slapped the stones again, a growl working its way up my chest and into my throat.

"I'm done with this shit," I snapped, my eyes closing. "Let me out!"

Ajax's minty aftershave washed over me in the next second, his pine-scented power tugging at my spirit. I could hear him whispering my name, guiding me toward him.

My brow crinkled.

Then my eyelashes fluttered.

And when the world settled around me, I found myself looking up into a pair of blue-black eyes.

Ajax.

My captor.

My Warden.

CHAPTER 6

AJAX

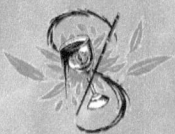

"Cami," I breathed, relieved to see her awake.

Az had gone to find Lucifer what felt like hours ago, leaving me alone with a shivering Cami.

She'd been gulping in air, almost as though she'd been struggling to breathe. Then she'd muttered something about being let out, causing her legs to kick wildly in response.

I'd tried everything I could think of to wake her from her nightmare, even casting Midnight Fae spells over her prone form in an attempt to free her. But whatever Lucifer had done to her had held her captive, making it impossible to free her.

She stared up at me now, her pupils dilating with palpable relief.

If seeing me made her feel at ease, then she must have been in some sort of hellish mental prison. Because I had to be one of the last people she wanted to be around.

Well, maybe me more so than Lucifer, Melek, and Az. But they weren't high bars to clear.

Cami groaned as she struggled to sit up on the couch, her eyes still a bit unfocused.

I reached out to help her, but she almost immediately swatted me away. "I can do it," she insisted.

The sheets slipped off her body, the fabric pooling at her waist as she pushed herself upward. Normally, I would have indulged in the view, but my primary concern was for her safety.

And her stability.

Something she seemed to be lacking as she wobbled in her upright position.

She grimaced as her bare toes touched the floor, her determined expression turning wary. It was almost as though she was uncertain of her reality, or like she'd forgotten how to use her body.

What the fuck had Lucifer done to her?

She finally managed to right herself completely, her sigh a distressed sound to my ears. Yet that sense of determination overcame her features once more as she attempted to stand.

Only to lose her balance in the next second.

I caught her by the hips and instantly pulled her down into my lap, my need to keep her safe overriding every other instinct.

She didn't protest.

Instead, she collapsed into me and buried her face against my chest with a groan.

I brushed my fingers through her hair, unsure of what to say.

Because I hated this.

I hated that I'd played a part in any of her pain. Cami shouldn't have gone through everything at the club, or what had transpired in the Marsh Lands, and certainly not whatever the hell had put her in this state.

This whole time, she'd just been trying to survive, and I'd been too wrapped up in my own shit to do anything about it.

Not anymore, I thought.

I'd been forced to stand by and watch those I loved suffer once before. I'd lost everything as a result.

I would not be repeating history with Cami.

She trembled as she tried to move, proving she was still unable to lift herself. Her body burned against mine as if she suffered from a horrible fever.

Fae did not get fevers. Humans did.

While Cami was supposedly a Halfling—half human, half fae—it seemed pretty clear to me that she was something else entirely.

"Do you...?" I trailed off, swallowing, still uncertain of how to comfort her. "Do you want to talk about it?"

Emelyn rarely had when she was upset. But sometimes she'd vented, and that had seemed to help.

"Not really," she muttered as she leaned more heavily against me. "Lucifer statue. Ocean. Vortex. Weird trial." She fell silent, her words not all that clear to me.

I was about to ask her to clarify when she began to tremble.

She was awake, but all I could do was stroke her back as she struggled with exhaustion and whatever magic was still making her burn up.

A growl rumbled in my chest. The state she was in was the clear result of her mistreatment.

Her *punishment* for doing nothing wrong other than being true to what she was.

Whatever that might be.

I didn't have to understand her origins to know that she didn't deserve whatever was coming next.

I should never have let that happen to her. Not that I could have stopped it. Lucifer was the Hell Fae King. Saying no to him wasn't possible. He owned everything in his realm. Everyone reported to him. Including me.

Although, technically, I'm still a Midnight Fae.

He might have given me the Warden role, but I wasn't one of his fae. That much had been obvious from the beginning. I'd just hoped he would one day take me under his wing, convert me to Hell Fae status, and make me one of his own.

But in what way did I expect that to happen?

I was his Warden. However, what did that actually mean? I wrangled Nightmare Fae. Beings I thought were beasts that belonged in cages.

Is that true, though? I wondered, thinking back on everything I'd witnessed these last few weeks. *Why are some Nightmare Fae given brides while others are locked up?*

Lucifer had never told me.

Because I'm not in his inner circle.

And everything with Camillia had just pushed me that much more out of it.

A month ago, I would have been eager to prove my worth, to find a way into his good graces, to earn his approval once more.

But something had changed.

I had changed.

What he'd done to Camillia tonight... It wasn't okay. He'd put her on display, and he'd told Az to hold me hostage while he humiliated her.

Binding my power. Rooting me in place. Forcing me to observe while he'd tried to break Camillia's spirit.

Just like Constantine.

Perhaps not to the same extreme. But Lucifer's quiet fury earlier had informed me that he could likely reach those depths, perhaps go even further.

He'd already tortured Camillia with those chains. Then he'd put her in some sort of coma. What would he do next?

What punishment would he eventually decide on?

Death, I answered myself. *He will absolutely kill her.*

Lucifer had made that much clear earlier.

Can I stand by and watch her die? I stared down at her shaking form, noting the way her eyes squeezed shut as though she was trying to hide from her own weakness.

Or maybe she was hiding from me—from *this*—her need to be held. Her need to be protected. Her need to be cared for.

Am I really caring for her by sitting here, waiting for the Hell Fae King to come back and do whatever he intends to do?

That coma she'd been in had obviously depleted her energy. She'd been shivering, *crying*, driving Az to act.

Yet he hadn't returned, and it'd been at least thirty minutes. If not longer.

What's taking so long? I wondered. *What are he and the Hell Fae King planning now?*

Az was on Lucifer's side. He always would be. Never mine. His actions tonight had proved that.

Which hurt a lot more than I wanted to admit.

But I wasn't exactly surprised. I knew the parameters of their bond. I would never come first for Az.

And neither will Camillia, I thought, my fingers weaving through her hair as I held her against my chest. *She hasn't come first for any of us. Including me.*

Lucifer had. Every step of the way, I'd supported him. Obeyed. Done mostly what he'd requested.

Then he'd set a trap with Camillia, waiting to see how long it would take me to end up in bed with her. Just so he could punish me.

However, it hadn't been just me he'd punished.

Camillia swallowed, her body feeling almost frail against mine. Weak. *Beaten down*. And I hated it.

This wasn't the fiery little Halfling who had challenged me when we'd first met. It was a shell of the woman she used to be. An exhausted soul who didn't deserve any of this.

She'd helped fight whatever entity had been ripping apart the Marsh Lands. She'd saved those fae.

And Lucifer had rewarded her with a coma? Thanked her by threatening to kill her?

Sure, she'd tapped into his power—something she should not be able to do—but maybe he should be looking at his *mate* for answers instead of Camillia.

Melek was the one who had done something to her. Bonded them. Played with fate. Indulged in tricks. Dragged her into his penchant for *games*.

Camillia had suffered enough.

And I was done sitting by while watching it happen.

I choose you, I decided.

Something shifted in my soul as a result of my declaration.

My alliances had been to Lucifer, to Az, and to the Hell Fae Realm.

But they didn't deserve my loyalty, not if this was how they treated women who were supposed to be their brides.

Not if this was how they *controlled* those who were unexpectedly powerful, just like Constantine had done. The Midnight Fae Council had viewed his actions as *normal*.

And it seemed the Hell Fae felt same about Lucifer.

I'd lived through the torment of watching all those I loved die at the hands of a closed-minded leader.

I'm not doing that again.

Gathering a limp Camillia in my arms, I squeezed her as shadows began to unfurl around us.

I knew what I had to do.

At my core, I was still a Midnight Fae. And there were still those I could trust in the Midnight Fae Realm.

They'd eradicated a powerful being like Lucifer. Opened their lands to those with gifts similar to Camillia's. Allowed a queen of mixed origins to rule.

They would provide us with sanctuary.

They would give Cami a fucking fighting chance.

The door creaked open, and I glared through the growing shadows to see Az and Typhos staring at me.

Az's eyes widened with shock, whereas Typhos, wearing nothing but a royal robe, settled his vacant stare on the female in my arms.

There was no going back now.

Az dared to appear hurt, like he couldn't believe I would leave him like this.

I'd joined him as the Warden with a role to track monsters and keep them in check.

But Cami wasn't a monster. *We* were.

This isn't what I signed up for, I thought.

Then the Hell Fae Realm dissolved around me as I shadowed Cami to the one place she would receive welcome.

To the one person who would understand.

I hope you're ready for us, Queen Aflora.

Because I'm coming home.

CHAPTER 7

AZ

Fuck.

The look on Ajax's face as he disappeared was one of resignation and determination.

He'd made a choice. *Cami.*

And now he was gone.

I blinked at the empty space before me, my mind whirling. The only evidence that Ajax and Camillia had just been there a moment before was the remnant shadows dissipating over the couch. *How the fuck had this gone so wrong?*

I... I hadn't meant... *I was doing my* job. *Why can't he understand that?*

My fingers flexed, my hand itching with the need to palm my heart. It was a maddening reaction, one I didn't have time for. Yet I couldn't help but feel... *betrayed.*

Except it was my fault. I'd pushed Ajax too far, and now... *This has to be repairable.* We had history. Over a decade of it. He couldn't—*wouldn't*—reject me after all that time over a female.

My Phoenix bristled inside, his reaction stirring a burning

sensation through my veins. He seemed to be saying, *He would and should.*

Because my bird was pissed, too.

Pissed at me for my decisions. Pissed at me for letting Typhos hurt Cami. Pissed at me for upsetting Ajax.

My inner beast wanted control, to fly, to seek his wounded *mates* and beg for their forgiveness.

They're not ours, I reminded him. *They're not Phoenixes.*

The damn bird snorted in reply.

I ignored him, determined to listen to my mind and not to my animalistic instincts. *Ajax just needs space. This will be fine. We'll... we'll fix it.*

"Hunt them," Typhos demanded, using the command reserved for my Phoenix when he wanted us to track down errant souls. "*Find* them."

"I will," I promised. "But not right now."

Typhos's brow inched upward as he glanced at me, his surprise palpable through the bond. He'd expected me to turn to ash and start tracking immediately. I usually did when issued a command, but I couldn't follow this one.

Not yet.

My Hell Fae King mate studied me for a long moment, his oceanic blue eyes swirling with questions he sought answers for within my mind.

I didn't push him out, didn't put up any walls, didn't try to hide. Because he needed to understand this conflict, needed to see how my loyalty to him might have jeopardized my relationship with Ajax.

My relationship with Cami.

My relationship with my Phoenix.

My jaw ticked, my bird pushing at my mental restraints in a blatant demand to be freed from his cage. But he didn't want to *hunt*. He wanted to *track*. And there was a fine difference between the two.

Hunting was reserved for dark souls—nefarious fae who had reneged on their deals with the Hell Fae King. Beings who had earned punishment.

Tracking was more of a pleasurable activity, one with a reward in mind. Locating Ajax and Cami was the reward in this case. My bird didn't like being separated from them. He wanted to join them. Be with them. Earn their forgiveness.

Bite them. Mate them.

My hands curled into fists. *Fucking. Phoenix.*

"I see," Typhos finally said after a beat, the two words an echo of what he'd said in his bedchamber when I'd told him what was happening to Cami. It'd taken me longer to reach him than I would have liked, mostly because he'd been too engaged with his prince to hear me. And I hadn't wanted to interrupt them.

Unfortunately, we'd been interrupted mid-conversation by Loch, the Kelpie King from the Underwater Kingdom. Typhos had issued a command to all the Nightmare Fae Kings to report any and all disturbances going forward, no matter how small.

Fortunately, Loch's reported disturbance didn't appear to be related to the ongoing portal issues. But it'd taken Typhos a few minutes to determine that. Once he had, he'd returned his focus to me.

Which had led us all here because Typhos had wanted to examine Cami himself.

"All I did was put her in a dreamlike state," he'd told me. "I don't want her anywhere near my magic."

I'd believed him. I *still* believed him. But that didn't mean Cami hadn't been glowing with power mere moments ago.

An unknown power.

And now she was gone.

On the run with Ajax.

He'll protect her, I told myself. Only, I wasn't sure if that thought was related to me pursuing them, Typhos wanting Cami dead, or the odd power that had been humming all over her skin while she'd slept.

I palmed the back of my neck, my chest suddenly tight.

This... I didn't know how to do *this*.

Typhos was my mate. My best friend. My *king*.

Ajax... Ajax was supposed to be a passing fancy. Yet he'd become so much more. And Cami...

I swallowed.

You're fucking with my head, I accused my Phoenix.

My inner beast huffed in reply.

And Typhos cleared his throat. "You pledged your fealty to me," he said, his words seeming to be for my animal more than for me. "*In blood.*"

"Fealty, yes," I agreed, sensing my beast's irritation. "But fealty doesn't mean blind obedience."

Which was precisely what my bird was trying to convey now—he might be my other half, my inner spirit, but that didn't mean we would always agree on a path forward. We were just usually in sync with one another, gliding along the same current in the wind.

However, Cami resembled a ripple in our airstream. A divide I couldn't ignore. Because it had me going one way and sent my bird in the opposite direction.

"Perhaps it would be wise to begin the pursuit in the morning. Give everyone a chance to thoroughly process tonight's events," Melek offered.

"You mean the event where a *Halfling* not only accessed my power but also used it?" Typhos asked, his focus still on me despite his reply being for his Hell Fae Prince. "An event that happened *after* I warned her not to touch my source again?"

"An event that saved lives in your kingdom," Melek replied. "An event that showcased a talent we need to investigate and analyze, not squander and destroy."

Typhos's jaw clenched as he shifted his attention to his royal mate.

Silence fell as the two of them engaged in a silent conversation, one I couldn't hear even with my link to Typhos's mind.

Just as Melek wouldn't be able to hear me speaking to Typhos.

Although, I could sense the emotions inspired by their conversation. And right now, Typhos was simmering with barely restrained anger. Outwardly, he appeared calm and collected, his expression almost bored. But inside, he was furious.

Fortunately, Melek was well versed in tempering the Hell Fae King's rage, something that became evident within minutes as Typhos's mind began to calm.

"Ajax chose the girl over us," Typhos finally said aloud, his gaze going from Melek to me. "He's reneged on our deal, Az. You know what that means. But if you wish to prolong his eventual agony, so be it."

My eyes narrowed. The Hell Fae King was baiting me by providing a choice. He was essentially saying, *Find Ajax now, and perhaps I'll lessen his punishment. Wait, and I'll take my wrath out on his sentence.*

"Camillia was never part of his deal with you," I replied.

"No. Our deal revolved around his promise to protect me and the Hell Fae, and he's turned his back on everything we've given him by choosing the Halfling."

"We promised to protect him, too," I pointed out. "Yet we failed him tonight. We reneged on the agreement first. Therefore, the deal was already null and void."

Typhos's eyebrows shot upward. "You dare accuse *me* of breaking one of my own contracts?"

"Yes." I stepped forward, my gaze holding his without remorse. Without fear. Without hesitation.

Because I was his Hell Fae Commander. His right-hand man. His *mate*.

He kept me here for a reason—to help him maintain balance. To guard him and his kind. To stand at his side for all of eternity and ensure no one ever hurt him again.

But he granted me that right because I'd earned it through my faith in him. And part of that faith involved an undercurrent of unerring honesty between us.

"Our actions tonight reminded Ajax of Constantine. I froze him with my power to protect him, but that's not how he perceived my actions. He felt we were forcing him to watch you torture Cami, just like Constantine did when killing Ajax's loved ones."

Typhos's nostrils flared at the mention of Constantine, his oceanic irises darkening with violent waves. "I am not Constantine."

"No, you're not," I agreed.

Constantine was an abomination-hating tyrant. Typhos was very much his opposite. Although, he could act as a tyrant in other ways. However, that wasn't the point of this discussion.

"Our actions tonight reminded Ajax of his past. He feels betrayed. And now he's reacting to that perceived betrayal."

Rather than elaborate further, I allowed him to hear my memory of Ajax's words from earlier, how he'd told me he'd never forgive me for my part in Typhos's punishment.

"Constantine once held me captive beneath a spell. Forced me to watch all those I cared about lose their will to live just before he cemented them in stone."

His dark eyes had glittered with pain as he'd looked up at me, the weight of his agony having settled heavily on my shoulders.

"Now you're forcing me to observe Cami lose her fight. She may not be my mate, or my family, but she's the first woman to

make me feel anything more than death in the last decade. And you are forcing me to watch her suffer. Tying me down. Making me powerless. Just like Constantine."

I'd winced. *"Ajax."*

"No," he'd bit out, refusing to let me speak. *"This is wrong. I'll never forgive you for this."*

And he'd continued upholding that vow in this room when he'd refused to talk to me for hours, something I mentally shared with Typhos now.

When Ajax had finally started to speak to me, it hadn't been any better.

"He's furious," I summarized softly. "But more than that, he's hurt. And if I go after him right now, it won't end well for any of us."

We'd fight, which would usually lead to sex. However, that wouldn't happen this time.

"I've never seen him this upset," I added. "We reminded him of an experience that nearly broke him."

"Only this time, he was able to save the girl," Melek interjected thoughtfully. "So he did."

Yes, I thought. *Yes, he did.*

My bird bristled once more, irritated that *we* hadn't saved her. That *we* had been the ones Ajax had sought to save Cami from.

It felt wrong.

Cruel, even.

She's not ours, I kept telling him.

But the damn Phoenix didn't want to listen. He was convinced that he'd finally found a worthy mate. One that could truly be *ours.*

Unlike the Hell Fae King before me.

He was mine in spirit. My best friend. A being I respected and loved in a brotherly type of way.

But he wasn't *mine.*

He belonged to Melek.

And Ajax belongs to me, I thought.

Sort of, anyway. Our dynamic was unique, to say the least.

Now our dynamic was forever altered because of Cami. Unless I could somehow fix this.

Fuck. I ran a hand over my face as I took a step away from Typhos. "I can't *hunt* them right now," I muttered, allowing Typhos to hear the frustration in my voice and in my mind. "But I promise to *track* them after I..." I trailed off, unsure of how to finish that sentence.

After I tamed my bird?

After I figured out what to say?

After I figured out how to fix this?

"I am not Constantine," Typhos reiterated, obviously fixated on that part of the conversation. "He murdered hundreds, if not *thousands*, of fae. He nearly annihilated an entire sect of Midnight Fae. All because he was power hungry and wanted to maintain his precious throne. I am *not* him."

"The Quandary Bloods possessed the ability to rewrite magic, which threatened his ties to the Midnight Fae Source," Melek replied, his multicolored irises flickering as he boldly held the Hell Fae King's gaze. "Constantine reacted to that *potential threat*. Similar to how you're reacting to Cami."

Typhos gaped at his prince. "I'm not reacting by trying to exterminate an entire breed of fae."

"No, you're not," Melek agreed. "But Constantine didn't begin that way either." He held up his hand to stop Typhos from speaking as he added, "I'm not saying you're him, Ty. I'm saying that Ajax is sensitive to that sort of behavior from a fae in power. Especially when directed at someone he has started to care about."

"I didn't even hurt her," Typhos argued.

"No, you dressed her in chains and put her on display—on a stage—while your Commander mentally held Ajax in place."

Typhos's blue eyes narrowed. "You weren't complaining about it when it happened, little prince."

"Of course not. I adore sensual punishments," Melek returned without missing a beat. "But there was something missing from this display, something I failed to understand at the time but realize now."

"And what was *missing*?" Typhos pressed, his muscular arms folding across his broad chest.

"Consent." The word fell like a bomb in the air, causing Typhos's jaw to clench.

"She's a prisoner. Prisoners have no rights. And further—"

"I've marked her as an intended mate," Melek interjected, cutting off the Hell Fae King. "That grants her more rights than most in this situation." Melek's serious tone was very unlike the typically playful fae.

It was enough to give Typhos pause.

Or perhaps it was Melek's words that finally broke through the Hell Fae King's thick wall of stubbornness.

"I know you're intimidated by her abilities," Melek continued in a softer voice. "And you're rightfully protective of your source. But Vita chose Cami for a reason. Your source is letting her in for a reason, too. Let's determine that reason before we enact judgment."

Typhos growled, his anger seeping out despite the tight leash he usually kept on his emotions.

However, he was among his trusted circle now. Which afforded him an opportunity to react as he saw fit.

There were no masks between us. Just truths.

And right now, these truths were ones Typhos didn't want to hear. But they were needed.

"Ajax and Cami will be fine for a night or two. Give them that time to heal. And give our Commander some grace, too." Melek glanced at me, his expression uncharacteristically concerned. "Your Phoenix needs to fly."

My beast needs a lot more than that, I nearly replied. But a hum of electricity cut me off, the sound coming from Typhos's mind. I was more in tune with him now than usual, thus allowing me to hear his reaction to an incoming call.

He was irritated.

Relieved.

Exhausted.

All those emotions rolled over me in magnetic pulses, his inner turmoil rivaling my own. Just for very different reasons.

He waved his hand through the air to call up a smoky screen. "It's Erebus," he growled. "I need to take this." His sapphire eyes met mine. "Two days, Az. I'm giving you two days. Then I want an update."

The Hell Fae King didn't give me a chance to reply, instead vanishing into one of his fiery clouds and leaving me alone with his prince.

Melek sighed, his long fingers combing his unruly blondish-brown strands away from his face. "He's stubborn."

"Yes."

"But he means well," he added.

"Usually," I conceded.

Melek nodded and echoed, "Usually." His hand fell away from his hair as he shook his head. "Camillia reminds him of Vivaxia. And not just because she's a woman."

"But because she can tap into his powers," I translated. "Like a siphon."

"Indeed," Melek replied, his lips curling down. "It can't be a coincidence that the Virtuous Fae have chosen to interfere with our lives now. Perhaps it's all related. Cami's arrival. Her unique skills. The portals. But I don't think it's *her*, necessarily. She seems innocent."

"So did Vivaxia," I pointed out, the name sending a chill down my spine. Just thinking of our shared past made time feel nonexistent, her cruel touch a lingering memory that refused to abate regardless of the thousands of years that had passed since I'd last seen her.

Evil didn't even begin to describe the diabolical fae who had nearly killed Typhos.

I'd known her true nature from the beginning. But everyone else had seen her as a docile, sweet little fae.

"Do you think Cami is like her?" Melek asked, his head cocked slightly to the side.

"Do you?"

"My judgment was impaired once. I'd prefer to lean on yours, Commander. Typhos is alive today for a reason, after all," Melek replied. "What do your instincts say?"

My fingers flexed, my mind at war with my bird's immediate claim—*She's ours. No, she's not. She is. She's not. She is.*

I closed my eyes and shook my head. "I don't know. My Phoenix is confused."

My inner beast snorted, almost as though he were mocking me for my claim. *You're the one who is confused*, that sound said.

Or that was how I interpreted it, anyway.

"Then fly and track them," Melek suggested. "You follow your instincts and I'll follow mine. Together, we'll develop a conclusion and go from there."

I arched a brow. "What are you planning to do?"

His lips curled, his usual playfulness returning in a blink. "What I do best—meddle." His feathers appeared in the next instant, the white plumes shimmering with golden dust. "Speak soon, Commander."

He vanished before I could comment, his exit similar to the Hell Fae King's, only he left a dusting of powder behind rather than smoke.

I supposed we all had our quirks.

Mine happened to be ash.

Which I demonstrated by following suit and teleporting myself outside of the palace grounds.

Because Melek was right—my Phoenix needed to fly.

I shifted and flew into the dark clouds, my Phoenix demanding that we track Cami and Ajax.

Not yet, I told him, causing my bird to grumble in indignation.

I might be in Phoenix form, but I was still very much in charge. However, that didn't stop him from threatening to take over.

It took considerable effort to maintain control, and I wasn't quite sure I'd succeeded because we seemed to be drifting toward the realm's gates.

Fuck, I could barely even tame my own beast right now.

My entire life had been turned upside down. All because of a female.

Cami.

I wanted to hate her for it. Hell, I *should* hate her. Yet, a part of me felt... *alive.* Like I hadn't actually been living until recently.

I hadn't realized it, but I sensed it now—my Phoenix had been bored before Cami came along. Nothing had piqued his interest.

For thousands of years, I'd settled into monotony and found excitement where I could as the Hell Fae Commander.

Until Ajax. Until Cami. They'd ignited a new spark inside me that I had never experienced before.

And I wanted more of it.

Of *her.*

Of both of them.

I'll find you, I vowed, talking to Cami and Ajax even though I knew they couldn't hear me. *I'll find you and we'll talk. Tomorrow.*

CHAPTER 8

AJAX

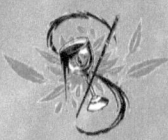

A CHORUS of hissing snakes confirmed that I'd shadowed Cami and me to the right place—just outside the massive wrought-iron gates of the new Midnight Fae palace.

Queen Aflora and her mates had built this place shortly after taking down the Midnight Fae Council. It stood for everything the Council hated—a home for abominations.

Abominations like the Midnight Fae Queen herself.

I muttered a spell at the hostile snake-vines, causing their stone-like bodies to slither in silence. I would have used my wand to cast them away, but my hands were otherwise occupied with holding Camillia.

They wouldn't bite, despite Camillia being an intruder. Mostly because I was the one holding her.

The protective vines would recognize me as an acceptable guest. Or they should, anyway.

Still, I moved through the gates slowly, not wanting to tempt fate. Fortunately, though, they left us alone.

I paused just beyond the threshold as a floral landscape came into view, the array of flowers and trees uncharacteristic of the Midnight Fae Realm. However, our queen was part

Earth Fae, so I supposed this landscaping style was to be expected.

"Ajax," my oldest friend greeted as he shadowed into the courtyard a few steps in front of me.

"Shade," I sighed. "Of course you knew I was coming."

"Of course I knew you were coming," he echoed, his lips curling to display a disarming pair of dimples.

It was a lie.

There was nothing innocent about this fae. His Death Blood aura—all dark energy and violet magic—betrayed his sinister nature.

I supposed it did the same for me as well, but Shade was a whole different caliber of dangerous, thanks to his Fortune Fae roots.

His icy irises glittered in the moonlight as his focus drifted down to the female in my arms. "You seem to enjoy keeping your Halfling in a nude state. It surprises me that she allows it, what with her being part human and all."

I glanced at Cami and winced. "Fuck." I'd completely forgotten to give her clothes, my focus having been entirely on leaving the Hell Fae Kingdom and coming here.

With another whispered spell, I conjured a blanket to drape over her, the fabric soft against my arms.

Shade gave me a raised brow. "You look like you've been through hell."

"Funny," I muttered as I shifted Cami in my grip, making sure she was comfortable as her head rested against my chest.

She seemed to be awake, but not exactly aware. Her long blondish-brown eyelashes fluttered a few times; however, she didn't quite focus on anything in particular.

When she shivered, I added a second blanket. The Midnight Fae Realm was much cooler than the Hell Fae Realm. It would take some getting used to after living in the blistering heat for so long.

"I wish I were joking," he murmured. "But you really look like shit."

"Your commentary is as helpful as always."

"What are friends for?" he drawled.

"Sanctuary, I hope," I muttered, causing him to cant his head to the side.

The unruly waves of his thick, dark hair fell over one of his ice-blue eyes while he considered me. He had a way of seeming to look right into one's soul when he did that. It had never unnerved me. But it did now.

Because he could say no.

He could refuse me entry, leaving me with nowhere to go.

Then what? I wondered.

I'd left the place I used to call home. Turned my back on my fellow Midnight Fae. And now I was back, hoping like hell that my oldest friend would help me. Help *us*. "Lucifer is going to kill her," I whispered. "He's probably going to kill me now, too."

Shade said nothing, his gaze still assessing. Perhaps he wasn't really assessing me at all, but the various paths drawn out before us.

I wasn't exactly sure how the Fortune Fae gift of foresight worked, especially when it came to Shade's abilities. His mixed heritage defined him as clearly *other*. His ties to Aflora and all their shared mates had altered him even more.

Who knew what he was seeing? What he was saying? What he was doing?

I swallowed, my arms tightening around Camillia almost protectively. Shade wouldn't hurt her; of that I was certain. But some of Aflora's other mates might not be so forgiving of our unexpected arrival.

"If I recall correctly, Zakkai's terms with Lucifer were to alter your magic to make you more Hellish in nature, not remove all of your Midnight Fae roots. Thus..." He trailed off with a shrug. "This is still your home, yes?"

"Is it?" I asked him, uncertain of the answer. Because I'd left this realm a decade ago, vowing to never return. Yet here I stood in the heart of the Midnight Fae Kingdom, essentially begging my oldest friend to offer Cami and me protection.

Lucifer would come for us, probably via Az.

How will Aflora and her mates react to that? Will they hand us over? Or will my rash decision to come here lead to catastrophic results?

"Let's not worry ourselves with semantics or potential futures just yet," Shade murmured, his gaze sparking with foreign knowledge. Sometimes I wondered if he could read minds, his intuitiveness a little too keen to be considered coincidence.

Alas, it was just Shade.

Power literally ran in his blood.

"This way," he continued, angling his head down a long path framed with black and blue flowers. They created a delicate-looking courtyard, at least upon first glance. But a longer look confirmed what I suspected—those flowers had thorns.

And not just any thorns—*bladed* thorns. Similar to the razor-like grass at Midnight Fae Academy.

Aflora had clearly married her Earth Fae heritage to her Midnight Fae Queen magic, creating a new form of life around her palace. That enchantment stretched out before me as we moved, my focus shifting to the burning thwomps in the distance. I snorted when their bare limbs puffed with cerulean smoke instead of its usual fire.

Then I paused when a flurry of color blinked in and out of existence all along the black thwomp branches. "Fire gnats?" I guessed, frowning at the flickering lights. They were usually little flame balls of irritation, but these reminded me of festive decorations.

"Hmm," Shade hummed, following my gaze and canting his head. "Aflora bespelled the palace walls to morph certain irritants into kinder species. In this case, she's made it so that all fire gnats that cross over the walls turn into lightning butterflies." He glanced at me. "If you think that's fun, you should see what she did to the stonepeckers."

My eyebrows rose. "Can't they just peck their way through the enchantment?" That was what stonepeckers did —they were birdlike creatures who used their long beaks to peck at rocks and other items to absorb spells. Pesky little buggers.

"Her spell constantly rewrites itself, making it impossible for the stonepeckers to absorb." His lips curled. "Which means they're constantly changing shape and species, too."

"I can only guess at why that amuses you." Because he clearly used them for something nefarious. This was Shade, after all.

"Zakkai hates them."

"I bet he does," I drawled.

"Zeph, too."

"So you love them," I surmised.

"Naturally." Devious twinkles entered his icy irises. "I've taught Florica how to hunt them."

"And what does she do with them when she finds them?"

"Hides them." His eyes smiled, telling me he very much liked *where* Florica chose to hide them. "One turned into a porcupined-sphinx the other day." His dimples flashed. "In Zeph's bed. While he was asleep."

Despite my dark mood, I couldn't stop my lips from twitching. Zeph had been a headmaster at the Academy during my final year there with Shade. As a Warrior Blood, he'd handled all the defensive arts training, and he'd been a bit of a dick at times.

Thinking about him being attacked by a porcupined-sphinx was mildly entertaining.

"What did he do?"

"Killed it and fed it to Raph." Shade's expression sobered upon mentioning Zeph's familiar—Raph, the three-headed snake. "Florica... is very much like her mother. She didn't take it well."

"I see."

"Zeph's still groveling."

"And you?"

He flashed me an innocent look. "I had nothing to do with it. I taught my daughter a valuable skill. It's not my fault Zeph doesn't appreciate her talents."

A huff of a laugh escaped me as I shook my head. Over a decade of being a mate-circle and clearly not much had changed.

What's that like? I wondered. *Having a family that tolerates all your quirks and choices? Even the ones that are downright devious in nature?*

I would never know.

Because my decisions were probably going to get me killed.

I glanced down at Cami, noting her now-closed eyes. She had her head against my chest, her delicate features making her appear more youthful than usual. Trusting, too. Kind. Soft. *Defenseless.*

My heart ached at the sight of her obvious exhaustion. Lucifer's antics had sucked the literal life out of the warrior in my arms, leaving behind a vulnerable female I hardly recognized.

I swallowed, a vow threatening to leave my lips, one I couldn't voice. Because I wasn't sure I could maintain it.

Lucifer will never touch you again wasn't a promise I could make, even if I wanted to.

In truth, I probably wouldn't be alive long enough to truly protect her.

But I didn't regret my decision.

My choice had been made.

There wouldn't be any further struggle with my alliances. No turmoil over honoring Lucifer's laws or the demands of my heart. I'd learned from my mistakes.

Mistakes that wouldn't be happening again.

The effect left me lighter, as if I could spread wings and take to the dark Midnight Fae skies.

I wonder if this is how Az feels when he's in his Phoenix form.

Probably not, because he squelched the poor beast any chance he had.

What I wouldn't give to offer him a taste of his own medicine.

Shade studied me for a long moment, his amusement having fled in the wake of whatever he saw in my expression. "We'll save the tour for later," he told me. "Come on."

I wasn't even aware we were going on a tour, but considering this was my first time here, a tour would have made sense. Except for the fact that I was carrying a now-unconscious female in my arms.

My old friend led the way in silence, his strides sure as he took us down the path of the courtyard past several other unique-looking animals and critters. All of them appeared to be magically altered, confirming Shade's commentary about Aflora's exterior spell. I wasn't all that surprised.

The former Earth Fae Queen loved nature and life, and her alterations to the landscape and palace exterior certainly demonstrated that. All the way down to the earthy stones and black bricks paving the path beneath my feet.

Shade halted at a set of obsidian-block stairs that seemed to frame the palace patio. "There are a lot of roots inside," he said. "Just watch where you step."

My brow furrowed. "Like tree roots?"

"Among other fauna and plant life," he replied, his shoulder lifting in his characteristic shrug.

The *roots* started on the patio, their vine-like widths weaving through black rocks and mossy textures all across the floor. Several of the stems led to trees that appeared to be part of the palace walls, causing my eyebrow to inch upward in curiosity.

A leafy overhang decorated a set of doors, the entry opening to a cozy living area boasting a myriad of windows. It seemed a bit wasteful considering the sun never appeared in this realm, but the moonlight did create a sort of romantic ambience in the oversized room.

"This is the family wing," Shade explained. "Seemed more appropriate for you to stay here rather than the guest wing."

"We'd be fine in the guest wing," I told him.

"You would," he agreed. "But having you here will be more fun."

"Because Florica might hide a stonepecker in our temporary room?"

He grinned. "No. Because it'll royally piss Zakkai off, and that's always fun."

"It's amazing that you're still alive," I told him.

"Understatement of the millennium," he returned without missing a beat. He led me down a hall toward a back staircase, then hopped over a particularly thick root before ascending to the second floor.

I resituated Cami in my arms and followed, part of me wishing I could just shadow to a room and lay her on a bed. Alas, I could only shadow to places I'd seen before.

Shade whistled as he walked, causing the walls to shift

around us to reveal several knob-less doors. When one finally appeared with a gargoyle's head at the center of it, he stopped.

"Sir Silber," Shade greeted. "Our guests have arrived."

"Guests," Sir Silber repeated, his voice gravelly as his rocky mouth and throat worked to utter the word. "How quaint."

The wood shifted before either of us could reply to the snarky gargoyle, the door opening to reveal the room beyond.

Little stone feet hit the floor, the gargoyle taking on his role as the room's protector. Most Midnight Fae employed gargoyles for this purpose. They thrived with security-related tasks.

He stomped off inside the opulent quarters, the plush, mosslike carpet softening his steps.

"Wow," I said, taking in the ornate fixtures inside and the massive balcony framing the back wall. "This is the guest room?"

"For visiting family and royals, yes," Shade said. "Sol and his mates often stay here, hence the giant bed." He gestured to the mattress large enough for a family of ten.

Sol was an Earth Fae mated to the Elemental Fae Queen. They had quite the mate-circle, not that I knew any of them well.

"Are you sure we should stay here?" I asked warily. "We're not really family..." It hurt more than I expected to admit that, but it wasn't untrue.

As much as I respected Shade, we hadn't exactly been close these last few years. I'd pushed him away, along with every other reminder of my past.

"We're not royals, either," I added, my voice a little more gruff than I'd intended it to be.

"Family is more than blood, Ajax," he returned. "And no, you're not royals yet. But your little mate might be one soon."

"My little mate?" I repeated. And what the hell did he mean by "soon"? "She's not my mate."

"No, I suppose she isn't yet." He turned and walked over to a table. "My grandmother sends her love, by the way. And cookies." He gestured to the treat—something that would usually make my mouth water because I fucking loved his grandmother's cookies—but I was still hung up on his cryptic bullshit.

"I'll never bite her without her consent." An action that would enact the mating bond against Cami's will. Which was precisely what Shade had done to Aflora. "Cami is not my mate, nor will she ever be my mate."

Primarily because she currently hated me.

But also because I refused to even consider the possibility of making her mine.

Claiming her could easily become a fantasy. But that wasn't our reality. We lived in a hell loop dictated by Lucifer's wants and desires. To believe otherwise would set me up for a world of pain.

"You're fortunate that your path allows you that freedom," he replied, a glint in his gaze. "Mine did not."

"I wasn't making a jibe about you and Aflora. I'm just saying..." *What am I saying?* I wondered. "I'm saying that... that what I have with Cami is different."

There.

That was the truth.

Because this really wasn't about how he'd mated Aflora. Consent or no, they'd worked everything out between them.

But Cami... I wasn't sure we could move on from our current problems, and I sure as fuck wasn't about to add to them by biting her against her will.

Even if mating her would make protecting her easier.

Not going to consider that at all, I told myself.

"We'll see," he murmured in that cryptic way of his. "G'ma left you a card with the cookies. Read it when you're able." He walked over to the windows overlooking the balcony. "There are blackout shades if you need them. Sir Silber will show you how to work them."

The gargoyle snorted. "Sir Silber will do whatever you'd like," the stone creature mocked. "Sir Silber doesn't need any introduction at all because he lives to serve."

"I did introduce you," Shade insisted. "Well, technically, I greeted you. The sentiment was there."

"Hmph," the gargoyle muttered.

Shade sighed. "I'll owe you a stoner, okay?"

My eyebrow lifted at the term *stoner*. Shade was referring to a leafy cigar filled with toxic herbs from the LethaForest—a dangerous woodsy area near Midnight Fae Academy.

"Make it three and I'll consider us even."

"Three?" Shade shook his head. "*Two* and you help Florica with her next assignment."

The gargoyle scratched his chin. "Thwomp torches?"

"Yep."

"Fine."

"Good." Shade stuck out his fist for the gargoyle to bump.

"Would you like me to set up the bed for the lady?" Sir Silber asked me, his lighter tone still holding a gravelly touch, thanks to his stone mouth.

"Yes, that would be appreciated." Cami didn't weigh much, nor did I mind holding her, but she needed rest, and that giant bed would definitely suit that purpose.

"Well, I'll leave you in Sir Silber's capable claws." He grinned as the gargoyle grunted from across the room. "Join us for midnight breakfast tomorrow, if you're both rested. I'm sure Aflora will want to meet your intended."

"She's not—"

Shade disappeared into a cloud of smoke, his chuckle an echo in the room as the wisps of his power vanished into thin air.

"Bastard," I muttered.

"He's better than the Architect," Sir Silber grated out from beside the bed. "That one actually scares me."

Yeah, I thought. *Me, too.* Not that I'd admit it aloud. Of course, I didn't really need to.

Zakkai was the Midnight Fae Architect and pretty much as powerful as Lucifer. Having the Midnight Fae on my side might actually be a good thing for when Az finally showed up. But convincing Zakkai to help would not be easy.

A problem for tomorrow. Maybe at midnight breakfast.

"Bed is turned down," Sir Silber announced. "There are already towels on the warming rack, if you want a shower or a bath. Do you need anything else?"

I shook my head. "No. Thank you for your help, Sir Silber. Feel free to take a break or go hassle Shade about your stoners."

The gargoyle bowed. "I'll be at my post."

That wasn't what I recommended at all, but I knew better than to argue with a gargoyle. Instead, I thanked him again and carried Cami over to the huge bed.

Sol was a massive Earth Fae, his boulder-like size intimidating. Yet this mattress could easily fit ten of him.

"Guest suite," I groused as I set Cami on the bed. "More like an orgy pad."

I flinched, not at all keen on thinking about that right now.

Well, Cami at the center of an orgy... that might appeal to me. She'd be an alluring goddess in the middle, her beautiful gray eyes flashing with the lightning of a passionate thunderstorm as she cried out in pleasure.

Yes, please, I thought.

Only, the vision sharpened, the participants of the fantasy becoming clearer.

Az driving into her from behind while she straddled me,

my cock buried in her sweet heat. Melek pumping in and out of her mouth.

And Lucifer commanding it all.

He'd sit in that chair—the one facing the bed in the corner of the room—wearing one of his trademark suits. The raw power of the Hell Fae King would shudder through the room, sending his dark hair billowing around his shoulders in energetic waves. Those dark glittering eyes would house violent intent as all of his focus homed in on Melek. On Cami. *On me.*

I shivered, the vision so vivid it almost felt real.

But Cami's soft breath pulled me back to the present, to her weary body curling naturally into the sheets.

I shook my head, the intense fantasy leaving me a bit dizzy. I couldn't tell if I'd just had a moment or if exhaustion was threatening my sanity.

Because that image in my head would never happen.

The only thing Lucifer would ever desire to demand would be our deaths.

"Fuck." I ran my hand over my face. "*Fuck.*"

Cami responded with a soft sigh as she nuzzled into the floral pillowcase—the design a stark contrast from the black and red tones of the Hell Fae Kingdom.

It wasn't exactly my preferred decor, but it suited Cami in this moment. And she seemed rather content, too.

Sleep well, little rebel.

Leaving her to her well-deserved rest, I ventured out onto the balcony.

The weight of my decision hit me with the breath of fresh air.

I've really done it now, haven't I?

The palace courtyard stretched out before me, boasting a wide array of trees, flowers, and life. So quiet. Yet so alive. Nature everywhere. All of it illuminated by the moon above.

Including a set of peach trees—something that wasn't native to this realm at all but was very human in nature.

I made a mental note to ask Shade about it later. That strange creation had to be Aflora's doing. Same with the patch of shrooms and purple leaf plants beside it.

Definitely Elemental Fae food, I thought. *Maybe that's Aflora's personal garden.*

How surreal, I marveled.

I'd never thought I'd come here.

Despite Shade's open invitation, I'd thought I'd settled on what my life would look like after meeting Az. He'd been death incarnate, more of the kind of invitation I had craved after Constantine's antics had shattered my heart.

When I'd first met Az, he'd challenged me to a fight and had seemed surprised when I'd accepted. A broad, inky black tattoo of his Phoenix had spread over strong muscles, and a gleam of dark magic had twinkled in his cruel, violet eyes.

I'd taken him up on his offer, expecting to die.

But I hadn't, and thus my role as Warden had followed.

Picturing the Commander made me grip the railing until it cracked.

I'd thought that taking the position of Warden had been a solution. If not death, then servitude to the Hell Fae King as a wrangler of monsters.

A purpose greater than myself.

Something that Emelyn would have been proud of—but if she saw me now, she would have been disgusted with me.

Where do I belong? Who am I? What kind of future can I hope to have?

I couldn't answer any of those questions. Not anymore.

I'd just made a life-altering decision.

One that could bring war to my friends here if I wasn't careful. *But what choice did I have?*

Cami couldn't be left in the Hell Fae Realm to be

mistreated, abused, and inevitably killed for no other reason than attempting to survive.

For being true to who and what she was. Just because none of us understood that didn't give us the right to snuff out her life.

Like Constantine would have done.

Cursing, I ventured back inside, my nose reminding me that Shade's grandmother Zenaida had sent along her famous cookies.

Because she'd known I'd come here. Just like Shade had known. Their penchants for fortune-telling were intimidating but useful.

Especially considering my half-starved state.

I plucked a cookie off the plate and studied the note card beside it. *Of course you sent along a note,* I mused, my eyes rolling in amusement.

Finishing off the cookie in a second bite—I was *very* hungry—I picked up the note.

My lips curled down at the words scrawled along the top. *A spell.* Not just any spell, but one meant for a Midnight Fae to wield with a wand. "Okay..."

There was a smaller handwritten inscription underneath it that read, *You may need this to tame a certain beast. Good luck.*

I considered it for a moment, wondering if Zenaida had predicted something I should be concerned about, but I was too exhausted to wonder what that might be.

It's been a long fucking day.

I took off my shirt, shoes, and socks and collapsed onto the couch. While the bed was more than big enough for Cami and me to share, I didn't want to risk upsetting her by making assumptions.

Especially since she was still pissed at me.

Not wanting to think about that, I opted to memorize the

incantation from Zenaida instead. If the old Fortune Fae wanted me to know this spell, there was a reason for it.

With that thought in mind, I uttered a perimeter enchantment, one meant to wake me in case anyone entered the room without my permission. Then I slid the card into my pocket.

This will have to do for now.

Cami needed rest and so did I. We would figure out a battle plan when we woke up.

Assuming she stuck around long enough for us to talk.

I pulled out my wand to alter the incantation to also wake me up if anyone left the room. *Just in case...*

CHAPTER 9

CAMI

STOP THAT, I thought, squirming. *Leave me alone.*

I swatted at my arm, but the creeping sensation continued to crawl over my skin.

Fucking ant. I swiped at it again, only for several more to appear. Or that was the way it felt, anyway.

Growling, I smacked the bugs, determined to make them disappear. I was too exhausted for this bullshit. Too depleted. *Too...* I frowned. *Too cold...*

My brow furrowed, the temperature one I hadn't felt since... *Since the day Ajax and Az tied me to a chair in the Midnight Fae Realm.*

I shot upward, my eyes wide as I took in my surroundings, my mind half expecting to see a familiar dungeon covered in writhing snakes.

Except... that wasn't what I saw at all.

Instead, I was surrounded by silk and floral-patterned sheets, as well as a room that looked like it had furniture growing out of the ground itself.

I blinked. *Where the hell am I?*

This definitely wasn't Lucifer's palace.

However, it seemed certain things had followed me from said palace.

Things like the smug-looking Melek lounging beside me in the foreign bed.

His eyes dropped to my breasts before he popped a grape into my open mouth. "Good morning, angel. Lovely to see you."

My lips curled down again as I followed his gaze. *Shit.* I snatched up a blanket to cover my nude state, only to remember that he'd seen me in those chains... *yesterday? The day before? Hours ago?*

Hell, I had no idea.

Regardless, this wasn't a new view for him.

And *that* pissed me right off.

Crushing the grape with my molars, I reluctantly forced the sweet morsel down my throat. Its vibrant flavor and juice hit the spot perfectly. I had to admit I was parched, and *hungry*.

But equally furious.

Maybe... maybe more furious.

However, my stomach chose this moment to growl, disagreeing with my priorities. *Eat first. Then chastise the Hell Fae Prince,* it seemed to be saying.

"Where am I?" I demanded before reaching out to take another grape from the bowl in Melek's lap. *At least he has clothes on.*

Of course, his expression seemed to indicate that he would much rather remove his clothes and join me under the sheets.

At one point, I would probably have been okay with that —just to see what he hid beneath those sexy suits of his.

Right now, though? No. I wanted nothing to do with this asshole.

Except for maybe garnering some answers.

And eating all those grapes. I grabbed another with the

thought, my eyebrow arching upward as I waited for him to reply.

"The Midnight Fae Realm. Specifically, the Midnight Fae Palace." He paused for a moment. "It's riddled with power. Can't you feel it?"

Yes, I thought, my jaw clenching. *It feels like ants crawling all over my skin.*

"Why am I here?" I inquired instead of confirming his comment.

"You would need to ask our dear Warden that question," he murmured, glancing over his shoulder at the living area beyond the bedroom. I appeared to be in an overly large suite, one wall framed by windows that opened to a balcony outside.

The moon in the sky gave me pause. *What time is it?*

"I would give him another hour or so of rest," Melek went on. "He's going to need it."

I frowned once more—the look one that would probably become permanent if I didn't start making other expressions soon—as my mind slowly pieced together the events of last night.

My dream.
Waking up to Ajax.
Collapsing.
Him shadowing me...

"Am I here for interrogation again?" I asked slowly, taking in the ornate room once more. It was certainly an upgrade from the dungeon.

"No, I believe Ajax's intent is to rescue you," Melek mused, his multicolored irises flashing. "He wishes to keep you safe from Ty. A bold move, I must say, if a bit hasty. But the objective is respectable."

He handed me the bowl of fruit.

"Here, eat. You'll need your strength as well. Because it won't take Az long to find you both, especially with how quickly I managed to track you." He cocked his head to the side, causing his blondish-brown hair to fall over his expressive eyes. "I wonder how you'll convince him not to drag you back to Ty. It's a shame I won't be able to stick around to observe."

He vanished with the words, leaving me scowling at his disappearance. "Typical," I muttered, eating a grape. "Always speaking in riddles and never giving me worthwhile information."

"Well, now that's just not true," he replied, his voice making me jump as he reappeared beside me with a tray in his lap. "Everything I tell you is worthwhile. It's not my fault you fail to interpret it." He held up a cup of coffee. "Here."

I really wanted to refuse him on principle, but the delicious scent curled around me in hypnotic swirls, making my mouth salivate.

Chocolate. Whipped cream. Coffee.
Delicious.

I snatched the mug and took a careful sip to test the temperature, then groaned as it soothed my sore throat— something I hadn't even realized was scratchy until swallowing.

Definitely dehydrated and starving.
Fine. I'll accept this meal.
But I will not accept him.
Even if he does have chocolate-covered strawberries.

Which he held out to me next. I took one because, well, it sounded good. However, that didn't mean I was buying into this whole act-of-kindness thing.

He watched me bring the berry to my mouth and bite down, his eyes tracking my tongue as I swiped it across my lips. He seemed to be in a particular sort of mood, one I really didn't want to play with right now.

"Are you here to take me back to Lucifer?" I wondered aloud. "Or are you here to fuck with me?"

Amusement flirted with his expression. "I definitely want to fuck you, angel. But—"

"That's *not* what I asked," I interjected.

"I'm here to check up on you," he continued, ignoring my interruption. "How are you feeling, little angel?"

My eyes narrowed. "Like my days are numbered, *Prince Melek.*"

"Hmm," he hummed, his amusement seeming to deepen.

That makes one of us, I grumbled to myself.

Because I was very much *not* amused.

Ajax had tried to rescue me. I remembered pieces of the supposed event, allowing me to somewhat believe that information. But that just meant he'd defied Lucifer.

Which, in turn, meant we were both dead fae.

I had no doubt that when the Hell Fae King found me, he'd drag me back by my hair and execute me in front of everyone.

Well, no. He'd probably send Az here to do the dragging part. *Then* Lucifer would execute me. Horribly and publicly. And he'd probably do so in a manner that required me to be naked since that seemed to be a common theme in my relationship with these men.

I picked up another strawberry, then focused on my coffee for a bit while the Hell Fae Prince studied me in silence.

He probably bespelled this fruit, I realized. *And now he's just waiting for it to take effect.*

I was naïve to trust him before and an idiot for trusting him now. But I was so damn hungry. "How long was I asleep?" I mused aloud.

"A while," he replied cryptically. Because of course this fae couldn't give me a straight answer to anything. Why would he ever prove to be helpful or forthcoming?

I finished the coffee and set the mug on the nightstand next to me. A bottle of water appeared beside it, making me roll my eyes before I refocused on the grapes. "You're not going to buy my forgiveness with food," I muttered.

"I'm not trying to buy anything, Cami. I just want to take care of you."

"Oh?" I arched a brow at him. "By what, exactly? Fattening me up before Lucifer puts me on display again?"

His multicolored irises flickered, an uncharacteristic note of emotion fluttering across his expression. It was too brief for me to define, just a slight tug of his lips that seemed to go against his usual smirk. Almost as though he'd been about to scowl.

"I realize Ty's actions were, well, *uncomfortable* for you. However, he had to do something to maintain order. His Warden and Commander took a bride without permission. That couldn't be overlooked, or other Hell Fae would react accordingly and steal their own brides."

"You mean capture captives who were already there against their wills and force them to mate? Which is precisely what the games are doing anyway?" I countered.

Melek's expression darkened. "Are we back to that intentional misunderstanding of events again? The one where you pretend not to comprehend the entire purpose of the trials?"

"Are you just going to ignore the fact that *most* of the females are unwilling?" I tossed back at him, aware that I was being a judgmental brat and not caring in the slightest. Because fuck him. And fuck his king.

Melek sighed and shook his head. "Fate works in ways none of us can comprehend, Camillia. Your display in the Marsh Lands proved that, yes?"

My jaw clenched. "That had nothing to do with fate."

"No? You just happened to be wrapped up in enough of Ty's magic to wield it and save an entire kingdom of Nightmare Fae? Fascinating how that worked out."

"What are you accusing me of?"

"I'm not accusing you of anything, little angel. I'm merely pointing out that fate worked in our favor last night. Which our Hell Fae King is now struggling to *comprehend*, similar to your reaction to the Hell Fae Bride Trials." I reached out to steal a grape from the bowl in my lap. "You and Ty have some strikingly similar traits. Stubbornness being a key personality quirk."

"I'm nothing like him."

"Interestingly enough, I think he would agree with you on that," he mused. "Of course, you're both wrong, but neither of you will admit it." He lifted a shoulder and relaxed into the headboard of the massive bed, his lounging position the epitome of nonchalance.

"Whatever, *Prince Melek*. If you're not here to drag me back to Lucifer, and all you really want to know is how I'm doing, then I'm fine for a dead woman, thank you. Please feel free to fuck off now." Was I being rude? Yes. But this asshole deserved it.

Lucifer had dressed me in chains and put me in a cage. *On a fucking stage.*

All to what? Humiliate me? Because I'd touched his precious source?

Then I'd used it to *help* him, and he'd reacted by essentially intending to kill me.

Sure, maybe Melek had temporarily saved me from the Hell Fae King's wrath. And yeah, it probably wasn't a good idea to piss off the one fae who seemed capable of saving me from the literal devil. But I was done playing these games with Melek.

Done being a pawn.

A toy.

Or whatever the fuck he considered me to be.

"Leave," I reiterated. "And take your cryptic bullshit with you."

His jaw clenched, my words clearly striking a nerve. But rather than disappear, he merely conjured himself a glass of wine and took an indulgent sip from the crystal rim.

"When Ty revealed his plans for your punishment, I'll admit that they intrigued me. Mostly because I have a particular fascination with bondage play, and chains seemed to suit that fetish."

"How nice for you," I deadpanned.

"But I've since realized that verbal consent in such an activity is equally important," he went on, again ignoring my interruption. "While our bodies may enjoy a certain sensation, that doesn't mean our hearts and minds do."

I stared at him. *What am I even supposed to say to that?* I wondered.

Fortunately, he didn't seem to want me to say anything at all.

Because he wasn't done.

"I'm sorry, Cami." All signs of his typical playfulness disappeared beneath the weight of his words. "Ty selected your sensual punishment as a means of trying to please me. He hasn't admitted that, of course, but his methods were clearly designed with my proclivities in mind. I think it was his way of showing support."

My eyebrows jumped upward. "Support for what? Torturing me?"

"Support for my intentions with you," he replied. "He's not been very pleased with my decisions where you're concerned, such as the gifts I've provided, the information I've revealed. Kissing you. But I think he was trying to create a little light in an otherwise dark situation. It's how he works."

"I..." I didn't really know how to respond to that now, either. This was probably the most straightforward Melek had ever been with me, and it still didn't make sense. "What intentions?" I finally asked because I still didn't understand what he wanted from me.

"My intent to mate you," he clarified, a note of patience underlining his words.

He'd said that to me before.

"Then we'll say I intend to be yours, if you choose to one day have me."

He'd made it sound like a choice. *Is it still a choice?*

"I'm not trying to overwhelm you," he murmured. "But I know you're upset, and I'm sorry. Truly. Ty is just trying to navigate all this change, and, to be blunt, he's not handling it well."

No shit, I nearly responded.

"I owe Ajax an apology, too. Although, Az and Ty—" Melek winced, his gaze suddenly narrowing at the living area.

I followed his gaze, thinking that maybe Ajax had heard us and was awake now. But he was still nestled into the cushions with one arm tossed over his face, his opposite lying across his bare torso.

Instead, Melek appeared to be focused on the entryway.

A chill ran up my spine, causing the hairs to dance along the back of my neck. *Is Ty here? Az? Someone else?*

Power radiated off Melek as a light dusting of gold sparks flickered in the air, the energy swirling toward the door.

"What is it?" I whispered.

"Zakkai," Melek murmured. "He's playing with my essence."

I swallowed, the name very familiar to me. *Zakkai, the Source Architect.* He was an intimidatingly powerful Midnight Fae with the ability to rewrite magic. He'd also administered a truth spell that had proved my innocence.

He'd called me powerful, and when asked to elaborate on what he sensed, he'd said, "An equal."

Whatever the hell that had meant.

"I shouldn't be here, and he's making sure I know that," Melek continued. "I'm showing him that I could choose to retaliate, but I'm not. Instead, I'm letting him play."

"And how's he reacting to that?" I asked warily.

"Unclear," Melek murmured, shrugging. "Anyway, I believe we were discussing apologies?" His pretty eyes swirled with energy and barely restrained power as he looked at me. "I'm sorry for hurting you, Camillia. I would never do so intentionally. All I want is to protect you."

My jaw clenched and unclenched, his sincerity pricking at my walls. But it wasn't nearly enough for me to forgive him. And definitely not Lucifer.

Too much had happened for me to trust either of them. *Any of them*, I corrected, my gaze flickering back to Ajax. *Well, maybe not all of them.*

Hell Fae Rule #10: Actions Speak Louder than Words.

And Ajax's actions thus far suggested he was more than apologetic; he was willing to sacrifice everything for me. Including his relationship with Az.

My teeth continued to grind together. I wasn't sure how I felt about Ajax's choices. He shouldn't have given up so much for me. Shouldn't have fled Lucifer's command. Now he would be hunted, too. Perhaps even killed.

Because of me.

I... I didn't like that.

"Would Lucifer believe me if I said I somehow cast a spell on Ajax and forced him to bring me here?" I asked Melek, my fingers curled and uncurled at my sides. "Or will he forfeit Ajax's life anyway?"

"He's not going to kill Ajax, Cami. He's not going to kill you either."

I glanced sideways at him. "I find that very hard to believe."

"I know. But Az gave him a lot to think about last night. And I'm going to ensure he continues to think about what Az said." Melek reached out, his fingers nearly brushing my cheek. But at the last second, he pulled back and shook his head again, another sigh parting his too-perfect lips.

Why does he have to be so damn alluring? I wondered.

I *hated* how attracted I was to him. I refused to be one of those females who forgave a guy for doing something wrong just because he flashed a charming smile.

Or uttered a heartfelt apology.

It might be a step in the right direction, but he still had a few miles of hiking ahead of him before I'd even consider forgiving him.

Although, his lack of cryptic commentary was another positive move forward.

"My aim is unity, little angel. A stronger future. To become impenetrable and indestructible in the eyes of our enemies," he said, ruining everything I'd just thought.

Because there went the *lack of cryptic commentary.*

"That tells me absolutely nothing, Melek." It was just a bunch of fancy words that made no sense whatsoever. *Whose enemies? Mine? Yours? And what's this talk about unity and stronger futures?*

"Perhaps it tells you everything, but you're not understanding all the pieces yet." He ran his fingers through his hair, the movement one that seemed almost uncharacteristic. Like he was stressed and trying to find the right words.

How very unlike Melek.

"I know you're mad, angel. You should be. Ty is trying to control you so he can better control his response to you. Keep fighting him. It's what you both need."

"Maybe what I need is to have nothing to do with him or

you," I countered. "Maybe I need to have nothing to do with *any* of you."

"If only that were an option, little angel," he replied with a sigh. "But the book chose you, which means, on some level, Ty's soul has marked you. None of us were ever given a choice in the events that followed."

If I had known that, I would never have picked up the damn book in the library.

"The only one who wasn't given a choice in this was me, the Hell Fae Bride captive," I said. "A consequence of a deal my father struck with the devil. Everything since that day hasn't been *by choice*."

"Back to that again, hmm?"

"It's all true," I retorted.

"Hmm, well, I think you've made plenty of choices, Cami," he murmured, his gaze knowing. "Plenty of *pleasurable* decisions, to be precise."

My lips parted. "Excuse me?"

"You heard me just fine, little angel." Some of that playfulness entered his gaze again as a pile of golden dust formed in his palm. "Unfortunately, however, I don't have time to continue this chat."

He blew the powder into my face in the next instant, making me cough. "What the fuck?"

"See you soon, little angel," he whispered, his lips suddenly against my ear. I flinched as his mouth brushed my temple. "Try not to kill Az when he shows up."

Then he disappeared in a wink, leaving me covered in his golden essence.

"*Melek,*" I snarled, my hands wiping futilely at my face. I didn't need a mirror to see that he'd just saturated my skin in shimmering sparkles.

A curse from the living area followed as Ajax jumped to

his feet, his wand at the ready and his gaze flying around the room as though searching for a threat.

He paused when his focus landed on me in the bed.

Both of his eyebrows shot upward, probably at the sight of my glittering skin.

Fuck, it was on my shoulders and neck, too. *And my breasts*, I realized, looking down.

Because I'd lost hold of the sheet when I'd started frantically wiping at my face. The fabric had been tucked under my arms while I ate, and now... yeah, now it was pooled at my waist.

Fuck it, I thought. *Fuck all of this.*

What did my nudity matter now anyway? Between the interrogation and the chain dress and now this... it just didn't matter.

So why not have sparkly boobs?

Ugh!

My head fell into my hands as I groaned loud enough for the entire Midnight Fae Kingdom to hear.

"Melek?" Ajax guessed.

I didn't bother to nod. Instead, I just muttered, "Obviously."

Then I flopped over in the bed and screamed into the pillow.

Fucking male fae.

I hated them.

All. Of. Them.

CHAPTER 10

CAMI

My throat ached, my screams more of a croak than an earsplitting sound.

Probably a sign that I need to stop throwing this tantrum and do something else, I thought, irritated with myself. But a part of me also felt relieved. I'd needed a chance to just let it all out. And fortunately, Ajax hadn't tried to stop me.

Unfortunately, he was leaning against the wall just inside the bedroom, his arms folded over his chiseled chest as he observed me with his dark eyes. From here, I couldn't see the rim of blue around those obsidian irises, which somehow lent him an even more sinister appeal.

"You brought me to the Midnight Fae Realm," I said, my voice raspy. I grabbed the water from the nightstand and downed half of the contents before I added, "Why the hell would you do that? Lucifer is going to kill you." *Because of me.*

Ajax merely shrugged. "It was the right thing to do. If he chooses to kill me for it, then he'll only further prove to me that my reaction was the right one." He stepped forward and held out a towel for me—one I hadn't realized he had tucked into his hand against his chest until now.

Rather than thank him for it, I set my water down and grabbed the towel, then used the damp fabric against my face.

Only one glance down at the item told me what I already suspected... "It's not coming off."

"No, it's not."

I ground my teeth together. "Fucking Melek."

"It seems to be... soaking in," Ajax said, his hands sliding into the pockets of his jeans.

"Soaking in?"

"It's disappearing, almost like lotion," he offered.

"Of course it is," I gritted out. "He probably just marked me with some sort of tracking spell." Although, he obviously didn't really need one since he'd already found me.

My face fell to my hands once more with a growl.

This was all so fucked up. Every minute of it. "I was just trying to help those fae," I told Ajax, not caring at all if the change in subject jarred him. "But I had to use Lucifer's power to do it."

"I know. I saw what happened."

"And so did he, but you see where that led," I grumbled.

"I can't begin to explain his reactions. Melek or Az would do a better job of that. I can only say that I disagree with what he did. And..." He shuffled his feet, the movement oddly boyish and very unlike the Hell Fae Warden that I knew. "And all I can do is apologize for my part in everything."

My eyebrows shot up. "You're apologizing, too?"

"Melek apologized?"

"Yes."

"Oh." His brow crinkled. "That... that must have been interesting to observe."

"It was certainly something," I admitted, still unsure of how I felt about it all. Melek had mentioned consent, just like he'd made it sound like a choice as to whether or not I would take him as a mate.

Then he'd doused me in his golden essence like some sort of claiming spritz.

I could feel it settling into my being, the power warming my skin and leaving behind a subtle kiss of electricity that hummed along my exposed arms.

With a curse, I tossed the towel to the floor. All of this... it... *ugh.*

I wanted to scream again, but my still-sore throat wouldn't allow me to enjoy it. So I grabbed the water and finished chugging it. The bottle vanished when I emptied it, along with the coffee mug and all of the other food-related items Melek had brought with him.

Including the grapes.

"What...?" I glanced around, then realized Ajax was holding a wand.

"If you want anything else, I can conjure it. But I don't trust Melek's food," he explained. "Or what I assume was food from Melek, anyway."

"It was," I confirmed in a low grumble.

Ajax nodded. "I don't know how he circumvented my spell to enter, but my magic caught him on the way out. That's what woke me up."

"Oh." Not exactly my most profound response...

"But him finding us this quickly is a problem. We're not just in the Midnight Fae Realm; we're in the Midnight Fae Palace. He skirted all the protocols to get in here, which means Lucifer can as well."

I didn't reply because I wasn't all that surprised. Lucifer was the literal devil. Of course he could traverse other realms with ease.

And Melek was... well, I didn't know exactly *what* Melek was, but he was definitely powerful.

Ajax blew out a breath and sat on the edge of the bed, his fingers twirling his wand in rapid movements. "Shade invited us to midnight breakfast." He uttered a spell to reveal the time. "That's in about two hours. Maybe they'll have some suggestions."

"Melek mentioned that Zakkai was playing with his powers." I wasn't sure if that information would be useful or not, but it seemed important. "So Zakkai at least knows Melek was here."

"I can't imagine he was pleased. Zakkai and Shade have always met with Lucifer in the paradigm, never here. At least not that I know of." He ran his free palm over his face, his exhaustion palpable. It made me wonder how much sleep he'd actually gotten, since I felt mostly rested.

Because he brought me here, I thought. *He chose to protect me.*

"Why?" I whispered. "Why did you bring me here?" I'd already asked him that, but I... I couldn't believe he'd actually done it. That he'd put his life on the line... *for me.*

No one had ever done that before. Hell, no one had ever come close to supporting me in any real way. Not even my parents.

Fuck, my dad had given me up to the devil for his Hell Fae bridal games.

My mom barely acknowledged my existence.

My best friends—if they could even be called that— probably didn't even realize I was gone.

Granted, I didn't really allow personal relationships.

Hell Fae Rule #4: Don't Trust Anyone.

But part of me wanted to trust Ajax now, even despite everything we'd been through.

His actions definitely prove his intent, I told myself, referring to rule number ten—*Actions Speak Louder than Words.*

"I had nowhere else to go," Ajax said as his wand disappeared into thin air. "I left the Midnight Fae Realm to escape my memories. But what happened yesterday...? What Lucifer and Az did?" He swallowed and shook his head. "They made me realize that those memories will always haunt me."

The pain in his voice made my heart ache for him. I... I should hate him, should hate *all* of them, but I couldn't fortify my walls with that necessary emotion right now.

He tried to save me, I kept thinking. *He sacrificed his relationships with Az and Lucifer... for me.*

That wasn't what I wanted at all.

No one should ever have to give up their loyalties for another person. No one should ever be forced to choose.

"I thought Lucifer just wanted to punish me," he went on. "I touched something that didn't belong to me. I acknowledged that. But I didn't expect him to punish you, too." His dark eyes burned into mine as he finally looked at me. "I should never have told you to put on those chains. I'm sorry, Cami. You have no idea how sorry I am... for everything."

The sincerity in his features rivaled Melek's from just moments ago, the two men making my head spin with their unexpected apologies.

Maybe I died, I mused. *Maybe Lucifer killed me and this is some form of the afterlife. But is it Heaven or Hell?*

I nearly laughed at the very human concept of death. I'd been to literal Hell now. I knew what that was like.

And this didn't feel all that hellish. It felt... kind of nice.

Of course, it didn't fully cure my anger. Lucifer had humiliated me while Ajax and the others had just stood by and watched.

But Ajax hadn't been a willing participant.

Az had forced him to comply with Lucifer's punishment, providing Ajax with his own personal sort of hell. He'd told me what had happened to his family and to Emelyn, how Constantine had forced him to watch them die.

Lucifer's actions hadn't been nearly that violent, at least not on the stage in his club. He'd just been maniacal and cruel. But I would eventually overcome the trauma of the incident. Hell, I was mostly over it already anyway.

So a bunch of Hell Fae saw me mostly naked on a stage. It wasn't any different from what they'd seen in the trials. They hadn't been allowed to touch me, only talk to me. And most of them hadn't even been all that inappropriate with their words.

Was I ever going to forgive Lucifer for his part in it? No. I probably wouldn't forgive Az either, especially knowing what he'd done to Ajax.

And Melek, well, I wasn't even sure where to begin with him and his cryptic meddling.

Whereas Ajax... I might be able to forgive Ajax.

Not yet. Not now. It was too fresh. But eventually, I probably could.

"I can't say I forgive you," I admitted. "However, my anger isn't so much directed at you as it is at Lucifer and Az."

He swallowed and dipped his chin in acknowledgment. "I understand." He huffed a humorless laugh. "I *really* understand. I'm pissed at them, too. They..." He trailed off and shook his head. "This isn't about me. Never mind."

"No, tell me," I said, rearranging the sheet to better cover my nudity and leaning forward a bit. "It'll distract me. Or maybe I'll be able to relate."

He considered me for a moment, then drew his leg up onto the bed to face me, his opposite limb hanging off the edge.

"I trusted them, and they burned that trust by taking away my ability to choose. They might not know everything about what happened to me, but they know enough. And using my past against me as punishment..." He scowled. "Intentional or not, I don't think I can forgive that."

"I don't know if I could either," I admitted.

Ajax and Az had a history, one I might not fully understand but certainly had noticed in our time together. For Az to be so obtuse, so *inconsiderate*, was inexcusable.

And Lucifer... well, I highly doubted he was oblivious to his methods. He knew what he was doing. *Evil incarnate.*

I might be a bit biased, all things considered, but Lucifer certainly seemed sinister enough to purposely design a punishment meant to pluck at the heartstrings.

Although, Melek had made it sound like the whole arrangement had been for his benefit.

"His methods were clearly designed with my proclivities in mind. I think it was his way of showing support."

Is he right? I wondered. *Or is it a combination of some kind?*

Ajax sighed and fell back onto the bed, his torso near my feet, only he was on top of the blankets, not beneath them like me.

"Fae, this is a comfortable mattress," he groaned as he brought his other leg up and curled into the bed. "Fuck, it's probably spelled for sex."

A laugh escaped me as he crawled into the center to collapse again.

"The couch must be spelled for backaches. Maybe it's some sort of warped punishment for being kicked out of this monstrosity of a bed," he continued. "Anyone sleeping on the couch clearly did something wrong."

"I didn't force you to sleep there," I pointed out.

"No, but it was what I deserved. Hence, the backache." He stretched against the mattress and sighed. "I think I'll live here now. Enjoy midnight breakfast with Shade. His riddles are almost as annoying as Melek's." His words were a mumble as his eyes closed.

"Maybe the bed is spelled for sleep, not sex," I mused.

"A bed this size is absolutely used for sex," he murmured back. "Group sex." One hand lifted to gesture at the chair in the corner. "With an audience."

"Sounds like you've been thinking about it," I hedged as I lay down beside him, still under the covers while he remained on top.

"Sex is a common thought while in your presence," he admitted, his thick eyelashes parting as he gazed over at me. "Pretty sure I'm addicted to you, Cami."

My lips twitched. "I'm not sure if that's an insult or a compliment."

"Definitely a compliment," he replied. "You're the first woman I've desired in over a decade. The first fae I've wanted to confide in, too. I think I've told you more than I've ever told Az, which I guess means he might not have fully realized how his actions would impact me. But..." He shrugged. "Doesn't mean I can let that go."

Sort of like how I might not be able to let Lucifer's punishment—and Ajax's involvement—go either. Just for different reasons.

"I'm going to do what I can to protect you, Cami," he promised. "I just hope it's enough."

I reached over to palm his cheek. "I appreciate the sentiment, Warden." And I did. Because I could tell he meant it.

Alas, we were both aware that Lucifer would win this battle in the end. Neither of us knew how to fight him, nor were we strong enough to even try.

Ajax angled his head to kiss my wrist, his eyes falling closed once more. "The instinct to bite you is killing me, Cami."

I started to pull away, but he caught my hand and held my wrist to his mouth.

"I would never bite you without permission," he vowed. "Even with my uniquely wired magic, it would initiate the

Midnight Fae bonds. And I refuse to take a mate without consent." His eyes opened, the blue rims around his irises flashing. "I'll prove to you that you can trust me, Cami."

He nibbled my pulse, not hard enough to break the skin, then placed a kiss on my open palm.

"It'll take time, but I'll earn it, if you let me."

Did I want that? Do I want to let him earn my trust? My affection? *My... heart?*

My throat worked as I studied him, my mouth suddenly dry. *Actions speak louder than words,* I kept whispering to myself. *And his actions... are very loud.*

How was this the male who had interrogated me before? Tying me to a chair, threatening me with snakes...

Only to be contrite afterward when he realized I hadn't deceived him. Hadn't broken his faith in me. Hadn't intentionally hurt him at all.

We'd grown so much since those moments, in so short a time.

How much more can we grow? I wondered. *What could life together be like?*

We would always have Lucifer hanging over our heads, likely numbering our days. Hell, we might die today. Tomorrow. Next week.

Did I really want to spend my last remaining hours being angry at the one fae who had actually tried to help me?

He hadn't known what Lucifer would do with those chains. Sure, he'd probably had an idea of what it would entail, but not the full picture of what would actually occur. How he'd been frozen by his best friend, forced to watch it all happen as Lucifer presented me on the stage like some sort of prize to be taken.

We were both suffering for very different, yet related, reasons.

And I really didn't want to waste time hating the only fae in this universe who had attempted to support me.

Too little, too late just didn't apply here. We hadn't known each other long enough for me to blame him for his choices. He'd done what he felt was right. Including assisting me in the end.

This wasn't about forgiveness.

This was about living.

Accepting.

Commiserating with someone whose fate was now darkly tied to my own.

Because he chose me. He chose to do what he felt was right. He tried to save me.

I moved my hand away from his mouth to cup his cheek once more, only this time my entire body moved with the action as I leaned into his strength. He'd been next to me without really touching me, and I quickly removed the gap between us.

His eyes held mine as I moved, his fingers loosely wrapping around my wrist while his opposite arm remained limp between us.

The sheets slid off me, revealing my nude state. However, his gaze didn't falter, his focus staying on my face instead of my breasts while I straddled him.

He was shirtless as well, affording me a delectable view of all that sinewy muscle, yet I kept my eyes on his, the intimacy of our connection unmistakable.

I held it even while I lowered to kiss him, my chest pressing against his as though they'd always belonged there. His lips parted beneath mine, his touch equal parts reverent and knowing. Like this was meant to be. As though our destinies had been tied together specifically for this moment, knowing exactly what we would need from one another. How we would need each other. Need *this*.

Maybe Melek was right about fate, I mused. *Or maybe Ajax is right about this bed being bespelled for sex.*

But I was done thinking.

Done fretting about the future, about the past, about Lucifer, about everything in between.

Now I wanted to scream in an entirely different way.

"Distract me, Ajax," I whispered against his mouth. "Give me a moment of peace."

"I'll give you anything you want, Cami," he replied. "I'll give you everything."

CHAPTER 11

AJAX

I<small>T WAS</small> a vow I shouldn't make.

A vow I wouldn't be able to uphold for long.

But at least I could carry the promise to my grave.

Because I had no doubt that Lucifer was coming for us. Melek having found us so easily meant Az would be on his way any minute now. However, I refused to agonize over the inevitable.

Cami wanted to live in this moment—something I somehow knew because I felt it in her kiss—and I fully intended to fulfill her craving.

I swiped my tongue against her lips, seeking permission for more. A deeper kiss. An unspoken declaration of partnership. An intimate moment meant only for us.

It was more than I deserved. More than I could ever have anticipated asking for. More than I'd ever realized I wanted.

But I needed her.

I needed *this*.

I needed the *moment of peace* she'd requested and anything else she'd be willing to give me.

Time was precious and we had so little of it left.

Unless we can find a way to deal with Lucifer, I thought. And I didn't mean by killing him, but a real deal. A contract that would allow us to live.

It was a fantasy, a dreamlike desire that would likely never come to fruition. Just like the sexual image I'd imagined last night about fucking Cami in this bed with Melek and Az while Typhos watched.

This bed is definitely enchanted, I decided. But fuck if I cared about that right now. I just wanted Cami. And I had her. Naked. Straddling me. Kissing me. Hands on my shoulders. Tits pressed to my chest. Fucking perfection.

I just need to get out of these damn pants.

Cami pressed down against my hips, almost like she was agreeing with my thought. Fuck, it was like we were connected even though I knew we weren't. We simply understood each other.

Her nails dug into my shoulders, her mouth responding to mine and allowing my tongue entry.

Our kiss was slow. Thorough. *Intentional.* A whispered promise between souls. *This is our moment and we're taking it for ourselves.*

It wasn't about forgiveness. It wasn't about moving on from our past or about healing. It was about pleasure. Escape. *Indulgence.*

She kissed me with a fervor, her passion crashing over me in a hot wave of intensity. I allowed her to drown me in it, to suffocate my instincts and quiet every ounce of doubt I could possibly possess. Not that there was much left.

This woman had broken through every one of my barriers and had forced me to *feel.*

I was irrevocably changed.

And I didn't have a single regret.

Rather than say the words aloud, I whispered them into her mouth with my tongue.

She moaned.

I growled.

Cami provoked every single one of my predatory instincts, her mere presence making my incisors ache. I hadn't been lying when I said I wanted to bite her. It was this intrinsic yearning deep inside that threatened to take control.

Claiming her would allow me to protect her.

Marking her as mine might secure us both. She'd be welcomed into Midnight Fae society. Granted access to the realm via our bond. Perhaps even gain new traits and powers as our souls joined.

Assuming I'm truly welcome here, I thought.

But that was a concern for another day. Another time. Not now. Not while I had Cami's sensual form pressed against mine.

I rolled us over, pushing her back into the mattress as I deepened our kiss.

She ran her palms over my shoulder blades in response, her nails scraping along my skin. A subtle claim. One I echoed by nibbling her lower lip. Not hard enough to break the skin, just an answering claim to rival her own.

Cami grinned in response, her thighs squeezing mine as she hooked her ankles together against my ass. "These pants need to go."

"Eager, little rebel?" I asked her, my lips curling to match her smile. "What happened to foreplay?"

"Our entire relationship has been foreplay, Ajax. Just fuck me already."

"Mmm..." I wanted to fuck her. Own her. *Bite* her. Make her mine. *Bond* us.

Too much, I told myself. *Too fast.*

We'd been through hell. *Literally. This... we shouldn't be... moving this...*

She arched into me, her body echoing her command and

making me curse. Cami seemed as lost to this connection as I did. Utterly captivated. Ready for everything. *Begging* for my touch. My cock. *My fangs.*

No.

It's this fucking bed, I realized. *It really is enchanted.*

Maybe even by Melek.

That last thought made me growl, the irritating concept giving me just enough pause to act. "Not here," I told Cami as I slid off the mattress and pulled her along with me. "The shower."

We needed to wash up anyway.

And if we still wanted to fuck in there, then I'd let it happen. Because that would mean this was real. That she truly wanted me and wasn't just acting under some sort of lust spell.

"The shower?" Cami repeated. "Ajax, that's for aft—"

I picked her up, cutting her off before she could finish, and cradled her against my chest.

She gaped up at me. "You're serious."

"I am." I started toward the en-suite bathroom. "You're covered in Melek's essence. Time to wash it off." *And make sure this is really what you want,* I added mentally.

Cami made a noise that had my lips twitching upward in amusement. It was one of equal annoyance and frustration, and I suspected it wasn't all directed at me.

I stepped inside the bathroom, my focus shifting to the oversized bathtub and then to the giant walk-in shower.

"Choices," I mused, debating between the two. "But I think I want you there." I gestured to the tiled wall with the ledges built in. There was a bench, too. "Three showerheads as well."

Cami followed my gaze, her gray eyes lighting up with expectation. "That does look fun."

"It does," I agreed, setting her on her feet. "But first, you need to take off my pants." It would confirm whether or not she truly wanted this. Give her a choice to back out. A moment of clarity to see beyond whatever lust-inducing spell the bed might have unleashed upon her.

Or Melek's golden glitter, I thought sourly.

Cami glanced back at me, her pretty irises flickering down to my jeans. "Do I get a reward if I strip you?"

"Several," I promised.

"Hmm." She drew her nail across my lower abdomen, her lip disappearing between her teeth as she sank to her knees. It wasn't at all what I'd expected when I'd issued my demand. A denial—because she'd come to her senses—had been one way I'd thought she might react.

But this?

I hadn't anticipated this.

Or that devilish glint in her eyes as she reached for the button of my jeans.

I swallowed, my throat suddenly dry. I wasn't sure if she wanted to please me or eat me. *Maybe she plans to torture me. Punish me.* Own *me.*

My heart skipped a beat at the thought, my veins immediately burning with renewed need.

I'd do whatever she desired. Bow. Beg. Please her for hours, days, *years.* Follow her lead in every way imaginable. Do whatever she wanted.

It was a terrifying realization. However, this female... she'd gotten under my skin. She'd inserted herself into my soul without a single bite.

How is that even possible? I marveled as she drew the zipper of my pants down. *When did she become mine?*

Was it because I'd tasted her blood? Because we'd been through literal Hell together?

My jeans whispered along my skin as she tugged them down, leaving me exposed to her in more ways than she probably knew.

Would it scare her if I told her? Confessed how my incisors ached with the need to mark her? How my Midnight Fae spirit longed to marry hers?

Who even am I? I wondered, shaking my head to clear it.

Except the yearning only grew that much sharper as Cami pressed a wet kiss to my cock. Completely unbidden. Entirely unexpected. But so damn perfect.

I fisted her hair on instinct, my balls aching from that subtle tease.

She rewarded me by parting those sweet lips and taking me into her mouth, her tongue gliding along the underside of my dick.

"*Fuck*, Cami," I breathed.

She hummed against my throbbing shaft, her devious gaze capturing mine. This female knew what she was doing, something she proved by playing with my piercings in a way that nearly drove me mad.

"I don't know what I did to deserve you," I admitted. "But I thank the fates every day for putting you in my path."

She nibbled the barbell decorating the head of my cock and pulled back to stare up at me. "You're only saying that because I had your dick in my mouth."

I huffed a laugh that sounded more like a growl and lifted her off the ground to set her on the counter.

"I'm saying that because all I want to do is bite you and claim you," I corrected her as I leaned down to nip at the raging pulse point of her neck. "I'm saying that because you've changed everything for me, Cami. *Everything*."

She'd made me *feel*.

Brought me back to life.

Given me renewed purpose.

Reminded me how to fight for what I believed in.

"You taught me how to breathe again," I told her reverently. "I didn't realize how lost I'd become... until you."

Heavy words littered with emotion. But I couldn't hide them from her. Couldn't hide the impact she'd had upon me.

I had never truly let Emelyn in, my walls always having been up because of our dark circumstances. She'd been betrothed to another fae. I was just a passing memory. It didn't matter that we'd fancied ourselves in love with each other. There had never been a chance for us.

Or that was what I'd told myself all those years ago.

Why I'd held myself back.

Except it was different then. Different *now*.

Yes, I'd loved Emelyn.

But Cami... *Cami is so much more.*

I won't make the mistake of holding back again, I thought now. *I won't let Cami down.*

She had to know the truth. *My* truth.

Especially because that truth was all I had anymore. Cami meant more to me than I could even comprehend. And I was done trying to determine the *whys* or *hows* of it.

We could belabor the point all damn day and never figure out a cause.

And fuck if I was going to waste more time.

I refuse to take these truths to the grave.

I pressed my palms against her thighs and spread her legs to step between them, my mouth trailing down over her breasts and pausing to nibble her delicious nipples. "You're so fucking perfect, Cami. Rebellious. Strong. *Determined.*"

She'd been the most difficult captive to catch for the trials. Then she'd created problems at every turn.

And I fucking loved her for it.

Those headaches were what had woken me the fuck up. Her truthful statements and claims were what had pulled me from the fog in my mind, forcing me to live in the present. To move on from the past. To consider a potential future.

I continued my path downward along her flat abdomen,

my tongue dipping into her belly button along the way. All the while, I told her what I was thinking, how she'd changed my perspective on life. Provided me with new opportunities. Redefined my entire existence.

"It's a lot, I know," I whispered, my mouth near her clit. "But, Cami, I mean it—I'm so damn thankful to have you in my life. No matter how long or short it may become, *you* were worth every moment of pain and suffering from my past. And you'll continue to be worth it in the future, too."

CHAPTER 12

CAMI

AJAX'S EYES were a dark swirl of emotion, his words a reverent kiss to my ears.

I... I didn't know what to say. He'd just poured his soul into those statements, allowing me through his barriers and to the core of his existence.

I could almost feel his pain as though it was my own, his resulting loneliness a tangible presence I more than understood.

Because I, too, had been alone most of my life. Although my loneliness had been for entirely different reasons, I still understood the plight of having no one else to rely on. No one else to trust. No one else to *love*.

However, we were in this together now.

Two rebels fleeing a dangerous court.

Two fae running from a lethal king.

Ajax had chosen me.

And now... now I wanted to choose him.

Our days were numbered. Why spend them alone? Why fight our emotions for one another?

Ajax's lips sealed over my clit, causing my back to arch as a scream left my lips. He growled in approval, his palms skimming up my thighs to my hips, holding me in place while he devoured me.

Fuck. I'd told him we didn't need any foreplay. I'd been wrong. Foreplay was *always* appreciated.

I grabbed the back of his head, my nails dragging through his dark hair. *So soft. So thick. So... ohhh.*

His incisors against my tender flesh sent a shock wave through my system, my breath catching in my throat.

Then his tongue followed, swirling against my skin to soothe the sting.

"Did... did you... break skin?" I asked, breathless from the sensations rolling through my body. *So close. Too close. Fuck, that... yes...*

"No." He repeated the nibble, the sharp end stirring another jolt, this one even more intense than the last. "I told you I won't bite you without permission. I meant it." He laved the hurt away once more. "I'm just indulging in your sweet pussy, little rebel. I love making you jump."

He did it a third time, causing me to moan. Because damn, that felt... *good.* Different. A little dangerous. And equal parts erotic.

"I like it," I admitted.

"I know." The two words were spoken against my slick heat, the confidence in his tone making my thighs tense.

He'd listed several of my attributes that he liked about me. Well, his confidence was one of the many characteristics I liked about him.

I also really appreciated his mouth. And his tongue. And his *hands*—both of which were gliding up to my breasts.

His thumbs teased my nipples as he taunted me with his vampiric kiss below.

I wanted more.

All of him.

Everything we could be.

"I want you to bite me," I told him. "*Really* bite me."

"That'll initiate the mating bonds," he reminded me, his response spoken against my clit.

"I know," I replied, infusing the same amount of confidence in those two words as he had moments ago. "I want you to bite me, Ajax."

His thumbs stilled against my skin, his focus shifting away from my heated center and upward to my face. "You want my claiming bite?"

I swallowed and nodded. "Yes." It came out less confident than before, but not because I didn't want this. I definitely did.

But what if I'd misheard him earlier? Or perhaps I'd misunderstood?

No. He keeps saying he wants to bite me.

Unless...

"Do you only want to bite me for my blood?" I asked him. I didn't know how often he needed to feed. Maybe that was why he wanted to bite me—to satiate his hunger.

He'd craved my essence before. Az had helped him by biting me for Ajax. And another time we'd used a knife.

Perhaps... "Can you conjure a blade?" I frowned, another thought occurring to me. "What happened to your wand?" He'd had it in the bedroom, but now it seemed to have vanished.

I shook my head. *Stop being ridiculous, Cami.*

"Never mind." I was rambling now, which was very unlike me. "Just fuck me. Forget I said anything."

Ajax lifted his head away from my core, his blue-black eyes studying mine. "Forget that you asked me to bite you?" His lips curled. "Forget that you asked me to *claim* you?"

"Ajax—"

"I'm not forgetting anything, little rebel." He grabbed the

counter on either side of my hips, his muscular form leaning into mine. "When I do this, we'll be connected forever. Are you sure you want that, Cami? Are you sure you want me inside you? Linked to your soul? Able to hear your thoughts and mind?"

I shivered, the intensity in his words touching my spirit and setting it on fire.

Because *yes*, I wanted that. All of that. With him.

To not be alone anymore. To have a partner. To survive with someone rather than on my own. To live out what little time I had left with a lover—*a mate*—instead of wasting it away in solitude.

But it was more than that.

I'd clicked with Ajax from the beginning, even when he'd been the intimidating and cruel Warden. Against my better judgment, I'd desired him even then.

And he'd been supportive of me in his own way, too. Confiding in me despite his nature not to trust anyone. Helping me with the trials. Even his behavior after he thought I'd betrayed him had been more sensual than harsh. And when he'd realized I was innocent... he'd groveled.

He'd made it up to me.

He'd been there for me.

He'd even tried to help me.

Then he'd saved me. *At the expense of everything else.*

Do I want to mate him?

"Yes," I told him, my hand cupping his cheek. It was probably crazy. Rash, even. *But...* "It feels right. This. Us. Right now."

I didn't want to debate it anymore. I just wanted this to happen. With *him*.

I moved forward to brush my lips against his. "Will you bite me, Ajax? Will you initiate the claiming bond?"

He shuddered beneath my palm, his lashes lowering as his gaze grew hooded. "I feel like this is a dream."

"Maybe it is."

"Maybe it isn't."

"It won't change what I want," I promised him. "Now tell me what you want."

"I'd rather show you." The words were a breath against my lips, and an absolutely perfect response.

Actions speak louder than words, I mused, the rule playing over and over again in my thoughts as his tongue dipped inside my mouth. The flavor of my arousal on his lips sent my pulse racing with need.

A need that only flared hotter as he lifted me in the air and carried me into the shower.

Cold stone tile met the overheated skin of my back, the trickle of warm water instantly falling all around us. I wasn't sure if the shower was motion sensor operated or if it was magically controlled, but I didn't care.

All that mattered was Ajax's kiss.

His hands.

His cock against my saturated sex as I wrapped my legs around his hips.

I groaned as he slid inside me, his expert movement only seeming to confirm how well we fit together.

This male. This fae. This *Warden*. I was lost to him. To the moment. To his touch. His measured strokes. His addictive kiss. *Those magical hands.*

He caressed me in a way that made me feel worshipped.

Took my mouth with a passion that stirred my very soul.

And held me with such care that I couldn't help but feel protected.

Secure.

Joined.

No longer alone.

His thrusts went deep, hitting me in the right place over and over again. My thighs tightened around him, my back arching as I moaned into his mouth.

This was more than sex. This was a vow. A promise forming between two souls with our bodies cementing the terms.

Mine, his movements said.

Mine, my core responded, clenching down around him. *Bite me. Take me. Make me yours.*

Ajax growled, probably because I'd communicated those thoughts with my nails in his back. He wasn't the only one who could draw blood.

His mouth ripped away from mine, his expression positively feral. "Tell me to claim you, Cami. Tell me and I'll do it."

"Tell me you want to claim me first," I demanded. Or I tried to demand it, anyway. It came out more sultry than I'd intended, but he was fucking me to within an inch of my life. And there was truly no better way to die...

"I want to do more than claim you." He drove into me. "I want to spend eternity with you. Even if that eternity is short-lived. Even if—"

I pressed my lips to his, silencing his talk of eternity. Would I spend eternity with him? Yes. But we both knew that might not happen, and I didn't want any false promises tainting this mating.

We were living in the *now*. The present. *Today*. "Claim me, Ajax," I whispered against his mouth. "Bite me and *claim me*."

"Fuck, Cami." His lips ghosted across my own, his hips slamming harshly into mine. "This might be a spell."

"It's not."

"What if it is?"

"Then let it enchant us," I told him. "*Bite me.*"

His responding growl vibrated my chest, his body tense

and hot against mine. I drew my nails down his muscular back, indulging in the hard, sculpted lines of his athletic physique. He was perfect. *And mine.*

I sank my teeth into his bottom lip on instinct, my need to provoke him overruling reason in my brain. Blood touched my tongue in the next instant, making me groan. *Mine. Mine. Mine.*

This might be a spell, he'd said.

Who the fuck cares? I thought now.

I was drunk on his essence. Wrapped up in this moment. Solidifying my future. *Picking my mate.*

No one could take this from me. *No one.*

Ajax groaned, his tongue tangling with mine as his decadent taste filled both our mouths. His grip on my hips tightened, his thrusts almost punishing in nature.

I could scarcely breathe. Barely think. Yet I'd never felt more alive in my entire life.

Now, I thought at him, vaguely aware that he couldn't really hear me.

But he would soon.

He would the minute he—

His mouth left mine, my world shifting upside down as my anchor to this reality left. A protest escaped me, the sound part moan, part mewl, only to end on a gasp as he nuzzled my neck. *There. At my pulse. His teeth... fangs... sharp... and...*

Stars burst across my vision, my clit pulsating in response to his *thumb.* I hadn't even felt his hand move, my focus on his mouth.

I clung to him, his name a chant on my tongue, my body shaking around him as my unexpected climax crashed over my being. It was intense. Hot. Insanity-inducing. *Pleasure.*

"*Ajax...*"

He circled my sensitive nub, his movements slowing as he drew out every inch of my ecstasy.

Then he tongued my pulse point. A tease. A promise. I wasn't sure. I just needed more. I needed him. I needed *this*.

His name left my mouth once more, my limbs straining as I tried to pull him impossibly closer.

He pressed his thumb into the top of my sex in response, the pressure on my swollen flesh almost too much. Moisture collected in my eyes, the power of the moment drawing out as rapturous waves continued to assault my being.

Drowning me in lust.

In overwhelming desire.

Stirring new cravings.

Suffocating me with molten sensations.

I'd never felt anything like it, his strength swirling around me in a whirlpool of madness.

A predator capturing his prey.

A Midnight Fae about to bite.

Shadows danced in the shower around us. Or maybe that was my vision going black.

Am I even breathing? I wondered, gasping for air. *Is this real?*

It'd better be fucking real.

Ajax's lips curled against my throat. "Say it again, Cami," he told me. "Tell me what you want. What you *need*."

I swallowed, my heart racing in my chest. There were only two words for me to say. Two words I'd already voiced, but in different ways. Now I would ensure he knew *exactly* what I needed. "*Mate me.*"

His sharp incisors pierced my neck in the next breath, his hard form engulfing mine as magic danced in the air around us. I could feel it twining our souls together, his fae blood mingling with mine as he swallowed my essence.

It was intoxicating. Overwhelming. *Very real.*

I hadn't expected to feel it so severely, for the bond to be this tangible. But the power of it whirled between us, humming over my skin, sinking into my very being.

Ajax released me, the dark blue rim of his eyes burning like liquid sapphires as he gazed at me. "Two more," he said, his thumb leaving my clit. "Two more and you're *mine*."

I gasped as he leaned down to bite my breast, his hands on my hips hoisting me higher on the wall and leaving just his pierced tip inside me.

"*Fuck*," I breathed, arching into him. He yanked me back down onto him in the next instant, his pulsing cock filling me to completion.

"One left, little rebel." The words were spoken against my mouth.

I trembled as he drew his fangs along my lower lip, the two tingling bites on my body already healing, thanks to my fae genetics.

"Where do you want it?" he asked me, his movements below stilling as he kept himself buried inside me. "Here?" The question was an exhale that mingled with my inhale. "Or do you have somewhere else in mind?"

My eyelashes fluttered as I fought to maintain his stare, my insides a hot mixture of need and anticipation. There were so many places I'd enjoy him biting.

But a primary location came to mind.

One that reminded me of our first time together.

When Az bit me instead of Ajax.

I angled my head, my fingers dancing up his back and over his shoulder before reaching my throat. "Here." It was the opposite side from where he'd already bitten me, in a position that wasn't exactly over my pulse, but still on my neck. "Claim me here."

His nostrils flared, his mind no doubt supplying him with the reason I'd chosen that spot. Maybe he could even hear the memory playing through my mind, how Az had held me up like an offering for Ajax's cock, supporting me while Ajax took me.

And biting me when Ajax couldn't.

But he could now.

He can bite me wherever, whenever, however he wants, I thought.

Yes, Ajax whispered back, his mind already connected to mine from the first two levels of his Midnight Fae bond snapping into place. *And I'm going to bite you everywhere, Cami.*

Then do it.

Ajax's lips curled against mine. *Don't have to tell me twice.* His head dipped down to my neck, his mouth skimming the spot I'd just indicated.

Electricity zipped down my spine as the third level fell instantly into place between us, the power almost seeming to precede his bite. But it was really just that quick, our souls rejoicing at the potential connection they'd sensed from the beginning.

Fated mates are not a thing, I marveled. *But this...*

Feels like fate, Ajax finished for me, his mental groan lighting my blood on fire. Or maybe that was his bite. Because a fresh wave of searing passion flooded my instincts in the next instant, my entire body going up in immediate flames.

Fuck me, I begged him. *Oh, Fae, fuck me.*

Ajax's palms branded my hips as he obeyed my command, his own punishing mine as he threatened to put me through the damn wall.

It was feral.

Perfect.

Exactly what we both craved.

A lethal coupling to solidify the marriage between our souls.

Mine, his movements claimed.

Mine, I returned with my hips. My nails. *My bite.*

He growled as I sank my teeth into his shoulders, my need to taste him an overwhelming yearning I couldn't ignore. So I didn't. Just like he didn't ignore his responding desire to fist my hair and yank my mouth up to his.

Our tongues dueled for dominance, our blood mingling in our mouths as our bodies engaged in a sensuous rhythm.

Warmth cascaded over my being, my nipples beading into hard points against Ajax's chest. I could feel another euphoric wave threatening to take me, to whirl me into oblivion, to drag me into the deepest depths of sensation and unadulterated heat.

It was even more powerful than before, the feelings doubled in strength. *Because I'm feeling Ajax's arousal, too,* I realized. *His need. His mounting release. The tension coiling in his lower abdomen. His hot passion threatening to explode.*

Oh, Fae... My thighs tightened around him, my mind locking on his as I indulged in his experience more than my own. It was so unique. So virile. So *animalistic.*

I could hear him growling inside, his fierce hunger a violent presence he kept hidden deep within. I wanted to play with that beast. Tempt it to come out and bite. Revel in its claim.

He snarled in response.

Then bit down on my lower lip, harshly, *savagely.*

I moaned. *More.*

Ajax's grip turned bruising, his dark side eagerly coming out to play as he traced my wound with his tongue. *I need you to come, Cami.*

Then make me come, Ajax.

He grinned against my mouth. *All right.*

Something about that response sounded sinister. Borderline cruel.

I didn't understand it until he lowered his lips to my neck again, his teeth skimming his claiming mark.

Ajax? I asked softly, not fully grasping his intent. *What are you—*

He clamped down and my entire being *froze*.

His earlier bites had been more superficial in nature. Claiming, but not too deep. And his pulls from my bloodstream hadn't been all that vigorous.

But now? *This*?

Oh, this was something else entirely.

He was truly biting me now, his vampiric kiss laced with some sort of searing venom that went straight to my core. I clenched around him, a maelstrom attacking my insides and forcing me right over the edge into catastrophic oblivion.

Screams rent the air.

My screams.

Blood pooled beneath my fingertips as I clasped Ajax's shoulders.

Spasms rocketed through my being, the tension flowing all the way to my toes.

Ajax's arousal crashed over me in the next instant, his orgasm all-encompassing and equally as powerful. Maybe even more so. His roar filled my mind, his euphoria a sweet addiction I hadn't even known I craved.

It was... amazing.

A union of ecstasy unlike any I'd known existed.

Because it's with my mate. My fae. My Ajax.

His forehead met mine, the vestiges of our shared passion still rippling over us in magnetic pulses. *Mine,* he breathed. *You're mine.*

You're mine, I echoed.

Neither of us added *forever*.

Neither of us bothered to put a time stamp on it.

Because we were living in the *now*. Today. This moment.

And this moment... was bliss.

It was perfect.

It was *ours*.

"Again," I told him on a rasp. "I need to feel that *again*."

"Yes," he agreed. "Yes."

CHAPTER 13

MELEK

"You shouldn't eavesdrop," a deep voice drawled from the shadows of the palace hallway. I'd been lurking outside the guest suite, indulging in the sensations of Ajax claiming Cami.

Fucking finally.

"I've been told it's rude," that voice added in a bored tone.

"Hmm, perhaps," I agreed, my wings ruffling at my back. "But the same could be said about meddling with another's power."

I materialized into my corporeal form, my feathers disappearing in a flash. Yet I suspected Zakkai had seen them anyway.

The powerful Midnight Fae might not be able to define my existence with a term—very few could—but he knew I was distinctly other. Which was likely why he'd been flirting with my magic for the past hour or so.

His tampering had started upon my arrival, but I'd mostly ignored him. It was my way of telling him I wasn't here to cause harm.

Of course, that wouldn't matter to him. I didn't belong in

this realm, and my presence here was breaking several Interrealm Fae rules.

I could visit—if invited.

And I hadn't been invited.

Which had been the point of Zakkai's meddling. He was letting me know that not only was he aware I was in his realm —*and in his home*—but he also had no qualms about taking advantage of my illegal visit by exploring my magic.

Most fae would be dead for touching my essence.

I might display a calm and nonchalant exterior, but I could more than protect myself against threats. Present company included.

Most fae made the mistake of fearing only Ty.

Zakkai's little exploration should have ensured he didn't make that common error in judgment. However, I suspected Zakkai didn't fear anyone. It wasn't arrogance on his part, simply confidence.

And confidence, I could respect.

"I'm going to be visiting often," I informed him. "At least for as long as Cami is here." I met his silver-blue gaze. "She's my intended. And now, it doesn't break the rules."

Because she was officially mated to a Midnight Fae. Which made her a welcome fae in this realm.

And as her other mate—the bonding level didn't matter— I was allowed to follow her here now, too.

"At least according to the new Interrealm Fae laws, of which this realm is now following," I added aloud. "Yes?"

Zakkai didn't reply, his gaze assessing as he tested my power once more.

I allowed the intrusion, amused by his continued attempts to play with my inner spirit. It didn't matter how many times he attempted to manipulate my magic; the strands simply snapped right back into place.

Because I was no ordinary fae.

Something he clearly already knew.

"Well. As I said, I'll be stopping by frequently for now," I went on, not bothered at all by his continued silence. "For at least as long as Ajax keeps Camillia in this realm."

Still nothing. Not even a hint of interest.

His stoic expression was admirable. As was his persistence in meddling with my abilities.

Zakkai was the strongest Midnight Fae in existence. Although, I suspected his queen rivaled him in his abilities. Her mating circle was exceptional.

Which was why I'd been very pleased when Ty began making deals with them—starting with his recruitment of Ajax and his deal with Zakkai to rewrite the Warden's powers.

However, that didn't mean Zakkai or his circle trusted us.

Perhaps that'll change someday.

Or maybe their distrust will be warranted.

Hmm. A lot of that depends on Cami and Ty.

I canted my head to the side. "I think the Interrealm Fae Ball might be a good deadline for us all. That'll give Ty a few weeks to calm down. It'll also provide me with enough time to ensure Cami's properly prepared to deal with him when they see each other again."

Of course, it would take some doing on my part to convince Ty to leave her and Ajax alone for that long. *Unless...*

"Would you and your circle agree with honoring Camillia and Ajax as guests for that long?" I asked Zakkai. "Because if you did, then they would be considered esteemed guests of the Midnight Fae Royal Circle. And no one would wish to dishonor such an invitation."

Not even a Hell Fae King, I mused to myself.

He folded his arms and leaned against the wall, still silent.

If he thought this would intimidate me, he was wrong.

I excelled at games. Especially ones involving power and posturing.

"Perhaps you'll determine my origin by the Interrealm Fae Ball, what with my frequent visits and all. Assuming Camillia and Ajax will be remaining here, I mean." I smiled. "I could tell you, if you prefer. That might be the only way for you to determine my ancient ancestry."

He plucked at another one of my Virtuous Fae strands, his grasp sharper than before.

Unfortunately for him, the tendril merely snapped right back into place like all the others.

"Most mixed fae have a myriad of power cords, all of which are woven together in haphazard methods that create a unique hybrid—or *abomination*, as some might call them," Zakkai finally said. "Your power cords are all intact. You're not a hybrid fae of any kind."

"I'm not," I conceded. "I'm a pureblood."

"A pureblood what?"

"You don't really want me to tell you that. Part of your enjoyment is in solving the puzzle." All Quandary Bloods—the specific sect Zakkai was from in the Midnight Fae Realm—adored riddles.

And I was perhaps the most fascinating one of Zakkai's existence.

Well, that might not be true. Ty might fascinate him just a smidgen more than I did.

Zakkai pushed off the wall, his arms falling to his sides. "How does Lucifer feel about his mate bonding himself to another?"

I lifted a shoulder. "You would have to ask him that question."

"I'm asking you," Zakkai replied. "I need to know how far Typhos Lucifer will go to retrieve Camillia De la Croix."

"To the end of the realms," I told him.

Especially when he realizes how right she is for our circle, I added to myself.

Aloud, however, I clarified by saying, "But I don't think he'll jeopardize his tentative alliance with you to retrieve her when she's under your protection via invitation. He's not one to force his way inside. He'll try to make a deal instead."

"And when that deal fails?"

My lips curled. "His deals never fail. However, should you be the first to achieve such a feat, he'll simply find a more clever way to bring her home."

"As you pointed out, she just mated a Midnight Fae. That makes this realm her home now. Indefinitely."

"True," I agreed. "But her mate has unique magic, yes?"

He said nothing. Not that I expected him to. After all, he was the one who had rewritten Ajax's connections to the Midnight Fae Source and the Hell Fae Source.

"Like I said, Ty's deals never fail. He's also a huge fan of loopholes." I glanced at the door that led to the guest suite before returning my attention to Zakkai. "I suppose that means Ajax has two homes, and so does Camillia. Which brings me back to my suggestion regarding *guests*."

Zakkai remained quiet, only this time I suspected he was talking to his mates rather than playing the silent game.

I let him do what he needed to do and relaxed against the wall, my focus shifting to my intended mate and the exquisite pleasure humming through her being.

Ajax was being very thorough. As he should be.

I closed my eyes and reveled in her ecstasy, my lips curling in anticipation of one day being the cause of such sensations.

Melek?

My smile grew. *My love. Your timing is as impeccable as always.* Despite having played with Ty only hours ago, I was very ready for more. And he no doubt sensed that, hence his mental call.

I need you in the Marsh Lands, he replied, his tone and words causing my grin to disappear.

Has something happened? I'd ventured out to find Cami while Ty interrogated an Unseelie that Erebus had found wandering the kingdom. That wouldn't normally have been an uncommon occurrence in the Marsh Lands, as that was where the Unseelie lived. But this specific one wasn't part of Erebus's court. He was an outsider.

And the father of one of the Hell Fae Brides.

I finally finished unweaving all the Virtuous Fae strands. Ty sounded exhausted. *But either I'm missing one or the magic erased his memories. Because he has no recollection of creating the portal despite being covered in evidence to the contrary.*

By that, he meant the Unseelie was covered in remnants of the portal spell, I assumed.

I need your eyes, he added. *I... I need to make sure I'm not missing something obvious.*

Meaning he was doubting his own work, something that was very unlike my Ty. *I'll join you shortly. And I'll bring you something to eat.* It would be my excuse for visiting him, something to help cover his needing my help with the interrogation.

Most of the Nightmare Fae assumed I simply took care of the Hell Fae King's needs and nothing more. It didn't matter that I was shrouded in power—power I didn't bother hiding, at that. They just presumed Ty did all the work for me.

I didn't try to dissuade those false notions. It was best to let them underestimate me.

However, speaking of underestimating, Zakkai was certainly not doing that where I was concerned. Instead, the Source Architect was still scrutinizing me in that emotionless way of his.

"You're beginning to make me feel like a research subject."

"You are," he replied. "I don't like unknowns. And you are very much an unknown."

"Well, perhaps you'll get to know me better during my

upcoming visits." I waited for him to correct me. When he didn't, I said, "I'll be sure to let Ty know that Ajax and Cami are currently guests of the Midnight Fae Queen and her mates."

No reply.

That wasn't a denial either, though, so I accepted it.

"You may need to add Az to that guest list," I added. "I not only heard Cami and Ajax mating, but I also felt it. So the Phoenix would have sensed it as well. I suspect he'll be here soon."

I was actually surprised he hadn't arrived already. His beast had to be close to taking over by now, his need to secure his mating intentions overriding everything else.

Although, if anyone could tame the dangerous animal, it was Az. Hence the reason fate had gifted him with his Phoenix side.

Of course, Az might not even realize the cause of his Phoenix's agitation. He didn't seem to understand that his beast had imprinted itself on Cami via Ajax, thus bonding the three of them for life.

Or perhaps it wasn't a misunderstanding at all, just denial.

Regardless, it would certainly prove entertaining in the coming hours or days.

"Good luck," I told Zakkai. "I suspect you're in for quite an experience."

Zakkai snorted. "Every day is an experience in this palace."

Given the magical embers floating all around us, I didn't doubt it. "See you soon, Architect."

I disappeared before he could comment to the contrary.

Not that he would. I intrigued him too much for him to dismiss me.

Oh, I had no doubt he'd try to kill me if he thought I was a threat. He'd fail, of course. But he'd definitely try.

He was protective of his circle. His family. His mate.

I understood. I felt the same way about my king and our future queen.

Which was why I approved of Ajax's choice for the temporary relocation. Cami would be safe with the Midnight Fae. At least for now. And it would give me time to persuade Ty to work with her, not against her.

Something that would become increasingly important when he realized Ajax had mated Cami. He wouldn't have felt it the way Az and I had.

But he'd find out soon enough.

Either from me or from Az.

Thank the fae for Interrealm Fae politics. That would slow Ty down a bit.

Hopefully, it would be long enough for him to see reason.

Otherwise, all of this would be for naught.

And Ty might just end up on the losing side of a deal...

CHAPTER 14

AZ

I FISTED my cock with a groan, the sound muffled by Ajax's sheets.

Why did I have to nest here? I asked myself. *I'm surrounded by roses and mint and* sex.

A growl rumbled through my chest as I rolled in the blankets, memories of playing with Ajax and Cami tumbling through my mind.

The scent of our sensual exploration still lingered despite it occurring well over a month ago. Or maybe it was all in my mind. An echo of the past.

I'd flown for hours, exhausting my Phoenix, placating my need to simply exist. To be *free*. Yet I'd ended up in Ajax's old room in the Hell Fae prison, my need to return to an easier time superseding reason.

And now I was being tormented with a sexual need so damn potent I could hardly breathe.

Fuck.

My Phoenix practically burned inside, his urgency a palpable flame threatening to singe my entire being.

I pumped my palm over my aching shaft while visions of Ajax fucking Cami pummeled my mind.

He was taking her hard, his thrusts forcing Cami to rub against me as I held her for his assault. Those creamy thighs felt so fucking good beneath my palms, her naked backside pressing into my throbbing groin.

"*Fires,*" I whispered, my throat working over a swallow as I painfully tightened my grip. I needed more. I needed *them.*

What the hell is wrong with me? I marveled. *Why am I losing control?*

Delayed gratification was one of my favorite games. I loved forcing myself to wait. It allowed the violence inside me to build to a crescendo—then I typically took it out on Ajax's ass.

Oh, but I'd love a chance to test Cami's stamina. See how well she could take my explosion of power. My strength. *My feral need.*

Would she cry?

Would she beg for more?

Would she respond in kind?

I suspected it would be all of the above. She'd try to hurt me like I'd hurt her. And we'd both end up in the throes of exquisite bliss. Drowning in painful pleasure. Overwhelmed by sensual torment.

I'd bite those rosy little nipples. Torture her clit with my tongue and teeth. Flip her over and pound that sweet pussy with all my might.

Then take her ass with just as much vigor.

All while Ajax watches, I thought, the fantasy playing out vividly in my imagination as I stroked my cock. *I'd make him clean her up for dessert.*

Then fuck her again.

While he took her cunt.

Sandwich her between us. Make her take us. Make her

come. Over and over again. Until she couldn't speak, couldn't think, couldn't *breathe.*

Fae, yes, I thought, picturing her tight little body all replete and bruised and bloody from our bites.

She'd be so damn satisfied.

So fucking beautiful.

So very much ours.

I groaned again, my head burrowing into Ajax's pillow as my shaft pulsed against my palm. *So good. So fucking good.*

But it wasn't Cami's sweet pussy or Ajax's addicting mouth. It was just my hand.

Which had to be enough.

For now.

My grip turned bruising as I throttled my dick, inflicting the perfect amount of harsh pressure I needed to explode.

Up and down. Twist. Fuck...

I would love to teach Cami how to do this, how to please me. Then I'd return the favor with my tongue, do whatever she desired to make her see stars.

Assuming she ever forgives me.

Fuck, I'm not thinking about that right now.

Just that tight cunt. Squeezing me. So damn wet. So perfect. So mine.

Ajax, too. His skilled mouth. That firm ass. His angry grunts. All that magic.

I wanted Ajax on his knees, worshipping Cami's clit as I fucked her from behind. I'd make him lick up every drop while driving into her mouth, the two of them writhing in the sheets, playing with each other while I watched.

So many fantasies.

So many *ideas.*

My thumb swiped my damp slit, my balls clenching with need. *So close. So damn close.*

Ajax's pillow nearly suffocated me as I bit down on the

fabric, my chest rumbling with intrinsic need. It was so intense. So unlike me. I usually had more control than this.

What is going on? Why am I so hot? Where is all this pent-up lust coming from?

My Phoenix was clawing at my instincts, his urgency mounting. He needed this explosion. This expulsion of power. It was burning me up inside. *Literally.*

I yanked on my dick, demanding that it respond, to unleash some of this insanity.

But all that did was make me burn hotter.

With a snarl, I released my shaft and panted against the sheets. Something was very wrong. I shouldn't be losing control of myself like this.

Talk to me, I told my bird. *What do you really need?*

I shifted into my Phoenix form and gave my beast the reins.

Do what you need to do, I said, only belatedly realizing how bad an idea that was when the world immediately disintegrated around me.

And reformed in a blink to reveal a bedroom decorated in florals and earthy tones.

Fuck. Of course my animal would bring us here—right to Ajax and Cami.

In the heart of the Midnight Fae Kingdom. *In the Midnight Fae Palace.*

I instantly harnessed my Phoenix, my human form taking control once more. He bristled in response, furious that I'd only given him a few seconds of dominion over our shared existence. But I was the dominant one. The *thoughtful* one. The one who understood reason.

Very unlike my bird.

Who had just ashed us into a territory where we may or may not be invited.

The interrogation had been different—I'd been Ajax's guest.

But right now? Not so much.

Especially since he was currently *inside* Cami.

On the bed.

My dick immediately hardened again at the sight, my need crashing over me in a fiery wave of dizziness. My beast growled inside, *hungry*. I echoed the sentiment, my stomach tightening at the sight of Ajax thrusting into Cami's slick cunt.

Fuck.

Fuck!

I told myself to ash out of here, to disappear, but my Phoenix refused me, too enraptured by the view of Ajax and Cami.

Her cries of pleasure.

His grunts of satisfaction.

Their sensual forms illuminated by the moonlight streaming in from the windows.

It was an intoxicating scene. An invitation my beast wanted to accept.

Not now, I kept saying, even as I took a step forward. *Stop this!*

But my animal wasn't hearing me. He saw what he wanted and fought like hell for control of our being, demanding that I *join. Fuck. Take. Bite.*

I shook my head, a snarl ripping from my throat as I fought my damn beast.

Which was precisely the wrong move.

Ajax was on his feet in an instant, his wand appearing in his hand, his dick glistening with Cami's arousal. The sight of it made my mouth water, my tongue begging for a taste of their joined passion.

Cami yelped, her delicate fingers snatching up the sheets

to cover herself in a move my Phoenix didn't understand. *Why hide?* he seemed to be asking.

But I knew why.

Because she fears us.

I could taste that fear in the air. Just as I could taste Ajax's fury.

I held up my hands. "Ajax, I—"

A spell formed on his lips. One I hadn't heard in thousands of years. My lips froze, my body following suit. *That...? How?*

I had to be hearing things.

He... he couldn't know...?

But as the words whispered around me, the enchantment taking hold, it became very clear that he did know. At least some of it.

Or all of it? I wondered, stunned by the magic cascading over my body. It was the beginning of a nightmare I'd woken up from ages ago.

A nightmare I'd *left*.

Vivaxia.

My vision wavered and clouded over with darkness as my Phoenix took full control of my form once more.

The familiar magic made me nauseous. I had no power over my own body, my spirit, my *will*. I was trapped as my animal self.

But my Phoenix wasn't in control either.

He was *tamed*. Beaten down. *Owned* by an ancient spell.

Owned by Ajax.

I gaped at him, unable to comprehend how he could do this to me. How he'd learned such a cruel enchantment. To *tame* me in this way... *Why?*

"*Kneel,*" he demanded.

My stomach plummeted as an invisible weight slammed

onto my shoulders. My bird immediately bowed, confirming Ajax's dominion over us.

Where the hell did he get this damn spell? From Vivaxia? A chill swept through my insides. *Oh, fires, is she here?*

Ancient memories taunted my thoughts, Vivaxia's voice a screeching sound I'd thought I'd permanently erased. *Hunt,* she'd often said. It was entirely different from how Typhos voiced the word. He offered it to my Phoenix as a reward, a game, a way to take back control. But with Vivaxia, that word had been a command. There had never been a choice. Never an option to refuse or stand up for myself.

She told me to bow and I did.

She told me to hunt and I did.

She told me to kill... and I did.

How could you do this to me? I wanted to ask Ajax. *Do you even realize what you've done?*

"How does it feel to have your will stripped from you?" Ajax asked me in a seething tone, one he typically reserved for misbehaving Nightmare Fae. Only, this was even more sinister in nature. *Angrier.* Underlined in a palpable fury that had my soul going cold. "Not very fun, is it?"

"What did you do?" Cami asked from the bed, her gaze wide as she looked between us.

Az? Typhos whispered into my mind. *I sense... pain.*

I swallowed inside, my heart throbbing from the intensity of the spell and the memories it had provoked. *Ajax...* I trailed off. *I...* I wasn't sure how to explain. If I told Typhos what Ajax had done, he would come for me. Come for *Ajax.* He'd kill him. No questions asked.

This enchantment hit too close to home.

"It's a taming spell," Ajax said, his focus on me while he responded to Cami. "Shade's grandmother left it for me, saying I might need it. Now I understand why."

I blinked. *Zenaida gave this to you?*

Azazel? Typhos prompted. *Ajax what?*

I... I found him, I started slowly. *I need a minute to focus.*

Typhos didn't reply, his silence telling me he was granting me my request for a moment.

Zenaida gave Ajax the spell, I repeated to myself. *Not Vivaxia. But then, where did Zenaida acquire it? How did she know?*

She was a Fortune Fae who had a deal with Lucifer regarding the paradigm that housed the Hell Fae Bride Trials. She'd helped create the magical territory in the Barren Lands. Only those who knew where to look could find it, and even then, not everyone could enter.

Why is she meddling in Ajax's affairs with me? I wondered. *Why give him such a hurtful spell?*

"What does it do?" Cami asked as she slid off the bed with the sheet still wrapped around her.

Ajax, however, remained stark naked, not at all bothering to hide himself from me or her. Although, he still had his wand pointed at me like he thought I might become a threat.

Does that mean I can potentially break the hold this spell has on me? Or is it because he doesn't fully understand what he's done?

"I'm not sure," he replied to Cami, essentially confirming my last question—*he doesn't fully grasp the severity of this spell.*

Which meant he hadn't intended to hurt me this way.

Or perhaps he had meant to hurt me in this way but hadn't realized how effective it would be.

"Um, what now, then?" Cami asked, her expression wary.

"I'm not sure," he repeated, walking toward me.

My Phoenix instantly looked away from him, submitting to the one with authority in the room. It was a trained reaction from centuries of abuse by the one who used to wield that spell.

It was a reaction I'd thought I'd broken.

Just like this nightmare was one I'd thought I'd removed from my mind.

But the enchantment brought it all back with a vengeance. *Fucking Zenaida. What have you done?*

Ajax crouched. My Phoenix didn't look up at him, remaining submissive in fear of being commanded again. The incantation fucking *hurt*. "It seems to have pushed Az into the background and let his Phoenix out." He waved his wand into my vision as he said, "*Sit*."

My jaw clenched inside as my Phoenix shifted back to *sit*, just like Ajax had commanded us to.

The obedient effect took me back to a time when this had been my life. When I'd had no sense of free will. Where every move I'd made had been at the sharp instruction of a vicious Virtuous Fae.

Her visage appeared in my mind, her cruel gray eyes glittering with venom. Her long, inky black hair framing her elegantly beautiful face.

She was stunning.

A female many fae craved and envied at the same time.

But I'd been all too familiar with the coldness of her heart.

And, in time, Typhos had also become acquainted with her cruelty and the pain she'd caused others. Himself included.

Betrayal hummed through my blood as Ajax chuckled. "It seems he'll do whatever I say, too."

"Like go back to the Hell Fae Realm and leave us alone?" Cami asked.

"Maybe." Ajax seemed to hesitate. "But the spell might wear off if he leaves. Then we won't have the element of surprise for when he returns."

"True." Cami's bare feet whispered across the floor as she started to pace. "So what do we do?"

"I don't know," Ajax replied, sounding conflicted. "I can dress him in chains and put him in a cage, if you want."

Cami paused midstride. "That is a very tempting offer."

"If I forced him back into human form, we could make him wrap a chain around his cock, too," Ajax added, the sinister quality of his proposal causing me to flinch inside. "Similar to what Lucifer did to you."

And that part made me wince.

Because he wasn't wrong.

Typhos's chains had been designed with the purpose of inducing Cami's arousal.

I supposed doing the same to me would only be fair, in terms of revenge.

But like this? I thought, swallowing once more. *Under the weight of my past? Using a spell that removes my free will and leaves both me and my Phoenix helpless?*

My bird released a soft, sad little sound, perhaps understanding the intentions swirling in the air. Or maybe he was echoing the pain piercing my heart.

Because this was more than a punishment. It was revenge. Harsh. Fucking cruel.

Just like Vivaxia.

CHAPTER 15

AZ

CAMI CROUCHED BESIDE AJAX, her sinful scent catching my Phoenix's attention and drawing his focus to her. She hadn't wielded the spell. Thus, he didn't fear her. If anything, he seemed to think she would help him.

Her gray eyes studied me, her expression giving nothing away as she took in my beast form. I wasn't a small Phoenix but a towering creature that looked down at her even while sitting.

She didn't seem to be afraid, though. Instead, she seemed curious. Awed, even.

Her open admiration had my bird preening in response, his pleasure humming through our joined being despite the haunting memories circling my mind.

"How long do you think this spell will last?" she asked quietly, not remarking on Ajax's offer to chain me up in a cage.

"I don't know." He didn't appear as taken with my beast as she did, Ajax's gaze wary rather than admiring. "I need to find a way to detain him because the second Az is free, he'll take us to Lucifer."

I frowned inside. *Is that what you think? That I'm here to drag you back to Typhos without remorse? Without even offering to have a conversation first?*

I'd told the Hell Fae King I would *track* Cami and Ajax. I hadn't agreed to *hunt* them.

But Ajax didn't know that.

And he hadn't given me a chance to explain it either.

Because he no longer trusts me.

I'd bound him with my power, and now, he'd bound me with his magic.

My Phoenix canted his head, his focus still on Cami as she continued to gaze upon him. He blinked a few times, his demeanor far softer than usual. Almost contrite, even. He knew she was upset, and he didn't like it. Just like he knew Ajax was mad, too. Which was probably why he didn't appear to be fighting Ajax's hold over us. He was embracing it instead.

Granted, he'd also done that with Vivaxia.

The enchantment required full compliance. It worked by wrapping around my soul and tethering the Phoenix spirit to the obedience spell.

Like a leash.

Or chains.

The thought had me frowning once more, the parallel between Vivaxia's spell and Lucifer's punishment shining brightly in my mind.

No, I told myself. *Lucifer is not Vivaxia.*

Just like he wasn't Constantine.

He'd devised a sensual punishment for Cami, one that had essentially put me and Ajax in our places as well. It hadn't been violent.

Yet the emotional damage...

Is that worse? I wondered.

Ajax no longer trusted me. Over a decade of companionship had been dismantled in one night. All because I'd been trying to protect him from making matters worse.

I'd just wanted us to survive the incident and move on.

However, my actions had done more damage than good.

But what if he'd reacted? What would Typhos have done to him in response? What would he have done to Cami?

Guilt welled in my chest as the female in question continued to stare at me.

None of this was her fault.

She'd merely been thrust into a life she'd never asked for, dragged into a set of trials she hadn't even realized existed, and essentially put on display like a trophy simply because of what she was.

Rare. Coveted. Powerful.

She and I aren't so different, I realized. *Because Vivaxia once did the same thing to me.*

"So Az isn't in charge at all right now," Cami said slowly. "Meaning whatever we command him to do... we're actually commanding his Phoenix?"

Ajax considered me for a long moment, then nodded. "The spell was meant to tame his beast, so I think that's the case."

"And you don't know the limitations or what else that spell is doing?"

"No."

"Yet you used it anyway?" she pressed, her brow furrowing. "What if it's hurting him?"

His eyebrows lifted. "You would care? After what he's done?"

"Well, no." She glanced at him. "I don't know." Her gaze returned to my Phoenix. "But his beast isn't the problem. His beast seems to actually like me."

I like you, too, I thought at her, irritated by the insinuation that only my Phoenix liked her. *How is that not obvious by now?*

I'd defended her in front of Typhos. Taken her side and *thanked* her for closing the portal. I'd only gone to him to ask him to help battle whatever magic seemed to be hurting her while she'd slept.

But I hadn't been given an opportunity to say anything before Ajax had disappeared with her.

And now that opportunity had been stripped from me again because of this damn spell.

My beast bristled, seemingly annoyed on my behalf as well. Perhaps he could sense my emotions, my dismay that she thought I didn't *like* her. My sadness over Ajax's lack of trust. My frustration over not being able to speak my piece.

Cami lifted her hand toward my Phoenix, causing Ajax to freeze.

"Cami," he cautioned. "I'm not sure that's a good idea."

Wow, I thought at him. *You really think my beast is going to attack her? He's fucking infatuated with her. All he's going to do is purr for her.*

Which, of course, he did, the vibrations loud and obnoxious and momentarily drowning out all other sound in my mind.

Cami's lips twitched as she gave my Phoenix a scratch behind the ear, like one would a dog. "You're kind of cute like this," she told me. Or I supposed she was talking more to my bird than to me. Maybe both. Who the fuck knew?

Ajax rolled his eyes.

My bird just purred louder, his beak nuzzling her wrist.

A rose in the evening shade surrounded by a field of mint and pine, I marveled as my Phoenix inhaled deeply. *Fuck, that's an addicting scent.*

No wonder my beast was purring.

It smells like home.

Like where we belong.

Where we want to be.

Forever and eternity.

I sighed inside, momentarily content despite the dangerous circumstances.

Cami sighed, too, the sound a melody to my bird's ears. "I think he's tired," she told Ajax. "He looks all dreamy and dru— *Ow!*" She snatched her hand back, her eyes rounding as she took in the fiery crescent bite mark embedded in her wrist.

Oh, fu—

Ajax tackled my bird to the ground before I could properly process what had just happened, his fist connecting with my beast's beak.

My Phoenix reacted with an excited caw, his bird brain completely misinterpreting this situation. *Mating time,* he seemed to think. Which was probably because most of my brawls with Ajax ended with us in bed.

He released a powerful pulse that sent Ajax sprawling across the floor, then lunged at the Midnight Fae in a playful maneuver to pin him to the ground beneath his beak.

Ajax roared.

My Phoenix purred.

And the taste of Ajax's blood filled my mouth, to join Cami's essence.

Fuck! I shouted at my Phoenix. *What the fuck are you doing?*

He'd just bitten both Cami *and* Ajax.

And now he was prancing around in a victory circle, cawing like a damn beast in heat.

Because now he wanted to *mate.*

However, when he tried to relinquish control to me, to allow me to take my human form and indulge in our new mates, he couldn't. The spell wouldn't allow it.

Ajax palmed his neck, his blue-black eyes glowing with fury as my beast started to pace, confusion melting into panic.

My Phoenix didn't understand why I couldn't take charge and finish this act.

Not that there was much to finish.

One bite was all it took to solidify a Shifter Fae bond.

One bite *in* animal form.

Which he'd done.

To Ajax and Cami, I marveled again. *Hellfire, this is bad. So fucking bad.*

Az? Typhos whispered into mind. *What's happening?*

I ground my teeth together. *Still need time. Please.* I wasn't sure what to say to him yet, how to explain everything that had happened.

And this... this definitely made things a thousand times worse.

Typhos didn't press me, his patience and understanding touching my spirit instead. But he had to know something big had just happened. Hell, he could probably feel the change via our Virtuous Fae bond.

We weren't bonded by my Phoenix, which I supposed meant my beast had never actually been mated to Typhos.

But my bird was absolutely mated to Ajax and Cami now.

How could you do this? I demanded of my beast. *How could you do this without my consent?*

My bird wasn't listening, though. Not that he could understand me anyway. He was too distraught by his inability to give control back to me.

He didn't like this spell.

The weight of the invisible chains.

The need to obey an outside force.

It'd been a long time since someone had done this to us. He hadn't fully comprehended Ajax's spell until this moment, and now that he did, he was gazing at the Midnight Fae in astonishment, his betrayal coming out in a low mewling caw of a sound that had my heart breaking in my chest.

How could you do this to us? my Phoenix seemed to be asking. *What have I done wrong?*

He knew we'd upset them. He knew because he could feel my own remorse. But he'd mistakenly thought coming here would cure everything. That biting his mates would fix the problems I'd created.

My beast didn't process emotions the way I did. Nor did he understand complex situations.

These are our mates, so I bite them, was his logic.

Consent didn't matter to him. He was too caught up in his animal instincts to consider the fact that Ajax and Cami might not want this. To my Phoenix, there was no other way forward.

Shit. I'd known how he felt, how close he'd been to taking over and claiming them as his, but I'd been handling the instinct. I'd been handling *him*.

However, Ajax's spell had bound me to the back of my mind, leaving my bird in charge.

And now...

"Now we're mates," Ajax hissed, his gaze narrowing at me. "You're really blaming this on me?"

I blinked at him from inside. *What? No. I'm not blaming anything on you,* I wanted to say. *How the hell did you even come to that conclusion?*

"Because your thoughts are fucking *loud*," he retorted. "My spell locked you out and gave your bird free rein. That's what you were thinking."

You can hear my mind? If I could, I would furrow my brow right about now.

Of course he can hear my mind, I thought in the next breath.

We were mates now. And Shifter Fae bonds required an *open mind*.

It was different from the Virtuous Fae bonds with Typhos,

where we vaguely picked up on strong emotions from one another but otherwise only communicated telepathically when we felt like it.

Shifter Fae bonds were a whole new brand of telepathy.

And it worked both ways.

Which meant I could hear Cami and Ajax, too.

Shit. There had to be a way to wall off our thoughts. *Think, Az.* My mother had taught me things as a fledgling. Ways to protect my mind, and to protect others as well.

I was too powerful for unfettered access to my thoughts.

One energy explosion could render my mates unconscious.

Cami was saying something, but I ignored her, too focused on closing off our mental connections. I had to limit it to telepathic conversation only. Just like I had with Typhos.

Ajax's deep tones filled the air, his response probably for Cami.

Or maybe it was for me.

However, I couldn't hear him. I was too busy searching the ancient history in my memories for the knowledge I craved.

I'd always wanted a mate, but after so many millennia of not finding anyone worthy of my Phoenix, I'd lost touch with that side of my past. Why maintain information that would obviously never apply?

But it did apply now.

Because my Phoenix finally chose his mates.

Had Ajax always been a candidate, and I'd just misinterpreted my bird's interest in him? Or was this all about Cami?

I'd bitten her for Ajax.

But I'd been in human form.

However, maybe... maybe it was all related? Maybe I'd provoked my Phoenix while playing with Ajax and Cami?

Or maybe she's been an ideal mate all along, and that's why I've been so drawn to her.

My Phoenix's primary goal was to *mate*. Not to just find a partner, but to *breed*.

Was Cami an ideal mother for my future progeny?

Is that why you wanted her so badly? I asked my bird. *To rut?*

Does it matter? another part of me wondered. *It's done. It can't be undone.*

I also didn't really want to undo it.

This—despite the circumstances—felt right.

My bird was in pain from the spell, his sense of betrayal still humming through our veins, but inside, my beast was finally content. He'd found the other half of his soul. *In Cami and in Ajax.*

They balanced my fiery spirit.

But do I balance them? I finally pulled myself out of my mind to take in my surroundings once more. Ajax stood before me, arms folded, expression murderous.

And Cami... I tried to look around, to find her. However, my Phoenix was sitting and staring straight at Ajax instead.

You issued more commands, I realized, sighing inside. At least these commands hadn't *hurt*.

I did, he confirmed, his mental voice sharp.

Oh. What was my Phoenix doing?

His eyebrows lifted. *Your Phoenix just forcefully* mated *us. Do I need more of a reason to tame him?*

I bristled at his tone and the question. *He was reacting on instinct. Similar to how you reacted when I arrived—to talk, not to take you back to Typhos, by the way.*

He snorted. *He ordered you to hunt us. You do realize I heard that part in your thoughts, right?*

I told him I'd track *you, Ajax. Not* hunt. *There's a difference.*

He rolled his eyes at me. *Sounds the same to me.*

Well, they mean very different things to my beast. I went back into the recesses of my psyche again, searching for the blocks I needed to wall off my mind.

Ajax's demeanor told me exactly how he felt about this *forced mating.*

And Cami, well, it seemed she'd left. I only knew that because of my link to her thoughts. I didn't want to intrude on her more than I already had, so I backed off and left her to think on her own.

Just as I left Ajax alone in front of me.

If he wanted to play an obedience game with my bird, so be it. I had a job to do. *Inside my mind.*

CHAPTER 16

CAMI

WHAT THE FUCK JUST HAPPENED?

One moment, I'd been admiring the Phoenix. And then... *and then he bit me.*

Mated me.

Claimed *me.*

Just like Ajax had. Except not. It was entirely different.

I was just bitten by a damn Phoenix. The thought kept circulating in my mind, my feet moving quickly over the floor inside the palace. I had no idea where I was going, and I didn't care. I'd told Ajax to spell me some clothes, and then I'd left.

"I need to go on a walk" was all I'd said to him before leaving the room.

It probably wasn't safe for me to be wandering here, nor was it very appropriate as a guest, but *fuck.* What the hell was I supposed to do? I needed air. To breathe. To be *free.*

Only, I'd never be free again because I now had *two* mates.

Actually, no. I had *three.*

Melek.

"*Fuck,*" I muttered aloud. *I suppose this is one way to die— connected to a bunch of male souls.*

They could all at least gift me a few hundred orgasms before Lucifer finally killed me. That'd be the kind thing to do in this situation, right?

I nearly laughed at the inane concept.

This is insane. I've lost my mind. And I have three mates.

"Absolutely nuts," I told myself as I turned down a random hallway. "This place is a maze." I'd only been wandering for a few minutes, but I was already lost.

"A tour might help," a soft voice replied from behind me.

I grimaced and glanced over my shoulder to see a woman with blue-black hair only a few feet behind me.

"Sorry, I overheard you as I was leaving my room." She gestured to a wooden panel that looked like a door, except it was missing a handle.

Actually, all the "doors" in this corridor seemed to be decorated similarly. "How do you enter and leave a room without a door handle?" I asked dumbly.

"The gargoyles handle it," she replied, her lips twitching. "It takes some getting used to." Her nose crinkled. "Actually, there are a lot of things that take a while to accept. Like the perpetual night sky. Lack of flowers. Fluffy animals that want to kill everything in their paths. Hmm." She shrugged. "But it's home."

I blinked at her. "Oh." This realm certainly seemed to have its quirks.

Something that became increasingly evident as I glanced around the corridor.

There were trees built into the walls. And their roots were all over the floor.

It was a miracle I hadn't tripped.

Perhaps I'd been more aware of my surroundings than I'd realized. I just hadn't taken in the scenery so much as moved through it.

My fingertips danced along the nearest tree, my mind

expecting it to be textured plastic, similar to a vase of fake flowers.

But no.

It's real, I marveled, stepping closer to the black bark. "What kind of tree is this?" I asked, confused by the color as well as its location.

"My re-creation of a burning thwomp tree," the woman replied. "I call them sturdy thwomps."

Sturdy thwomps? I repeated to myself. *An odd name.* "They're pretty."

"Thank you." She sounded pleased by my compliment. "My garden is full of them, if you want to see more. Although, there are other things there, too. Like peach trees."

I glanced at her again. "Peach trees?"

"One of my oldest friends loves human peaches. He made me a fan of them, too. So now I grow them."

"Oh." I was a fae of a lot of words today, apparently.

No idea why, I thought sardonically.

My fingers curled into a fist as I looked at the source of my current frustration. The fiery crescent mark on my wrist had already cauterized, but it didn't appear to be fully healing.

Your bite is going to leave a scar, isn't it? I thought at Az.

He didn't reply, his mind quieter than before.

I frowned. *Az?*

Nothing.

I turned to face the hallway I'd just wandered down, like I could somehow find the room I'd left however long ago. *Ajax?*

Yeah? he replied instantly.

Did you knock Az out? I asked, my heart skipping a beat. Ajax wouldn't kill him... right?

No. But I can, if you want.

I frowned. *I... no. I don't want that.* At least, I didn't think I did. *I can't hear him.*

He's erecting some sort of mental wall, Ajax muttered. *Or*

193

that's what I've gathered from his mind, anyway. He was thinking about what a power explosion would do to us if he kept his mind exposed.

Oh. There was that brilliant word again. *Is he okay?*

I couldn't see Ajax, but I felt him bristling. *He's fine.*

Are you okay? I hedged.

Silence fell for a long beat. Then I heard Ajax mentally sigh. *Yeah, I'm okay, little rebel. You?*

I pinched my lips to the side. *I don't know. I'm kind of—*

"Did one of my creatures bite you?" the female asked suddenly, reminding me of her presence. Her cerulean blue eyes were focused on my chest. Glancing down, I realized I'd pressed my fist to my heart, but it was rotated a little to reveal the dark crescent mark in my skin.

"No, it was a Phoenix," I told her.

Her eyes widened. "A Phoenix? Truly? They're usually so docile."

I couldn't help the responding laugh that escaped me. It was more sarcastic than humorous, but the thought of Az being *docile* was absolutely hysterical. "Not this Phoenix," I assured her. "This one is intimidating and downright dominant."

"Dominant?" she repeated with a frown. "I suppose they can be perceived that way. They're majestic, regal beings that..." She trailed off and tilted her head. "Wait, you're talking about a man, aren't you? Not the actual animal?"

"Well, his *animal* is the one that bit me." I rotated my hand to give her a better view. "And I'm guessing this isn't going to disappear since apparently we're now mated for eternity."

Which had been why I'd left the room to go on this walk. *Right.* I glanced around, eager to continue that course, my need to think and escape overwhelming everything else.

"Hmm," the female hummed, seemingly oblivious to my

desire to flee. "Mated against your will. I may know a thing or two about that."

My instinct to run away momentarily halted as I looked back at the woman. "You do?"

"Oh, yes." She scowled a little. "I also know how it feels to be bitten without consent."

All right. She had my attention. "Who are you?"

Her lips twitched. "Aflora."

My lips parted. "Aflora. As in... *Queen Aflora*?" *Fuck.*

What is it? Ajax asked immediately, my mental commentary having apparently gone straight to him.

I really needed to figure out how to control that.

Cami? he prompted. *Are you all right?*

I think I just met the Midnight Fae Queen, I told him. *Aflora* wasn't exactly a common name, and it was one I'd overheard a few times now.

"I prefer to go by Aflora," she murmured, her nose crinkling again as though she'd tasted something sour. "No title necessary."

Are her mates there? Ajax asked.

No. It's just her, I replied after glancing around. *Why?*

Wondering if I need to rescue you.

I... I'll be fine. At least, I hoped I would be. "You were mated against your will?" I asked Aflora, still stuck on what she'd said about knowing a thing or two about that.

"Yes, via a bite." Her long eyelashes fluttered as she shifted her focus to my wrist. "But mine was on my neck."

I studied her flawless skin. "Looks like you healed."

She nodded. "Midnight Fae marks show on the soul, not on the skin."

"I think mine will be both."

"I think so, too." Her expression turned thoughtful. "Do you need help?"

I swallowed and shook my head. "No." Mostly because I

had no idea what kind of "help" she could offer. And I wasn't exactly hurt, just... conflicted. "I just wanted some fresh air."

Her lips curled. "Well, can I at least help with that?" she offered. "I can take you to my gardens."

"Oh, um, I don't want to impose." She was a queen. She probably had "royal things" to do. "I can... find it."

She laughed and shook her head. "Really, it's no bother. I was on my way there anyway. I need to find Dragonya for Florica."

Dragonya? I echoed in my mind. *No idea what that is, but...* "Okay."

"Excellent. Follow me." She moved around me in a long skirt that swirled against the ground, the black fabric rustling as she went.

It certainly seemed like a fitting outfit for a vampire queen.

Meanwhile, I wore a simple pair of jeans, a tank top, and a leather jacket. My boots were flat, too. A practical outfit for a stroll. Very un-queen-like. It was what I'd asked Ajax to conjure for me. And I—the commoner—didn't regret it even when faced with stunning royalty.

Melek would probably love her, I mused. *She'd match his and Lucifer's penchant for suits.*

They would be insane to touch her, Ajax returned, obviously overhearing my thoughts again. *Zakkai is fucking terrifying. Even they know that. And he's just one of her four mates.*

The one who bit her without her permission? I guessed.

Ajax snorted. *No. That would be Shade. And how did you know that?*

She mentioned it.

Ah. He paused. *I suppose you would have that in common.*

He turned into a Phoenix and claimed her?

Ajax coughed a laugh. *No. He just pinned her against a wall and seduced her with his vampiric charm. Then sank his fangs into her neck.*

Without her consent?

Without her consent, he confirmed. *And he did it all without even giving her his name, too. The Midnight Fae Council was pissed.*

And Aflora?

Also pissed.

No shit, I thought. "How did you not kill him?" I asked aloud as we reached a widened hallway that seemed to be leading to some sort of grand foyer ahead.

"Who?" she asked, notably startled.

"The mate who bit you without consent."

She gazed back at me for a moment, her steps slowing. "I'm an Earth Fae at heart. We tend to favor peace over violence."

"So you just... let him mate you...?"

She laughed, the sound reminding me of magical chimes. "No. He groveled. *A lot.* They all did."

"All of them...?" My eyes widened. "Multiple men mated you without consent?"

And I thought my situation was bad...

"No. It... No. Only one did that. The others..." She twisted her lips to the side and shook her head again. "Honestly, it's a really long story. But it had a happy ending. And I wouldn't change anything about it now."

The primary piece of her history that I knew about dealt with her and her mate-circle destroying an evil Midnight Fae —Constantine.

If I were in her shoes, I supposed I wouldn't regret that either.

"Not to sound like Shade—who, by the way, is the willow stump that bit me against my will—but fate can be cruel sometimes. However, it almost always works out in the end."

"Willow stump?" I asked her.

"She means asshole or jackass," a masculine voice said as a

male moved out of the shadows just as we stepped outside. "I heard my pet name, thought you might need me."

Aflora rolled her eyes. "You've been stalking me since I left the room."

Shade placed a palm over his heart, his icy eyes widening with fake innocence. "Me? Stalk you? I wouldn't dream of it, little rose."

Aflora made a noise. "I'm showing our guest to the gardens."

"A guest you haven't properly met yet." Shade gave me a pointed look. "Most people introduce themselves before demanding a name. Especially when the person is a *guest* in another's palace."

"You're chastising me?" I arched a brow. "After I learned how you forced your mating bite on Queen Aflora?"

"Just Aflora," the queen interjected. "And it's fine, Shade. I know this is Cami. She doesn't need to introduce herself."

"It's the formal and polite thing to do," he drawled.

"Shade? Discussing *formal* and *polite* things?" a second male asked from behind us. "Have I stepped into an alternate reality?"

I glanced at the newcomer—a tall male with auburn hair streaked with gray and white strands. His burnt-gold eyes flickered with humor as he moved through the threshold to join us outside.

Aflora sighed. "I just wanted to go for a walk with Cami."

"I thought you were looking for Dragonya?" Shade asked, confirming he'd heard that part of our conversation.

"Yes, that, too." She arched a brow at the male. "*Someone* threw a fireball into my garden, and Dragonya ran off after it. I need to make sure there's no damage and bring the little familiar back to our daughter."

"Ah, a fireball, you say?" He stretched his arms over his head, causing his fitted shirt to lift a little around the midsection. Aflora's gaze followed the action, her cheeks pinkening at the sight of her mate's muscular form.

I couldn't say I blamed her—the Midnight Fae was hot. Hell, both of them were.

But Shade was more my type, with his bad-boy looks and devilish charm.

Shade's the one you're friends with, right? I asked Ajax, recalling the camaraderie they'd displayed during my interrogation.

Yes. Why?

No reason, I lied.

Ajax and Shade certainly had the same vibe. Only, Ajax seemed more dangerous somehow. Maybe it was the Hell Fae influence that gave him that sinister appeal.

"Stop distracting our queen, Shade," the other male said. "She was in the middle of showing Cami around."

"And you would only know that if you were stalking me, too," she replied without missing a beat, her arched eyebrow now directed at the golden-eyed male.

He held up his hands. "I was looking for Shade."

Aflora's expression confirmed she didn't believe that for a second.

And neither did Shade—something his responding snort indicated.

"Zeph wants to spar," the male added. "So I'm calling in that favor."

Shade snorted again. "Clever timing."

"Isn't it?" His golden irises seemed to glitter despite the burnt coloring. "Better get going. You know how much our former headmaster hates tardiness."

"All the more reason to be late," Shade drawled. "Be useful and hunt down Dragonya for our daughter so our mate can focus on the guest." He vanished into a cloud of smoke before anyone could reply.

Aflora narrowed her gaze at the space he'd just occupied, and I had the distinct impression that she was saying something to him mentally.

If it were me, I'd be telling him I didn't need anyone doing anything for me.

"Kols," the other male said, holding his hand out toward me.

I stared at it. "I'm sorry, what?" *Kols* wasn't a term I understood.

"It's short for Kolstov."

"Okay..."

"His name," Aflora clarified, helping me to understand.

"Oh." I eyed the male's open palm and warily gave him mine in return. "Cami. Short for Camillia. But please don't call me that."

"Then call me Kols instead of Kolstov," he replied, releasing my hand.

"Deal, Kols."

"*Deal*, Cami," he echoed before glancing at Aflora. "*If* you need my help with Dragonya, let me know. Otherwise, I'll leave you to your garden stroll."

She offered him a relieved smile. "Thank you."

The male winked and walked back into the house rather than vanishing into a cloud. He softly shut the door, leaving me alone with Aflora on the stoop.

"Shall we, then?" she asked, gesturing to the black brick path before us.

"Sure," I agreed. "Why not?"

Seeing the grounds would help me think. Or perhaps it would just be an escape. Regardless, it was definitely what I needed right now.

I'm here if you need me, Ajax murmured, his words reminiscent of the ones Kols had just given Aflora.

Thank you, I replied, understanding Aflora's sentiment.

CHAPTER 17

CAMI

AFLORA LED the way in silence, seeming to understand that I needed a few minutes to process everything that had happened.

It was all a lot to take in.

I just needed to breathe.

To reflect on what Az had done.

To determine the best way forward.

Not that there was much I could do about the mating now. His Phoenix had staked his claim, bonding us for eternity. I'd heard that in Az's mind, understood that there was no choice in the matter.

We were officially connected.

The strange part was—I didn't feel all that upset about it. It confused me because I should be furious. Yet I wasn't.

Maybe it was hearing all those immediate thoughts in Az's mind that had calmed whatever ire I would have otherwise felt. But he'd been just as conflicted, just as alarmed and surprised by his Phoenix's actions.

He's suffering, too, I'd realized almost right away.

The spell Ajax had cast over him hurt, had brought up

some sort of past I didn't quite understand, and left him vulnerable. His Phoenix had reacted to that vulnerability and completed a bond he'd apparently already initiated via Ajax.

An animalistic reaction.

Not an emotional one.

Az—the man—hadn't meant to take my choice away. And his bird didn't really know any better.

Was I angry? Yes. But I also understood.

So confusing, I muttered to myself as Aflora led me to her gardens.

Although, they weren't really *gardens* in the traditional sense of the term. It was more like a gothic forest, littered with leafless branches, random peach trees, and flowers that *burned*.

I blinked at it all, stunned by the beauty of the landscape. It was fresh out of a fantasy book with all the foreign wildlife prancing around.

And wow, she hadn't been kidding about having phoenixes. They weren't black like Az's beast, but fiery red and orange. They lit up the night sky as they flew overhead, their majestic forms glowing with flickering embers.

"Az is a lot bigger than that," I told Aflora as I watched one land on a perch nearby. "Like twice the size."

"Probably because he's a Shifter Fae rather than a proper phoenix." She wandered over with her hand outstretched, some sort of flower forming in her palm. The creature bent to pluck it from her fingertips, its sharp beak careful not to nip.

Unlike another Phoenix I know, I marveled.

He's not enamored with or imprinted on her the way my Phoenix is with you, Az replied quietly, our link apparently open once more.

I didn't immediately reply, instead poking at the connection he'd created and trying to determine how deep it went. But it seemed I couldn't hear anything from his mind now. That, or he just wasn't thinking of anything at all. *Did you finish your wall?* I asked, referring to the one Ajax had mentioned.

I'm still building it, but the preliminary layer is there, yes.

To keep us from hearing your thoughts?

To keep you from feeling my magical outbursts, he corrected. *I can dismantle it at will, but it needs to be there to keep you both safe.*

I wanted to accuse him of lying, but I couldn't. Because I'd overheard part of his realization before I'd left the room earlier. He'd been so stunned by his Phoenix's antics that he'd left his mind wide open to us, providing me with a deep insight into his nature. His intentions. His fears. His insecurities.

It'd been... overwhelming.

Yet something about it had also been somewhat forgiving.

My body had been on display in front of all those Hell Fae, and it didn't even come close to having one's mind suddenly ripped open for others to explore. It'd been almost invasive to have that kind of access to his mind.

However, it'd helped me understand him a bit.

Forgive him? No, not really.

But I'd heard his frustrations with Ajax for not understanding his purpose, his need to protect him from Lucifer's potential wrath. Az's duty to honor his commitment to the Hell Fae King.

His hurt and loneliness at Ajax's lack of comprehension.

His sadness over Ajax accusing him of being like Constantine.

Az wasn't Constantine. And Az didn't feel Lucifer was either.

Although, deep down, he acknowledged that Lucifer's actions had been similar, and for that, he was eternally sorry.

A part of him was terrified that Ajax would never forgive him.

That part of him might have even coaxed his beast into biting Ajax, to ensure he couldn't escape him again.

I'd overheard all of that and so much more in the brief moments after our connection had snapped into place. I had no idea what Az had pulled from my own mind, if he'd even had the same sort of access. But it'd sounded like his immediate focus had shifted into protection mode once he'd gotten over the initial shock.

"It took me a while to understand the intentions of my mates," Aflora said after the phoenix took another magical flower from her palm. "They were essentially protecting me, by either pushing me in training or establishing boundaries to guard our secrets. But it was all a learning curve." Her cerulean eyes met mine. "For them and for me."

I nodded. "Most relationships work that way."

"They do," she agreed. "But powerful relationships often come with complex obstacles. It seems you're reaching one or two of them now."

"We have some, yeah," I muttered, thinking of Lucifer's desire to kill me. Az's errant Phoenix. Ajax having turned his back on the Hell Fae. Melek's cryptic bullshit. "Just a few obstacles."

Aflora dipped her chin in understanding. "I'd tell you it gets easier, but sometimes, I'm not so sure. Obstacles keep things interesting." Her attention went to a nearby tree, her eyes slitting with a glare. "*Very* interesting." A whistle sounded from her lips in the next second, the unexpected echo having me cover my ears as her power whipped around us in unanticipated waves.

Cami? Az and Ajax asked at the same time.

I gritted my teeth. *Don't do that.*

I sense panic, Az said.

Are you okay? Ajax inquired at almost the same time.

I pressed my palms to my ears, protecting my hearing from

Aflora's whistle while also trying to shove both of the male voices out of my head. *I'm. Fine.* Or I would be if the noise would go the fuck away.

What's happening? Az demanded.

Where are you? Ajax echoed.

Seriously? I'm. Fine.

But of course they didn't listen.

Because Ajax brought Az—still in Phoenix form—and both of them appeared in the courtyard in the next breath.

Followed immediately by Shade and Kols.

I shook my head. *Un-fucking-believable.*

I opened my mouth to comment on *overprotective males,* when a snarl sounded from the peach trees ahead, causing my eyebrows to lift.

Aflora didn't appear all that bothered, but both Kols and Shade took a step backward to flank her while Az and Ajax did the same to me.

What the hell was that? I wondered.

No idea, Az replied, his beast releasing a low warning snarl.

A wand appeared in Aflora's hand, similar to what Ajax had done a few times in my presence now. *So Midnight Fae conjure their wands?* I asked him. Or maybe I was asking *them.* I still wasn't sure how this telepathic link thing worked.

Yes, they both replied in unison.

Can you hear each other when you're talking to me? I wondered, thinking that maybe we were just in some sort of mate-circle now in my mind.

No, they echoed, making me frown.

Right. I really needed to figure this out. And soon.

But the hissing sound whirling through the air definitely took precedence.

Aflora stepped forward as a fiery ball appeared, the violent sphere bouncing in a chaotic zigzag along a path between two trees.

Kols cursed.

Shade smirked.

And Aflora whistled once more.

I winced, then gaped as a large black dragon appeared with a tongue lolling from the side of its snout, its gaze hyper-focused on the *fireball*.

Oh, I thought, that word becoming an ingrained part of my vocabulary. *That must be the fireball Aflora mentioned earlier.*

She mentioned a fireball? Ajax asked at the same time Az inquired, *What fireball?*

I think Shade conjured it and threw it out the window for Dragonya *to chase. And I'm guessing that dragon is* Dragonya. Not exactly an original name, but it somehow seemed to fit the creature with wide wings lumbering toward us.

Aflora sprang into action, stepping between the dragon and the fireball, her arms folding in a motherly manner. "*Stop,*" she demanded.

Dragonya immediately responded to that tone, its paws digging into the earth as it skidded to a halt mere inches from Aflora's form. Rather than appear contrite, the dragon gave the female a big lick against the cheek before plopping into a seated position and panting like a very large puppy.

"Dragonya!" a little voice cried as a small girl ran into the garden with two males right on her tail.

Florica, I recalled, having met her briefly during my interrogation in this realm. She immediately threw her arms around the dragon just as a large white wolf ran up beside them.

My eyebrows shot upward, but no one reacted to the wolf's sudden appearance.

Nor did they seem to notice as a crow, a bat, and a falcon swooped in to land on a few branches of a nearby tree.

Familiars, Ajax explained to me softly, probably catching

the profound confusion on my face. *Midnight Fae all have animals as familiars. The dragon appears to be Florica's familiar, which I would normally find hilarious if that beast weren't so close to you. Because of course Shade's daughter would have a violent, unruly creature as a familiar.*

I frowned. *All Midnight Fae have familiars?*

Yes.

Then where's your familiar? I asked, glancing at him. *Is it a Nightmare Fae of some kind? Because those are the only beasts I've seen you socialize with in the Hell Fae Realm.*

His lips flattened. *My familiar has remained here. Where it's safe.*

So you do have a familiar?

Yes.

Where is it?

He lifted a shoulder. *I haven't seen it in years.*

It's very strange hearing your questions for Ajax but not his responses, Az whispered into my mind. *Does he have a familiar?*

Yes, I told him. *But he hasn't seen it in years.*

Ajax's lips curled down. *Are you sharing that information with Az?*

He asked, I replied.

That's not his information to know, Ajax returned.

Then you talk to him, I said, exasperated. *I'm not getting in the middle of you two.*

Too late for that, Az drawled.

Not. Helpful. Irritation colored my mental tone.

He *put you in the middle,* Ajax snarled. *Or rather, his Phoenix did.*

I sighed heavily out loud and in my mind. *Yes. His Phoenix bit us both. But that doesn't mean I'm in the middle of your issues with him. I know he hurt you. And then you hurt him* with that spell. *And now we're all hurting. But I don't want to be the go-between in this conversation.*

I wish it were that simple, Ajax replied as Az said, *I'll talk to him.*

"*Enough,*" I said out loud. "You're both giving me a headache, and I'm not dealing with this right now."

Rather than allow either of them—or the other Midnight Fae—a chance to respond, I turned on my heel and started down a random path.

They could all play with the dragon.

Or whatever.

I need time, I told them. *Just... give me that, please.*

They both fell silent for a long moment before they agreed, their word choice exactly the same. *Okay.*

CHAPTER 18

AJAX

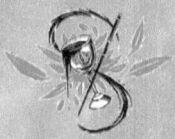

WHAT A FUCKING MESS, I thought, dragging my hand over my face.

Not the dragon part—although, that was certainly something—but everything with Cami.

With Az.

With Lucifer.

With *fate.*

I blame you for this, fucker, I told Az, my gaze narrowing his way.

His Phoenix fanned out his feathers as he took in my expression. *You're agitating my bird.*

"*I'm* agitating *your bird*?" I huffed a laugh. "Are you fucking serious right now?"

The creature faced me fully, his chest puffing out in a way that made him look twice as big. Which was fucking impressive considering the beast was already huge.

Don't do this, Az said. *It won't end well.*

I hate to break this to you, but it's already not going well, I snapped back into his mind. "*Sit down,*" I demanded out loud.

The Phoenix visibly winced, then did exactly what I'd commanded it to do, only for a jolt of agony to hit me right in the heart. I flinched away from the bird, my hand going to my chest to inspect the wound.

Except all I felt was the shirt I'd thrown on before shadowing out here.

Frowning, I glanced down, my torso aching from some unknown attack.

It's me, Az gritted out, his bird flinching again. *It's that damn spell. It* hurts *to comply.*

My frown deepened, an uncomfortable sensation building in my chest at the pain in Az's words. *You... you deserve it,* I forced myself to say. *After what you did to me... it's only fair.*

Az grunted in my mind but didn't deny it. He didn't say much at all.

But his Phoenix seemed to be glaring at me.

I glared right back. "You bit me without permission."

Because you're his chosen mate, Az muttered. *I've tried to harness his instincts, but Vivaxia's spell pushed me into the back of my mind, giving my animal complete control. He bit you to keep you from running from him again.*

Who the hell is Vivaxia? I asked him. "Zenaida gave me this spell," I added out loud. "I told you that."

"What spell did Zen give him?" someone asked softly. A female. I glanced up and suddenly remembered our audience —Aflora and all her mates.

Shade was standing beside her with a bag of popcorn in his hand—a bag he appeared to be sharing with Zakkai and Zeph because both men were currently chewing. "Something about taming a beast," Shade drawled before taking a fistful of kernels and popping them into his mouth.

"You're kidding with this shit, right?" I gestured to the bag in his hand. "Is my life a joke to you?"

"Not a joke," he replied. "But I assumed you were about

to fight the giant Phoenix, and I wanted some sustenance to go with the entertainment."

The dragon behind him poked his arm, causing Shade to conjure a bone in his hand that he quickly tossed back to the beast. He—or maybe it was a *she*—caught the bone and curled up on the ground with Florica on its back, the creature happily munching away while the little girl gazed up at the moon.

"Can we have some privacy, please?" I asked them.

Zakkai considered us for a moment and shrugged before turning away to kneel beside Florica. "Let's take Dragonya back to Daddy Shade's den and create more fireballs."

The smirk dancing over Shade's lips immediately melted away. "No."

But Florica was already cheering in excitement, which had the dragon leaping up in immediate alarm. Zakkai picked up the bone and chucked it toward the palace before flashing Shade a quick smile.

Shade cursed and immediately shadowed after the now-flying dragon, Florica squealing with joy on its back the whole time.

Zeph and Kols shared a look while Aflora sighed. "You're all giving me a headache now. Why are men so obnoxious?"

"Hey, I didn't do anything," Kols argued.

"Uh-huh," Aflora murmured.

"I also haven't done anything," Zeph added, his deep voice one of his defining traits. That and his green eyes—the same color as his magic. "But I'm about to do something."

Aflora glanced at him, her eyebrows lifting. "Zeph—"

She yelped as he lifted her off the ground and into his arms. "You look famished, pixie flower. Kols, go grab the blood paste."

Kols grinned. "Yeah, all right. Meet you back at the room?"

Zeph nodded.

Aflora turned pink.

And I faced Az again while shaking my head. *At least they're all distracted now,* I thought at him, some of my ire seeming to have disappeared in the last few minutes of whatever the fuck that was.

Remind me not to procreate, Az replied, then winced as his bird growled in response. It seemed the man was at odds with his animal's instincts.

Despite everything, my lips twitched. *Procreating is probably the best thing that's ever happened to Shade, apart from his mating to Aflora.* He might still be an obnoxious dick, but he'd grown a lot over the last decade. *He was such a rebel back in the day.*

I think he's still pretty rebellious.

Yeah, I guess he is, I agreed, shaking my head again. *A dragon for a familiar is quite something.*

Hmm. Az didn't sound as impressed. *What's your familiar?*

My jaw ticked. *None of your damn business.*

Touchy subject? he taunted.

Do you want me to kill you? I demanded, my fingers curling into fists at my sides. *Because I will. I can. Especially while you're under this spell.*

I'll just ash back to life, he returned. *So, sure. If that's what will make you feel better, then kill me.*

My jaw clenched. *It won't make me feel better.*

Then why waste the energy? he asked. *Besides, you need me to help you protect Cami. Killing me will make that temporarily harder.*

I glared down at him. "How the fuck are you going to help me protect Cami? You're mated to the fucking threat."

Typhos isn't going to hurt her.

"Right. I believe that," I deadpanned. "Your Phoenix just

mated her. He'll probably see her as an even bigger threat now because of it."

Or maybe he'll see that she could be a valuable ally, Az pointed out. *Maybe you should give me a chance to talk to him and see what I can work out.*

My eyebrows lifted. "Like I would trust you with that. The last time you *worked something out* with him, Cami ended up in chains on a stage, and I was forced to sit there and watch while bound by your powers."

Something both Typhos and I realize was wrong, Az said. *He was trying to sensually punish us both. Not hurt us. But when I pointed out the similarities to what Constantine did, well, why do you think Typhos let me take my time in tracking you?*

I ground my teeth together, unsure of how to reply to that. It almost sounded more like an apology than an explanation or an excuse, which was strange because Az wasn't the apologetic type.

He knows something is going on now, that I'm hurting from something that's happened to me, but rather than barge in to fix it, he's trusting me to handle the situation—because I asked him to give me time. Does that sound like someone who's a threat to Cami?

"I saw the way he looked at her last night. He wanted to kill her."

Yes, while in the throes of chaos and confusion from the portal issue. She used his power to close it. He wasn't seeing reason then. But he should be calmer now. We can talk to him.

I snorted. "You'd like that, wouldn't you? Convince us that it's safe to go back to the Hell Fae Realm for a *chat*." Like that was going to happen. "Cami's safer here. It's also her call to make, not mine."

Az didn't immediately respond, his Phoenix giving nothing away. His mind was quiet as well, confirming he'd finished erecting his wall—or was perhaps close to the completion of his little mental project.

I hoped that wall of his kept him out of my thoughts, too.

I know I've broken your trust, Az said softly. *I deserve your anger. So does Typhos. But we can fix this, Ajax. Please let us fix this.*

Fix what? I asked him mentally. *What is this to you?*

Us, he replied without hesitation. *You, me, Cami. Our future. Our* mating. *I realize my bird took our choices from us, but there's no going back. We can only move forward. And to do that, we need to fix this issue between us.*

"I don't think that's possible," I told him on a breath, my legs suddenly itching to move. So I did. Not far. Just pacing around in front of the still-seated Phoenix. "You froze me in place, Az. You made me watch while Lucifer humiliated her. How could you do that to me? *To her?*"

It was so fucking cruel.

So damn *wrong*.

"She hasn't done anything wrong. It's not like she's purposely tapping into Lucifer's powers. It's just... happening. You've witnessed it. You know it's not nefarious. It's simply... *her.*" Yet Lucifer had been hell-bent on punishing her for it, his need to put her in her place overriding practical thought.

He should have *thanked* her for helping with the portal.

Instead, he'd nearly killed her for it.

And Az... "You're his mate," I whispered. "Your loyalty is to him."

Not anymore. The two words were soft in my mind, Az's mental voice sounding pained. *My Phoenix chose you and Cami. My Phoenix mated both of you. While I may still be soul-bound to Typhos, my animal spirit is yours.*

I stopped pacing to look at him. "What the hell does that even mean?"

It means I'm bonded to you both as my Shifter Fae half,

while my Hell Fae side is what's tied to Typhos. My soul is essentially divided. That's the only way I can explain it.

"So you're still connected to him."

Yes. I'll always be connected to him. But now I'll always be connected to you and Cami, too. Which means my loyalty... is to all of you. Not one over the other.

"And if we die?" I asked him. "What then?"

My animal spirit dies with you.

I gaped at him. "And what the hell does that mean?" It was pretty much the same question I'd just asked him, but for an entirely different reason now.

Exactly what I said. A Shifter Fae can't live without his chosen mate. If you or Cami dies, my animal spirit will pass with you. And while I might have other fae pieces in me, my Phoenix is the largest part of my soul. Thus... He trailed off, the rest of the sentence not really needed.

But I finished it for him anyway. "You'd die, too."

Yes.

I studied him, searching for any hint of a lie. But all his Phoenix did was gaze back at me, his black eyes giving nothing away. "If you're lying to me..."

I'm not. But I understand that you can't trust me yet. Just tell me what you need, Ajax. I'll do it. I vow it.

My eyebrow inched upward. "That's a dangerous proclamation."

Then test it, he dared me. *Give me a task. Tell me what to do, and I'll do it of my own free will.*

My gaze narrowed. "Meaning you want me to lift the spell so you can prove you mean it." I shook my head. "Wow. You almost had me believing you, Az. *Almost*. But there is no way in hell I'm lifting the spell. The moment I do, you'll just drag us back to Lucifer. Then it'll be game over."

"Maybe he will, maybe he won't." Cami's voice came from

the trees, preceding her return. She gave me a critical look before focusing on Az. "I want to see what he'll do."

I gaped at her. "You want me to release him?"

"Yes. I want to give him a chance to prove his loyalty."

"And when he breaks our trust again?" I demanded. "What then?"

"Then we'll know," she replied, her gray eyes flickering toward me. "I don't want to live in a world of what-ifs and wondering who to trust. I want facts and undeniable truths. No games. No prolonging the inevitable. No guesses. Just straight answers. Release him and we'll know. End of discussion."

"If I release him, he will take us to Lucifer," I reiterated. "I'm certain of it."

"Maybe," she repeated. "But we both know I have to face him at some point. So release Az, and he'll either escalate the inevitable or prove his worth. It's our best play. It's our *only* play."

"I could keep him in a cage." I'd offered that once before, but she hadn't really accepted it. I'd absolutely do it. However, I'd probably forgo the chains.

"For how long?" she asked, suddenly sounding tired. "Hours? Days? Weeks?" She gave his Phoenix a sad look. "How is that fair to his beast? He's not the one who chose to freeze you with his power. It was Az. And it's Az who wants a chance to earn our trust back. I say we let him try. It won't be an easy road, but I think he knows that."

I do, Az whispered into my mind.

You've been talking to her, haven't you? I realized. *She figured out how to control her mental links.*

No. I left her alone when she went on her walk.

My eyes narrowed slightly, suspicion overwhelming my mind. "Have you been talking to Az?" I asked Cami, needing her to tell me the truth.

"No. But I saw enough of his mind to know he's regretful over what happened. I also know that spell you're using is hurting him a lot more than Lucifer's chains ever hurt me." She took a step toward me, her expression matching the weariness in her voice. "Free him, Ajax. It's the only way we'll know his intentions."

My jaw ached from me gritting my teeth, my frustration over this choice exhausting me almost as much as it was exhausting Cami.

I hated that she was right.

We wouldn't know Az's intentions until I freed him.

And how long would this spell tame him, anyway?

I had no idea.

"All right," I said, focusing on Az. "You want to try to earn my trust back?"

His Phoenix blinked as Az said, *I believe I've made that clear, yes.*

Now isn't the time for condescending responses, I retorted.

Just get to your terms, Ajax. Tell me how to make this right.

My lips curled, but it wasn't in amusement. It was in sinister expectation. Because he'd vowed to do *anything* to fix this.

Which gave me freedom to demand whatever I wanted.

"Okay, Az. I'll free you. But I want you to convince Lucifer to leave us alone. *For good*. And when you come back, I want you to give your Phoenix control again. Human form, animal form, I don't care. But the bird will be in charge while you watch from the inside."

For how long? Az asked warily.

"Until we decide to trust you again," I replied, folding my arms. "Which might not be for a *very* long time."

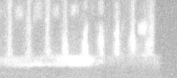

CHAPTER 19

AZ

Convince Lucifer to leave Cami and Ajax alone—for good.

Give my Phoenix control until Ajax and Cami trust me again.

The two terms whirled around in my mind, my analytical side processing them and breaking them down into a myriad of loopholes. It was an automatic instinct created by millennia of knowing several of the universe's most experienced deal-wielders.

There were so many ways to interpret the demand to encourage Lucifer to leave Cami and Ajax alone. *Typhos is my other mate,* I reminded Ajax. *Lucifer will always be part of my life.*

"I know," Ajax replied. "But he won't be part of my life or Cami's. That's the deal."

You want me to convince Lucifer to stop pursuing you and Cami, I carefully rephrased. *For good. And in return, you'll give me my freedom.*

"I also want you to give your Phoenix complete control."

Yes, that, too. Until you trust me again.

His eyes narrowed. "That's never going to happen, but yes."

"What's never going to happen?" Cami asked.

"Me trusting him again," Ajax translated before informing her of what else I'd said, including my rephrasing of convincing Lucifer not to pursue them.

Cami shrugged, her expression wary. "That's fine with me."

But is it enough for you to eventually forgive me? I asked her softly. *To trust me?*

She glanced at me, causing my bird to perk up with interest. He was utterly infatuated with the female and practically ready to sprawl out on his back, belly up, for her.

When she didn't immediately smile at him or acknowledge him, he sighed.

My Phoenix didn't understand why she was still upset with him. In his mind, he'd *fixed* the problem by biting her. She was his now. So why wasn't she as enamored with him as he was with her?

I knew why, but I couldn't even begin to explain it to him. It was too complicated. He didn't think in complex terms, just instincts.

"I don't know if I can forgive you or trust you," she finally said. "This... is a lot, Az."

I know, I told her. *And I'm sorry. But there's nothing I can do to reverse the bond. It's here to stay. For eternity.*

"You mean until Lucifer finds me and kills me."

This time, I was the one who sighed, not my Phoenix.

Lucifer's not going to kill you, Cami. Your death would kill my Phoenix. It would hurt Melek. It would hurt Ajax. And while Ajax might not believe it right now, Typhos does care about him, too. He cares about all of us. He just has a unique way of showing it.

She snorted in response. "That's one word for it."

He's ancient. His methods for showing he cares are a bit archaic, I admitted. *But this isn't about Lucifer right now. It's about you and me. Tell me what you want from me. Tell me how I can start earning your trust. I know it'll take time. I just want to know where to start, Cami. Please.*

Because there was no going back now. I had to find a way to move forward, or my Phoenix would suffer. *I* would suffer.

I needed Cami and Ajax more than they would ever know.

I cared about them, too.

I want to make this work, I told her. *I realize it wasn't planned for any of us. But it happened. We either accept it or spend our entire lives fighting it.*

She sucked her bottom lip in between her teeth, her gaze contemplative.

What are you saying to her? Ajax asked me, his tone holding a hint of irritation at being left out of the conversation. Or maybe he thought I was trying to convince her of something.

I'm asking for her terms, I informed him.

He didn't say anything in reply, instead looking at Cami, who then glanced at him with a nod. *Yes,* she said. *He wants my terms.*

The words were for Ajax, not for me.

Because he'd apparently just asked her to confirm what I'd told him.

I really did mess things up with him, I thought for the thousandth time. It wouldn't matter how many times I explained why; he'd still hate me for it.

So I would just have to earn back that trust.

Starting with convincing Lucifer not to pursue Cami and Ajax.

"I want you to train me," Cami said suddenly, causing my bird to perk up. He liked her tone. Or maybe he understood her words. "I want you to train me how to defend myself against Lucifer or anyone else who might want to hurt me."

Ajax nodded. "That's a good term."

Yes, I thought to myself. *Yes, it is.*

Anything else? I asked her.

"You asked me where to start." She shrugged. "That's where I want to start."

Fair enough, I agreed. *I accept your initial terms.*

When she wanted more later, either we'd negotiate an agreement, or I'd just do whatever she asked. It would depend on the request.

I accept your terms, I added to Ajax.

"Good." He looked at Cami. "You're sure about this?"

"It's our only option. I'm not putting his Phoenix in a cage. It's cruel."

Ajax grunted, clearly disagreeing, but he didn't comment. Instead, he pulled a card from his pocket and scanned it with his gaze.

Then he sighed and uttered the words I'd only heard a handful of times in my existence—the reversal spell.

It was slightly altered from the one Vivaxia once used, but so was the taming enchantment he'd voiced before.

How did Zenaida get these spells? I wondered as renewed life flourished through my lungs. I'd only been trapped for an hour or so, but it'd felt like years, the weight of the incantation resembling hooks in my spirit as it held me captive in its invisible binds.

When the last one snapped free, my beast immediately relinquished control and allowed me to shift into my human form. I stood and stretched, my limbs feeling battered and bruised by the remnants of that horrible magic.

My hands tracked over my legs and arms, trying to rid myself of the spiderweb sensation it left behind.

All the while, Ajax and Cami watched, their expressions

equally concerned. But it wasn't my well-being they were worried about, just their own.

And that hurt almost as much as the spell had.

I deserve it, I reminded myself. *But I will make this right.*

"When you want to communicate with a certain mate, think of only that mate," I told Cami. "You'll eventually see the various channels in your mind. It's an important skill that will help safeguard your thoughts."

I was well versed in it because of my links to Typhos.

Had I not known how to open and close our telepathic link, he would already know about Ajax and Cami. Fortunately, he'd only sensed a mild disturbance because the bond had been through my Phoenix. And my animal only connected to Typhos when I needed to expel excess energy.

Very unlike Melek, who was bonded to Typhos entirely by Virtuous Fae bonds. When Melek had connected himself to Cami, Ty had very much sensed it because it was the same magic the two of them had used to mate one another.

"Try practicing with Ajax while I'm gone," I added to Cami. "Consider that my first training tip."

Leaving her to discuss it with Ajax, I disappeared and headed to the Hell Fae Realm to find Typhos.

Not exactly the first lesson I expected, Cami said into my thoughts as I arrived at the Hell Fae Palace.

No, but it's an important lesson, I promised her. *Otherwise, Typhos would hear everything I've been saying to you and Ajax.*

Well, technically, that wasn't true. My bond with Typhos was via his Virtuous Fae magic, not my Phoenix. Therefore, his access to my mind was automatically restricted. I could let him in as I saw fit, but I had natural mental blocks in place to stop him from going too deep.

Instead of keeping those details from Cami, I chose to share them, explaining how my Phoenix had never mated him, thus our bonds were different.

The only thing I didn't elaborate on was the type of fae magic Typhos had used to bond me to him. I simply let her assume it was a Hell Fae mating link rather than reveal Lucifer's origin.

That wasn't my story to tell.

But safeguarding your mind is still a valuable skill, I concluded. *You never know when you'll need to be able to compartmentalize your thoughts.*

An image of Vivaxia tumbled through my mind, her beautiful visage unwelcome.

She seemed to be haunting me a lot today.

Stupid fucking spell.

Cami fell silent, not replying to the comments about how it would be a useful skill. Instead of pushing her to accept my first training lesson, I focused on my other task of finding the Hell Fae King.

I engaged our mental link. *Typhos.*

I'm in my lair, he responded, obviously aware that I'd returned to the palace.

Rather than walk to his underground office—otherwise known as his lair—I ashed. It was faster. And I didn't need time to gather my thoughts.

There was only one way to approach Typhos with this, and that was to be direct and to the point.

"Azazel," he said when I appeared in the posh living area adjacent to his large obsidian desk. His lair was reserved for private matters, the area underground not even frequented by the palace Hellhounds.

Lucifer only came down here when he had something secretive to work on. I suspected his presence here now was related to the portal situation in our realm.

The maps on his desk confirmed it, his handwriting indicating all the places we'd been attacked and potential future weaknesses. A stack of folders sat off to one side, a feathered pen hovering above them with magic ink highlighting the sharp tip.

"New deals?" I wondered. He typically worked on those in another area of the palace, but perhaps these were unique.

"No, old ones that I'm reviewing." His sapphire eyes locked on me. "Erebus caught the Unseelie responsible for the portal in the Marsh Lands. It was one of the bride's fathers. He was covered in Virtuous Fae magic, yet has no memory of the attack at all."

My eyebrows lifted. "Do you think he was a pawn?"

"I don't know. So I'm searching for other potential fae who might not approve of their daughters being enrolled in our program. Perhaps they're working together. Or maybe someone is using them. Melek is still reviewing our latest case, just to see if I missed any Virtuous Fae strands."

"Do you want me to stop by as well, see if I scent anything?" I asked, exhausted by the potential task but also willing to take it on if it would help end all this madness.

Typhos studied me for a moment, his dark gaze not just assessing but also knowing.

We'd been together for a very long time, which meant he could read all my tells. However, this situation was different. *Very* different. And unlike anything else we'd ever experienced.

Pushing away from his desk, he came around to take over one of his leather chairs. "Tell me what happened with Ajax and Camillia first."

Sighing, I sat across from him and told him everything. Including the part about my Phoenix biting Ajax and Cami.

Hiding the truth wouldn't help anyway. Age and experience had proved that to me millennia ago.

Typhos didn't interrupt me while I spoke, not even when I mentioned Vivaxia's spell. However, I felt his fury pulse through our bond when I mentioned her name and the memory of what she'd done to me countless times before.

I finished by telling him Ajax's terms.

"And Cami wants me to train her," I concluded right as Melek appeared in the room. His blondish-brown eyebrow arched, curiosity coloring his features, but he didn't comment, simply wandered over to the bar to pour himself a drink.

Interestingly, he chose ice water instead of something alcoholic.

He fixed three glasses and brought them over without a word before taking over the sofa across from us.

Typhos remained quiet while his prince moved around the space, his focus on me rather than Melek.

"Train her how?" Typhos asked, his tone giving nothing away, just like his expression. Yet I could feel his anger humming through our bond like a live wire. It'd been thrumming since I'd mentioned the spell and hadn't weakened at all, just continued to build.

"To protect herself against you and any other perceived threat," I told him, not hiding the details. Because every bit of information mattered when agreements were made.

"And do you intend to see that term through?"

"Yes." There was no point in concealing my intentions. Typhos deserved to know. He also needed to understand. "My Phoenix mated her. My animal's spirit is bound to hers. Protecting her is now as important to me as protecting myself. So yes, I will be training her. Ajax, too, if he'll let me."

Which wouldn't be anytime soon, given the current state of our relationship.

Fortunately, I'd essentially spent the last decade teaching him how to fight.

Of course, physical prowess meant nothing around Typhos. His fights were never physical; they were psychological in nature.

"I see." He picked up the glass Melek had poured for him

and took a long swallow, his gaze assessing. "Your Phoenix has complicated matters."

There wasn't anything I could say to that other than "I know."

"I disagree," Melek interjected. "I think they've improved matters. Now you have even more control over the girl. You're connected to her by me and Az."

"You keep assuming that these connections are not some sort of manipulation," Typhos returned, a hint of his anger deepening his tone. "Az's Phoenix finally found a mate after several thousands of years, and it just so happens to be the same female you've bonded yourself to. That's not a coincidence."

"I never called it a coincidence." Melek smiled. "I merely pointed out that the circumstances have improved the situation by affording you more control."

Typhos set his now-empty glass down. "So long as she's not actually the one gaining control over both of you, which remains to be seen."

"I really don't think that's the case," I confided. "My Phoenix bond lets me see her mind. She was stunned when my animal bit her. It was very genuine."

"Then maybe someone is using her in a fashion similar to the Unseelie father," Typhos suggested.

"To what end?" Melek asked. "She *helped* you, Ty. Why would she do that if she wanted to hurt you?"

The Hell Fae King's jaw ticked, his irritation palpable.

He didn't like to be wrong.

But more than that, his instincts warned him that something wasn't right. And until he figured out the cause, he'd continue to investigate this.

"I don't trust her." The words weren't unexpected, but the admission was, especially since Typhos uttered it in a soft, barely there whisper. "I don't trust *this*."

Melek slid off the couch to kneel at his king's feet, his palms flattening against Typhos's suit-clad thighs as he peered up at him. "Trust takes time, my love. We all know that."

I nodded, agreeing with Melek. "We all distrust things we don't understand. And Camillia De la Croix is definitely an unknown entity. But my Phoenix trusts her implicitly. He saw something in her that was worth his bite, and you know he doesn't choose lightly."

"It has to be a spell," Typhos said. "She has all of you acting out of sorts. These rash decisions are unlike you."

I assumed *all of you* included Ajax.

And that last part wasn't entirely true—Melek was the prince of rash decisions.

"Maybe it's a spell," Melek echoed. "Or maybe it's fate. But we deserve the chance to determine the cause. We deserve the option to indulge in these instincts and to trust them. We deserve the right to know Cami. She's special. Let us try this our way, my love. Let us be free with her and open with you."

I stayed quiet, Melek's plea exactly what I wanted, too.

He was asking Typhos to let us get to know Cami, to see if what we felt toward her was real, and in return, we'd keep him informed. Just like I had now.

Give us the freedom to date her, and we'll tell you if you can trust her, was essentially Melek's request.

"You pointed out once before that if she betrays me, it'll be my pain to bear. I accept that risk. It seems Az's Phoenix does, too. Let us know her. Please." Melek bowed his head toward Typhos's knees, his utter submission a gift from him to the Hell Fae King.

Because Melek didn't submit to just anyone.

Hell, I submitted to no one. But I suspected my bird might try to submit to Cami.

Typhos sighed, his fingers combing through Melek's thick hair. "What exactly do you want me to do, Melek? She touched my source. Do you wish for me to forgive her? Set her free? Allow her to come back? What are your terms? Be specific."

Melek considered him for a few seconds before looking at me.

I knew what the terms needed to be.

But I let Melek lead. His penchant for dealing with Typhos gave him an edge I didn't possess.

I usually obeyed orders because I agreed with those orders.

Melek rebelled—even when he agreed with the directive—because he enjoyed rebelling.

Rather, he enjoyed the punishment that followed.

I didn't play those games with Typhos. *This is all you,* I thought at Melek. He couldn't hear me. But we'd known each other long enough that he could no doubt read the words from my expression.

Ajax had tasked me with halting Typhos's pursuit of them. He hadn't told me how to accomplish it, just that I needed to get it done.

So I was using the assets at my disposal—my asset being Melek.

"I have a list," Melek began, his gaze glittering as he returned his focus to Typhos.

"I imagine you do," the king drawled as he relaxed into his chair as though it were a throne. He waved a hand and said, "Proceed."

"You will not harm Camillia. This includes physically, psychically, mentally, the hiring of an external party, the ordering of an external party, and strategic plotting of any kind that may result in even the tiniest amount of pain or harm to Camillia De la Croix."

Typhos arched a brow. "That's quite a term."

"I'm not done, my love," Melek murmured. "You will also

do whatever you can to make amends with Ajax. We need him."

"We do?"

"We do," Melek echoed. "He's mated to my intended. And he's mated to your mate. He's officially part of our circle now. You must make amends with him."

Typhos scratched his chin. "Anything else?"

"You will give me and Az freedom to woo Cami as we see fit. No interference. No meddling. No *rules*."

Typhos grunted. "I'm not the meddler, little prince."

Melek's lips curled upward. "That's a lie, my love. You just meddle in different ways."

"Hmm." The hum of sound resembled a deep rumble from Typhos's chest, his sapphire irises glowing with power. "Those are a lot of demands, Melek."

"Yes," the prince agreed. "And I'm not negotiating on a single one."

Typhos's eyebrow inched up higher. "I see. And what do I receive in return for all of this? How will it benefit me?"

Melek's smile grew. "You'll receive a Hell Fae Queen."

CHAPTER 20

AZ

Typhos didn't return Melek's smile. "I have no desire or need for a queen, Melek. I'm more than content with you."

"You have every need for a queen," Melek returned, his grin slipping from his features as he grew serious—a trait that seemed to be coming out more and more these last few days. "The portal incident proved your need for a queen, Typhos."

"He's right," I said, backing up Melek. "Cami helped you when you needed it. With proper guidance and care, she could help you again."

Typhos snorted. "A fluke."

"It wasn't a fluke, Ty." Melek reached for the king's face, his palms cradling his cheeks. "You've carried the weight of this realm for too long. You need more support. *Cami* is the solution. I just need you to give her a chance to prove it."

Typhos's jaw ticked. "You have a lot of faith in a girl you hardly know."

"And you have a lot of prejudice against a woman you've barely spoken to," Melek returned. "She's special, Ty. It's like she was made for *us*."

"Which is precisely my concern," Typhos replied. "There's something not quite right with her. And it's more than having a magic pussy that you all seem to want to fuck."

My Phoenix bristled inside, not liking the crude tone the king had just used when talking about his mate. I swallowed down the urge to punch him for it, my mind seeking reason while my beast demanded action.

Typhos's focus shifted to me, our link no doubt betraying the flare of anger simmering inside me. "You don't approve of my assessment?"

"My Phoenix doesn't, no," I replied. "He might not understand your terms, but he understands your tone. And he's feeling very protective of his mate."

"It's not just a queen you'll receive," Melek interjected, his palm leading Typhos's focus back to him. "It's a mate-circle. A place of power to help you balance the scales. Your kingdom has grown and stretched you far too thin. You need us, Ty. You need our support. You can no longer handle all this on your own."

Typhos's hands curled into fists. "I'm fine."

"You're not," Melek insisted. "I'm inside you, Ty. I can *feel* the weight of the source on your shoulders."

"It's my burden to bear."

"It's *our* burden." Melek removed his hands as he fell back to his haunches, his expression hard as he looked up at the king. "What happens if the source swallows you whole? How do you think that'll impact the Hell Fae Realm? How do you think it'll impact *me*?"

Typhos's gaze narrowed, the tendons of his neck seeming to bulge as the veins became more prominent in his hands. Melek had struck a nerve. Several, actually.

However... "He's not wrong," I told Typhos softly. "I can feel that weight, too. I just didn't realize how heavy it was until recently."

Melek was more in tune with the Hell Fae King. He also tended to think in futuristic terms, his proclivity for meddling giving him an advantage when it came to assessing situations before their time.

"You can draft a cancellation clause," Melek offered. "If things prove too dangerous, or if for some reason you feel our judgment is truly clouded, you can act. But you'll need to provide substantial proof of your suspicions."

It was a dangerous clause to add, especially as it would mean every term could be nulled and voided depending on Typhos's interpretation of events.

But Melek seemed to be banking on his certainty that this would work—if Typhos just gave Cami a chance.

"There will be repercussions to terminating our agreement," Melek added. "It'll come at the expense of the Phoenix's soul, as well as pieces of my own. And Ajax... he won't survive. So your suspicions would need to be absolute before you could act, or you'd risk losing more than you've ever had."

A hint of uncharacteristic fear echoed through my bond with Typhos, the king realizing the veracity of Melek's words.

He was also likely comprehending that it was too late for him to even attempt to negotiate this deal. The pieces were already in place, the agreement having been struck between all of our souls.

There was no choice here. Either he accepted and tried to make it work, or he refused and risked destroying his small circle of trust.

Because my Phoenix would pull me toward Cami and Ajax, my need to protect them already riding me hard.

And Melek wasn't going to give up that easily. He only involved himself in affairs that meant something to him, and Cami clearly meant a great deal to him.

Typhos ran a hand over his face, his exhaustion hitting me

like a tidal wave through our connection. These security issues were taking their toll, as was the growing power of the realm. It had reached capacity, making it nearly impossible for him to manage.

How had I missed that? I marveled. There'd been signs, but he'd always come out on top. He'd also accepted my Phoenix energy without blinking.

However, I'd been using Ajax more and more over the last decade, my needs mounting as time moved on. I'd assumed it was my attraction to Ajax that had caused me to need him so fiercely, and perhaps that was true on one level.

But it seemed my Phoenix had sensed Typhos being at capacity, too.

Which had led me to seek out Ajax as much as I had. Grow closer to him. *Trust* him.

No wonder you chose him, I thought at my bird. *You knew he was an ideal mate because of how he accepted your power.*

I'd been moving in a daze these last few years, not paying attention to anything other than my own physical needs.

Cami had woken me up.

She'd changed everything.

For the better, I realized.

Az? she asked suddenly, causing my spine to straighten.

Cami? Are you all right? My Phoenix paced inside, concerned.

I'm fine. Just practicing my first lesson. She sounded pleased with herself.

My lips twitched. *Good girl.*

Don't be condescending, she snapped.

I'm not. I'm happy you're practicing, I told her solemnly.

"Azazel?" Typhos prompted, his voice drawing me back to him. "Are you well?"

I blinked at him, my brow furrowing. "Yes, sorry, Cami was talking to me."

That eyebrow of his cocked upward again. "About?"

"She's practicing her telepathy." I lifted a shoulder. "She was struggling with it earlier, her mental responses going to me and Ajax at the same time. I told her to focus her mental channels."

"I see." He blew out a breath and palmed the back of his neck. "This..." He trailed off, his head shaking slowly. "You've left me with no real choice here." His attention went to Melek. "You did this on purpose."

"I can't take all the credit, my love," Melek murmured. "Az and Ajax played their parts."

"Yes, and I have no doubt in my mind who set those pieces in motion," the king replied.

Melek said nothing, neither confirming nor denying the accusation.

Which probably meant he was guilty.

On any normal day, I'd likely be pissed to have been dragged into one of his little games. Yet I felt oddly content with how everything had turned out.

My Phoenix was... calm. Happy, even. He seemed to be hovering right alongside me, our spirits joined in a way I had never really experienced. Even my energy levels seemed tranquil, my usual need to expel excess power nowhere to be found.

I'm at peace, I realized, frowning. *Because I have mates? Or is this a temporary reprieve after today's events?*

"I accept your terms, little prince," Typhos finally said. "As well as the cancellation clause. But I reserve the right to renegotiate later, just as I reserve the right to alter course should Ajax or Cami require it."

Melek considered him for a long moment, likely evaluating those words and searching for whatever loopholes Typhos was creating by uttering them.

There were several that came to mind, specifically about

how Typhos could manipulate Cami and Ajax to *alter course* from the agreement. But he would attempt to do that even without the added clause.

Typhos was a strategic genius.

However, so was Melek.

Hence the reason they paired so well together.

Melek placed his palms on Typhos's thighs and stood, then leaned down to brush his lips over the king's mouth. "It's a deal, my love."

I didn't move forward to join them, just added mentally, *I accept, too.*

"This will satisfy your agreement with Ajax?" he asked aloud.

"You can't pursue him or Cami. And I need to be given time to earn their trust." Once I did, my deal with Ajax could be altered, and we could discuss Typhos again.

Or that was my hope, anyway.

"It seems I need to make amends, too. How am I to do that when I can't pursue him?" Typhos asked.

"I'm certain you'll devise an appropriate course of action, my love," Melek said as he straightened. "But worst-case scenario, we'll see them at the Interrealm Fae Ball in the Midnight Fae Kingdom."

Typhos glanced up at him, his eyebrow lifting once more. "We will?"

Melek grinned. "Yes, we will."

"I don't recall saying I would attend that event, little prince."

"No, I took the opportunity to confirm our attendance when speaking with Zakkai earlier. Or I implied it, anyway." Melek shrugged. "With Ajax and Cami being royal guests, they'll definitely be in attendance. So it'll provide the perfect opportunity for a reunion, yes?"

Typhos sighed, his eyes rolling upward as he settled more heavily into his chair. "Interrealm Fae politics. You would find that to be the *perfect opportunity,* wouldn't you?"

Melek grinned. "I would, yes."

"Fine." Typhos waved a hand. "Ajax and Cami can remain in the Midnight Fae Realm as *guests.* But you're staying here with me and helping me determine the cause of these security breaches." Those words were for Melek. However, the ones that followed were directed at me. "And you will keep an eye on Ajax and Cami for us."

I dipped my chin. "I will."

"And train Cami," Melek added. "Which I have some ideas for. I'll share them with you on your way out."

Typhos gave him a look. "More meddling?"

Melek pressed a palm to his chest, his posture the picture of innocence. "Me? Never."

Typhos just shook his head again and pushed away from his chair. "Go. Meddle. I need some time to process all of this anyway."

Melek stepped into the king's muscular form, his palm returning to Typhos's cheek. "Everything I do, everything I've done, is for you, Ty." The sincerity in Melek's voice had me wishing I could disappear. This was a moment I didn't want to intrude upon.

"You say that," Typhos whispered. "I'm trusting that you mean it."

"I do." Melek brushed his lips against Typhos's again, then stepped away to focus on me. "Go find some pants and let's take a walk."

I glanced down at my naked state. I'd been so caught up in my tasks that I'd forgotten my clothes. *Shifter Fae problems.*

"Unless you prefer wandering naked?" Melek prompted. "I don't mind."

I snorted at his flirty commentary. "Meet me at my hut." Rather than wait for a reply, I ashed back to my place.

Melek appeared as I was zipping up a pair of black jeans. He observed quietly, his expression no longer playful, while I pulled on a shirt and then some socks and boots for my feet.

"I won't take up much time, Az," he said as I headed toward the door of my cabin. "I think we're both on the same page here."

"Somehow I doubt that." I opened the door, only for him to close it and slide between me and the wood, his multicolored gaze flickering with a myriad of secrets.

"You need to use your training with Cami to show her who Ty really is," Melek told me, a hint of uncharacteristic severity in his tone. "It's the only way we're going to come out of this intact."

I stared at him, our even heights putting us at eye level with one another. "It's going to take a lot more than *understanding* to ensure we survive this, Melek."

"Yes, I know. However, I have my hands full with teaching Ty. I need you to take over with Cami. I'll still assist when I can, but I need you to take the lead on this."

"Take the lead?" I repeated. "From you?"

"Who do you think has been guiding her where Ty is concerned?" Melek asked, his expression serious. "She needs to understand Ty, Az. And right now, she has him all wrong."

I gritted my teeth. Because he was right—she didn't really know Ty at all. "I guess that means your guidance failed?"

A hint of anger flashed in his multicolored irises, his eyes narrowing. "I haven't had much help."

"Maybe because you've been playing this game on your own."

"It's not a game," he returned. "It's about saving Ty. About saving *us*. And I'm tired of waiting for you all to understand that." He shoved me back, the violent move very unlike Melek. "Show her who Ty is, Az. Help her. It'll protect her in the end. It'll protect us all."

He didn't give me a chance to argue, just vanished without a trace.

Az? Cami whispered, distracting me from my scowl.

Cami?

Did you hear any of that?

Any of what? I asked her, my Phoenix prowling inside, his instincts on immediate alert. *Is everything okay?*

Yes... She drew out the sound. *How about now? Did you hear that?*

Your questions about my hearing?

No, my comment about the snake-vines.

I frowned. *What? I haven't heard you say anything about snake-vines.*

Excitement filtered through our connection.

Cami?

It's working! she told me. *I'm controlling my mental voice.*

Amusement touched my mouth despite the gravity of the situation. *Then I guess it's time for our next lesson, little warrior.*

And I had an idea of what that should be.

To understand Typhos, Cami needed to realize that Typhos Lucifer never lost. Regardless of what someone did to him, he always came out on top. No matter what.

So to accept him, she had to learn how to speak his language.

The first phase was in comprehending that the physical didn't matter.

Then the second phase would be an introduction into his mind.

I'm coming back, I told her. *When I arrive, my Phoenix will take over again. But I'm staying in human form.*

Okay, she replied.

I repeated the details to Ajax. He didn't acknowledge me or respond.

With a sigh, I returned to the Midnight Fae Realm.

It's going to be a long few weeks.

CHAPTER 21

CAMI

I STARED at Az on the couch, his long body seemingly uncomfortable.

He'd chosen to rest there when he'd come back from his meeting with Lucifer, leaving me and Ajax alone for the day. *Or night*, I corrected myself. *Whatever time it is.*

This realm had no sunshine. It was impossible to guess the time without it.

Not that it mattered.

Ajax and I hadn't slept at all since Az's return yesterday, both of us waiting for Typhos to magically appear and whisk us off to the Hell Fae Realm. But nothing had happened.

We'd eventually eaten, Ajax saying something about how we'd missed midnight breakfast with Shade and the others. I hadn't wanted to venture out, too concerned over what would happen next, so we'd stayed in the room and eaten in the bed.

Ajax had said he could have just ordered something from the kitchens, but instead, he'd conjured our meal because it was easier. He'd also used his magic to remove all the resulting crumbs.

Now we were enjoying a huge pizza at the table near one of the balcony doors.

I really don't think Lucifer is coming, I thought at him. *That, or he's playing some kind of long game. But I feel like we're just wasting time right now, waiting for the inevitable.*

Ajax picked up a slice of pizza, his gaze on Az. *Do you really think he's going to train you?*

It was a subtle shift in topic, but it seemed to be weighing on his mind. *I don't know. There's only one way to find out.*

I agree. He pulled his wand from his pocket and whispered a spell under his breath.

My brow furrowed as I watched a snake appear on Az's chest.

Ajax...

Shh. I've done this before, he told me.

I held my breath as the snake slithered upward, its tongue reaching out to touch Az's chin. His hand flew upward in response, the snake suddenly in Az's mouth as he shook it around like a giant worm.

My eyes widened as Ajax broke off in a fit of laughter.

The snake vanished in the next breath, leaving a panting, *angry* Az on the couch. His black eyes gleamed as he glared at Ajax, the Phoenix clearly pissed at having been woken in such a manner.

"Well, at least I know your bird is definitely in charge."

Az spit on the ground, the movement animalistic in nature despite being in human form.

"Oh, I disagree. That was hilarious," Ajax drawled, clearly responding to Az. "But it's time for you to get up anyway. Cami needs training and Shade keeps messaging me."

I frowned. *Shade's been messaging you?*

He's been touching my ear with some sort of tickling spell, he replied. *Or I assume it's him, anyway. No one else knows how to be that annoying.*

Az pushed off the couch, his tall form intimidating and drool-worthy as he stretched his arms over his head. He'd taken off his shirt, choosing to sleep in just a pair of black jeans, leaving his feet bare as well.

I didn't want to be attracted to him. I wanted to *hate* him.

But... it was kind of hard when he resembled sex. His dark hair was mussed, his face sleepy, his body *perfect*.

Ajax and I had been in the middle of playing when Az had arrived yesterday. We'd never had a chance to finish our time together. We'd been too caught up in everything that had happened since.

Keep looking at me like that and my Phoenix is going to want to engage in a different kind of training, Az said into my mind, his voice resembling a low purr.

Looking at you like what?

Like you want to eat me, little warrior.

I'm not looking at you like that.

You are, he replied as he bent to pick his shirt up off the ground. *And given that my Phoenix mated you yesterday, he's absolutely looking at you the same way. He seems pretty keen on breeding.*

Breeding? I repeated.

But he didn't elaborate. Instead, he focused on his shoes, then wandered over to steal a piece of pizza.

"Did I say you could eat?" Ajax asked.

Az grunted in reply and took a huge bite of the pizza slice.

Ajax narrowed his gaze.

Az ignored him, finishing the piece before I could blink.

Then he grabbed a second one and pointedly ate it in front of Ajax.

"I'm starting to think you're in charge again, Az," the Warden drawled. "Already reneging on our deal?"

I waited for a response, but all Az did was continue eating.

Did he reply to you mentally? I asked Ajax.

Yeah. He says his bird is hungry and if I didn't want him to eat, he shouldn't have put a pizza out on the table like an offering, Ajax muttered.

Do you believe him? I wondered.

No. He glanced at me. *Do you?*

I'm not sure what to believe anymore, I admitted.

Silence fell as Az devoured a third slice, then he stalked over to the small kitchen area adjoining our suite and opened the fridge. He pulled out a jug of juice a second later and started drinking directly from the carton. *That seems animallike,* I mused.

Yeah, Ajax agreed, his hand lifting to bat at his ear. *If Shade tickles me one more time, I'm going to kill him.*

Probably not the wisest move in his palace, I pointed out. *Especially when he has a powerful mate-circle.*

Pretty sure Zakkai would reward me if I killed Shade, Ajax muttered, standing. "Fine. *I get it,*" he said, swatting at his ear again and drawing out his wand to mutter some sort of spell.

I half expected to see a snake appear again, but nothing happened.

What did you do? I asked, frowning.

Sent Shade a little gift.

The Midnight Fae in question appeared in the suite a moment later, a bat on one shoulder and an owl on the other. "If you're going to send your familiar after me, perhaps check in with the animal first to see if he still even likes you."

Az turned around slowly in the kitchen, his nose twitching as he sniffed the air. His gaze immediately landed on the two winged creatures, a low growl vibrating from his chest.

Or perhaps he was growling at Shade.

It was hard to tell.

I almost asked Ajax, but he was too busy staring at the owl on Shade's shoulder.

Are you okay? I asked him, concerned by the pale quality of his features. For lack of a better phrase, he looked like he'd just seen a ghost.

Ajax didn't reply to me. Instead, he swallowed and took a step forward.

The owl's features ruffled in response, his little beak turning away in a clear snub.

My eyebrows lifted. *Well, that little thing has a personality on it, doesn't it?*

"You've been looking after him," Ajax said aloud, his words seeming to be for Shade.

"Of course I have. He's Draco's best friend. Just like you're my best friend." Shade cocked his head to the side. "Want to take a walk with us?"

Ajax swallowed again, then cleared his throat. "I, uh..." He shook his head, then looked my way. *Are you okay to stay here with Az for a bit?*

I glanced at the still-growling male in the kitchen. He was hyper-fixated on the owl now. *What's wrong with your Phoenix?* I asked Az.

He doesn't like the competition for your attention, Az gritted out. *He wants to rip the owl apart.*

Oh. I frowned. "Az's Phoenix doesn't appear to like the owl. So maybe a walk is a good idea?" I said aloud to Ajax.

"You two will have to learn how to get along," Shade drawled, glancing between the owl and Az in the kitchen. "Kuro might be giving Ajax the cold shoulder now, but once they repair the divide, I suspect he'll be following Ajax everywhere again."

My brow furrowed, my mind finally piecing together all of Shade's statements. *Wait... Is the owl your familiar?* I asked Ajax.

Yeah. His mental voice sounded gruff. *Kuro is mine.*
Why's he so angry with you?
He thinks I abandoned him here, Ajax muttered.

Did you?

Sort of. It's complicated. He cleared his throat. *He... he reminds me of my past. And I left all of that behind. Including him.*

A hint of remorse filtered through our link, making my heart ache a little for him. *You were healing.*

No. I was running, he replied. *Hiding from my pain. And now I'm paying the price for it.*

He cleared his throat again. "Yeah, let's go on that walk," he said before I could comment. Then he focused on Az. "If you harm so much as a hair on her head while I'm gone, I'll kill you. Understand?"

Call for me the second you think something might be wrong, he added mentally. *I'll be here.*

I nodded. As crazy as it was to try to trust Az, it was the only way to test him. We could sit here and watch him all day, waiting for Lucifer to attack or for Az to try to drag us to hell.

Or we could give him a chance to uphold his side of the bargain.

The latter might be the more dangerous option, but this was the only way we would know his true intentions.

Az bristled in the kitchen as Shade headed toward the door. "Have fun," the Midnight Fae murmured, winking before disappearing through the wood.

Literally.

Like he walked right through it without so much as casting a spell.

When Ajax followed, I lifted my eyebrows. *We can walk through the door?*

It's the Midnight Fae Realm. Nothing is what it seems here, Az replied, his bird still posturing in the kitchen. After a few seconds, he sniffed again, then went back to guzzling his juice carton.

The image had my lips curling into a grin I couldn't fight. Watching him like this was pretty humorous.

I feel you laughing at me, he muttered.

You're about to dump juice all over your face.

My Phoenix has more control than you think, he returned as his bird set the now-empty carton down. *Ready to begin your next lesson?*

"Sure," I replied out loud. "Is it another mental exercise?"

I felt him smirk in my head and caught the answering excitement in his black eyes. *No. This one will be physical. Let's go find an appropriate room to play in.*

Thirty minutes later, it was clear to me that the vines, flowers, and trees decorating the palace were more than ornamental fixtures. I swore they were alive, perhaps even monitoring our every move.

But no one stepped out to stop us; just a handful of gargoyles asked if we needed directions.

When I inquired about a sparring area, a little stone creature led us to a room where scorch marks lined the dark walls. Whereas most of the palace was covered in trees and florals, this place was a contrast of hard, stone interior. Little else occupied the space, suggesting that either whatever had been in here had been burned, or it had been purposefully kept empty.

It was the only space that wasn't covered in roots and other plant life that would have made training rather difficult. Maybe this had once been a sparring area, but I had a feeling that more recently it had been used as one of Florica's playrooms.

Because a lone teddy bear rested on its side in the middle of the room. The skylight above seemed to illuminate the toy, telling me the poor little bear had seen better days. Patches of fur had been burned off, and one of its buttons was melted, but it was clearly well loved by a certain little faeling.

I hadn't had many stuffed animals as a child—at least, they hadn't lasted very long. My mother had given me some, but my father had felt that attachments to soulless objects made me soft, so he'd preferred to infest them with demons that would then try to stab me in my sleep.

That had not gone over well.

"Is this one of Florica's playrooms?" I asked the gargoyle. I was questioning it more because I didn't want to intrude as a guest if Florica still intended to use it.

"One of many," the little creature confirmed. "I'll add a marker so others know the room is in use. If you need anything, call for Sir Fletcher."

With that, the gargoyle left.

Apparently, this space was ours. Hopefully, that was all right.

"Hmm," I hummed, bending to pick up the bear. "I don't want to risk anything happening to this." The last thing we needed was to upset a little girl who liked to play with fire. Not to mention the mother of said girl—who happened to be a very powerful queen.

I turned over the bear in my hands as I headed toward a bench along one of the walls, then nearly dropped it as the beady black eyes burned red.

What the fuck? I thought, alarmed.

At first, I assumed it was my childhood trauma flaring up, but Az's Phoenix hissed. He didn't give me a chance to react as he grabbed the stuffy and sent it careening across the room.

It exploded a moment later into a burst of fire, adding another scorch mark to the wall.

"Remind me never to have kids," I said.

Because I did *not* envy Aflora.

This "playroom" was evidently where Florica worked out her fire starter tendencies, including enchanting her toys to resemble firebombs.

The Phoenix made a strange sound as if I'd just pained him.

Az had been silent this whole time, but I nearly jumped out of my skin when his voice popped into my head. *Please, please don't bring up the topic of offspring to my Phoenix. Who is mated to you, in case you forgot.*

I turned to find the Black Phoenix looking back at me. The dangerous, ancient beast that I seemed to have gravely offended was clearly upset. His dark eyes burned with glittering embers, and shadows swirled around his feet as his mouth parted on a pant.

"I didn't mean..." My voice trailed off when the Phoenix's fists clenched.

He's an animal, Cami, Az explained. *The entire endgame of mating a capable female is offspring. Ajax is a fellow warrior —one charged to eventually protect any faelings—but you, you're more than that. You're the first female he's found to be compatible in thousands of years.*

My eyes widened. "*What?*" I screeched. A part of me wanted to react to the "thousands of years" comment. I hadn't realized Az was *that* old, even though that technically made sense if he'd been with Lucifer from the beginning, but the news about the claim on my *reproductive organs* felt more pressing.

The Phoenix tilted his head, a fraction of his anger ebbing with Az's words. He seemed to find it obvious that I was to be the mother of his future child.

Or faeling.

Or... birdling?

Ugh.

Rage flared inside my chest. "Let me get this straight. The only reason you've been so nice to me, protected me, and *bit* me, is because you want my *uterus*?"

I wasn't sure if I was talking to Az or his Phoenix.

No, I was definitely talking to his Phoenix. This whole time he'd been on my side, but not in a million years would I have imagined *this* was why.

His head tilted the other way, the Phoenix seeming to be hurt by my conclusion. *Of course not, Cami. You're perfect.*

A bit of my anger evaporated at that simple statement.

Because I could feel the emotions and assurance that came with it. He hadn't hesitated. He hadn't stumbled.

He meant it.

You... You think I'm perfect?

The Black Phoenix had control over Az's body, and he lifted a hand to trace his fingers over my lower lip.

We both do, Az confirmed. *Which is why I'm not surprised my Phoenix wants to breed you, but that doesn't have to be anytime soon. Or any time at all, if you don't want it.*

The Phoenix made a sound of disagreement, but it was more like a disgruntled noise, one that said, *It's just a matter of time. You'll see.*

I would let Az deal with his horny bird, one that acted on instinct.

If Az said that he'd mated me for more than just my ability to procreate, then I'd believe him.

As his finger continued to graze my lip, I didn't realize my tongue had flicked out to taste him until I'd already done it.

Careful, Az purred in my head. *Or my bird is going to—*

He leaned in to kiss me, but I dodged out of the way. "What are you doing?" I asked, both disturbed that I'd almost let him and thrilled by the prospect.

I reminded myself that I was supposed to be mad at Az. That he had magically bound Ajax and forced him to watch while I'd been on display in the Hell Fae Kingdom.

But I was also his mate, so my body certainly wasn't listening very well to that logic.

This must be what Az struggles with on a daily basis. His primal instincts were literally half of his soul.

He ashed behind me, sneaking in a nip on my earlobe, making me yelp. *Training starts now, Cami.*

When I turned around to swat him away, he wasn't there.

He ashed again, this time clipping my shoulder with his teeth. "Ow!" I yelled, growing irritated.

He did it again, then again, biting me in more sensitive places.

My hip.

My wrist.

When he caught me by surprise and sent me tumbling over, he lightly bit me on the inside of my thigh.

"Stop it, Az," I hissed.

Tell that to my bird, he said in my head. *Ajax put him in charge. If you want him to stop, then* stop *him.*

I realized this was part of Az's training, meaning he wanted me to fight back.

That, I could do.

I threw a punch at him, but he simply ashed out of view.

The Phoenix appeared behind me, earning a growl from my chest as I turned on him. The momentum of my body wasn't in my favor, but as I suspected, he ashed out of sight again.

Nice try, Az said. *But Lucifer can disappear and reappear wherever he wants, similar to Ajax—just like my Phoenix can ash. You're not going to win in physical combat no matter how much experience you may have. Not against one of us.*

"Only if you allow yourself to be distracted," I replied, catching the Phoenix looking down my shirt as I threw myself at him again.

His Phoenix's dark eyes flicked up to me before he molted out of existence, only to reappear a few feet out of reach.

"Stop running," I told him, growing even more irritated.

Not really at him, but at the fact that he was much harder to catch than I'd realized.

Not until you understand, Az cryptically replied.

I came at him, this time with a low kick that should have caught him off guard.

He ashed out of sight again.

Maybe he thought he could wear me down.

"You want to play this game?" I said, tracking him when he glanced to the left. "We'll see who gets tired first." As everyone liked to remind me lately, I wasn't even half human. I was something *other*, and I could play this game all night.

The Phoenix didn't respond. He simply ashed again, so I followed—but I'd been wrong about the direction he'd chosen. He reappeared on my right instead of my left.

Fake-out maneuver, I decided.

Maybe he was evading me right now, but I was learning. So I chased him, trying to find a pattern to his endless tactics. After at least thirty minutes, the room swirled with soot from his magic that made it hard to see. I tore off the bottom of my shirt and wrapped it around my forehead, occasionally using it to rub the particles from my eyes as sweat rolled down my temples.

There has to be a pattern.

Despite my best efforts, I couldn't find one. Every moment I thought I had him, he ashed out of the way again.

The rays of the moon shifted as we danced, informing me that hours had gone by. Despite my hearty breakfast, lunch must have passed some time ago, and my stomach rumbled in complaint.

But I wasn't going to stop. Not until I won.

While I had decent stamina, my chest was heaving by the end of it. Sweat made my shirt cling to my skin, and all I wanted to do was scream.

I'd had ample sleep, but it had been plagued by

nightmares. Not to mention all I'd been through just the day before.

And the days before that.

I was beaten down, even if I didn't want to admit it. Exhaustion made my arms and legs feel like weights. I was only growing slower, while the Phoenix looked just as he had this morning. Tired, yes, but his fatigue was more emotional than physical.

And right now, he seemed determined to make me *understand*. Whatever that meant.

He watched me with those dark, pensive eyes. A pristine shirt unbuttoned at the top was somehow free of the ash that drifted through the room. Every time he reappeared, he paced around me, taunting me with his predatory stare, and then he vanished again.

He hadn't even broken a sweat, the bastard.

The Phoenix appeared in front of me a moment later, close enough for me to strike. I tried—by all the gods, I tried—but my strength was gone. My knuckles brushed his cheek, and I collapsed into his arms.

"You're an asshole," I grumbled as I allowed my eyes to shut for a minute. "Just... need to catch my breath. Then I'm going to kick your ass."

Mm-hmm, Az murmured.

The Phoenix kissed the crown of my head, not appearing to be bothered by the sticky ash that clung to my damp skin.

My Phoenix thinks you need a shower. But I disagree.

"Good. Because I still have some ass kicking to—" I began, but Az cut me off.

You need a bath, Az corrected. *And a massage.*

"I hate you both," I murmured, mostly because I had no fight in me to decline.

A bath and a massage sounded fucking fantastic.

The Phoenix effortlessly scooped me into his arms as he ashed again, and this time we reappeared in my room.

Except, Ajax was waiting for us, and he glowered at us with his arms outstretched. "I'll take it from here. Hand her over."

"No," the beast said. The word was quiet but edged with violence.

I knew it wasn't Az talking. Az didn't want to let me go any more than his beast did, but his bird finally had me in his arms—fae arms—and he wanted to pet me.

Protect me.

Finish what he'd started.

And right now, Ajax was standing in the way of that.

"Please," I grumbled against his chest. "No more fighting." I really didn't want to be in the middle of one of their quarrels again.

Sometimes it was fun, but at the moment? I suspected it would end in a bloodbath between mates. We had more pressing matters to deal with, like a furious Lucifer, who could find a loophole—at any second—in the deal Az had made with him.

And after meeting Queen Aflora and our other hosts, I really didn't want Lucifer to melt this place to the ground. Not that Zakkai would let him, but I knew what Lucifer was capable of.

I didn't want to see how far he would go when he decided to come for me.

Ajax held out his arms. "Don't make me ask again." The threat hummed between us. Ajax still had access to the taming spell. He wouldn't use it, not unless he had to.

The Phoenix's jaw flexed as if he was going to resist, but maybe Az was trying to reason with him. I could hear the hum of power that went with his coaxing voice, as well as a thread of magic I didn't understand.

I found myself following it, curious as to where it led.

To his soul.

His soul burned, and not just because he was part Phoenix. Because we'd hurt him.

The notion felt ridiculous after all he'd done, but it seemed like I was missing something, too.

How much did we really know about Az? About his past? About *why* he was so damn loyal to Lucifer?

It made me wonder if we'd gone too far. If I wasn't careful, I might start feeling sorry for him.

Or entertaining other feelings, too.

No feelings, I chided myself. Not after learning I was a glorified Black Phoenix baby maker.

But he said he mated me because I'm perfect...

Ugh. I felt so damn conflicted.

Magic worked underneath Az's skin, and for a moment, it felt similar to strands in a web. It stretched and went taut before he finally moved and held me out to Ajax.

Did Az do something? Is he up *to something?*

Due to the terms of the agreement, the Phoenix was still in full control. Az must have reasoned with him, or otherwise done something to force him to comply. But there wasn't any reasoning with a bird, was there?

Then how had he gotten the beast to listen?

Too tired. Don't care...

I felt weightless as the two males exchanged me, like some sort of precious gift they shared.

Az's voice swept like a caress in my mind in response to that thought. *When you realize this is forever, Cami, I won't be sharing you. Not at first, anyway. Our mating will be just the two of us. Ajax will join after, and then the both of us will make you come until you black out or beg us to stop. Even then, we won't.*

A swallow worked down my throat as I tried to pretend I hadn't heard Az say that.

But I certainly had.

And if I was being honest with myself, I liked it.

I'm so fucked.

CHAPTER 22

CAMI

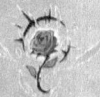

Az's Phoenix had complied. Although, based on the low burn of hatred in his dark eyes, he didn't like it.

Ajax easily held me in his arms, and I couldn't help but relax into his embrace. I felt so *tired*.

I wasn't sure if Ajax knew about the *breeding* issue. If he did, I imagined he would have been pissed. So maybe he hadn't considered it.

Instead, he appeared satisfied that the Phoenix had obeyed his order. The deal we'd made seemed to be working as intended—keeping Az in the back of his mind while his bird remained in control. Although, that was proving to be annoying and possibly problematic.

His bird acted on instinct, and given the crescent shape mark on my wrist, it felt dangerous to have him in charge for long.

But he would be until we trusted Az, and that certainly wasn't ever going to happen. Was it?

"What was the focus of your training today?" Ajax asked as he peered down at me.

His gaze jerked to Az before I could answer, making me

assume that Az had answered mentally. They seemed to talk for a while until Ajax frowned.

Az's features were unreadable as he molted into his beast form and then ashed out of view.

Az? I asked, but he'd put a wall up again.

"What did you say to him?" I murmured as I tried not to fall asleep on Ajax out of sheer exhaustion.

Ajax narrowed his dark blue eyes as he regarded me. "I asked him why his beast looked like he wanted to peck my eyes out. He said he would handle it, then added that we needed time to heal, so he was going to give it to us."

"Then why do you look so pissed?" That didn't sound so bad.

"Because his bird is damn disrespectful."

I sighed. "*Ajax.*" Whatever else they'd discussed had really pissed him off.

Had he found out about the breeding issue?

What breeding issue? Ajax asked with quiet lethality.

Shit.

"It's... I don't want to talk about that right now. Whatever just happened between you guys, can we make it a truce? I don't want this to turn into a dick-measuring contest."

"We're not measuring dicks," Ajax said with a straight face.

I rolled my eyes, then closed them because everything *hurt*.

"He's doing what we asked of him. Lucifer hasn't come to burn this place to the ground, we weren't dragged back to Hell, and Az and his Phoenix have been trying. He started my training, even though I'm not entirely sure I learned much today."

Other than the fact that I'm not going to survive a one-on-one fight against Lucifer.

I felt like that was something I already knew, but tonight's training really made that hit home.

Ajax huffed. "He thinks just because he mated you, he can have you."

"And my babies," I murmured, nuzzling into him. *Gods, he smells so good. Like mint. I should lather him with white rum and see if he tastes like a mojito.*

Ajax raised an eyebrow. "What? Is that what you meant by *breeding*?" he asked, startling me from my strangely specific fantasy.

"Yes? No? Just... I'm too tired for this conversation, Ajax," I murmured.

A low growl vibrated in his chest, but he didn't press me further regarding my comment about babies. "*Anyway*. I'll still help you with that bath and massage, if you want it. I've had... a day."

I blinked up at him through bleary eyes. "Where did you go?"

I most certainly wanted to take him up on his offer, but now I was curious.

He shrugged. "I'll tell you, but first, let's get you washed up. You smell like a toasted marshmallow."

I wrinkled my nose. "Excuse me?"

"You heard me," he said, a small smile appearing on his kissable lips.

He carried me to the oversized bathroom and helped me undress and untangle my twisted ponytail. It felt natural, like we did this every day.

And since his teasing me about marshmallows made me hungry, he also conjured food for me—as well as a low table and a lengthwise cushion for me to sit. The spread was gorgeous and included a traditional marshmallow-and-graham-cracker s'more with melted chocolate that was human-worthy.

I ate everything on my plate while a huge basin with built-in benches filled up with water. We didn't use the shower this time. A bath would be much more relaxing. And I didn't mind that I was naked while I ate, either, especially when Ajax hand-fed me grapes.

I didn't tell him that Melek had done the same thing. That would probably only add to his dick-measuring complexities.

And while I hadn't seen Melek's dick, I had a feeling it would compete.

Stop thinking about dicks, I chided myself.

Yes, stop, Az purred in my head, apparently having dismantled his wall in time to hear my thought about dicks. *Unless you're thinking about mine, too. Then, please, continue. And Melek's dick is bigger than Ajax's, since you were wondering,* he added, making me choke on a grape.

"You okay over there?" Ajax asked.

He only wore a towel when he endured Typhos's anger for you, so it wasn't that hard to see, Az continued. *Well, it was definitely* hard. *And by "endured his anger," I mean Ty fucked him. Brutally. While thinking of you, no doubt.*

I rubbed at my temple as if I could push Az out while Ajax stared at me, waiting for an answer. "Mm-hmm," I murmured, pretending that I wasn't getting all hot and bothered.

For some reason, the idea of seeing Melek take on Lucifer in that context was... intense. And knowing that they were thinking of me wasn't entirely unpleasant.

"Yep. Totally fine," I said, grabbing a finger sandwich.

Enjoy putting things in your mouth, little warrior. I'm sure Ajax will make for a nice dessert.

I stared at my sandwich and frowned.

Why was he teasing me? Az was so fucking confusing. One minute he was furious, and the next he wanted to play games.

Ignoring him, I finished eating while Az went back to whatever he was doing. I didn't feel so bad now that Az had left me in Ajax's care, which included food.

And a bath.

It steamed and rippled with its invitation, complete with multicolored rose petals, because of course everything in this place had flowers in some shape or form.

But I didn't mind it.

Ajax ushered me into the shower first under protest, which quickly died on my lips as I finally felt clean. It would have been a shame to get soot all over the pretty petals. "Okay, yeah. Maybe a day of chasing Az's stupid Phoenix around a fire-scorched room wasn't the best idea. All it did was wear me out. And cover me in ash."

"If wearing you out was the lesson for today, I could have done that," he said with a mischievous grin as he guided me back to the bath. "And it would have been much more fun."

Ajax stripped off his clothes, not seeming to mind that I took full advantage of the view. My gaze lingered on his hardening cock that proudly displayed a barbell I loved to feel inside me.

If he was trying to distract me from feeling like a total failure, it was working.

"Now, turn around," he said, swirling his finger.

Rolling my eyes again, I complied, then slipped into the warm water.

Oh, Fae, this is nice.

My muscles relaxed as the soothing heat swept over me. Ajax joined me, then settled onto one of the underwater benches as his hands worked magic on my shoulders.

The petals floated around us as Ajax's body lingered behind mine, only his hands touching me as he kneaded the sore knots.

I moaned in response. "Where did you learn to massage?" I asked, leaning into his strong grip.

He chuckled. "I'm just reacting to your body. When I do... this," he said, pressing on a particularly tender spot. I responded with a guttural moan as pleasure and pain surged through my muscles. "And you sound like that? I know I've done something correctly."

"Yes. Do that again," I mumbled.

Ajax continued working his magic hands, wringing moans from me and sending my toes curling until I was completely languid against him. I would have melted into the perpetually warm bath had he not remained a rock behind me.

Is he rock-hard for you, too? Az teased.

Fucking male.

He was supposed to be letting Ajax and me heal, but he wasn't doing a very good job of leaving me alone.

Probably because I kept thinking about sex, which was a siren call to Az and his bird.

Get out of my head. I'm trying to enjoy my evening, I thought back, then imagined a massive wall.

I sensed something beating against it, then the echo ceased.

Two could play at these mind games.

Victorious that I'd walled Az out, at least temporarily, I settled in closer to Ajax. I rested my head on his shoulder as his chest pressed against my back. The sensual promise of his barbell nudged against my spine, as did the length of his arousal, but he didn't stop his massage.

Which had now gone to my chest, not that I was complaining.

"I'm sorry I left you alone with him," he murmured as he worked on the tender spots just on the sides of my breasts, deeper into the pectoral tissue. I flinched as he reached another achy spot. He eased up on the pressure but kept working at the area until I relaxed.

"I doubt much training would have happened had you been there," I countered. "You two only seem to be able to fight."

Or fuck, my brain added.

Az might have heard my addition, but he didn't intrude on my moment with Ajax again. I could sense him resting somewhere now, more content being in his bird form than his fae one.

I could also tell that it was effortless to let the Phoenix take over that way. And in effect, it made it easier for him to ignore all the roiling emotions I also felt swirling in his fiery soul.

I wasn't the only one who had been forcibly mated, I realized. It had occurred to me before, but now it was really starting to sink in.

The Phoenix had bitten me, as well as Ajax.

Az hadn't decided to do that, leaving him just as helpless as us in all of this.

Not that I'm going to feel sorry for him. Cheeky bastard.

"I hope he wasn't too difficult," Ajax continued while his massage moved to cup my breasts more fully.

My nipples beaded in response, dying for his attention.

"He was trying to tell me something," I said with a sigh. With a full stomach and now a warm bath that included a naked and flirty Ajax, it helped me to not be so sour about my brutal night with Az. "Something that I heard loud and clear. Lucifer is untouchable."

Which made me feel even more like we weren't going to make it out of this in one piece.

Ajax hummed, his warm breath against my ear making me shiver. "It's an important lesson. I learned that one the hard way."

I sighed, losing the ability to care about Lucifer and my problems.

But Ajax was still tense, even if his movements were aimed at giving me relaxation and pleasure. His arousal was obvious, but something was definitely bothering him.

"Are you going to tell me what you were up to today?" I asked.

His hands swirled over my breasts, pausing just as his fingers brushed my nipples. Pleasure made my toes tingle. "Shade tricked me into going to visit my parents."

I leaned my head back so I could peer up at him. "Your parents?"

He nodded. "Their statues at the graveyard, anyway. Emelyn is buried there, too."

Oh. Shit.

"Ajax, I'm sorry. I didn't mean—"

He slid one hand between my legs and pressed directly on my clit. I sucked in a breath, all questions thrust immediately from my mind.

"I'd rather focus on you right now," he whispered in my ear, his touch circling the inside of my thigh while his left hand continued to brush my nipple. "On us."

Yes, please.

My thought hadn't intended to go to him, but he heard it and obeyed my desire by kissing my neck, then *biting*.

I loved that he could bite me now. As much as he wanted, anywhere he wanted. As *often* as he wanted.

Me, too, little rebel.

Me, too.

CHAPTER 23

AZ

CAMI MIGHT HAVE WALLED me out, but her pleasure still thrummed through my veins, satiating my beast throughout the day. While he wanted to join, Ajax's emotional state had proved that they needed this time together right now.

They would help each other heal.

And eventually, they would hopefully help each other trust me again.

My Phoenix and I went hunting in the interim, the craving for fresh meat coming from my inner beast more than me.

We swooped through the Midnight Fae Realm, our wings wide and casting violent shadows along the ground. There were so many creatures here to choose from, but the magic wafting off of them gave my Phoenix pause.

He didn't like the scent.

Too flowery, I decided. *Like the Midnight Fae Queen.*

Perhaps hunting wouldn't happen today.

Maybe I could steal some food from Ajax.

They appeared to be finished with their fifth—*or was that*

their sixth?—session. They'd definitely need something to eat soon.

Or perhaps I could just steal something along the way.

The Midnight Fae Palace had an open kitchen and a very spacious dining room.

I was in the middle of flying there when Ajax said, *I can sense you hovering.*

If I were in human form, I would have lifted a brow at him. *I'm flying above the palace right now.*

Hence the hovering, he muttered.

I snorted and continued on my journey, shifting into my human form when I reached the kitchen. I'd given my bird control, but we seemed to be working together more than against each other, causing us to align with one another in our every movement.

It was... strange.

Foreign, even.

But I liked it.

Mating had completed me in a way I hadn't anticipated. The only thing missing now was the actual *relationship* that usually came with claiming a mate.

Releasing a long breath, I snatched a plate of eggs and bacon from a random burner and ashed back to the hallway outside the bedroom. *Let me know when I can come inside,* I told Ajax as I sat on the floor to eat my stolen meal.

He didn't reply, but I heard the shower turn on in the room.

Cami's moans soon followed, causing my bird to purr with approval.

Show-off, I muttered at Ajax.

She tastes so damn good, Az. Like you wouldn't believe...

Asshole, I returned.

His chuckle reverberated in my head, making my lips twitch a little. Mostly because that sounded like the Ajax I knew. Which hopefully meant we were getting closer to making up.

I reveled in Cami's pleasure as I continued to eat, my cock hard between my legs. It took significant effort not to reach down and stroke myself. But I really didn't want to provide any of the lurking Midnight Fae with that kind of a show.

Instead, I finished my breakfast and waited for permission to enter like a good little pet Phoenix.

It almost reminded me of Vivaxia and all the times she'd commanded me to roost in solitude.

But this was different. There was an undercurrent of anticipation now as I waited for Ajax to grant me entry.

His climax finally echoed in my mind, his hungry growl one that had my balls tightening in response. Because I knew that sound. I *loved* that sound.

Fuck, you're killing me, I told him, my hands fisting in the air as I refused to let them roam.

Good, he replied, his mental voice breathless.

A litany of sensual threats lined up in my thoughts, most of them ideas for how to repay the favor later.

Someday, I placated myself. *When I've earned the right to touch him and Cami again.*

Then I would have my revenge.

For now, I dealt with the pain—both in my groin and in my heart.

I pressed my palm over the offended organ in my chest, my eyes squeezing closed. I *hated* how things were between me and my mates. It all felt wrong.

However, I didn't have a choice. I had to embrace it. I had to *fix* it.

Once we're dressed, we can discuss today's training, Ajax said. *But no more "lessons." You're going to teach Cami and me something useful. Something we can use when we fight Lucifer.*

I nearly sighed.

The entire point of our last lesson was that there was no fighting Typhos. I also wasn't even sure I was capable of teaching something that could harm one of my mates.

Rather than focus on all that, I repeated, *Us? Does that mean you'll be joining the fun?*

Ajax scoffed in my mind. *I wouldn't call it* fun. *But I'd rather spend the night with you than with Shade.*

His admission intrigued me. *Oh? Did Shade do something?*

Yes. He didn't elaborate.

Want to talk about it?

No.

Right, I replied.

And it's none of your business, Ajax added, like he was reminding himself that I wasn't someone he could confide in anymore. Not that he had confided in me much over the last decade anyway.

Unfortunately for him, it sort of *was* my business now that we were mates. Even before, I'd always felt close to Ajax. Not quite protective—because he didn't need protecting—but possessive, perhaps.

And I did not like the idea of Shade meddling with my mate.

Rather than push it, I simply replied, *Okay.*

I'd drag more out of Ajax when the time was right.

I have an idea for today's training, I said, focusing on that instead of Ajax's issues with Shade.

Good, Ajax replied. *Cami is almost ready.*

Almost? I echoed.

A spike of pleasure followed, telling me he was about to engage in yet another round.

Seriously? I growled.

My cock immediately hardened again, my body—and beast—intrigued by the arousal thrumming through my veins.

Ajax was trying to prove a point, one I heard loud and clear.

I'll be waiting outside, I hissed at him.

You can have your fun, I added as a thought, only for myself. *Because it's just a matter of time before I repay the favor.*

I found a pair of pants and shoes waiting for me outside, the size too perfect a match to be a coincidence.

Shade, I guessed.

The fabric was probably bespelled, but I put it on anyway. Then I paced, waiting for Ajax and Cami to join me.

When they did, I didn't say a word, instead cocking my head to the side and leading them to a place at the edge of the palace grounds.

It was a location I'd spotted while flying—a space outside the precious courtyards and closer to the wild. There was a forest just beyond the clearing, the vast wilderness riddled with power and a variety of creatures. I'd considered hunting there, but Aflora's essence seemed to be laced into every leaf. And I didn't want to offend the Midnight Fae Queen by accidentally killing one of her pets.

I paused in the center of the clearing and faced Ajax and Cami.

Today's lesson would require enough wood for a fire, but not so much as to create an inferno. The damp leaves would make things sizzle, although it wouldn't be enough to quench the flames.

Not when I planned on releasing something that neither Ajax nor Cami had ever experienced before.

An arrangement of rocks strangled by roots gave me the

perfect place to work. I stood between two massive trees that had found purchase despite this area's difficult terrain.

"So, you said you had an idea for today's training," Ajax said, folding his arms. "What is it?"

He wore his battle leathers today. I knew they would be equipped with many hidden blades, as well as his wand that was tucked away, probably in his boot. It interested me that he didn't wear his Midnight Fae robes now that we were back on his home grounds. It suggested he still didn't feel comfortable here.

I considered that for just a moment before focusing on Cami.

Time to train, I thought at my Phoenix.

He immediately took the reins, my animal lifting my arm and snapping my fingers together. A tree at the edge of the clearing went up in flames a second later, causing Ajax and Cami to spin around.

Put it out, I told them.

They glanced at each other before looking at me. "I thought you said that learning to fight Lucifer wouldn't have anything to do with fire," Cami said.

Put it out, I repeated as my Phoenix puffed out my chest. *There's a point to it. I promise.*

Cami scowled and Ajax appeared even less amused. "Aflora isn't going to appreciate you burning up her property," he informed me. "I'll make sure she knows this was *your* idea."

I snorted inside. *Fine. Now stop wasting time and put out the damn fire.*

It was vital for today's training, assuming they could survive the first task. They needed to master this lesson in order for the next step of my plan to fall into place.

A plan that I hoped ended with deliverance.

Not death.

Although, when Cami unleashed her first attempt to calm

the flames, it became apparent that this was going to take a while.

Because instead of cooling the flames with water or something similar, she used warmth to stoke them higher.

"That worked on the Marsh Lands portal," she said, her lips twisted.

This isn't a portal, I said into her mind. *It's Phoenixfire.*

But she didn't listen.

Instead, she tried a similar spell, making me sigh inside.

At this rate, we were all going to burn.

CHAPTER 24

CAMI

I DON'T GET IT, I snarled in my mind, tired of this endless game of fires.

Every effort I'd made to extinguish the Phoenix's flames had only made matters worse. At least Ajax had worked a spell to keep the fires from expanding and consuming the whole property. He could contain it and keep it from spreading, but we couldn't put it out.

As evidenced by the five trees that had ignited and now sizzled into vibrant displays of reds, blues, and golds.

I'd never seen fire like this. It reached for the sky, the branches blistering with flames that left the air smelling like burnt embers.

Put it out, Az said for the thousandth fucking time.

"I'm fucking trying!" I snapped back, memories of my childhood coming back to haunt me.

That everglade exercise with my father—where he'd dropped me in the middle of the swampy lands and set everything on fire around me—seemed to have been a defining event from my past.

Or maybe it was because playing with flames was a fun pastime for the Hell Fae.

Regardless, I officially hated fire.

Ajax panted beside me, his torso bright pink. He'd peeled off the top part of his battle leathers because the fireproof material had started to melt into his skin.

Shit. How am I supposed to handle this when even Ajax is having a hard time?

The heat from the fires was way too hot now, threatening to consume us if this continued much longer.

Ajax paced the ash-covered ground, his frustration palpable. Every now and then, he hurled insults at Az, but the Shifter Fae said nothing.

Aflora is going to be furious, I thought, eyeing the flaming trees.

Look closely, Az sighed into my mind. *What damage has been done?*

I blinked at the glittering leaves on the branches, my lips curling down. The tree wasn't really burning...? *How...?*

Just put out the fire, Cami.

If you say that to me one more time... I wasn't sure how to finish that threat.

The Phoenix seemed unfazed by the heat, which made sense. Because this was Phoenixfire, after all.

And I had no fucking clue how to combat it.

I had tried everything. Water spells. Warmth spells, like I had done with the fires in the Everglades and the Marsh Lands.

Ice, dirt, sandstorms—*everything*.

Not everything, Az corrected. Apparently, I was now failing lesson one—safeguarding my thoughts.

If you're talking about Lucifer's source, no. I'm not touching that with a ten-foot pole, I said. *That's a lesson I've already learned.*

Az hummed in my mind. *I wasn't talking about that, no. If anything, that would make the fire hotter, not squelch it.*

Great. So then what the fuck are we supposed to do? Even Ajax had tried a few tricks, but none of them had worked.

"How does this help us learn anything about fighting Lucifer?" I demanded as I brushed sweat from my brow. Maybe there was a lesson to be learned here, but I wasn't comprehending it.

The Phoenix simply watched us with those intense black eyes of his. I knew Az was back there somewhere, too, even if I couldn't see a glimmer of the purple irises of his spirit.

If I tell you, then it'll ruin the point of today's training, Az said, infuriating me more. *Did you learn nothing from the last one?*

The last lesson had been that Lucifer was untouchable. I wasn't sure what that had to do with this.

Unless...

Maybe I'm not supposed to fight it? I thought, causing Ajax to glance at me. Because yeah, he'd probably overheard that, too. Just like Az undoubtedly had. I'd fix the *safeguarding* problem later.

"Maybe we need to work together," Ajax suggested.

The Phoenix went still at his comment, which suggested that Ajax was onto something.

I nodded. "Okay. Take my hand."

Ajax did as I requested, slipping his fingers through mine while the fires roared all around us.

I couldn't see the moon anymore. The smoke blotted out the sky, and even the ground beneath my boots felt hot and unsteady. The warmth bled through the soles and scorched my feet. I did my best to ignore it, but I wanted nothing more than to escape this growing inferno.

But Phoenixfire didn't burn like real fire did. It didn't spread in the same pattern. It seemed to jump to new locations, flaring up without warning before delving into the earth again.

Each time it sparked to life, my heart leaped and intense heat swept through my system.

The Phoenix walked straight through the flames, seeming at home in them as they turned blue around his fingers. His clothes burned off his body, making me swallow when I took in his naked form.

Pay attention, little warrior, Az said with a pleased lilt to his voice.

My jaw clenched, and I yanked my attention back to Ajax's blue-black eyes. "Follow my lead," I said.

Ajax nodded.

I recited a spell, one that I'd just thought of after watching Az step through the fire.

Fire walker.

The spell was one that was about indulging the flames instead of fighting them. Once, my father had set a trap, and the only way out of it had been across hot coals.

I'd nearly burned off my feet before he'd given me the damn fire walker spell.

Reciting it now gave me mixed feelings. I hated how much I used the things I'd learned from my father. So much of my childhood had been a battle and a literal fight for survival.

But in his own way, he'd been trying to prepare me for what he'd known was coming.

Bet you didn't know it would end up like this, though, I thought.

Still, it would be stupid not to make use of what I had learned. If I ever found my father, I would give him a piece of my mind and show him exactly what I thought about his deal with Lucifer.

One more reason to stay alive.

The fires crept closer as I recited the words, making my

skin ache with its intense heat. I adapted the fire walker spell to consume my whole body and allow my skin to swallow the flames.

A cool breeze rushed over my skin when Ajax countered it with a shield spell. I stopped chanting and opened my eyes to look at him.

"No, let the fire come," I told him.

The Phoenix grinned, showcasing a row of straight white teeth.

Yes, that's my good girl, Az praised. *You're learning.*

My teeth ground together at his use of *good girl,* but I was too focused on the fire to chastise him.

Ajax frowned beside me, but his protection spell dropped a moment later.

I knew he was trusting me, and I hoped like hell this didn't get us both killed.

But I also knew Az wouldn't let that happen. He was trying to teach us something.

And he'd said himself that his Phoenix's soul was now intertwined with ours. Killing us would hurt his own animal, something I doubted he'd ever allow to happen.

Heat flared all around me, becoming unbearable.

I gritted my teeth.

Agony raked up my legs, then my hips, as the flames grew.

"Az!" Ajax shouted, a warning bite in his tone.

The Black Phoenix joined us as he stepped through the fire. He rested one hand on Ajax's shoulder, then another on mine.

Accept it, Az instructed, confirming what I'd thought would finally help us put these fires out.

The only way to end them was to *consume* them.

Digging my nails into Ajax's palm, he gave me an encouraging nod, one I could barely see, obscured as it was by the billowing air.

Setting my jaw, I tried to accept the burn, but it felt as if my skin was blistering and unfurling against the flames.

Fiery daggers scraped up my body, ruthlessly spearing into my skin, and the fire entered me. A scream erupted from my throat as I threw back my head.

I was burning alive.

It hurts!

Hold strong, Cami, Az encouraged. *You're doing it. And you're... beautiful.*

I couldn't see what I looked like, and I didn't fucking care. All I knew was agony. All I knew was *pain.*

You're beautiful bathed in my flames, Az said. *You both are.*

I was pretty sure he was a sadistic maniac, because I most certainly was dying a gruesome, horrible death. Ajax endured the claw of my nails, but surely he was burning alive just like I was.

I think I hate you, I told Az.

I accept your hatred, he returned. *But don't stop, little warrior. Embrace the heat.*

The pain consumed me, but after what felt like several minutes of agony, I realized that I should already be dead.

Yet I was very much alive.

And my skin isn't melting.

Ajax heaved a breath, echoing my own exertion. He held on to me while Az remained at our side.

The fires cooled, but not because they'd been quenched.

They'd disappeared... *into us.*

Dark, black streaks marred the ground, spanning out in a massive pattern that had been formed by the flames.

We stood in a triad circle, three points on overlapping magical waves that formed a knot.

Magic unfurled and I blinked up at it, seeing those threads again.

Is everything made of string? I wondered.

Lucifer's source had felt like a bright strand. And then other magical elements seemed to consistently introduce themselves to me. Maybe it was more of Lucifer's source interfering with my mind, or maybe this was simply how magic worked.

And I can see it.

"This is... fascinating," Ajax admitted. His dark eyes glowed with new light, making him impossible to look away from.

Az was right. It *was* beautiful.

"Why have you never used Phoenixfire on me before?" Ajax asked Az, being the first to back away. His hands dropped to his side, causing ash to fly through the air around him. His clothes had been burned off, just like mine. Like we had all been reborn. "It would have made sparring more interesting."

The Phoenix's hand remained on my shoulder, but his focus was on Ajax.

"It would have killed me?" Ajax asked, seeming to repeat Az's mental answer. "Then why didn't it kill me now?"

This time Az's response entered my mind as well. *Because you're mated to me.* The beast's dark gaze swept over me and then Ajax. *You both are.*

And now, somehow, it felt real that we belonged to him.

Not just Az, but to the Black Phoenix. His bite had claimed us, but his fires had *purged* us.

Swallowing, I watched as the threads of magic slowly faded away, but the new burn inside my soul remained.

Yesterday had been about learning that I couldn't touch Lucifer.

Tonight had been a lesson in accepting the flames instead of fighting them.

What lesson are you trying to teach, Az?

Because this certainly didn't feel like a way to protect myself against Lucifer.

It felt more like a lesson in letting others in and giving them access to my very soul.

Acceptance, he whispered back to me. *It's a lesson on acceptance and trust.*

And how will that protect me in the future? Because all it did was leave me feeling more vulnerable than ever.

You now have access to my Phoenixfire, Cami. Trust me— it'll protect you when you need it. Simply call upon that mark in your soul, and it'll be yours to command. Just like my ashes and my beast.

CHAPTER 25

CAMI

TWO WEEKS LATER

The dreams had started the night of the Phoenixfire.

At first, I'd frozen, thinking the dream had been real. That Lucifer had found me. But as I'd slowly processed my surroundings, I'd realized that nothing about the situation had made sense.

I'd been naked—that much hadn't surprised me.

But he'd been... *smiling*.

His lips curling in promise. His words whisper-soft against my exposed skin. His compliments a sensual kiss to my senses.

Something had happened when Az marked me with his Phoenixfire. Something drastic. I couldn't define it. But it'd somehow brought me closer to Lucifer.

Or perhaps it was simply my growing connection to Az that was wreaking havoc on my mind.

He was linked to Lucifer, which made me somewhat connected to him, too.

Melek as well.

Both males seemed hell-bent on making me see their Hell Fae King in a new light.

Between Az's lessons on survival—all of which seemed to

link back to Lucifer in some way—and Melek's sporadic visits, I'd discerned the similarities and determined that their common goal wasn't just to teach me how to survive against Lucifer, but also how to *understand* him.

Which had to be why I kept dreaming of the intimidating male.

Oh, but I wasn't only dreaming about him; I was *romanticizing* him and his power.

Because every time I closed my eyes, a different side of Lucifer was there, waiting for me. One that was so unreal I doubted it was even a side of Lucifer that actually existed.

Whether it was real or fabricated, tonight proceeded exactly as the rest had. I was trapped inside my own mind as I mindlessly *consumed* raw power. Flames kissed my naked skin, leaving me caged in by muscular arms that burned with rugged fire.

I looked up to see the Hell Fae King gazing down at me. His wings were real in this dream. They spread behind him, magnificent and full, with white plumes that appeared plush enough to sink my fingers into. The urge to test the soft down for myself made my fingers itch.

But I didn't dare move.

We rested on a bed of liquid flames. The sheets might have resembled red satin in another life, but everything moved and curled with heat. Nothing about the dream felt ethereal, though.

It was all too real. Heat washed over me, seeping into me as some unknown void yawned from deep within my soul and sucked down the power, filling me with fiery energy and dangerous embers.

Imbibing the flames only caused them to grow fiercer, *stronger,* threatening to drown me in magnetic energy and hot intensity.

All the while, the flawless Hell Fae King hovered over me with his sensual grin, his blue eyes sparking with dark hunger.

My surroundings didn't concern me, even if they should have. It was the male who held my body captive beneath his own that owned my full attention.

Strength and power rippled through his perfect body. Danger sent a warning jolt up my spine, urging me to run.

But all I could do was stare up at him in awe while I soaked it all in.

The heat.

His eyes.

His desire—and mine.

Lucifer was more terrifying than the Black Phoenix. His irises glittered like dark blue diamonds, and his gaze scalded me with ruthless passion.

Yes, he was terrifying. But he was just as alluring as Az's beastly bird.

You want this, don't you? Lucifer always asked that question.

And I always replied the same way. *Yes.*

In my dreams, Lucifer was a god, but I was the one he worshipped. He was always over me, bathing me in his light as his beautiful wings spread out behind his shoulders.

And he gave his power to me in these dreams. He didn't threaten me for touching his source.

Here, he offered it willingly. The power built and I drew it in. I was hungry. Thirsty.

I wanted it all.

He gave it to me in my dreams. He didn't fight me or hate me. His source accepted me, so he did, too.

And he expected that channel to go both ways.

Take it all, Camillia, he told me. *Let it burn in your soul until only my mark remains.*

My mouth parted on a gasp when I gave in. Whatever

barriers I'd kept in place crumbled into ash, leaving me naked before the Hell Fae King.

Then the pleasure hit. Just like it always did.

Oh...

My toes curled as electric heat settled between my thighs. A soft grin from my king told me he approved of my reaction to his power.

But why is it always like this?

Why are you always... here?

With me?

"Cami?" a voice asked, causing my lips to curl down.

Don't listen to him. Stay with me, Lucifer said.

Yes, I thought. *Yes, yes.*

Only... I could feel a hand... one that didn't belong to the Hell Fae King. It wasn't unwelcome. If anything, it was a calming touch.

Keep drinking, Lucifer urged. *Don't stop. You're so close.*

My frown deepened. *So close to what?* I'd already detonated, hadn't I? Was I supposed to—

"Cami," that voice said again, causing my body to shake.

I blinked, confused. Then frowned even harder as the sapphire irises melted into a set of new eyes.

Ajax? I thought.

His gaze wasn't burning with Hellfire. Instead, his irises were rimmed with blue flames.

"Another dream?" Ajax asked softly, his arms moving around me as he pulled me into his chest, his lips ghosting across my brow.

I swallowed and nodded.

I hadn't hidden these dreams from him. Nor had I hidden Melek's visits. I'd been completely open with Ajax.

And Az, too.

To an extent.

Az was still sleeping on the couch, though. And he frequently left to give me some privacy with Ajax.

"Same thing?" Ajax pressed. "Absorbing power while he...?"

I nodded again. "Yeah."

Ajax was trying to be supportive, but I knew the dreams bothered him. Especially since I often woke up from them screaming... *with pleasure.*

He was convinced Melek had bespelled me with some sort of dream potion.

He probably wasn't wrong.

But I still wondered if it was linked to the Phoenixfire, only because that was the night these strange dreams had begun.

The energy inspired by the dream clung to me, making my skin burn. That, at least, was real. The pink hue radiating over my flesh was a stark contrast to the cool room's pleasant breeze. I had no idea where it came from—probably from deep within my own soul—but it glowed every time I awoke.

And it freaked me out.

Because this couldn't be a good sign.

It also wasn't normal.

I licked my lips, trying to rid myself of the warm sensations. "Do you think these dreams have anything to do with the source?" I asked, unable to hide the quiver from my voice. We'd talked about it briefly before, but not too much in depth.

However, this dream had been even more intense than the others.

I'd been so *hungry*, sucking in Lucifer's power like I needed it to survive.

And it terrified me.

Because I'd *craved* his power in my dreams.

Just like I'd craved *him*.

"Maybe," Ajax murmured, his fingers running through my hair. "Or maybe it has something to do with our bond to Az. You keep dreaming about hot power, which could easily be related to the Phoenixfire."

True, I thought.

"It could also be some residual connection that they share seeping through the bonds," he added.

That sounded convoluted, but I supposed that was a possibility, too. Az and Lucifer were mates. I could be impacted by that somehow. It wasn't exactly like the two were run-of-the-mill fae. Who knew what kind of changes Az's bite would cause within me?

Or Ajax's.

My Warden—now my protector, my *mate*—ran his thumb in gentle circles on my hip as we rested naked together in the bed. The moon floated in its usual space in the sky, making it impossible to tell the time. But I suspected another night of training would soon be upon us.

Ajax satisfied me nearly every day—because it could be our last, right?—but no matter how thoroughly he fucked me or how many times he made me come, I still often awoke to an orgasm gifted by an ethereal Hell Fae King.

Sure, my courtship with Ajax hadn't exactly been founded in love. More like a realization that we could die at any moment, but after two weeks of pure *Ajax,* it was a relationship I was starting to enjoy.

It could be more.

It could be *real.* But I felt like I would never find out what Ajax and I were capable of because these damn dreams were ruining my mood.

"It could also be from Melek," Ajax mused aloud. "The sensuality would certainly come from him. Because Az and Lucifer are not intimate in that way."

Oh, right. That made sense. The king and the prince were

definitely a romantic pair, and Melek had marked me as his intended.

Maybe it was a combination of everything.

Or maybe I'm missing something important.

I shook my head, the Melek theory not adding up. "If this was because of Melek mating me, then these dreams should have started a long time ago."

Ajax hummed. "There's that golden sparkle jizz he sprayed you with. Maybe it's related?"

I groaned. "We don't know what that did." But it was also a possibility I couldn't ignore, even if the dreams hadn't started until a few days after that incident. Maybe it had taken time to kick in.

Melek could certainly be doing this to fuck with me, or *meddle*, as he was so fond of saying.

Or it had nothing to do with him and everything to do with my fucked-up connection to Lucifer's source.

I could very well be doing this to myself.

Sighing, I flopped onto my back and stared up at the ceiling. It had taken me a while to notice the little seedlings planted in the stone rock. They only bloomed right at moonrise before falling into slumber again.

They made a little noise when they did that, too. Like an alarm clock. Although, with these dreams of mine, I had my own orgasmic wake-up call that never failed.

"Is it just Lucifer? In the dreams, I mean," Ajax asked.

I rolled my head to look at him. He rested on one arm as he peered at me with a sense of concern.

And maybe something else. Concern, yes, but also dark intrigue. Ajax had a fucked-up relationship with sex. The idea of me with Lucifer and Melek might even turn him on, as long as he got to play.

Too bad the only thing Lucifer wanted to impale me with was a sword.

Melek, though, had made his interest clear. The Hell Fae Prince had been dutifully visiting me almost every day, supplying me with homework to mix in with Az's instruction, along with sensual remarks. But it was the homework that confounded me. I'd entirely expected Melek to tease me with sex.

The documents he brought with him were all examples of old deals with the Hell Fae King. I had a nice stack of them under the bed now. Melek had insisted on me reading every deal of significance I could get my hands on.

Because, apparently, the only way I was going to get out of this was by playing his game, if Melek was to be believed.

"Just Lucifer," I confirmed, looking away again.

Because I couldn't face him when I spoke the truth.

I hated Lucifer. I hated his deals and his damned source.

But every dark morning when I went to sleep, I dreamed of him over me, consuming me.

Owning me.

No, not just owning.

Giving, too.

He gave me *everything* in my dreams.

Then, unless Ajax interrupted like tonight, I woke up from an intensely powerful orgasm, feeling like I was going to die.

Being fucked to death might be a good way to go.

I shook my head to clear my sleep-crazed thoughts. *Pull it together, Cami.*

"Let's just get tonight's training over with," I murmured as I hauled myself up, letting the sheets fall and pool around my hips.

I was growing weary of all this. Az's training always seemed like a puzzle I couldn't quite figure out until the end.

And even then, it wasn't something I felt would be

particularly useful against Lucifer. Either he was toying with me, or I wasn't getting what he was trying to teach me.

But I was Az's mate, meaning I could feel his genuine intentions. So Az was definitely *trying* to teach me something. But all it did was leave me exhausted and confused.

Not to mention, my daytime escapades with Ajax left me without much sleep. While my body was satisfied, both of us seemed like we were chasing a high to avoid the inevitable.

We were living on borrowed time until the devil found us.

Or rather, when we found him on our terms. We had a deadline now that we knew when we would be seeing Lucifer again.

The Interrealm Fae Ball.

He would be outside of his realm—which was rare, apparently. He'd be weakened, without his normal guard, and vulnerable. We would have all sorts of fae around us.

Elemental Fae. Winter Fae. Fortune Fae. Paradox Fae. Midnight Fae, of course, being the hosts of the incredible event.

There would be Shifter Fae, too. I wondered if Az would meet any others like him, but it sounded like most of the Shifter Fae were things like wolves and, if I had heard correctly, peacocks.

Perhaps minus the peacocks, we would have a good number of powerful mixed fae of all the known breeds—and likely a few unknowns. If I'd learned anything from my experiences, it was that not all the fae kinds were fully accounted for. They were either lost to the annals of time or in hiding.

Which made the Interrealm Fae Ball important to "abominations," and it seemed like something Lucifer should support.

But he liked to do things on his own terms, and this whole process was likely too democratic for him.

No threat of burning alive by Hellfire. No gnashing of teeth. No decrees.

Lucifer had an invitation, and under normal circumstances, he wouldn't attend, probably because he knew it put him in a vulnerable position.

But this time, he would.

To come for *me*.

After two weeks of training, I had one week left to prepare myself for an encounter with the Hell Fae King.

Az promised he was preparing me for that moment, but he wouldn't specify exactly what I was supposed to do when I met Lucifer.

His answers were always evasive.

Melek, however, kept bringing me deals.

Is there really no other way out?

Ajax held my hand and pressed a kiss to my palm. "I'll grab us breakfast. Maybe an update on Florica's shenanigans will cheer you up, too."

A smile flirted on my lips. He wasn't wrong. When the little darling wasn't hiding stonepeckers in beds—thankfully, not ours, as she seemed to like Ajax—she was setting something on fire or testing out a new spell that wreaked havoc.

A spell that Shade had taught her, no doubt.

"Maybe," I agreed, stifling a yawn behind my free hand. "And one of those mushroom bread things."

He shot up an eyebrow. "A shroom loaf?"

I shrugged. "What can I say? Aflora's tastes are rubbing off on me." The Elemental Fae cuisine was foreign to me, but I liked it.

A genuine smile crossed his features, dazzling me. Lucifer's warm heat finally bled from my skin, and a small shiver ran up my spine. I welcomed the chill as I adjusted to the room's actual temperature.

Ajax would no doubt warm me up again when he returned with midnight breakfast.

"Careful, little rebel. If you keep looking at me like that, I'll feed you something else."

"Is that an offer or a threat?"

Instead of answering, he leaned in, claiming my mouth with his.

I hummed against him as he enveloped me in a powerful kiss, and then he was gone, his shadows inking around me like a caress. One that said, *Be back soon, little rebel.*

"I must say, this lovesick-puppy look on you is rather charming," a familiar voice preened. "I'm glad to see things are going well with the Warden."

CHAPTER 26

CAMI

Snapping to attention, I jerked the sheets over myself again as I stared up at Melek.

Who had appeared in my room, once again.

Uninvited—but that never stopped him.

I chose to ignore his *lovesick puppy* comment, as well as the urge to correct him that Ajax wasn't the Warden anymore.

Somehow, Melek seemed to hide his existence here from my other mates.

Az was still asleep on the couch.

Ajax was off retrieving food.

And neither had felt my instant shock at Melek's arrival.

I had no idea how Melek had done it, but he'd clearly found a way to mask my reactions to his random visits.

Maybe that's what his sparkle jizz does? I marveled. *Who the hell knows?*

My gaze fell to the stack of documents tucked against his side as I realized the reason for his visit, and I groaned. "Oh, goody. More deals, I presume?" I gave him a raised brow. "You know, Argumentation and Debate class wasn't my favorite subject, and it's no better with a Hellish spin."

The cases I had reviewed in class might have been dull, but at least it was for a justice system with a goal of putting the bad guys behind bars.

These deals from Melek were all about foolish fae selling their souls to the literal devil. Every time I saw one of Melek's examples, it turned my stomach.

Because it only reminded me of what my parents had done.

My political science undergraduate program and pre-law status at the University of Florida had prepared me for a lot, but so far, it wasn't enough. Clearly, I still had a lot to learn.

I just wasn't so sure if Melek as my teacher was the answer to my problems.

He gave me one of his disarmingly seductive smirks. "If this bores you, there are other things we can do."

My flat stare didn't waver, but the heat of reminiscent Hellfire returned to my skin.

Maybe Melek knew how to get to me, or maybe he *was* to blame for my stupid dreams.

I tilted my head, carefully crafting my words in my mind. So far, Melek's deals had at least taught me the importance of word choice. "You know, I learn a lot better 'on the job,' so to speak. Why don't you and I make a deal? You know, for practice."

His multicolored eyes sparkled. "I'm not sure you're ready for that, sweet angel. Who do you think penned most of these deals?"

"No more dreams," I demanded. Whether or not he was responsible, perhaps he could do something about them.

He set the pile of documents on the nightstand and sat on the edge of the bed. His focus homed in on me, remarkably reminding me of Az's predatory stare.

I had better tread carefully, but I wasn't lying. Melek

would be great practice when it came to deals, and at least I knew he didn't want to kill me.

Worst-case scenario, he might trick me into bed—but would that be so bad?

Fuck, Cami. Think of Ajax.

Except, when I thought of Ajax, all I could see was his dark intrigue.

Damn it.

Melek took my hand and turned over my palm. He ran his fingers down the lines as if reading my future.

Or, more likely, he was memorizing parts of my body. That seemed like a Melek thing to do. He was becoming infatuated with me, but I kept reminding myself that it was like a dog with a bone.

Once Melek sank his teeth into me, I would be a broken toy, tossed aside never to be whole again.

Or maybe I would be his treasure, to be adored and protected.

I shook my head, not letting those errant thoughts take control. Because they weren't real; they couldn't be.

If anything, I would be a trophy to put on display somewhere for all to see.

Like a certain cage in a bar while I had been dressed in chains.

Melek was Lucifer's. And anything that belonged to Lucifer was corrupted.

Including Az, I reminded myself.

"Tell me about your dreams," Melek said, drawing me back to him.

I shook my head. "No. The deal is for you to stop the dreams. You don't need to know what they are." Melek was powerful. I had no doubt he could take care of my Lucifer lust problem when I was trying to rest—whether or not he was responsible for it.

He tilted his head, his eyes sparkling again as blondish-brown hair fell over his gaze. "You're right. I only ask because I'm curious."

I pinched my lips closed as he continued to stroke my palm. It was such an innocuous place to touch me, but it didn't get past me that he was caressing the place where Ajax had kissed me.

How long had Melek been watching?

If he'd heard the whole conversation, he didn't need me to repeat what my dreams were about. He already knew.

The wicked gleam in his eyes suggested he wanted me to say it out loud. To illustrate the fantasy for him as if this was another sensual game.

"Can you do it or not?" I asked, keeping on topic.

Melek's smirk evolved into a grin. "Very good, Cami. It's important when making a deal not to be distracted. Ty will certainly try to lure you off course to direct a deal in his favor."

I nodded, accepting his praise, then quietly waited for him to answer my question.

His long lashes fluttered over his sharp cheekbones as he looked down, inspecting my palm.

"Depending on the nature of your dreams, I can attempt to suppress them. At the very least, I can offer you an anchor to reality, one you can pull on when you wish to escape. That's a technique that might take practice, if the dreams are of a magical nature. But I will require insight into your soul to offer any assistance. That's where dreams come from, after all."

I didn't want to give Melek any sort of foothold into my soul, but if I was being honest with myself, I was desperate. And he had made himself a regular resident in my life anyway.

He's also my mate, so he already has access to my soul, I thought.

Still…

"Giving you access to my soul in exchange for a good night's sleep doesn't sound like a very fair deal," I countered.

He nodded. "Who's to say I don't already have access to your soul?"

I'd suspected as much, but the confirmation didn't exactly leave me with warm feelings.

"Although," he continued, "this would deepen the connection between us, indeed, and allow me enough insight to help you with this matter. It would also allow me to better protect you. Is there an amendment you'd like to make to your end of the bargain so we can proceed?"

He was being nice to me. He could have pressed the issue, but his offer informed me that amendments were always possible until the deal was forged. When it was time to make my deal with Lucifer—assuming I had one to make—I could backtrack if needed.

His gaze sparkled. "If you want to broker a deal with Lucifer, you're going to have to offer him something he can't turn down. A deal he *can't* resist." He kissed my palm. "You, my little angel, are definitely irresistible to me."

Too bad I wasn't irresistible to Lucifer, or the simple solution would be to offer up myself.

Not a deal he would be intrigued by, surely, nor one that Ajax would possibly allow.

I wrinkled my nose as I rolled words over in my mind, thinking of the right sequence for Melek. "My end of the bargain would need to match the risk. I propose that you stop the dreams and—"

He held up a finger. "I can only offer you assistance to stop them yourself with the anchor, as well as a suppression spell."

Chewing on my lip, I amended, "Okay, you assist me in stopping the dreams myself and provide a suppression spell, as well as a vow that Ajax cannot be killed by you, Lucifer, or anyone you or he commands."

There, that should be specific enough.

He raised a brow. "I have done nothing but try to protect both you and Ajax, little angel. However, I cannot bind my soul to a deal I cannot uphold. Lucifer is a creature of his own mind. As much as he listens to me, you're the one who will ultimately decide Ajax's fate."

Back to cryptic shit again.

"What does that even mean?" I sighed.

His fingers now moved to my wrist, stroking the raised bite Az's beast had left behind. "I can promise you this. I will place a seed in Ty's mind, one that I've been toying with for a while now. It's dangerous, but perhaps it's exactly what we all need."

I swiped my free hand over my face, not caring that my sheet fell again. *I'm doing all of this for a fucking* seed?

"Will this seed of yours result in Ajax's life being spared? No matter what happens to me?"

Melek seemed to ponder my question, then slowly nodded. "Yes, if it grows into a tree that bears fruit, paired with the correct deal you make with Ty on your end. It's the best chance Ajax has. And you."

I knew this deal wasn't in my favor, but if there was any hope in hell—literal Hell—that Ajax could come out of this mess alive, I wanted to take it.

He'd done the same for me. He'd thrown away everything he had just to save me. He hadn't known if his risk would pay off, if we'd be accepted here, or if there would be any future to be had at all. I owed him one, and I paid my debts.

"Then the terms are set," I said with a nod. "You will help me create this reality anchor, as well as give me a dream suppression spell, and you will place a seed in Lucifer's mind that will be the best chance for Ajax's life to be spared."

Gods. That sounded like a load of crock.

Assistance. Seeds. Chance.

Whereas my end of the bargain was much more solid, and even more painfully evident as Melek repeated it aloud.

"And you will recite the incantation we spoke before while we cut our palms, one that will deepen our soul connection, to allow me to better protect you."

It was interesting, though, that he included his protection in his terms. Maybe it was to show me that the deal might be more even than it appeared to be.

"This sounds an awful lot like your *vow of protection*." Actually, it seemed a lot like a blood vow.

"Because it is," he said with a sensual smirk. "It's the next level of that particular spell, anyway. Do you remember the words?"

How could I forget? The incantation had released an initial burst of power within me, feeling like I had dipped my toes into both frost and fire at the same time.

While my training underneath my father's tutelage had made foreign spells natural on my tongue, there was something different about the words I had once repeated back to Melek.

Nadeehar Laki Nafsi.

It wasn't just about protection. That incantation, paired with Melek's kiss on my cheek, had fundamentally connected us. His talisman fueled me with power, and even now with it tucked away in the nightstand, I could still feel his essence curling around me like Ajax's shadows.

The truth was evident now. It wasn't the talisman that gave me Melek's power. It was nothing more than a medium to strengthen a connection that was already there.

Now, I couldn't deny what was happening as Melek's gaze dipped to my lips.

This was a mate-bond. I knew what he was doing. That

much had already been illustrated. That the so-called vow of protection had been the first step to mating me. But just like the bite of a Black Phoenix, it was already permanent.

I couldn't back out of it anyway.

And hopefully, it behaved the same way as the Midnight Fae bonds, thus requiring three steps to reach fruition instead of one or two.

I didn't think my soul would accept Melek at the final level, even if I wanted to, but the second might be possible.

Something to consider, because this might work in my favor.

Growing closer to Melek would place me in an advantageous position against the Hell Fae King. It was Melek who had prevented my execution—something I imagined would not have been possible had his *vow of protection* not been in place. Lucifer had hesitated not just because of Melek's protests, but because I was linked to Melek's soul.

Killing me would hurt him.

And that gave me leverage—leverage that would only deepen if I took the next step with Melek.

"Little angel?" he prompted. "Do you remember the words?"

I cleared my throat and nodded. "Yes. I do." The words sounded stupidly like a marriage vow.

My skin tingled as energy hummed in the room. The hairs on the back of my neck stood on end, and I knew I was stepping into dangerous territory.

I became acutely aware that I was, once again, naked. Melek seemed to time his visits around the state of my wardrobe.

Or lack thereof.

A beautiful dagger flashed into existence in Melek's palm. Another appeared beside me on the bed.

Feeling numb, I picked it up.

He placed the tip of his own dagger at the top of his palm, then waited for me to do the same.

"We must say the words together, and at the same time. You must also trust me, or this won't work."

Do I trust Melek?

No. Yes. Maybe.

Melek didn't want me to die. He seemed to care about Ajax, too. In his own way.

I also suspected he'd helped convince Lucifer not to come after us.

Az had obviously helped, too, but Melek was the one Ty really seemed to listen to. At least from my observations.

Regardless of all that, it was clear to me that the Hell Fae Prince wanted something that none of us could see—and that obviously involved ensuring that we kept breathing.

Melek might be many things, but he wasn't a liar.

If I did this, he would take the next step required to save Ajax's life, and that alone was worth it to me. He had said it was dangerous but also something we might all need. Whatever that had meant.

"I'm ready," I said, done debating it. *This is for Ajax. And also for me.*

Melek nodded, then slid the blade down his palm.

I copied him as our lips moved, speaking the incantation together.

"*Nadeehar Laki Nafsi.*"

A punch of power hit me in the chest, making my eyes widen. My hair flung from my face, and Melek's pupils dilated to pinpricks as immense power filled the room.

Our blood glittered into magical sparkles, drifting up into the air and mixing together in a clear representation of what I had agreed to.

The blood vow paired with our words secured fiery ropes around my soul, making me wonder if this was what it felt like for Az.

But it wasn't constricting. If anything, it felt freeing, as if I had been yanked up high into the clouds to look down on a new dominion.

One where I was queen.

Careful, little angel. Don't let the power go to your head.

I blinked a few times, grounding myself.

Was that Melek in my thoughts now? *Fucking hell.*

Except, I wasn't grounding myself. I was floating above the bed.

As was Melek.

The magic of our union whirled around us, winding and spinning as it tied together in a multitude of knots. Melek grinned as they turned into silver ropes that fell to the ground.

They disappeared a moment later, as if I'd imagined the odd manifestation.

"Those... will be saved for later," he said with a wink.

He placed a burning kiss on my hand, the gesture anything but chaste despite the location.

Then he straightened and pressed his lips to my ear. "When this is over, you'll be begging me to use those on you, little angel. And when I do, I'll show you what pleasure your body is truly capable of." He licked the edge of my ear with sensual promise as he added in a more serious tone, "Your deal-making skills are good, but they need work, little angel. Talk to Az. Ask him about Vivaxia..."

And then he vanished, his magic curling around me just like Ajax's shadows.

I drifted to the bed, only to realize that the deals Melek had brought with him were now scattered from one end of the room to the other.

And for the first time, I could see the hidden, bloodied fingerprints next to the signatures.

I could *see* the blood vows.

Fuck. What have I done now?

And who the hell is Vivaxia?

CHAPTER 27

MELEK

IF I HADN'T LEFT my little angel right that instant, I would have used the silky silver rope to bind her. Pleasure her. *Secure a knot directly over her clit.*

Then I would have suspended her from above, tugged on all the right places, and elicited sounds from my little angel that she didn't even know she was capable of making.

All while tasting her pert nipples, nibbling her lips and her tongue, and sensually tormenting her until she forgot how to breathe.

What have you done now, my prince? Ty's question pushed into my mind like a wave of sensual heat.

My aroused state had likely piqued his interest. As well as the influx of power within our bond.

He absolutely knew what I'd done. But rather than immediately respond, I focused on my deal with Cami. Never mind that this part of the deal was something I would have done on my own, had I thought of it.

The placement of a seed that could change everything.

Similar to the seed I'd just planted in Cami's mind

regarding Az. Merely mentioning Vivaxia's name would force him to show her what he'd been hiding all along.

Some meddling and a little blood vow, I whispered to Ty.

There was nothing *little* about it, something Ty knew. But I liked to tease, especially when I was in a good mood.

Like right now. I still tasted Camillia's ambrosia on my mouth.

I couldn't wait to taste the nectar between her thighs.

Mmm.

Ty's quiet power thrummed on the other side of our connection. He might have been angry, or he might have expected this of me. *So you chose to take your bond to the next level? Is this a move to provoke me, little prince? After everything you already had me agree to?*

Humming while I walked the halls of the Midnight Fae Palace, I curled my finger around one of the vines. It hissed at me but didn't bite, mostly because I was too powerful even for the palace's wards. Not because I was welcome.

Zakkai's essence continued to pluck at me, like it always did when I walked these halls, just to remind me that he knew I was here. If he so chose, he could boost the palace's power, rewrite it, and try to match my level. But he chose not to, which was the loudest message of all.

He permitted me here. For now.

That would change if Typhos decided to pay a visit without permission.

But I knew my king.

He wouldn't storm in; that wasn't his style. Ty respected protocol and much preferred order to chaos. He would also respect the deal he'd made to not pursue Ajax and Cami. But he could certainly find a loophole, given enough time, to extract Cami before the plan was set.

Hence, my timing.

This *little* deal with my angel was exactly what I'd needed. What we *all* needed to prevent catastrophe.

And, hopefully, to save us all.

Provoke you? No. Quite the opposite, I told Ty. *I'm trying to help us.*

I could almost hear his laugh on the other side. *And how do you find* this *helpful? Do share.*

He wasn't angry, which told me he'd expected me to do this. I'd already marked Cami as my intended, so strengthening what was already there had been inevitable.

My timing, though, was intentional. And that was likely what irked him.

Ty had enough on his plate right now without me *complicating things*—at least, those were his thoughts. They were loud enough for me to pick up.

You'll see, I said. *It won't be any fun if I outline it for you, my king. Now, I'm bringing Ajax home for you to propose your deal, just as you had sent me here to do. So do put on your welcoming face.*

Ajax was still a Midnight Fae. I couldn't kidnap him, but I could try to convince him into returning for a visit. I just had to tread carefully. Not only was he welcome in this realm as a Midnight Fae, but he was also currently the guest to the most powerful family in the realm.

I'm always welcoming, Ty promised. His words sounded more like a threat, though.

Of course you are, I continued. *But remember, we can't keep him. Even if he agrees to the deal, he's still a flight risk.*

There, that was the little seed Ty needed.

Hmm, he said, sounding disinterested, but I sensed the spike in his curiosity. *Are you suggesting I should change the terms?*

Ty and I had carefully reviewed the deal he would propose to Ajax. But something was missing.

Giving Ajax back his position wasn't going to be enough. Neither was citizenship as a Hell Fae. While that was something Ajax seemed to have wanted for a long time, everything had changed now that he had Cami. All he wanted to do was protect her—which had been my hope all along.

And, currently, there was one very obvious way Ajax could do that, if Ty proposed it correctly.

Not change, I told Ty. *But you might consider an addition to give you the best control over the situation. Simply having Ajax and Cami in the palace wasn't enough before, and I don't want to assume it would be now. If Ajax chose to hide Cami again, he could, and we'd have no idea where he went.*

As good a hunter as Az was, we were in danger of losing him, too.

It would be up to me to find Ajax and Cami again.

Which I could do.

But I much preferred not chasing them through the realms.

Silence spanned out as Ty considered what I was alluding to. There was only one way Typhos Lucifer could know where Ajax was at all times.

Perhaps, he finally agreed. *Bring him for our talk. I'll be waiting.*

I could almost hear Typhos stoking the fires of his power now as he retreated from my mind, ready to burn the Warden down. But I knew he wouldn't touch him. He wouldn't want to risk his terms with me and Az.

Which was why he'd found a way around the deal.

Or rather, a way through it.

If Ajax accepted Ty's proposal, my king would have the one thing he truly desired—*control.*

My little angel had given me an idea. One that just might save Ajax from the wrath of the Hell Fae King.

An altered deal. One Ty couldn't resist.

I had planted the seed, as promised. And, hopefully, my little seed would grow into a fruitful tree.

Like a bad omen, the ex-Warden's presence loomed down the hall, blacking out the white flowers with the warning of his shadows.

His blue-black eyes burned with power. I wondered if he knew how he had already changed by mating Cami.

Because the telltale blue-black of his eyes flickered with bursts of gold and red.

And if the week ended on my terms, Ajax's fires would finally burn at their full potential.

He'd become one of us.

Ajax approached me holding a tray of food, I assumed for Cami. I magicked it out of his hands and sent it to her room while making a mental note of the new additions to her evolving preferences. Ajax wasn't the only one changing.

He glanced at his hands, then at me, and sighed. "Why are you here, Melek?"

"For you," I said, deciding to be straightforward. "Ty's requesting an audience."

His jaw ticked, not because he was surprised, but because he wasn't thrilled by my announcement.

"And why would I do that?" he asked.

I casually leaned against the wall and crossed my arms. I had no doubt we'd both be heading back to the audience chamber in the Hell Fae Kingdom shortly. I always got my way. "Because Ty has a deal for you, and it's one you're going to want to consider."

A dark eyebrow shot up. "What kind of deal?"

I clicked my tongue and wagged my finger. "You're going to have to talk it out with Ty. I assume you want to negotiate the terms, and I can't do that by proxy."

I could, actually, but I needed Ty to come to the inevitable conclusion I had reached.

There was only one way we all got what we wanted.

"And Cami?" he asked. "You just expect me to leave her unprotected?"

I smiled. Cami was safe, at least until the ball. I'd made sure of that.

"She has Az, doesn't she? She's his mate, too. And she has protection as a guest of the Midnight Fae Royal Circle. She's a Midnight Fae herself now, thanks to you. If that's not protection enough, I don't know what is." I stroked my chin. "And it would be a real shame if you didn't have enough time to consider all the facets of this deal before the ball. Especially when it could protect Cami like you seem so keen on doing."

If he was wise, he'd make sure the wording was perfect.

The Hell Fae King was a master of loopholes. Vivaxia was to thank for that.

And I fully expected Cami to help Ajax with the deal that Ty proposed. I'd been giving her examples of past deals not just for her sake but also for our dear Warden's.

Ty thought we had lost him, but we could get him back if this played out correctly.

"Hmm," he said. "Protect her how?"

"Come with me and find out."

"I'm just supposed to trust you?"

"Yes," I replied, pulling out a card from Ty. "He gives you his word that he won't keep you there. He really does just want to talk."

Ajax glanced down at the writing, his brow furrowing at the elegant script. "A one-way ticket out of Hell?"

I lifted a shoulder. "Ty knew you'd be hesitant."

"And he expects me to believe the writing on a card will save me?"

"Considering his penchant for deals and the fact that he used his favorite pen to craft that note for you, yes." I studied him. "He doesn't want to hurt you, Ajax. He just wants to talk. Ask Az. He'll tell you."

"That would require me to trust Az."

I tsked. "You might be mad at him, but you know deep down that his Phoenix wouldn't let you leave if he thought you might be in danger. Your life is tied to his now."

Ajax's jaw ticked, his blue-black eyes flashing as he tongued his lower lip.

Energy hummed in the air, suggesting that he was reaching out to Az, just like I'd recommended.

I waited, not bothering to mention the consequences of what would happen if Ajax didn't consider hearing Ty's deal. I didn't need to threaten him, and that would only cause division when there needn't be any.

Ty would eventually find a workaround to the Interrealm Fae law that protected Ajax and Cami. It would likely have something to do with their new mate-bond with Az. Given Ty's mate-bond with Az, that made things a bit murky.

Zakkai had allowed my presence here, in part, because Cami was my intended. Az belonged to Ty, and it would be his right to come for him—and perhaps those he was mated to, as well, under the right circumstances.

Whatever those circumstances might be, Ty would find the crack he needed to shove open the door.

Ajax's fists clenched as shadows curled around his feet. One of his hands held his wand, and it glowed with amethyst power that took on a new golden hue.

He leveled a stare at me, one filled with barely restrained violence. "Promise that I'll return. *Tonight*."

"I promise that you'll return tonight," I echoed. Interrealm Fae law was clear in this matter. Ajax was categorized as a Midnight Fae and a royal guest. As such, Ajax was not to be kept hostage. That didn't work in Ty's interests.

Not today, anyway.

Ajax didn't voice his acceptance.

But I saw the resigned agreement in his expression.

I held out my hand, my magic glittering as I began the trip to the Hell Fae Kingdom. "He's in the throne room," I advised him. "Want a lift?"

Ajax ignored my outstretched offering as shadows engulfed him like a void, devouring him whole. He was more than capable of traveling between realms with a simple thought.

I curled my fingers as I smirked and followed him home.

CHAPTER 28

CAMI

A TRAY of food had appeared on my bed while I'd been showering and dressing, the shroom loaf suggesting it'd come from Ajax.

Except he was nowhere to be found.

Where are you? I asked him, the room seemingly empty apart from Az on the couch.

I'm dealing with Melek, he muttered. *I'll be back when we're done.*

My lips turned down at the sides. *Dealing with Melek how? What does he want?*

What does Melek ever want? To meddle, of course.

I chewed my bottom lip. A meddling Melek was never a good thing.

I'll be back in a bit, Ajax added after a beat.

He's taking you somewhere?

Yeah, he replied. *Just a quick trip.*

Where?

It's Melek. It could be anywhere, he replied. *But I'll be fine, Cami. Promise.*

That seemed like a promise he shouldn't make. However, I

couldn't exactly tell him what to do here. He might be my mate, but I didn't own him.

If the roles were reversed, I'd never let him stop me from doing something I wanted to do. The Marsh Lands was a pretty good example of that. And he'd let me do what I'd needed to do without interference.

I supposed I should repay that favor now, even if it felt... *wrong*. It hadn't exactly felt right to Ajax then, either. But he'd trusted me.

So I'd trust him now.

Be careful, I whispered to him.

I'm always careful, little rebel. Which is why I'm going to turn off our connection for a bit. I don't want to risk Melek interfering.

My frown deepened, my instincts rioting against that idea. But I wanted to trust Ajax.

I also wanted to see what Melek would do.

He'd promised to *plant a seed* for me. Perhaps this was related to that?

You'd better not hurt him, Melek, I said, thinking of my... *mate.*

I would never dream of harming him, little angel, he replied, causing my eyes to widen.

So we are mentally connected, I realized.

We're a lot more than mentally connected, Cami, he returned.

I need to close myself off now, Ajax told me. *I'll let you know when I'm back.*

Shit. Okay. Be safe, I reiterated.

Always.

Silence engulfed my mind a moment later, confirming that Ajax had walled off our communication just as he'd said he would.

But it still felt weird. I didn't like it.

See you soon, little angel, Melek murmured, his voice a kiss to my senses. *I'll protect our Warden. You have my word.*

My jaw clenched. *I'm not sure I trust your* word, *Melek.*

Then consider this a show of good faith. His voice warmed my thoughts, his presence in my mind different from Az's and Ajax's. Melek's tones were silkier in nature, reminding me a bit of that silver ribbon he'd created after our blood vow.

What even was that? I wondered.

A promise for the future, Melck hummed back at me. *Goodbye for now, sweet love.*

Sweet love? I repeated, my eyebrow arching.

Silence.

Sighing, I shook my head and took in the state of the room. *Guess I'd better clean this up, then.*

There were documents everywhere.

All of them signed in blood.

I shivered as I started collecting them, the foreign words translating into coherent sentences within my mind. It shouldn't be possible. Yet it was. I could read all of them. Each and every sordid deal.

I definitely prefer Az's training, I thought, glancing at the still-sleeping male on the couch. His expression appeared to be locked in a grimace, his discomfort palpable.

He was too big for that sofa.

It almost made me feel guilty. The bed was more than big enough for all of us. But... *We're not ready for that.*

I wasn't sure we would ever be ready for it again.

Although, Ajax and Az had been getting along better. Of course, that was relative. Ajax had moved from *hatred* to *tolerance* in his approach. And Az had been uncharacteristically docile.

Except when training us.

Then he was a dick.

But an insightful dick.

Sort of. He was definitely trying to teach me something, but it felt an awful lot like he was preparing me to deal with Lucifer rather than defend myself against him.

Although, it seemed *deals* were Lucifer's battle of choice.

They also appeared to be his indulgence.

And they all centered around a key point: there was a price to pay for Lucifer's power and "protection."

I had no doubt there would be a similar price for me to pay to Melek at some point. Beyond tying our souls together, anyway.

His power still hummed along my skin, the sensation reminiscent of his fiery kiss. I could also see a golden sheen forming along my exposed arms, the sparkle glittering in the incoming moonlight.

A shower hadn't removed the glitter.

If anything, the more time away from Melek, the brighter the residual dust shone along my skin.

I traced the spot on my hand where he'd kissed me a few weeks ago, the gold seeming to shine there like a residual print. It hadn't been like that before, yet now it glowed like a claiming mark.

Similar to Az's crescent bite. Only that wasn't gold in color. It was just an indent in my wrist that was clearly never going to heal.

Damnable men.

Constantly marking me.

And leaving me aroused, I thought, my gaze narrowing as a vibration crept up my spine. Melek's bite had left me warm. *Too warm.* And this electricity humming over my skin was beginning to tingle in a very sensual way.

Is that part of the bond? Or is that just Melek?

A groan sounded from the couch as Az stirred, his arms lifting over his head in a gorgeous display of muscle.

My mouth watered at the sight, my thighs clenching with renewed need.

Definitely a leftover gift from Melek, I thought, irritated. *Or maybe even my dream...*

Fortunately, we had training planned for today. I had no idea what it was, but I never did. Az was in charge.

Or rather, his *Phoenix* was leading the way.

Although, it seemed pretty clear that Az was feeding the beast ideas. Or perhaps they were working together.

While I craved the distraction, I was also exhausted. *Partly due to orgasmic dreams with the Hell Fae King.* Something I absolutely was *not* going to tell Az about.

Huffing, I grabbed a stack of the documents and stepped outside to enjoy the moonlight. I needed some fresh air.

Apparently, Az felt similarly.

Because he joined me outside, his dark eyes on the gardens below as Sir Silber popped into view with a tray of coffee mugs. His presence made me realize that I'd forgotten all about my breakfast in the other room.

But the scent of caffeine trumped my need to eat.

It also trumped my need to review these deals.

I set the papers off to the side while Az retrieved a cup— which he handed to me first. Then he grabbed the other for himself, his chin dipping in a polite nod toward the gargoyle.

"Thank you," I said since Az couldn't.

The gargoyle bowed and disappeared.

Az's focus returned to the courtyard, his mind silent while he indulged in his coffee.

I swallowed the caffeinated heaven while allowing my gaze to travel over his stunning physique. Just because I wasn't one hundred percent happy with him didn't mean I couldn't *admire* him.

And there was *a lot* to admire...

He wore a simple pair of black pants, leaving his Black

Phoenix tattoo on display—the imprint stretching across his muscular chest. A delectable "V" disappeared into his waistband, tempting my eyes to travel downward.

However, I inspected his unique mark instead.

It wasn't one made of ink like a traditional tattoo. It was something that represented his beast's spirit, and it gleamed with power, occasionally twisting with shadows or moving on his skin, just subtle enough for me to question if I had imagined its movement.

I had the absurd urge to trace the mark with my tongue to see if it tasted like his magic—I imagined it to be hot and silky like a stiff drink. My fingers ran over my wrist, feeling the raised bite mark from his beast, as desire licked through me like fire.

I can feel that, little warrior, Az said inside my head, his voice a low sound that reminded me of his Phoenix's purr. *It's not like Ajax to leave you wanting.*

Flames caressed my cheeks. He could probably sense my arousal through our bond. Even if he couldn't, maybe he could *smell* it.

Fucking Melek, I muttered to myself, careful not to transmit that thought to Az or anyone else. Not that Melek or Ajax appeared to be listening to me right now anyway.

I cleared my throat, my gaze flittering around the balcony, away from the sexy Black Phoenix. I needed a distraction. Something. *Anything* to change the topic at hand.

Because no way was I responding to his last line.

A deal, I thought, snagging one from the stack of papers I'd set aside in favor of my coffee mug.

I had no doubt he could feel what I had done with Melek, but he was giving me privacy on that matter. Instead, he seemed intent on remarking on my needy state.

Taking Melek's lesson to heart, I thrust one of the documents toward Az. "Can you read this?" I asked dumbly.

I had no idea which deal it was, but it didn't matter. We just needed a diversion. Something to keep me from staring at his too-perfect form.

Your magic is driving me crazy, I thought at Melek.

Hmm, he hummed in return. *Enjoy it, little angel. It becomes you.*

So you can still hear me, I muttered back at him. *Good to know.*

Shh, sweet angel. I need to focus on Ajax right now. Be my good girl and play with the Phoenix.

My eyes narrowed. *I am* not *your good girl.* And what was with all the men in my life suddenly using that phrase? What part of me made them think I was *good* at all?

You're absolutely my good girl, Melek replied. *You're just misbehaving right now. And that's fine. But you should know, Ty is the one who enjoys punishing brats, not me.*

I nearly lost my coffee mug, my jaw unhinging. *Excuse me?*

Melek's responding chuckle kissed my thoughts, then he disappeared, leaving me wondering exactly what he'd meant by all that.

And how the fuck I was supposed to focus now that... that... imagines of being punished by Typhos were flooding my mind?

Fuck. I pinched the bridge of my nose and forced myself to inhale, my opposite hand shaking around the handle of my coffee mug.

Az cleared his throat, reminding me of his presence.

And of course he was still shirtless. Why would he have bothered putting on clothes?

Where did you get this? he asked me, holding up the document I'd given him, his other hand tightly gripping his coffee mug.

There was no doubt in my mind that Az could sense my flustered state—and likely knew part of the cause—but there wasn't a hint of teasing or interest in his features. Just a severely serious look, one that matched his mental tone.

"Melek," I answered honestly.

The Phoenix's eyes flashed up to meet mine, startling me.

Because that gesture had been distinctly human.

What else did Melek tell you? Az demanded. *What happened between you two?*

I swallowed. *What hasn't he done to me?* I nearly replied. But I really didn't want to get into the energy exchange now, or the residual heat simmering across my being as a result of said exchange.

I also didn't want to explain our deal.

So instead, I thought about the last thing Melek had said —the question he'd instructed me to ask Az.

"He mentioned *Vivaxia*," I told him. "He said I should ask you who she is, so who's Vivaxia?"

Pain shot through my chest, knocking me back a step and drawing a gasp from my lips.

What...? I palmed my sternum, searching for the source of the injury. But I found nothing. No blood. No hole. Nothing to indicate a physical blow whatsoever.

Because it didn't come from the outside, I realized. *It came... from the inside.*

My attention flew to Az, his body oddly still. His eyes were unfocused, his hands balled into fists and his coffee mug now in pieces on the floor.

And his chest didn't flinch. Not even with an inhale or exhale.

The pain... it was *his* pain.

I blinked at him while he remained rigid. But Az's internal state was anything but firm. A storm raged inside him, while numbness touched my chest. No, not mine, *his*.

And that *was* physical.

"Breathe, Az," I told him, his lack of oxygen seeming to filter through our bond.

He didn't immediately comply, forcing me to say it again, his agony causing my voice to come out as a rasp. Because I could *feel* everything.

Are the walls still in place? I wondered dizzily. *Did he ever finish crafting them?*

Should I be feeling all of this?

Az? I asked, coughing out loud. *Az... I can't...*

He inhaled sharply, his dark eyes snapping to mine. "What did Melek tell you about Vivaxia?" he demanded.

"He... he just told me to ask..." I trailed off, my brow coming down.

Az had just spoken to me.

Out loud.

My eyes widened as I stared at him.

Some of his relaxed confidence returned as he interpreted my shocked expression.

"Hold on. How long have you been in control?" I demanded. Because Az had just answered *out loud*. The hairs rose on the back of my neck as my heart thundered in my chest. The urge to run from a predator made my knees weak.

I locked them, but my fingers itched at my hip for a blade.

He broke his side of the deal.

He broke his promise.

He lied.

Shit.

Betrayal slammed into my gut, making me realize that I'd stupidly begun to trust Az—*Lucifer's Commander*.

I'd grown too comfortable.

I'd made a mistake.

Because he'd been on a leash, first with a spell, then within the terms of a deal. Now, I understood how much false comfort that had really given me.

Damn it. Where's my knife?

"A knife would be useless against me, little warrior," Az said, his voice sounding tired. "And to answer your question, I've been in control for a while. Well. Sort of. It's complicated."

"Complicated," I repeated. "Right." It couldn't be a coincidence that he was revealing this to me now. When I was alone. *While Ajax...* My eyes widened. "You sent him away, didn't you? You and Melek... Where the fuck is Ajax?"

Az took a step backward. "What?" He studied me for a moment. "What are you asking, Cami? Who did I send away?"

"Ajax," I seethed, *really* wanting a blade. "Melek took him somewhere. Because you're working together, right?"

He held up his hands in a gesture of surrender— something I would normally find humorous, but after learning the truth, I wanted to hurt him. Kill him for his betrayal. *Find Ajax.*

"Hold on... Ajax asked me if it would be safe for him to go with Melek. I told him it should be fine because Typhos doesn't renege on deals. He won't hurt Ajax."

What's going on, little angel? Melek whispered into my mind. *Why are you seething?*

You know why I'm seething, I snapped back at him. *You and Az are working together to hurt Ajax. You both lied to me!*

Silence fell, confirming my suspicions.

"Cami," Az began. "I... I'm not plotting against you or Ajax. I swear it. I vowed to give my Phoenix control until I regained your trust, and I did that. I gave him control. It's just... Mating you and Ajax did something to me."

"Really? It did some things to me, too," I drawled, my sarcasm evident.

"Yes," he conceded. "But I mean it changed my relationship with my Phoenix. We're... we're closer now. I've been giving him the reins, just like I said I would. But I haven't been able to lock myself in the back of my mind. I've just sort of been hovering next to him while he calls the shots. Then you caught me off guard, and I... I took over on instinct."

"How did I catch you off guard? By mentioning Vivaxia?"

Violence flashed in his gaze. "You'd be wise not to throw that name around when you don't know what it means, Camillia."

Ajax is safe, little angel, Melek breathed into my mind. *I haven't lied to you. And I'm guessing Az hasn't either.*

"I didn't reveal that I was in control because I'm technically not in control. My Phoenix and I... we're equally in charge," Az added before I could reply to Melek. "I wasn't sure how to explain it. Honestly, I'm still not sure how to explain it."

My teeth ground together.

This all seemed a bit too *convenient*.

He's Lucifer's Commander. Can I really trust him? He's essentially the devil's pet Phoen—

Az visibly flinched, his anger slamming into me on a tidal wave of pure wrath.

I took a step back, my chest suddenly tight.

Az must have heard my thought.

And it must have pissed him off.

I just wasn't sure why.

But his now-purple eyes raged with fury as he moved toward me, his shadow stretching up the wall beside us. I gulped as that shadow developed ominous wings that spread out to stroke the writhing vines along the palace exterior.

Az might be in his fae form. But his Phoenix was clearly present, too.

"I am not a *pet*," he told me, then lifted up the document that he had clenched in his fist. "I don't know what game you and Melek are playing, but *this* is Typhos's very first deal. You might not know what it is, but Melek sure as fuck does."

I blinked. "I..." I'd chosen that page at random. It'd been in the pile on the floor. I wasn't even sure what it said.

"This deal was the first of many that Typhos made with Vivaxia, my former *owner*. This one, specifically, made it so I'd never be anyone's *pet* ever again."

That shut me up.

My gaze dropped to the document, but the page was too crinkled for me to read. Not that it mattered. I could *see* the vision of the deal in Az's mind, his walls either nonexistent or temporarily dismantled.

Because he was showing me a vivid image of Lucifer penning the deal.

The blood, I realized. *It's Lucifer's signature.*

And in this case, the bloodied text beside it was the signature of another powerful magic-wielder. *Vivaxia.*

The first deal of many, I thought, repeating Az's words.

This was Lucifer's very first deal, and it had been to free Az.

Az's anger faded into hurt as silence stretched out between us. His Phoenix keened in the back of my mind as if the memory I was forcing him to rip open was an ache that would never heal.

I... I didn't want to hurt him. Either of them.

"Do you want to talk about it?" I asked by means of an apology as I rested a hand on his, my heart suddenly in my throat.

Clearly, I was missing an important part of Az and Lucifer's history. Which wasn't unexpected. They had millennia of experience together. And Az hadn't provided me with a lot of stories regarding their past.

Melek had shared a bit during my tour of the palace.

But other than that, I really didn't know Lucifer outside of his dislike for me.

Az's dark eyes fluctuated between black and purple as if he was trying to give the Phoenix back control.

As if he was trying to run.

But he didn't ash into a feathery beast. He didn't fly away like the emotions in our linked bond told me he wanted to do.

His debate also gave me insight into what he meant about his Phoenix sharing the reins rather than holding them. *They're fully bonded,* I marveled.

Mating me and Ajax had essentially married Az to his beast. They'd always been one, but finding the missing pieces of his soul had strengthened his animal's spirit. It had also cured some sort of ache inside, one that had put them on opposite ends.

However, now they walked the same path.

Az couldn't give his beast full control, I realized. *Even if he wanted to.*

But he'd tried—for Ajax. For me. For *us*.

I could see it all there, splayed out in his mind, the truth mine for the taking.

And it wasn't a lie.

He'd opened up his soul for me to explore. Perhaps not on purpose. Or maybe he had. The intention didn't matter. What mattered was the information he allowed me to find.

The truth he displayed for me even while hurting.

His loneliness. His painful past. The way my words had cut him.

Vivaxia and *pet* kept swirling in his thoughts, the two of them resembling knives against his psyche.

Distant screams echoed in my mind as flashes of memories that weren't my own filtered into my head.

Az's screams, and those of his Phoenix.

Gods, what had he been through?

This Vivaxia woman must have been a force to behold if

she'd instilled this kind of emotion in Az, simply from the mere mention of her name.

Az dropped the document to his side.

"Do I want to talk about it?" he repeated, sounding hoarse. "No. But maybe I should. Maybe my history with Typhos is what you need to hear to better understand him. To better understand *me*."

I swallowed, the emotion in his tone matching the frustration I felt inside him.

He didn't talk about the past. Not because he avoided it, but because it was just so ancient.

However, his mind told me he was realizing the importance of it now. How we couldn't move forward without me knowing these crucial details about him.

Typhos would always be part of him. He'd always be someone Az admired and respected and cared for, and this history was the key to understanding *why*.

I gathered all that from his thoughts, the reveal leaving me breathless.

"I've been trying to show you who Typhos really is, but it doesn't seem to be working. Now I know why. You need his history. *Our* history."

His violet irises glimmered with determination and a tiny flare of hope—as if he could finally recount his past and do something good with it.

"It's a long story, if you want to hear it. So I will tell it to you on one condition."

I *did* want to hear it.

More than anything.

Gingerly, I took the document back from Az and rolled it up. "And what condition would that be?"

"That you don't interrupt me until I'm finished."

CHAPTER 29

AJAX

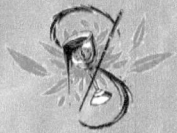

I DIDN'T GO to the throne room.

I went to Zenaida's house instead.

Lucifer expected me to obey his "request" with haste, but I no longer reported to him. He'd removed my title. Treated me like an outsider. Told me I couldn't have Cami because I wasn't a Hell Fae. Yet expected me to bow to him as my king.

No.

That wasn't how this was meant to work.

I'd wanted a new home. A place to remake myself and forget my past.

"You're running away," Shade had said to me all those years ago. And he'd said it right here, in front of Zenaida's house. "I understand. But at least own what you're doing, Ajax."

"Not all of us have a home to return to, Shade," I'd bitten back. "My family and the woman I loved are dead. Gone forever. *Annihilated* by a sadistic fuck who called himself a king. I have nothing left for me there. I'm done. I'm moving on."

He'd considered me for a long moment, then he'd nodded. "You need to find your family. Then you'll come home."

I'd snorted at him, assuming at the time that he just hadn't understood a damn thing about my situation.

But then he'd said something at the cemetery that had me wondering if it'd actually been me not understanding him. That maybe he'd actually foreseen something in that moment that had convinced him to let me take this path.

"Perhaps you should bring your new mates here for a visit," he'd suggested as he'd settled on top of a random tombstone with my familiar on his shoulder. "Introduce your new family to your old family. Let them see your home. Let them know *you*."

Fortune Fae had a knack for riddles.

And Shade uttered them in spades.

"Are you going to flutter about or come inside for some cookies?" a soft female voice asked from behind me. "I made your favorite—oatmeal chocolate chip. Even made sure they were dark cocoa chips, too."

My lips twitched at Zenaida's familiar presence as I faced the dark-haired woman. She might be Shade's grandmother, but she didn't look a day over thirty.

Midnight Fae aging slowed significantly in our twenties, most of us living to be five or six thousand years old.

Zenaida was still quite young, despite having been born over a millennium ago.

"Hello, dear," she greeted me. "Playing hide-and-seek?"

My lips curled. Of course she knew why I was here. "Just wanted to drop in and thank you for the spell."

Her eyebrow arched. "What spell?"

I gave her a look. She knew which one I meant—the taming spell—so I didn't bother clarifying. "It worked."

"Did it?" she asked, blinking her large, blue eyes.

I nodded. "But it seemed to hurt him."

Her nose crinkled. "In what way?"

"I think it brought up memories of a time that spell was used to harm him." Thinking about Az's reaction had me swallowing uncomfortably. I'd been angry. *Very* angry. And the thought of making him feel what he'd inflicted upon me had definitely appealed to me at the time.

But now...

I wasn't sure what I wanted now.

He'd done everything I'd requested these last two weeks. Beyond that, he'd been forthcoming and had allowed me more than one glimpse into his mind.

He'd wanted me to know him. To understand him. To *forgive* him.

I hadn't yet.

However, I wasn't angry anymore. I still didn't agree with what he'd done, but now I had a better understanding of why he'd done it.

He truly thought he'd been protecting me.

Because he cared about what happened to me.

He cared about what happened to Cami.

And that had been before our bond was in place.

Now, he was downright possessive of us. Yet I'd felt him tempering his instincts, telling his bird to *wait*. But I suspected he would explode soon.

Part of me was looking forward to that explosion. It would be hot and dangerous. *And orgasmic.*

But another part of me was terrified of it.

Because that explosion would burn the connection into our souls, cementing it for eternity.

And then there would truly be no turning back.

Not that we could break the bonds anyway, but the moment I accepted our fate, the second I let the intensity of it inside me, everything would change irrevocably.

Assuming Lucifer lets me live, I thought sourly.

Ignoring his summons probably wasn't my wisest move, but I needed him to understand that I wasn't his to command anymore. Zakkai had restructured my connection to the Midnight Fae Source, to allow me entry into the Hell Fae Realm.

But I wasn't a Hell Fae.

I wasn't the Hell Fae Warden.

And I wasn't part of Lucifer's inner circle.

Truly, I belonged nowhere.

Although, Shade had made it clear that I was more than welcome to remain in the Midnight Fae Realm—indefinitely.

"It's odd that you would provide him with a spell that would harm the Hell Fae Commander, Melek," Zenaida said as the Hell Fae Prince appeared. "I imagine there was a lesson involved of some kind?"

I frowned. *Wait...* Melek *provided the spell?* "The card said it was from you," I interjected before Melek could comment. "And there were cookies."

"The cookies were from me." She smiled. "The spell was not."

My teeth ground together as I glared at Melek. "You put the card there?"

He wavered a little, his gaze searching the sky for a moment before he shook his head. "Not quite. Or rather, not directly, anyway."

"You gave it to Shade," I muttered, shaking my head. Of course Melek would seek out Shade. Those two could probably take down monarchies all over the fae realms with their shared penchant for meddling.

"Hmm," Melek hummed, neither confirming nor denying my guess. "The Midnight Fae Palace is quite fascinating. All that magic. Even now, I can feel the residual kiss of power. Almost as though I left some things behind... which I suppose I did. Certain agreements, anyway."

I arched a brow at his gibberish. "Agreements?"

"Ancient things," he murmured. "Don't worry. Az will handle it."

Both my brows hiked upward. "He'll handle what, exactly?" I stalked toward him. "What did you do?"

"Careful, Ajax. Camillia is safe," Zenaida interjected. "But you won't be if you keep the Hell Fae King waiting for too long."

"She's right," Melek agreed as I stared him down. "On both counts. But I assure you, Cami is fine. I would never do anything to hurt her. Or you. We're all connected now. Our souls. Harming you or her would be akin to harming myself, which I'm not going to do."

That reveal gave me pause.

He's bonded to Cami.

I already knew that.

What I hadn't considered was how my bond to Cami would be linked to Melek. Just as my bond to Az would link back to Lucifer.

I slowly faced Zenaida, my mind whirring with this newfound understanding. "He can't hurt me."

"He can't," she echoed, fully aware of who I meant. *Typhos Lucifer.*

I hadn't realized why I'd come here exactly, just that it'd felt right. Perhaps because Zenaida had pulled me here.

But apparently, I'd been seeking validation. Confirmation that Lucifer wouldn't harm me. *A need to know that it's truly safe to meet with the Hell Fae King.*

Except Zenaida had said I wouldn't be safe if I kept him waiting. "Why?" I asked her now. "You said he can't hurt me. So why won't I be safe if I keep him waiting?" Those felt like conflicting concepts.

"I never said that Typhos would be the threat to your safety, Ajax." Her black hair seemed to wave all around her slender shoulders, her petite size betraying her Omega status. But being an Omega in Fortune Fae society didn't mean she was weak or powerless.

Quite the opposite, in fact.

Zenaida was one of the strongest fae I'd ever met.

A large male stepped out of the house, his silver hair gleaming in the sunlight. *Kodiak.* Zenaida's Fortune Fae Alpha mate. Only, his eyes weren't slitted like a normal Alpha's. However, he had Alpha fangs—two sharp points that he showed off as he grinned at me.

"Zen said you might want to take these to go," he told me, handing me a brown bag. "Something about an important meeting."

"Right." That meant I wasn't going to get any more information out of Zenaida.

Typical Fortune Fae, always cryptic.

Just like her grandson.

"Thank you, Zen," I said softly.

"Of course, darling." She walked over and put her arms around me in a hug.

Kodiak watched with interest, probably because it was strange for a Fortune Fae Omega to openly hold someone like this. *Touch* inspired foretelling, and a lot of Zenaida's kind were careful about what futures they evoked.

After several beats, she released me, her blue eyes glistening with unshed tears. "Choose wisely, Ajax," she whispered. "Love fiercely."

With those somewhat ominous words, she turned and headed toward the house.

"Oh." She looked back at Melek. "Bespelling that contract for Az and Camillia was quite clever. We should play chess sometime."

"I would enjoy that," he replied.

"As would I," she returned, the tears in her gaze having vanished behind her smile. "See you next week."

My brow furrowed. "What's next week?" I asked Melek after she and Kodiak entered the house.

"The Interrealm Fae Ball," he replied. "However, something tells me that's not what she means. Or maybe she does." He shrugged. "I suppose we'll find out soon enough. But first..." He held out his hand, his eyebrows waggling.

I shook my head. "No." I would shadow myself. He could follow.

Because, apparently, he was good at that.

Which... Hold on... "How did you know I was here?"

"How do I know anything at all?" he asked, amusement dancing in his features.

With a growl, I shadowed again.

Trying to get answers out of Melek was like trying to turn a boulder into sand.

Grueling. Frustrating. And too long a task to make the end result worth it.

Whatever.

I had a Hell Fae King to meet with.

Then a mate to go home to.

Home, I repeated to myself, my lips curling. *I like the sound of that...*

CHAPTER 30

AZ

A FEW MINUTES EARLIER

AZAZEL? Typhos's deep voice was tinged with concern—an emotion I seemed to be hearing a lot from him lately. *Are you all right?*

I finished pouring myself a fresh cup of coffee, courtesy of the ever-present gargoyle. The helpful creature had set two new mugs and a French press decanter on the table inside, probably because he'd heard me drop my former cup.

The ceramic pieces had also vanished within minutes, my uncharacteristic slip of the hand having been concealed and cleaned up without me having to lift a finger.

Definitely a useful little beast, I thought as I fixed a mug for Cami, too. She sat on the couch I'd been using as a bed, her long legs tucked under her as she patiently waited for me to join her.

Az? Typhos prompted again, his worry touching me through our bond. The Hell Fae King had always cared about me. But this appeared to be a new level of attentiveness from him, almost as though he knew something I didn't.

I'm fine, I told him. *Just rattled.*

He was quiet for a moment. *Are you sure? I can sense your distress.*

Hmm, I hummed back at him as I handed a mug to Cami. *Your prince has been meddling, and he left me with an unexpected surprise. One I didn't quite appreciate.*

Typhos's responding sigh was so powerful that I could almost *feel* it. *What has Melek done now?*

He told Cami to ask me about Vivaxia.

A jolt of electricity sizzled through our bond, the mention of the female who had caused his fall an instant trigger. But just as fast as his anger had arrived, it died, the Hell Fae King reining in his temper before I could experience the brunt of his fury.

It was always like that with him where Vivaxia was concerned, almost as though he felt the need to throttle his reactions to her name while in my presence. Probably because he thought I had more of a reason to hate her than he did.

And perhaps he was right.

But in truth, we both had equal cause to despise the woman.

How did you reply? he asked me after a beat, his mental voice carefully neutral.

I haven't really answered yet, just requested a moment to regain my composure. But I intend on telling her everything.

Silence fell once more, Typhos's reaction dulled, suggesting he was harnessing his emotional response to my admission. *Define "everything,"* he finally said.

My history, I rephrased. *Which will include telling her some of yours.*

I see.

She needs to know, I stressed to him. *She's my mate, Typhos. My Phoenix chose her. I don't have a choice. She has to understand me to accept me. Just as she has to understand you to accept us.*

It was a lesson I hadn't realized she needed until now.

A lesson in the truth.

That was the missing piece to all of this—Cami's comprehension of the past. She needed insight into why Typhos made certain decisions today. Why he preferred to work with deals. How his very first deal had indebted me to him for eternity. Why my life—and now hers—would forever be intertwined with his.

My prince is playing with fire, Typhos growled. *He's mated her on the next level, too.*

Yes, I'd noticed as much when I'd woken up and joined Cami on the balcony. My power had immediately responded to the stronger outlet inside her, my Phoenix humming with approval.

Melek deepening their mating only makes it more important for her to understand who we are, I told Typhos as I settled beside Cami on the couch. *I know you don't trust her, Typhos. I know you're not ready to let her in. But my Phoenix is done waiting.*

As was evidenced by my bird biting her without a second thought.

It seems Melek is done waiting, too. The words were a sigh in my mind, Typhos's exhaustion palpable. Yet there was an undercurrent of power that hummed through our bond. Like a live wire he wasn't quite restraining.

I couldn't tell if that was related to residual emotions or if it was a hint at his unraveling control.

I trust your judgment, Azazel. But I maintain my right to intervene the moment I determine Camillia's true intentions.

She doesn't want to hurt you or me, Typhos. I would know otherwise because I can hear her mind, I whispered to him. It hadn't been intentional, but when she'd mentioned Vivaxia, my barriers had temporarily fallen. She'd experienced my shocked pain, just as I'd experienced her reaction to it.

And her residual concern for Ajax, her thoughts that I'd been working with Melek to lull her and Ajax into a false sense of security.

That prospect had upset her far more than the realization that my Phoenix and I had been sharing control all this time.

It told me exactly how she felt about Ajax. She cared about him. Deeply. Although, I suspected she hadn't quite discerned that yet.

Her decision to mate him seemed to be based on a misconception about her lack of time left.

Soon she'd understand that she'd mated him for very different reasons. That the two of them were meant to be together.

Just as they were both meant to be mine, too.

My Phoenix had figured that out before me, his animalistic instincts keen and determined and not swayed by logic or reason. He'd wanted them, so he'd taken them.

Over the last few weeks, I'd slowly deciphered the cause, my stubborn mind unfurling like my Phoenix's wings.

Ajax had always been compatible. It was why I'd used him as I had—as a sparring partner capable of managing my brand of heat. But neither of us had been ready to acknowledge or accept the inevitable. Hell, he still wasn't ready.

However, Cami's arrival had expedited my bird's processing of events.

He'd immediately identified her as a fighter, someone who could challenge him and give him renewed purpose.

It'd started when the Hellhounds had failed to capture her, thus requiring Ajax to hunt her down.

And it'd solidified when I'd been tasked with finding her less than a week later.

My Phoenix had been enamored with the chase, his inability to track her nearly driving him mad. Her father had led us on a similar mindless pursuit, but it hadn't been the same.

My beast had wanted to destroy her father for that game. Fuck, he *still* wanted to destroy the male.

But not Cami. No, he'd wanted to *praise* her for crafting such a unique and difficult hunt. He'd decided she was his then.

A cunning, beautiful female with the heart of a warrior.

She wouldn't fall for me easily. She'd require me to work for it, even with my Phoenix's sensual traits.

Just as Ajax would make me grovel until either he decided to forgive me, or I made him forgive me. At this point, it seemed like it would be the latter.

A few weeks might not be long in the grand scheme of things, but it was so much more than that.

My Phoenix had finally marked his mates, yet I hadn't been allowed to physically complete our claim because Ajax and Cami were too angry and hurt for me to do so.

Telling Cami the truth now might help that along.

But that wasn't my true intent.

All I wanted was for her to understand not just me but Typhos, too.

And, hopefully, this history lesson was the key to achieving that understanding.

Let me know if you need me. Typhos's soft words were very unlike the Hell Fae King. But he knew how sensitive this topic would be for me. And he was offering his strength should I need it.

Thank you.

He didn't reply, the connection not necessarily closed, but not fully open either.

Cami sipped her coffee while she watched me, her patience a virtue I longed to reward. Which I supposed I would—with the truth.

I joined her while indulging in the coffee for a moment, then set my mug aside and twisted on the couch to face her. It forced me to draw up one knee, my opposite leg dangling off the side while my foot remained on the ground.

Her gaze flickered down to my exposed tattoo, her appreciation evident in the way her pupils dilated. But rather than tease her for it, I said, *I need to start by telling you about the Virtuous Fae. However, I can't say the words aloud.*

It was hard to know who might be listening in on this conversation.

And I didn't want to risk anyone else overhearing it.

She dipped her chin in understanding, her mind otherwise quiet.

I'd asked her not to interrupt me until I finished. It seemed she'd translated that to mean no speaking at all.

Or perhaps she was demonstrating her acceptance of my request.

Regardless, I was thankful for it. Because I needed silence to process everything I had to say—*a whole history of pain.*

The Virtuous Fae are the first fae to have ever existed. Because of their magic, the various species of fae kind were born. They were creationists, I suppose. Similar to what humans see as deities. Except the faedoms don't know that they ever existed. They assume their fae sources are the ultimate creators, and in essence, they're right. But those sources were created when Typhos fell.

Rather than elaborate, I carefully deconstructed the wall between us and allowed her to see the moment in history from my point of view.

Only, as I began to play the memory for her, a similar one ignited in her own mind—a recounting of that day from Typhos's perspective.

I arched a brow. "Did Melek show you that?"

She shook her head. "No," she answered aloud. *The book did,* she added mentally. *I thought it was a dream, though.*

Not a dream, I told her. *That moment created all the faedoms—it's the moment the Virtuous Fae Source shattered into pieces.*

I showed her the aftermath, how those pieces became their own sources of power throughout the realms, creating all of fae kind.

Virtuous Fae are fae with creation power. They're essentially beings who can make any form of magic imaginable. Some are more powerful than others, but the key to their abilities is the energy they harbor inside. And Typhos has more energy than most Virtuous Fae. He's a beacon of light—and that light is power.

I tried to show her what I meant by displaying a memory of Typhos wielding that light to save a fallen Shifter Fae. Like most of my kind, she'd been created as a passing amusement by some Virtuous Fae. When that Virtuous Fae grew tired of his "pet," he stabbed her with a silver blade and left her to die.

Typhos saved her, I explained. *By reigniting her light.*

Cami's eyes widened as the vivid memory played out for her in my mind.

Is that how you met? she asked. Then immediately said, *Never mind. Sorry. I didn't mean to interrupt. Keep going.*

I smiled. *It's fine. But no, that's not how we met.*

I lifted my arm and stretched it out along the back of the couch, my side leaning deeper into the cushion.

As I said, the Virtuous Fae essentially own creation magic. Similar to the concept of gods in the Human Realm. It seemed to be the best analogy, given Cami's roots.

When she nodded, I knew she understood.

So I continued.

But they're ancient beings. And many of them were bored. That's why Shifter Fae and a few other species were made—to amuse the Virtuous Fae. But all those species were seen as lesser beings. Their purpose was essentially to worship their betters.

Cami lifted her mug to her lips, and I suspected it was to cover up a frown.

I couldn't blame her—the whole concept of making a life as a diversion didn't sit well with me either. And I'd lived through that era of history.

As you can imagine, the "lesser" beings started confiding in one another. That led to relationships and the eventual creation of more life, as well as the development of new powers and fae types. The Virtuous Fae allowed it, partly because they were too arrogant to see the potential for rebellion.

They'd also been too entertained by their pet projects to notice much else.

I guess it might be similar to how humans disregard animal behaviors, but imagine the animals were actually fae with growing powers, and you might see how that could become a conflict.

Cami snorted, her mind telling me she could definitely visualize that potential outcome.

My kind was one of the original creations, I went on. *My mother was a Black Phoenix. There are not many in existence, similar to a handful of other shifter types. So my mother's mate wasn't a Black Phoenix. He was a combination of several fae breeds.*

Which would today be referred to as an abomination.

Or a Hell Fae.

He had Paradox Fae, Corpse Fae, and Ghoul Fae in him, I went on. *But the type really isn't important. What you need to understand is that all of these fae—these* amusements *created by the Virtuous Fae—were part of the original Virtuous Fae Source. Because it was that magic that was used to manufacture all these fae breeds.*

So when Lucifer fell... She trailed off.

When he fell, the Virtuous Fae Source shattered into all those pieces, giving the new fae breeds their own beacons of power, I finished for her. *But the largest piece remained with Typhos. And that piece is now the Hell Fae Source.*

Her eyes widened as if she was finally starting to understand the full extent of Typhos's power.

But it's part of him, she said slowly. *Right?*

Yes. Because he's a Virtuous Fae. As is Melek. Perhaps that last bit wasn't mine to share. But Melek was the cause for this entire conversation. So he could fucking deal with me spoiling his surprise.

However, Typhos isn't just any Virtuous Fae. He's one of the strongest in existence. His light energized the original source. That's why such a large section of it broke off into his spirit when he fell. Unlike Melek, for example, who has no connection to a source at all anymore—because the Virtuous Fae Source no longer exists. It's scattered among the faedoms as each realm's unique source of power now.

So what happened to all the other Virtuous Fae?

I shrugged. *We don't really know. Typhos's fall came with a blinding light. And we woke up in the pits of Hell—a realm the Virtuous Fae had created for their unwanted or imperfect pets.*

The Nightmare Fae, she realized, a memory of Melek talking to her about Typhos's fall trickling through her mind. She hadn't understood much of Melek's story at the time, but now it was beginning to make sense to her.

Typhos took that Hell and made it his own, creating a variety of kingdoms for the Nightmare Fae and weaving magic into the atmospheres to make them hospitable enough for them to thrive.

This part she seemed to understand because of Melek's previous lesson. Perhaps that was what he'd meant when he'd said he'd been trying to teach her—he'd attempted to explain the Hell Fae Realm, but he'd left out the important details about how any of it even existed.

I filled those gaps now by showing her bits and pieces of my memories. But it was a careful dance, one that required me to watch my mental steps.

Because the last thing I wanted was to introduce her to the horrors of my youth.

It wasn't out of shame or fear so much as an intrinsic need to ensure she never experienced that kind of pain. Especially not through me.

The reason I'm telling you all of this is so you understand the impact of what I'm about to share. Because while Typhos's fall resulted in the establishment of all fae kind, it was never his intention for that to happen.

Of course, he certainly didn't regret any of it now. If anything, he was quite proud of how everything had come to fruition.

But his intentions and how everything played out was a conversation for another day. What mattered today was the answer to the question Cami had originally asked me—*Who's Vivaxia?*

Typhos's fall was triggered by a corrupt deal. A greedy fae wanted to steal his energy—his light—*and to do that, she needed Typhos to willingly die.* Which was no easy feat for a Virtuous Fae. *So after years of pretending to be his mentor, she tricked him. And he fell.*

That wasn't the whole story, but it was enough. Typhos could elaborate upon it at a later date.

The fae who caused his fall was Vivaxia, my former owner.

CHAPTER 31

CAMI

FORMER OWNER...? Those two words whirled around in my mind, the concept one I couldn't wrap my head around.

Az was too dominant to have an *owner*.

How? I nearly asked. How *could someone own you?*

Apparently, I wasn't very successful at keeping those thoughts to myself, because Az huffed a laugh and drew his fingers through thick hair.

"Trust me when I say it wasn't a voluntary arrangement." He uttered the words out loud, his deep voice riddled with sardonic undertones.

This part of his past was clearly painful for him to relive. But I couldn't seem to bring myself to tell him to stop. I wanted to know this. I wanted to know *him.*

Vivaxia found me when I was in my early twenties. She was instantly intrigued by my mixed genetics and asked if I was interested in making a deal with her. I was proud and a bit naïve, so I agreed to hear her out.

His violet gaze took on a distant gleam, his cheekbones even more pronounced as he clenched his jaw.

She offered to upgrade my mother's nest to something more

accommodating, as well as to set her up with various necessities and superior goods, all of which were meant to improve her quality of life. His eyes narrowed a little. *You see, my father... was no longer in the picture. My mother wasn't his only mate. And he chose his Paradox Fae mate over my mother.*

Oh. He sounds charming, I muttered.

Az's lips twitched. *Hardly. But he's been dead a long time. I rarely think of him.*

His commentary made me wonder if Az had been the one to kill him, but I didn't want to interrupt him again. I'd already done it a few times by accident, essentially nullifying my promise not to say anything until he finished.

Fortunately, he didn't seem to mind my curious questions.

Unfortunately, my mother didn't have much. And as a result, neither did I. So Vivaxia's offer to improve my mother's quality of life appealed to me, especially since she would be doing so as a favor to me, thus making me feel like I had an opportunity to take care of my mother.

Hmm, I hummed to myself, careful not to share my thoughts with him. *I think I know where this is going...*

There was only one thing she wanted in exchange for all of this, and as I'm sure you've guessed, what she wanted was me, he said, his eyes gleaming while he spoke into my mind.

Yeah, that was my guess, I thought, but I didn't send him the response. Or I tried not to, anyway. Having all these "channels" in my head was interesting to manage, to say the least.

As I already mentioned, I was proud and naïve, he went on. *Proud because I wanted to be the man of the nest. Naïve because I didn't ask Vivaxia to clarify what she meant. I just assumed she wanted me for sex. I was wrong.* Very *wrong.*

I shivered as a handful of his memories reached my mind, the barrier between us seemingly gone. Except he was controlling what he showed me, and I knew from his thoughts that he was doing that to protect me.

He didn't want to hurt me.

Which meant he had some images in his mind that I probably never wanted to witness.

And I didn't think they were about things he'd done to others, but what had been done to him.

She wanted my Phoenix, not me—the man. The muscles of his arm flexed as he lifted his hand to run his fingers through his hair. *She cast a spell on me that forced me to shift, then she controlled my animal's every move. Like a glorified puppet.*

Ajax's spell, I whispered.

A stronger variant of it, yes. He swallowed, his pain trickling through our bond as he thought about how much it had hurt to hear those words from Ajax's lips. *I suppose we've both done things to one another that elicited dark echoes from our past. Neither of us intended to harm the other in that way, though. At least, I don't think we did.*

I don't think you did either, I admitted. Az had been trying to protect Ajax by suppressing his urge to interfere with Lucifer's punishment. I understood that now.

Just as I was beginning to see that nothing with Lucifer was what it seemed.

Vivaxia liked to parade me around, Az said, moving on with his story. *One of her favorite demonstrations involved my death.* His violet irises burned as he stared at me. *Phoenix Fae are immortal, but we can still temporarily die. And when we do, we go up in flames. Then we rise again from the ashes.*

That sounds... painful.

His lips curled, his arm stretching out along the couch again. *It depends on how I die, but I'm not afraid to burn, little warrior. In fact, I* crave *it.*

I shivered. Only Az could turn such a dark topic into a sensual one.

But it's the aftermath that hurts the most, he said, sobering. *When a purebred Black Phoenix dies, his or her memories die with them. They're truly reborn, unless they have a mate, in which case the memories trickle back in via the mating bond. Almost as though a Black Phoenix's mate saves pieces of their soul for that purpose alone.*

I stared at him, my eyes widening. *So you forget everything when you die?*

No. I'm not a purebred. As a result, my memories are typically safeguarded by my other half. And when those memories start to trickle in, they resemble bullets to my mind. Slamming into me either all at once or one after another.

I gaped at him. *That...* I had no words. No idea how to respond. That... that sounded *excruciating.*

The speed of recovery typically depends on how quickly I die, he went on. *An immediate death means I'll regain my memories in one catastrophic hit to the brain. A slow death results in bullet-like sensations piercing my thoughts for hours or days on end.*

I flinched. *God, Az. I... I don't know what to say.*

There's nothing to say, little warrior. His gaze glittered like fiery violet-colored diamonds. *But "God, Az" is a pleasing sentiment.*

I blinked, his sensual remark unexpected and somehow perfectly timed. Because it made me laugh out loud despite the sensation churning my insides. "I wouldn't bet on that."

"Oh, I would," he returned, his voice a low purr of sound. "Someday soon, you'll understand why."

My stomach clenched for an entirely different reason than before, his silky words wrapping around me in a caress of unanticipated heat.

Az studied me, amusement still teasing the edges of his full —very kissable—mouth.

Typhos attended one of Vivaxia's demonstrations, he said,

his statement not matching the hungry gleam in his features. But he seemed to want to finish his story.

And I very much wanted to hear the conclusion.

She invited him over with the goal of seducing him. I think it would have worked had she not involved me. But seeing her torture me—her pet—*created a detour in her plans. Instead of immediately bedding him like she'd intended, they ended up discussing their first deal.*

He gestured to the group of papers on the dining table, the one we'd discussed on the balcony sitting on top of the stack.

The contract you showed me earlier is the deal in question. His brow came down a little. *I suspect Melek has something to do with you* randomly *selecting it from the pile.*

My lips twisted to the side. *The pages were scattered across the room when he left. I didn't put them in any order.*

He dipped his chin. *I'm sure magic did that for you without you knowing.* He ran his fingers through his hair again and sighed. *Regardless, it's not a coincidence that you handed me the contract surrounding my proposed freedom. Only, I was never really free at all.*

What do you mean? I'd pretty much given up on waiting to ask questions. Fortunately, he didn't seem to mind.

Typhos requested a change in ownership, essentially asking Vivaxia to let him have her pet. She agreed on one condition— that he spend a night in her bed doing whatever she desired.

My eyebrows lifted. *And he agreed.*

Of course. Vivaxia was a desirable female, and a night of sin wasn't much of a hardship for him. Only, he made a fatal error in his acceptance. He didn't set a term for how long I would become his. So she gave me up for one night, then showed up the following morning to take me back.

Oh. One night in her bed in exchange for one night of

transferred ownership. I grimaced. *I'm guessing that's not what he had in mind.*

Not at all, Az murmured. *Of course, Vivaxia knew that. But she didn't actually know why at first. She thought he just fancied playing with me. It was more than that, but she was too arrogant to think of any other reason.*

Because she saw you as an animal, not a person, I translated.

Yes. But Typhos saw me. And he vowed to me in secret that he would do whatever it took to free me.

Why? I wondered. *Not that I blame him, but if he was raised in this environment where Virtuous Fae are superior, why would he consider helping a "lesser" being?*

Because he's always believed that power doesn't equate to superiority.

That seemed surprising, given my experiences with the Hell Fae King, but I didn't comment.

Typhos feels that those born with certain gifts need to protect their creations, not torture them. And he never agreed with what happened to the beings marked as defective. *He has always believed that all life should be cherished and rewarded, unless the soul has committed a sin, in which case the soul has earned its torment. Hence, his version of punishment for those who renege on his deals.*

The dark souls, I realized. *That's why some of those Nightmare Fae have black auras.*

You can see them?

I nodded. *Sometimes.*

He considered that for a moment. *Interesting.*

Silence fell between us, his astute gaze stirring goose bumps along my arms. Despite the serious nature of our conversation, I couldn't help but indulge in the view before me—a shirtless man with defined chest muscles, sculpted abs, and low-slung pants that fit his thighs rather nicely.

Melek's residual energy was clearly messing with my libido.

Or maybe it was the dream.

I really didn't know, but having Az sit so casually across from me like this almost felt like an invitation. One I was considering accepting.

He's my mate, I told myself. *Of course I want him. But can I trust him?*

His nostrils flared, suggesting he'd overheard those thoughts.

I really need to master this whole channel thing, I thought with a sigh.

Yes, you do, he agreed, his tone serious. *And yes, you can trust me.*

I swallowed, willing myself not to reply or to think because he would just overhear every word.

After that first deal, Typhos became obsessed with besting Vivaxia, Az continued, giving me a reprieve from my thoughts. *Thus began their long relationship where she played the part of his mentor, all while he attempted to beat her and she tried to find a way to steal his light.*

His light being his energy, I replied.

Yes. That had been her goal all along. She recognized his power and wanted it for herself. So she began testing the limits of her deals, seeing if there was a way to borrow his abilities. Meanwhile, he bargained for more nights with me. As I said, she thought it was because he fancied me as a pet. It pleased her to no end to be able to use me for her personal gain.

My jaw clenched, the notion of Az being used in such a way souring my mood considerably.

She thought he was fucking me, Az went on. *My Black Phoenix is sensual. A lot of her admirers wanted me for that reason. But Typhos was the only one she granted the privilege to because she thought he would be easier to manipulate if he was distracted by my Phoenix charms. Because of that, she let my leash slip a little more each time she gifted me to him for a night, knowing that I needed the ability to shift into my humanoid form to properly please Typhos.*

What was he actually doing? I wondered.

Talking to me like an equal, Az replied quietly, his gaze momentarily lowering as if he was embarrassed to admit those words. *He wanted to know how I'd become hers, and I told him about my mother.* He swallowed then, his expression hardening. *It turns out, my deal with Vivaxia held the same flaw—a time clause.*

His violet irises flashed as he met my stare again.

The nesting accommodations only lasted a week. That was how much effort Vivaxia felt her side of the deal was worth to imprison me for life. The fury in his mental voice burned into my thoughts, his words inspiring a similar reaction on my end.

But a note of concern also followed.

Because if Vivaxia hadn't upheld her part of the bargain... *What happened to your mom?*

His jaw clenched. *She wilted.*

CHAPTER 32

CAMI

I STARED AT AZ.

She wilted.

What... what did that mean?

Did she...? I trailed off, swallowing and attempting to find the courage to finish my question. *Did she die?*

But he'd just said Black Phoenixes were immortal, right?

Black Phoenix females are very protective of their young. And she blamed herself for me accepting Vivaxia's deal. My mother... He pause for a moment, his throat working. *She burrowed herself in her nest, refusing to eat, to preen, to live, for decades. By the time Typhos found her—after I told him about my deal with Vivaxia—my mother was a shell of her former self.*

My heart hammered in my chest, my eyes pricking with the sudden urge to cry. I wasn't close to my parents, but it was clear that Az cared a great deal for his mother. That he blamed himself just as much as she'd apparently blamed herself.

She's better now, he added softly. *She lives in Lunar Fae Realm.*

Lunar Fae? I repeated, unfamiliar with them. *Another breed of Nightmare Fae?*

He shook his head. *No. They're a unique breed of wolf shifters. One of the Alphas imprinted on my mother. She lives with him now. She's happy. That's what matters.*

And she knows you're safe? I guessed.

Yes. But our relationship has never been the same. She essentially grieved me as though I'd died. He flicked an invisible piece of lint from his pants. *I suppose that was a mutual experience. All those deaths took their toll on my spirit. Eventually, I taught myself to just stop caring. If it didn't bother me, it didn't hurt so much.*

I was beginning to see why Az favored pain with his pleasure.

As well as understand his need for dominance.

He'd never let anyone control him ever again. And with good reason.

Anyway, the reason I'm telling you all this is to help you better understand my relationship with Typhos. He saved me, Cami. He saved my mother. Without him... I'm not sure where I'd be today. Perhaps Vivaxia would have eventually figured out how to thwart my immortality and kill me for good.

I shivered at the thought. *I'm glad she didn't do that.*

His resulting smile was almost soft. Or as soft as it could be with his sharp cheekbones and chiseled features. *I'm thankful she didn't kill me as well. But for as horrible as she was, she taught me a lot of valuable lessons. Typhos, too.*

So how did he end up beating her? I wondered. *How did he eventually save you?*

He didn't really. Instead, he fell into the pit the Virtuous Fae had created for their rejected creations, Az replied with a shrug. *But something he did changed the course of history. And while I could explain it, I think that story really needs to be shared by him.*

Hmm, I see. So today's training *is meant to intrigue me about Lucifer's past so that I'll ask him about it,* I deadpanned. *Good to know.*

Today's discussion is to help you understand me, Cami. And to do that, you need to understand Typhos, too.

And where does Melek fit into all this? I asked him. *He's a Virtuous Fae, you said. So... he was obviously there, right?*

You can ask him for that story, Az replied. *Consider it my payback for his meddling.*

I relaxed into the arm of the sofa behind me with a sigh. "All of you enjoy telling me half-stories, don't you?"

"No, actually, not all of us. I told you *my* story. The others can share theirs." A hint of finality underscored his tone.

While I wanted to press him, I couldn't deny the fairness of his statement.

He'd shared his past, and it wasn't his responsibility to share the pasts of the others.

"Thank you for telling me all this," I said, meaning it. "I... I know that couldn't have been easy for you."

"It was easier than I expected it to be," he admitted. "Perhaps because it all happened so long ago. Or maybe because I'm joined with my Phoenix, and he trusts you. Therefore, I trust you."

"And Ajax?"

"The way my bird reacted to Ajax when he'd wielded a version of the taming spell told me that, deep down, my soul trusts Ajax. Otherwise, I would have been pissed, not hurt." Az palmed his chest, as though reliving the pain that spell had reignited.

I could feel the residual ache inside him, our bond allowing me to experience the sensation as if it were my own. Just as I could sense Az rebuilding his walls, not to shut me out but to protect me once more.

His energy was fiery. Potent. *Hot.* At the back of his mind, he kept thinking about his need to expel his fire, yet marveling at how it felt tamer than usual.

Out loud, however, he continued discussing his Phoenix's reactions.

"My beast isn't weighed down by humanlike thoughts or emotions. He knows what he wants. And some of that primitive knowledge is helping me heal now. There's no fighting what we are together, and honestly, I wouldn't want to fight it even if we could."

"You and your Phoenix are stronger now," I said. "Because you're together."

"I meant us, Cami," he replied softly. "There's no fighting what you and I have together now. And even if I could, I wouldn't fight it. My Phoenix is right. You were meant to be our mate. Ajax, too."

I frowned. "But how do you know that? We don't... we don't really know each other... right?"

Az's intense gaze held mine. "I imagine trust isn't something you come by easily. I've read a bit of your file and know that your parents essentially abandoned you in your youth, forcing you to live on your own. So perhaps it's difficult to accept a fate like ours. But our souls... they know each other very well. Deep down, I sense that."

A startled laugh escaped me. "Are you saying we're soul mates?"

"Yes," he replied seriously. "I am."

My eyebrows shot upward. "That doesn't exist."

"In the Human Realm, no. But in the Fae Realm, it can and it does." He leaned forward on the couch, his violet irises swirling with inky flecks, the man and the Phoenix joined as one. "I've wanted you from the moment I laid eyes on you, Cami. You fought Ajax while every other female in that camp ran the opposite direction from him. You're strong. A warrior. *My* warrior."

My amusement died in a breath, my heart seeming to halt with his words. He'd uttered them with such conviction, such *certainty*, that I... I didn't know how to respond.

I'd expected him to say something about wanting to fuck me the moment he'd met me. Something about my looks or the lust that burned hot between us.

Not his comments about my strength.

"You're unlike anyone I've ever met, Camillia," he added, his palm wrapping around my hand near my leg as I continued to hold my knees up like a shield between us. "You're fierce. Intelligent. *Aware*. And there's a kindness inside you that calls to my Phoenix. A softness I long to explore. Because I suspect you rarely allow anyone to see that side of you. I want to know you better, Cami. I want to be with you."

He gave my hand a squeeze and released me.

"But I know you don't trust me yet. That's okay. Patience is something I mastered long ago. And for you, I think I would wait an eternity if I had to."

My chest warmed all over, his declaration echoing in his mind, his earnestness a palpable presence in our bond.

He meant every word.

I... I didn't know how to handle this side of Az. This sentimental male. He was always so harsh, borderline *cruel*, and intensely sensual.

But this... *this is who Az will be with me.*

When alone.

When it was just us.

The man and the Phoenix with their mate.

I could sense his residual need for dominance lurking beneath this sentimental exterior, his intrinsic heat beckoning him to take what was rightfully his. But he tamed that craving with a thought, the man very much in control of his own feral nature.

The juxtaposition between his virility and his tenderness left me breathless.

It had me dropping my hands to my sides, my body seeming to operate of its own volition as I slid up onto my knees.

He watched me from beneath hooded eyes, his expression giving nothing away. But I *felt* his hunger. His *need*.

However, he let me lead.

He didn't reach out for me, didn't tell me to stop, didn't tell me to come closer, just observed me through those beautiful irises as I moved toward him.

His expression didn't change as I grasped his shoulders and straddled his lap. He didn't grab me. Just left one arm stretched out along the back of the couch, his other limb loose against his side.

I cupped his handsome face between my hands, my eyes searching his, my mind openly communicating my intent.

His acceptance came through our bond, his understanding of what I needed a kiss to my senses.

He refused to let anyone control or master him again. It was why he craved dominance, why needed to be in charge.

However, he granted me this one moment to do whatever I wanted to him.

This one searing *kiss*.

I pressed my lips to his, my thighs clenching around his hips as electricity hummed between us.

He reminded me of a wildfire, his touch hot and destructive, his trajectory and path unknown. Yet there was something so intensely beautiful about it. So alluring that I couldn't stop myself from embracing his flames.

Each stroke of our lips seduced me closer, enticing me with its promising heat.

I won't hurt you, those flames seemed to say. *Caress me.*

Indulge in me. Let me brand your soul. I promise to overwhelm you. Tempt you. Please *you*.

My tongue slid into his mouth, my body giving in to the yearning as my arms wrapped around his neck.

He didn't take charge. He let me lick him at my own pace, my lips memorizing his, my fingers teasing his thick hair, my breasts pushing against his hard chest.

It was a tender embrace.

One I maintained.

But like all wildfires, our embrace eventually burned out of my control. And Az stepped in to temper the flames, his tongue gentle against mine, guiding me into our kiss and deepening his touch upon my soul.

I no longer understood why we'd been waiting. Why I hadn't indulged in this maelstrom brewing between us.

This fae was mine.

My Phoenix Fae.

My Az.

My mate.

His arm came around me, his touch resembling a blazing band enveloping my upper back as his opposite hand went to my hip.

Caging me.

Claiming me.

Captivating me.

I want another lesson, I whispered into his mind.

Name it, he replied, his tongue still sliding purposefully against mine.

Teach me how you fuck, I told him. *Teach me how to please you.*

It was a dangerous proposition, one that would undoubtedly destroy every conception I maintained in regard to Az and sex.

But that was okay.

Because I wanted to know him. To know this. To know *us*.

To know what we could be together.

Show me what you need, I added. *Show me what it means to be yours.*

CHAPTER 33

TYPHOS

SEVERAL MINUTES EARLIER

Ajax and I are on our way, my love, Melek murmured into my mind.

Hmm, I hummed back. *Was the visit to Zenaida your idea or Ajax's?* I didn't bother hiding that I knew where they'd been. I'd felt their returning presence the moment they'd entered my realm.

Keeping tabs on me? Melek teased.

Always. It was an honest reply, one I didn't feel the need to hide. Melek was mine. Of course I paid attention to his disappearances and locations.

Just like I knew he kept visiting Camillia in the Midnight Fae Realm.

Although, I hadn't mentioned my knowledge of it to him.

If he wanted to play with his intended, then so be it. So long as he remained safe, I wouldn't involve myself in his choices.

Even if I did disagree with many of them.

Melek's amusement warmed my mind, his mental voice otherwise quiet. Because, apparently, he wasn't going to reply to my initial question regarding Zenaida.

Forever playing games, I sighed back at him.

You love them almost as much as you love me.

Hmm, I hummed again as I teleported myself to the throne room. I'd chosen this location for today's meeting with a specific purpose in mind.

Most of my constituents didn't even know I had a throne room. But there was one—a very unused and dusty one—that I utilized when meeting with my lieutenants and other royal fae.

Unlike most throne rooms, this one wasn't about power.

It was about equality.

A place where I invited those I admired and respected to meet with me.

Everyone allowed into this room had a throne to sit upon, not just me. Which I supposed made it resemble more of a glorified conference area, except there was no table. Just an ornate floor made of fire and obsidian rock.

Ajax had been invited to meet with me in this room before, which meant he should hear my message loud and clear.

Because here, he would sit at my side.

Not bow at my feet.

His shadows preceded his powerful form, his essence seeming to blend into the fiery walls of my chambers. It was different from before, his unique energy typically at odds with my own.

However, today his aura appeared to be dancing with mine. *Growing.* Inflamed with mutual appreciation.

Well, now that is interesting, I mused, eyeing the way my essence responded to his. *Interesting indeed.*

I took over my preferred throne, my curiosity piqued by this unexpected change. It seemed mating Camillia had altered Ajax's magic, his new energy surprisingly compatible with my own.

Melek materialized a moment later, a sinful smile tugging at his perfect lips while he followed Ajax into the room.

Are you going to tell me more about your visit with Zenaida? I asked him. *Or perhaps about how you coaxed Az into a conversation about Vivaxia?*

My prince's amusement grew. *I believe Ajax was seeking validation from Zenaida. As for Az, I think that conversation was long overdue.*

And you felt it was your place to introduce that conversation?

I simply supplied Cami with the means for introducing it herself, he countered. *Az needed a way to earn her trust. He—like you—was too stubborn to figure it out on his own, so I provided a solution. That's not meddling, Ty. That's helping.*

I snorted. "Your definition of *helpful* is *meddling*," I told him out loud.

Melek merely smiled once more and took over the chair to my right. "Did you find Zenaida's taming spell to be meddling or helpful, Ajax?"

My gaze narrowed. You *gave Zenaida the taming spell?*

Not exactly. No elaboration. No remorse. He merely stared at Ajax, waiting for him to reply.

"You mean the spell you left for me with Zenaida's cookies?" Ajax replied, his own eyes slitting into a glare. "Why would you help me hurt Az?"

"I didn't help you hurt him. I helped you tame him." Melek glanced at me. "See, Ty? *Helping,* not meddling."

My jaw ticked. *So then you gave Ajax the spell Vivaxia used on Az?*

A variant of it, he drawled. *One Az could easily break had he actually attempted to.*

Have you lost your fucking mind? I demanded, entirely focused on Melek now rather than the deal I'd been about to propose to Ajax. *Do you have no consideration for Az's past? The damage that spell could cause?*

Melek finally sobered, his multicolored eyes swirling with a myriad of truths and secrets. "The spell was written in a way that Az could break. But he trusted Ajax not to take advantage of his power, thus he never actually fought it. The purpose was to reveal the truth, and I believe the spell accomplished that."

"What truths?" I asked him. "Ones *you* think Camillia is worthy of hearing?"

"Yes." There was no hint of teasing in his tone now. "They're truths Ajax is worthy of hearing as well."

Camillia needs to know the history of your fall, and our Commander needs to be prepared for the coming turmoil— something he cannot do if he is weighed down by the past, Melek added into my mind. *The Black Phoenix has finally found his mates. Telling his history to someone safe will help him process that history once and for all.*

I am his mate, I countered. *He could always talk to me.*

You're not his Phoenix's *mate,* Melek replied.

Oh, I supposed not. I had bonded Azazel through my source using the Virtuous Fae spell—but that only tied me to the fae. Not the beast within.

His soul had always been divided. However, mating Camillia and Ajax had changed him. I couldn't define exactly what had changed, but I could sense it. Almost as if his soul had united and was growing stronger every day.

Yet he hadn't needed to use me to expel his power.

Actually, I barely noticed his burn. It felt as though he'd found another way to maintain his energy.

Via his new mates.

Is that why Ajax is so much more appealing now? I wondered, eyeing the stoic Midnight Fae. He stood there, hands clasped behind his back, clearly waiting for me to say whatever I needed to say so he could leave.

Very unlike the Warden of the past.

Very much like a potential new mate.

A male I might just want to add to my inner circle.

Because he stood before me now as an equal. Not an infatuated Midnight Fae with a hero-worship complex. He'd seen me as a king before—a powerful king he'd wanted to serve for eternity, no matter the cost.

Now he was looking at me like I mattered very little to him.

A fascinating change, one that had my lips curling despite everything that Melek had just revealed.

Your meddling has turned into gambling, Melek, I told my little prince, my gaze sliding to his. *Are you sure you've drawn the right hand?*

Melek relaxed into his chair, his head lolling back to expose his throat in a way that made me want to *bite. Come, my love. You know I'd never play cards without a few aces up my sleeve.*

Hmm.

Melek was toying with fire, but perhaps he felt that he needed to.

Too much in my kingdom—my *life*—was in danger of falling apart.

The Nightmare Fae used to hold me up on a pedestal, admiring me from afar, but the events of late were breeding disquiet among the ranks. They were concerned.

Rightly so, I thought, scowling inside.

However, I never ruled for power. I ruled to serve those who needed protection. And if I couldn't do that, then I would lose far more than my crown.

I would lose myself.

Ajax's jaw flexed as I considered his hard features. He represented a past I recognized in my soul.

A time when I'd thought all was lost. *My wings. My fizzling light. All those dead fae.*

Melek was the one who had pulled me out of the shadows, helped me find my way in the dark.

Ajax had looked to me for a similar anchor a little over a decade ago. I'd provided him with the tools I'd thought he'd needed. But seeing him now, I realized how wrong I'd been.

It hadn't been his position or his home within my realm that had helped him survive. It'd been Az.

And now... now Camillia appeared to be the one who had returned his light.

Or perhaps both Camillia and Az had rekindled his spark, their matings giving him a renewed purpose in life.

Regardless, it seemed I'd failed him.

I shouldn't have put Camillia on that stage, I told myself. *She was his light. And my actions had nearly snuffed it out.*

Perhaps not literally.

Well, no, I had absolutely planned to kill her. But that was after she'd touched my source again.

That night at the club had been my version of a playful punishment. However, none of it had been playful to Ajax.

And seeing what I did now made it very clear to me why he'd chosen Camillia over his loyalty to me. He loved her.

I'd threatened that.

I'd threatened *her.*

Which made me the enemy here. The one he no longer admired or trusted. Yet he still stood here now resembling an equal. *A king.*

Az's Phoenix had chosen wisely, at least where Ajax was concerned.

With Camillia—that remained to be seen. Although, I was beginning to understand the appeal.

Melek had told me to consider making Ajax an offer for more than just his position. I'd thought of nothing else since he'd said it, my mind wielding all sorts of possibilities and promises that I could bestow on Ajax to win back his favor.

However, none of those were good enough now.

Not when faced with an equal. A changed immortal. *A male in love.*

There was really only one thing I could offer him that would make him consider returning to his post, returning to *me.*

"I want to offer you a deal, Warden," I said, driving straight to the point.

"Ajax," he corrected me. "I'm no longer your Warden, if I recall correctly. And even if you do consider me your Warden, I resigned the moment I left."

The words were delivered with precision and no hint of fear.

Yes, definitely an ideal candidate for my circle, I decided. Because Az spoke to me in the same way.

As does Cami, a small voice whispered into my mind. One that sounded a lot like my mental tone, but Melek's words.

Except my prince was focused on Ajax, not me. I could feel his intense stare as though it were my own, his anticipation palpable.

He'd played his hand.

Now he wanted to see how I would play mine.

I suspected I was about to lay down the cards he'd sorted for me, which would normally make me want to shock him by doing something unexpected—just to increase the excitement of his games.

But I was tired of the one we were already lost within.

I needed a change.

I needed a way forward.

I need a stronger circle. Without it, I might lose my

kingdoms and the fae within them. Because whoever was behind all these attacks was far more clever than any adversary of my past. They were using others—manipulating them with Virtuous Fae magic—to attack my home, my *fae*.

To battle them, I would need to be at full strength. I couldn't achieve that when my powers were being stretched all over the realm, fixing these destructive portals, and healing my battered fae.

Ajax was an asset, one I should have promoted long ago. Welcomed into the fold. *Made into a Hell Fae.*

But I'd kept him on the outside. Choosing to use him where I could without ever really letting him in.

That changed now.

"Camillia De la Croix has accessed my power more than once. Her ability to siphon and use my source is something I cannot stand for in my position," I told him.

His lips parted, his stoic facade fracturing beneath what I imagined would be an argument in her defense. However, I stalled it with a raise of my hand.

"That said, I'm willing to guarantee her safety in my realm," I stated, beginning the terms of the deal. "I'm willing to overlook her abilities and offer her a home here. With you. If you wish to return."

His jaw snapped shut, shock seeming to render him mute.

"While I'm sure you're enjoying your stay with the Midnight Fae Queen and her mates, you can't remain there forever. Sure, you could find a Midnight Fae home somewhere, but what would you do? What purpose would you serve? Is that what Camillia wants?"

I could tell by his lack of a reply that he wasn't sure how to respond to any of my questions. Probably because he'd assumed I'd simply drag him and Camillia back here to finish what we'd started after the last attack.

He likely hadn't even considered alternatives. Which implied that Camillia hadn't either.

Rather than comment further, I waited for him to process everything I'd said.

Melek remained quiet as well, his silence confirming his intrigue. He was eager to see how the cards would fall, my little meddler a fan of observing the endgame.

Eventually, Ajax cleared his throat and asked, "How? What would your terms be?"

"You would resume your position as Warden," I told him. "And you would need to become an official Hell Fae. That's the only way I can allow you to claim a Hell Fae Bride."

His eyebrow inched upward. "A Hell Fae Bride?"

"Any bride of your choice," I stressed. "Including Camillia."

His chin notched upward, his expression distrusting. "Except she's no longer a bride. You announced that to your Hell Fae constituents."

My lips curled, impressed—yet not all that surprised—by him catching that detail. "Part of my terms would be her reinstatement as a bride."

"Before or after I become a Hell Fae?" he asked, impressing me yet again by setting specific terms.

"After." I cleared my throat. "Strictly speaking, this would all be a formality at this point, but I can't afford to deviate from this requirement. If my Hell Fae believe they can mate brides at will, chaos will ensue. And given everything else going on in my territory, I'm not sure I could handle that, too."

It was a statement of vulnerability that I wouldn't voice to just anyone.

Hopefully, Ajax understood that this admission meant something—that I trusted him. That I wanted to let him in.

"What else?" he asked, his gaze narrowing.

"You and Cami can reside within the palace or wherever you desire so long as it's within the Hell Fae Kingdom. I don't want her staying in the prison."

Mostly because I knew Melek would want to visit her, and those accommodations were not appropriate for my little prince. Or his chosen female mate.

"That means you'll need to commute to the prison," I went on. "So I want you to hire a Warden apprentice to help you share the burden. I'll give you full discretion as to whom you hire."

This would allow him to spend significant time with his mate and not just work all the time. He required balance. It was clear that would help him thrive.

And I needed him to thrive.

He swallowed. "You're going to ask something significant from me in return."

My lips curled. "Yes, Ajax. I am."

He nodded, his expression more resigned than curious. "So you're offering me and Cami safety, Hell Fae citizenship—for lack of a better term—and my old position back. Anything else?"

"Is there anything else you desire?" I countered, arching a brow.

"I just want Cami to be safe," he admitted. "Which she is right now in the Midnight Fae Palace."

"Yes," I agreed. "And I'm not threatening to harm her. But I am offering you an alternative—a purpose and a good life—with your bride. One that I suspect Az will very much want to be a part of, too."

"So you're doing this for him?" Ajax asked.

"I'm doing this for all of us." For Az. For Melek. For *me*. "We need a solution and I'm offering one. But it'll require your acceptance."

His jaw ticked as he studied me. "All right, I'll bite," he

said, suspicion darkening his features. "What would you ask of me in return?"

Melek's excitement heated our bond, yet he didn't outwardly show it.

He knew exactly what I was going to say.

Because I'd walked right into his play—his cards practically flickering in the air before me.

Only, they weren't cards. They were words. Promises. A way forward. *A new path.*

"In order for me to offer you solace, a home, your Warden position, access to the Hell Fae Source, and your Hell Fae Bride of choice, you'll need to become my mate, Ajax." It was the only way to guarantee everything I'd promised.

But he needed to understand what mating me would entail.

"Mating me means that you will give me access to your soul, your mind, and the ability to know exactly where you are at all times. It also means I'll be closer to Camillia De la Croix because we'll share three mates—you, Az, and Melek. That will allow me to keep better tabs on her power, and hopefully find ways to protect my own. *Without* harming her."

His lips parted, his surprise palpable.

I reveled in that look, the one telling me that he had never in a million years expected me to request this.

Because it meant he would actually have to consider his response.

And I loved a deal that required thought.

However, this agreement had a deadline—the Interrealm Fae Ball.

My lips curled as I set the final term. "You have one week to decide, Ajax. Choose wisely. It could be the last decision you ever make."

The Story Continues with Hell Fae Prince...

About Hell Fae Prince...

Ribbons are fascinating.
They curl and twine, yet unravel so beautifully.
Especially when wrapped around a woman's sensual form.

Alas, I've woven so many intricate knots around Camillia De
la Croix that I worry she'll never allow me the privilege of
untying her.

My pretty little captive is stubborn. Powerful. So delectably
perfect.
I've wanted her for many moons now.
To taste her.
Captivate her.
Dress her in ribbons and devour her.

But just as I'm about to make my move, to finally show her
who I really am, she's taken from my grasp to a place I thought
long destroyed.
And I'm the only one who can bring her back.

However, it's going to require a full mate-circle to provide me with the power to do so.
Typhos. Az. Ajax. Me.

Can I convince them all to play nice?
Or are we destined to spend eternity without our beautiful mate?

Don't worry, little angel.
I'll find you. I'll k*ll for you. And then...
All of us will worship you.

Authors' Note: *Hell Fae Prince* is a dark paranormal romance with four tormented mates and no choosing required. If you like your antiheroes dominant and sexy, you've come to the right realm—the Hell Realm, where the romance is hot and no forgiveness is required. This book is part of a five-book series and ends on a cliffhanger.

USA Today Bestselling Author Lexi C. Foss loves to play in dark worlds, especially the ones that bite. She lives in Chapel Hill, North Carolina, with her husband and their furry children. When not writing, she's busy crossing items off her travel bucket list or chasing eclipses around the globe. She's quirky, consumes way too much coffee, and loves to swim.

Want access to the most up-to-date information for all of Lexi's books? Sign up for her newsletter here.

Lexi also likes to hang out with readers on Facebook in her exclusive readers group. Join Here

Where To Find Lexi:
www.LexiCFoss.com

J.R. Thorn

Reverse Harem Paranormal Romance - Never Choose.

J.R. Thorn is a Reverse Harem Paranormal Romance Author who loves coffee, stormy weather, and heated discussions with her inner muse. She can often be found scribing her steamy stories in her writing cave far away from the prying eyes of her toddler, husband, two vocal cats, and canine pack!

www.AuthorJRThorn.com